喚醒你的英文語感！

Get a Feel for English !

喚醒你的英文語感！

Get a Feel for English !

Jazz Up Your English
Places Things
People Events
Issues Technology
英文閱讀能力養成
從跨學科知識、字彙記憶、文法練習到理解測驗，
結合英美雙口音朗讀與對話，輕鬆打造閱讀素養力！
Mastering English Reading
貝塔｜語測
檢測學習平台
高點｜美語系列

目錄

CONTENTS

導 讀

Introduction

學習目標

眾所周知，學英文學到一個階段會遇到停滯期，此時你會覺得自己的英文還不錯，但還不夠好；基礎知識你都了解，但你會想了解更多。這就是所謂的「學習高原 (learning plateau)」，學習者通常在中級程度左右會面臨此障礙。那麼，問題來了：如何才能跨越此高原達到下一個層次？如何才能成為英文的高級使用者？

高級英文使用者的指標有三項增加：詞彙量、文法複雜度以及使用時的流暢性與恰當性，本書將在這三個方面助你一臂之力。

大家也都知道，隨著閱讀量變多，詞彙量和文法複雜度也會跟著增加，而這是因為閱讀時，已知的單字和短語會自然而然地浮現腦海，並強化所學的內容。在閱讀的過程中，眼睛也會觸及到新單字。現在，你可以透過「注意」來加速這個過程。我所指的「注意 (noticing)」與「觀察 (observation)」不同，「注意」將意識運用到所見事物上。「注意」使無意識變得有意識，有意識的學習是幫助記憶的關鍵。藉由本書的閱．聽練習，希望能發揮此作用：注意與各種主題相關的詞彙和文法。書中所有任務 (Task) 都是為了讓你注意到以前可能沒有留意過的細節。一旦注意到某個單字或短語在文本中的出現方式，並經過反覆接觸，新語言就會成為自己詞彙庫的一部分。此外，同樣重要的是，這樣的練習可培養思考習慣。下次當你閱讀自己選擇的文本時，注意的習慣將有助於擴大詞彙量。

在進一步討論之前，了解書中採用的語言學習模型很重要。貫穿全書的語言模型稱為 Leximodel，我在教學中使用 Leximodel 已有 30 多年，對各種類型和程度的學生都產生了良好的效果。為了順利進入狀況，請務必看完以下介紹再開始本書的「閱之旅」。

The Leximodel

可預測度

在本節中，我要向各位介紹 Leximodel。Leximodel 是從全新角度看語言的方法，所根據的概念很簡單：

Language consists of words which appear with other words.
語言由字串構成。

此說法淺顯易懂，意即，**Leximodel 的基礎概念就是從字串的層面來看語言，而非以文法和單字**。爲了讓各位明白我的意思，我們來做一個 Task 吧，作答完畢再往下看。

Task 導讀 1

想一想，平常下列單字後面都會搭配什麼字？請寫在作答線上。

listen ____________________
depend ____________________
English ____________________
financial ____________________

第一個單字旁你寫的是 to，第二個字旁寫的是 on，我猜得沒錯吧？我怎麼會知道？因爲一種稱作「語料庫語言學 (corpus linguistics)」的軟體程式和電腦技術做過語言分析之後，發現 listen 後面接 to 的機率非常高 (98.9%)，depend 後面接 on 的機率也相差不遠。換句話說，listen 和 depend 二字後面接的字幾乎千篇一律，不會改變（listen 後接 to；depend 後接 on）。由於機率非常高，這兩組詞可視爲 fixed（固定字串），也由於這兩組詞確實是固定的，當書寫 listen 和 depend 二字時，後面沒有接 to 和 on，即可說是寫錯了。

接下來的兩個字——English 和 financial——後面該接什麼字則較難預測，我猜不出你在那兩個單字旁寫了什麼字。不過，我可以在某個特定範圍內猜，你可能在 English 旁寫的是 class、book、teacher、email 或 grammar 等字；financial 旁寫的是 department、news、planning、product 或 stability 等字，卻無法像方才對前二字那麼篤定了。原因何在？因爲以統計預測 English 和 financial 後面接什麼字，準確率相對地低很多，很多字都有可能，而且每個字的機率相當。因此 English 和 financial 的字串可說是不固定的，稱之爲 fluid（流動字串）。由此推斷，語言不見得非以文法和單字來看不可，你大可將語言視爲一個龐大的語料庫，裡面的字串有的是固定的，有的是流動的。

總而言之，根據可預測度，我們能看出字串的固定性和流動性，如圖示：

〈The Spectrum of Predictability 可預測度〉

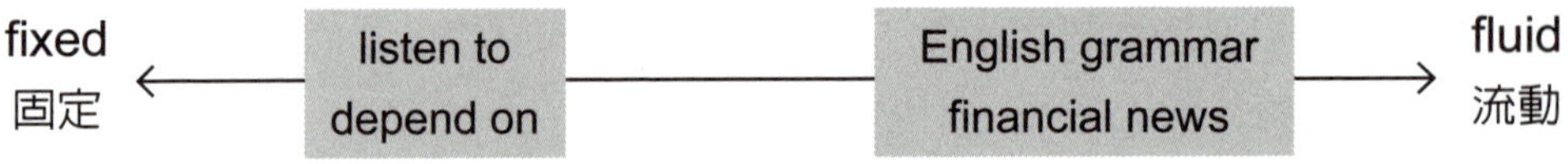

字串的可預測度即爲 Leximodel 的基礎，因此 Leximodel 的定義可追加一句話：

Language consists of words which appear with other words. These combinations of words can be placed along a spectrum of predictability, with fixed combinations at one end, and fluid combinations at the other.
語言由字串構成。字串可根據可預測度之程度區分，可預測度愈高的一端為固定字串，可預測度愈低的一端為流動字串。

你可能會想：我曉得 Leximodel 是什麼了，但這對學英文有何幫助？我怎麼知道哪些是固定字串，哪些是流動字串？它如何讓學習英文變得更容易？別急，放輕鬆，從今天起英文會愈學愈上手！

字串（multi-word items，以下簡稱 MWI）可分成三大類：chunks、set-phrases 和 word partnerships。這些名詞沒有相對應的中譯，因此請務必記得英文名稱。我們仔細來看這三類字串，各位很快就會發現它們眞的很容易了解與使用。

Chunks

首先來看第一類 MWI——chunks。Chunks 的字串有固定也有流動元素。... listen to ... 即爲一個很好的例子：listen 後面總是接 to，此乃其固定元素；但有時 ... listen ... 可以是 ... are listening ...、... listened ...、... have not been listening carefully enough ...，這些則是 listen 的流動元素。... give sth. to sb. ... 是另一個很好的例子：give 後面得先接某物 (sth.)，然後接 to，最後再接某人 (sb.)。因此 ... give sth. to sb. ... 在這裡是固定字串。不過在這個 chunk 中，sth. 和 sb. 這兩個位置可選擇的字很多，這是流動的，例如 give a raise to your staff「給員工加薪」和 give a presentation to your boss「向老闆做簡報」。看下圖你就懂了。

They	listened are listening have not been listening carefully enough	to	the presentation.

We need to give	a proposal a present some thought to	to	the client Mandy the new plan	.

部分為 fixed　　部分為 fluid

相信你能夠舉一反三，想出更多例子。當然，... give sth. to sb. ... 也可寫成 give sb. sth.，但 give sb. sth. 本身又是另一個 chunk 了，同樣是固定和流動的元素兼具。看得出來嗎？

Chunks 通常很短，由 meaning words（意義字，如 listen、depend）加上 function words（功能字，如 to、on）所組成。現在你可能已經知道很多 chunks 了，只是自己還不自知。再做一個 Task 吧，看看是不是都懂了。注意，務必先做完 Task 再看答案，千萬不要作弊喔！

Task 導讀 2

請閱讀下列短文，找出所有的 chunks 並劃底線。

Everyone is familiar with the experience of knowing what a word means, but not knowing how to use it accurately in a sentence. This is because words are nearly always used as part of an MWI. There are three kinds of MWI. The first is called a chunk. A chunk is a combination of words which is more or less fixed. Every time a word in the chunk is used, it must be used with its partner(s). Chunks combine fixed and fluid elements of language. When you learn a new word, you should learn the chunk. There are thousands of chunks in English. One way you can help yourself to improve your English is by noticing and keeping a database of the chunks you find as you read. You should also try to memorize as many as possible.

中譯

每個人都有這樣的經驗：知道一個字的意思，卻不知如何正確地用在句子中，這是因為每個字幾乎都必須當作 MWI 的一部分。MWI 可分為三類，第一類叫作 chunk。Chunk 幾乎是固定的字串，每當用到 chunk 的其中一字，該字的詞夥也得一併用上。Chunk 包含了語言中的固定元素和流動元素。學習新單字時，應連帶學會它的 chunk。英文中有成千上萬的 chunks。閱讀時留意並記下所有的 chunks，將之彙整成語庫，最好還要盡量背起來，不失為加強英文的好方法。

答案

現在請以下列語庫核對答案，如果沒找到那麼多 chunks，可再看一次短文，看看是否能夠找到語庫中所有的 chunks。

素養加分語庫 **導讀 1**

... be familiar with n.p. ...
... experience of Ving ...
... how to V ...
... be used as n.p. ...
... part of n.p. ...
... there are ...
... kinds of n.p. ...
... the first ...
... be called n.p. ...
... a combination of n.p. ...
... more or less ...
... every time v.p. ...
... be used with n.p. ...
... combine sth. and sth. ...
... elements of n.p. ...
... thousands of n.p. ...
... in English ...
... help yourself to V ...
... keep a database of n.p. ...
... try to V ...
... as many as ...
... as many as possible ...

語庫小叮嚀

- 語庫中的 chunks，be 動詞以原形 be 表示，而非 is 或 are。
- 記下 chunks 時，前後都加上 ...（刪節號）。
- 注意，有些 chunks 後面接 V（go、write 等原形動詞）或 Ving（going、writing 等），有的則接 n.p.（noun phrase，名詞片語）或 v.p.（verb phrase，動詞片語）。

Set-phrases

好，接下來我們來看第二類 MWI：set-phrases。Set-phrases 比 chunks 固定，通常字串較長，其中可能同時包含多個 chunks。Chunks 大都是沒頭沒尾的片段文字組合，但 set-phrases 通常包括句子的句首或句尾，甚至兩者兼具；換句話說，有時 set-phrases 會是一個完整的句子。Set-phrases 在電子郵件或會議和簡報的英文口語中很常見。請看下列語庫並做 Task。

Task 導讀 3

下列語庫為電子郵件中常用的 set-phrases，請把你認得的勾選出來。

素養加分語庫 導讀 2

- ☐ Thank you for sending me n.p. ...
- ☐ Apologies for the delay in getting back to you, but ...
- ☐ Thanks for your reply.
- ☐ Just to let you know that v.p. ...
- ☐ Just to confirm that v.p. ...
- ☐ Please confirm that v.p. ...
- ☐ I look forward to hearing from you.
- ☐ If you have any queries, please do not hesitate to call either ... or ...
- ☐ If you have any questions about this, please do not hesitate to contact me.

語庫小叮嚀

· 三類 MWI 中，固定性最高的就是 set-phrases，因此學習時務必鉅細靡遺地留意其中所有細節。

· 有些 set-phrases 以 n.p. 結尾，有的則以 v.p. 結尾。

學會 set-phrases 的一大優點是，使用時不必考慮文法。只要把它們當作固定的語言單位背起來，並依本書所介紹的原原本本照用即可。現在我們繼續來看第三類 MWI：word partnerships。

Word partnerships

三類字串中，word partnerships 的流動性最高，其中包含兩個以上的意義字（不同於 chunks 含意義字與功能字），而且通常是「動詞＋形容詞＋名詞」或是「名詞＋名詞」的組合。Word partnerships 會隨著文章主題或業務部門而改變，但所有主題和部門的 chunks 和 set-phrases 都一樣。比方說，假如你從事的是製藥業，那麼你用到的 word partnerships 就會跟在資訊業工作的人不同。做完下面的 Task，你就會明白我的意思。

Task 導讀 4

請看下列字串，依據其 word partnerships 判斷各組所代表的產業。見範例。

①

risk assessment	share price index
non-performing loan	low inflation
credit rating	bond portfolio

產業名稱：銀行金融業

②

bill of lading	shipping date
shipment details	letter of credit
customs delay	customer service

產業名稱：________

③

latest technology	repetitive strain injury
user interface	input data
system problem	installation wizard

產業名稱：________

假如你在上述產業服務，你一定認得其中一些 word partnerships。

答案

② 進出口貿易業　　③ 資訊科技業 (IT)

現在 Leximodel 的定義應該要修正了：

Language consists of words which appear with other words. These combinations can be categorized as chunks, set-phrases and word partnerships and placed along a spectrum of predictability, with fixed combinations at one end, and fluid combinations at the other.
語言由字串構成，這些字串可分成三大類──chunks、set-phrases 和 word partnerships，並且可依其可預測的程度區分，可預測度愈高的一端是固定字串，可預測度愈低的一端是流動字串。

新的 Leximodel 圖示如下：

〈The Spectrum of Predictability 可預測度〉

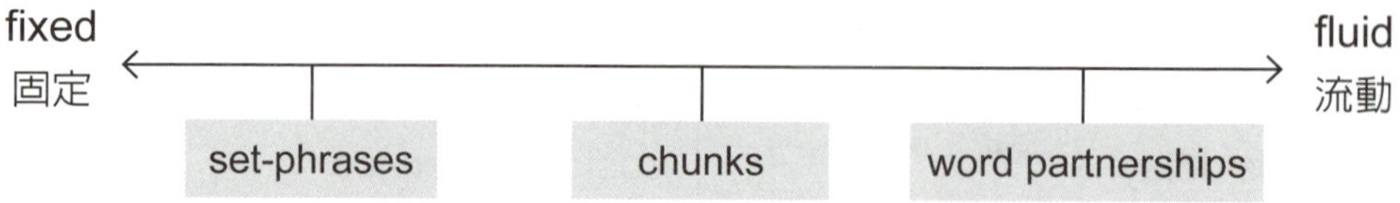

學英文致力學好 chunks，文法就會進步，因爲大部分的文法錯誤其實都是源自於 chunks 寫錯。學英文時專攻 set-phrases，英文功能就會進步，因爲 set-phrases 都是功能性字串。學英文時在 word partnerships 下功夫，字彙量就會增加。因此，最後的 Leximodel 圖示如下：

〈The Spectrum of Predictability 可預測度〉

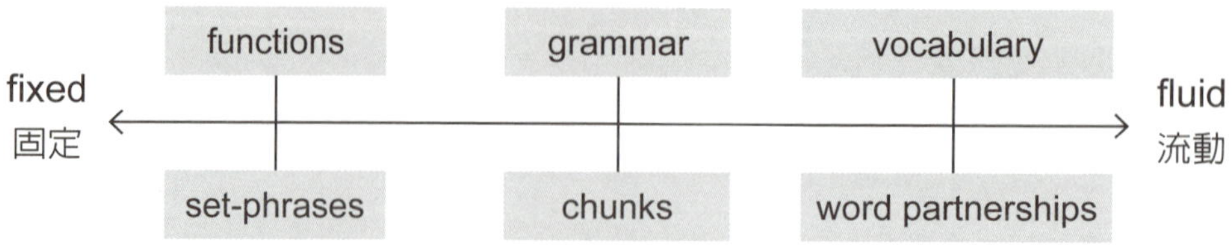

Leximodel 的優點與其對學英文的妙用，就在於無論說、寫英文，均無須爲文法規則傷透腦筋。學英文時，首要之務是建立 chunks、set-phrases 和 word partnerships 語庫，多學多益，再也不必費神記文法，或思索如何在文

法中套用單字。這三類 MWI 用來輕而易舉，而且更符合大腦記憶和使用語言的方式。在本節結束之前，我們來做最後一個 Task，確定各位已完全了解 Leximodel。完成 Task 前，先不要查看語庫。

Task 導讀 5

請閱讀這封電子郵件和底下的摘要，找出所有的 chunks、set-phrases 與 word partnerships，並分別用三種顏色劃底線，最後完成下表。見範例。

Dear Marge,

Thanks for your email, which I received yesterday. I have been very busy so I have not had time to look for the media review data you asked for. I hope I'll have time to get it to you tomorrow.

Regarding the customer satisfaction survey, this will be ready next week. In your email you mentioned that you are worried about the focus groups. Don't worry! We are currently organizing some people for the focus group to test the TV commercial and have already booked the research house for Saturday 28th at 9.00. I saw the draft version at the production house last night and the result looks good.

If you have any more questions, please don't hesitate to call me.

I'm looking forward to seeing you at the focus group on Saturday.

Regards,
Oliver

郵件訊息摘要

奧利弗和瑪姬都在廣告業工作。奧利弗寫信給瑪姬，對他因太忙而未寄送媒體評估數據致歉。他向瑪姬回報了專案的進度。客戶滿意度調查即將準備就緒，研究機構已訂妥，並且正在組建焦點小組來測試奧利弗公司製作的產品。他認為廣告的初剪看起來不錯。

Set-phrases	Chunks	Word Partnerships
Thanks for your email ...	... be ready ...	research house

中譯

親愛的瑪姬，

謝謝妳昨天的 Email。我最近很忙，沒時間去找妳要的媒體評估數據。我希望明天有時間給妳。
關於客戶滿意度調查，下週準備好。妳在信中提到妳很擔心焦點小組。不用擔心！我們目前正在組焦點小組來測試電視廣告，並已預訂 28 日星期六 9 點的研究機構。昨晚我在製作室看了初剪，成果看起來不錯。
如果妳還有任何疑問，請隨時來電。
期待在週六的焦點小組會議上見到妳。

祝好，
奧利弗

答案

請以下列語庫核對答案。

素養加分語庫 **導讀 3**

Set-phrases	Chunks	Word Partnerships
Thanks for your email ...	... have been very busy ...	media review data
Regarding n.p. ...	... have time to V ...	customer satisfaction survey
In your email you mentioned that v.p. ...	... look for ...	focus group
If you have any more questions,	... asked for sth. ...	TV commercial
, please don't hesitate to V ...	... get sth. to sb. ...	research house
I'm looking forward to Ving	... be ready ...	draft version
	... be worried about ...	production house
	... are currently organizing ...	last night
	... have already booked ...	looks good
	... book sth. for DATE ...	
	... see sth. ...	

語庫小叮嚀

- Set-phrases 通常以大寫字母開頭，以標點符號（如句號、問號）結尾；刪節號（ ... ）代表句子的流動部分。
- Chunks 的開頭和結尾都有刪節號，表示 chunks 大多為句子的中間部分。
- 所有的 word partnerships 都至少包含兩個意義字。

假如你的答案沒有這麼完整，別擔心。只要多練習，就能找出文本中所有的固定元素。不過你可以確定一件事：等到你能找出這麼多的 MWI，那就表示你的英文真的非常好！很快你便能擁有這樣的能力，熟能生巧！

本書使用說明

本書架構分爲六大部分，主題廣泛，包括：

- 地方 Places
- 人物 People
- 節慶 Events
- 事物 Things
- 科技 Technology
- 議題 Issues

利用本書練習時，請將重點放在 word partnerships 和 chunks 上，尤其是 word partnerships。各主題皆收錄五個單元，除了英文學習外，也提供一些基礎知識，可從頭到尾順著看完，也可選擇感興趣的主題跳著看，相信你會覺得既有趣又充滿收穫，自然養成閱讀素養。

各單元配置了相同類型的練習模式。首先請閱讀一篇文章，閱畢請動動腦做閱讀測驗。接著，我規劃了幾個 Tasks，例如從文本中找出 word partnerships、填空寫作、連連看等，這將有助於鍛鍊「注意力」；這類 Tasks 連同文章頁底的 VOCABULARY 的目標是擴大主題詞彙量。

接下來，我設計了一個著眼於文法的練習。這並不難，因爲大多數文法你都會在之前的學習中遇到，其中一些文法 Tasks 將重點放在 chunks，一些將重點放在動詞時態或動詞的其他特徵。練習結束後會搭配寫作 Task，請在不同但相關的句子中實際應用，這將幫助提升文法複雜性。以上所有 Tasks 都請不要跳過，答案都在各單元的最後一頁。

每個單元皆以對話作爲結尾，內容主題與閱讀文本相同但用字較淺顯易懂，也可當作聊天來閱讀。這將使你清楚知道如何在口語和聽力中正確運用 word partnerships，並加強流暢度。關於音檔，各單元的閱讀文本由我親自以英國口音錄製，同時聊一聊我的觀點；末尾的對話則由美國口音老師配音，讀者可透過這兩種不同腔調，進一步強化聽力。

祝學習有成，閱聽愉快！

Quentin Brand

Part 1

Photo by Anthony DELANOIX on Unsplash

地方

PLACES

Unit 1

巴黎
Paris

在本單元中，你將了解歐洲的一座城市。

研讀完你應達成的學習目標包括：

□ 學到一些可用以談論本主題的 word partnerships
□ 練習了一些介系詞 chunks

Reading

Task 1 1-1

請閱聽這篇文章並回答下面的問題。

In recent years, Paris has been steadfastly carving its path towards environmental **sustainability**, aiming to **emerge** as Europe's greenest city by 2030. With **innovative initiatives** and ambitious goals, the City of Lights is not only envisioning a greener future but actively taking strides to achieve it. From hosting the 2024 Olympics to **implementing groundbreaking** projects like its underground cooling system, Paris is demonstrating its **commitment** to environmental **stewardship** on multiple fronts.

The 2024 Olympics presented a unique opportunity for Paris to **showcase** its **dedication** to sustainability on a global stage. As the city prepared to welcome athletes and visitors from around the world, it prioritized eco-friendly practices in event planning and **infrastructure** development. From utilizing renewable energy sources to promoting public transportation and cycling, the aim was to minimize the **carbon** footprint associated with the games and leave a positive environmental **legacy** for future generations.

One of the standout features of Paris's green agenda is its innovative underground cooling system. As the city grapples with rising temperatures due to climate change, traditional cooling **methods** can strain energy resources and **exacerbate** environmental **impact**. In response, Paris pioneered an underground network of chilled water pipes that circulate cold water from the Seine River to cool buildings and public spaces.

This groundbreaking system not only reduces reliance on energy-intensive air conditioning but also helps **mitigate** the urban heat island effect, where cities experience higher temperatures than surrounding rural areas due to human activities and infrastructure. By **harnessing** the natural cooling properties of water and **leveraging** existing infrastructure, Paris set a **precedent** for **sustainable** urban development.

Beyond the Olympics and cooling systems, Paris implemented a range of initiatives to promote sustainability across various **sectors**. The city invested in expanding green spaces, improving air quality, and enhancing public transportation networks. Initiatives like "Paris Respire" transformed certain neighborhoods into car-free zones on weekends, promoting walking, cycling, and **community engagement**.

Furthermore, Paris committed to phasing out fossil fuel-powered vehicles and transitioning to electric and alternative fuel vehicles. With incentives for electric vehicle **adoption** and the expansion of charging infrastructure, the city aimed to reduce air pollution and **combat** climate change while fostering innovation in the automotive industry.

In addition to governmental efforts, Paris's green transition was supported by active citizen engagement and **collaboration** with businesses and organizations. Grassroots movements, community gardens, and sustainability-focused events contributed to a culture of environmental **awareness** and action. Meanwhile, partnerships with industry leaders enabled the development and implementation of **cutting-edge** technologies and solutions.

Looking ahead to 2030, Paris's ambition to become Europe's greenest city is not without its challenges. Addressing issues like waste management, **biodiversity** loss, and equitable access to green spaces will require continued dedication and collaboration. However, with a clear vision, strong leadership, and a commitment to innovation, Paris is well-positioned to lead the way towards a more sustainable future.

VOCABULARY

sustainability [səˌstenəˋbɪlətɪ] *n.* 永續性
emerge [ɪˋmɝdʒ] *v.* 出現；成爲
innovative [ˋɪnoˌvetɪv] *adj.* 創新的
initiative [ɪˋnɪʃətɪv] *n.* 倡議
implement [ˋɪmpləˌmənt] *v.* 實行
groundbreaking [ˋgraʊndˌbrekɪŋ] *adj.* 開創性的
commitment [kəˋmɪtmənt] *n.* 承諾
stewardship [ˋstjuwɚdˌʃɪp] *n.* 管理
showcase [ˋʃoˌkes] *v.* 展示
dedication [ˌdɛdəˋkeʃən] *n.* 奉獻；專注
infrastructure [ˋɪnfrəˌstrʌktʃɚ] *n.* 基礎建設
carbon [ˋkɑrbən] *n.* 碳
legacy [ˋlɛgəsɪ] *n.* 歷史地位；影響
method [ˋmɛθəd] *n.* 方法
exacerbate [ɪgˋzæsɚˌbet] *v.* 使惡化
impact [ˋɪmˌpækt] *n.* 影響
mitigate [ˋmɪtəˌget] *v.* 減輕（危害等）
harness [ˋhɑrnɪs] *v.* 利用
leverage [ˋlɛvərɪdʒ] *v.* 發揮重要功效
precedent [ˋprɛsədənt] *n.* 先例
sustainable [səˋstenəbl̩] *adj.* 可持續的
sector [ˋsɛktɚ] *n.* 部門；行業
community [kəˋmjunətɪ] *n.* 社區；群體
engagement [ɪnˋgedʒmənt] *n.* 參與
adoption [əˋdɑpʃən] *n.* 採用
combat [ˋkɑmbæt] *v.* 對付
collaboration [kəˌlæbəˋreʃən] *n.* 合作
awareness [əˋwɛrnɪs] *n.* 意識
cutting-edge [ˋkʌtɪŋˋɛdʒ] *adj.* 尖端的
biodiversity [ˌbaɪoˌdaɪˋvɝsətɪ] *n.* 生物多樣性

Comprehension questions

Q1: What is the main topic of the article?

A. the underground water cooling system in Paris

B. some features of the city of Paris

C. the 2024 Olympics

Q2: What is the main topic of the second paragraph?

A. renewable energy

B. an eco-friendly Olympics

C. sustainability

Q3: How does Paris reduce temperatures?

A. everyone uses air conditioning

B. there is an underground water cooling system

C. harnessing the natural cooling properties of water

Q4: How did the city promote sustainability?

A. it expanded its green spaces

B. it collaborated with businesses

C. it formed partnerships with industry leaders

Q5: What is Paris's ambition for 2030?

A. to implement cutting edge technologies

B. to provide strong leadership

C. to become Europe's greenest city

答案在本單元最後一頁。如果答錯了，請再確認一次文章內容。

稍後，我們將開始來研究 word partnerships。正如我在導論中所說，與其一個一個地記憶單字，以 word partnership 為單位來學習成效更好，因為我們從來都不是單獨使用某一個字，而總是將單字與其他單字一起併用。

中譯

近年來，巴黎堅定不移地走上環境永續發展的道路，目標是在 2030 年前成為歐洲最環保的城市。透過各種創舉與宏大的願景，這座光之城不僅僅只在構想更環保的未來，而是積極地採取行動。從主辦 2024 年奧運會到施行地下冷卻系統等創新計畫，巴黎正在多方面展現其對環境保護的承諾。

2024 年奧運會對巴黎而言是一個獨特的機會，可以在全球舞台上展示其對永續發展的奉獻精神。當準備迎接來自世界各地的運動員和遊客時，這座城市在活動規劃和基礎設施開發方面優先考慮了環保實踐。從利用再生能源到鼓勵民眾出門搭乘大眾運輸和騎自行車，其目的在於將與奧運會相關的碳足跡減至最少，並為子孫後代留下正面的環境遺產。

巴黎綠色議程中最引人注目的特色之一是其創新的地下冷卻系統。隨著氣候變遷導致氣溫上升，傳統的冷卻方法可能會增加能源負擔並加劇對環境的影響。對此，巴黎率先建置了地下冷卻水管網路，將塞納河的冷水循環起來，為建築物和公共空間降溫。

這項突破性的系統不僅減少了對高耗能空調的依賴，還有助於緩解都市熱島效應，即由於人類活動和建築物、道路等因素，城市的氣溫高於周邊鄉村地區的現象。透過利用水的自然冷卻特性和現有基礎設施，巴黎為永續城市發展樹立了典範。

除了奧運和冷卻系統之外，巴黎還實施了一系列措施來促進各領域的永續發展，致力於擴大綠地、改善空氣品質和加強公共交通網路。例如「巴黎呼吸 (Paris Respire)」此計畫將某些社區變成週末無車區，鼓勵步行、騎自行車和社區互動。

此外，巴黎承諾逐步淘汰燃油車，轉而推廣電動車和替代燃料車。透過鼓勵採用電動車和擴建充電設施，除了減輕空氣污染、因應氣候變遷，同時也促進汽車產業的創新。

不光是政府在努力，市民的積極參與及企業組織的協作也為巴黎的綠色轉型提供了支持。草根運動、社區花園和各類環保活動促進了環保意識的提升與實踐，而政府也與產業領袖合作，推動尖端技術的研發與應用。

展望 2030 年，巴黎成為歐洲最環保城市的雄心壯志並非毫無挑戰。廢棄物管理、生物多樣性喪失和綠地公平分配等問題皆需要持續的關注與多方配合。然而，憑藉著清晰的願景、強大的領導力和創新精神，巴黎已走在邁向永續未來之路的最前端。

文法甦活區

Task 2

請用上篇文章中的 word partnerships 完成下表。見範例。

environmental	sustainability
	initiatives
ambitious	
	future
unique	
	planning
infrastructure	
	transportation
carbon	
	agenda

只要對照文章，便可輕鬆找出答案。

接下來，我們要利用上列 word partnerships 練習寫作。在下一個 task 中，你可能必須以不同的順序加以使用。

Task 3

請用 Task 2 表格中的 word partnerships 填入下列空格。

1. By switching to renewable energy sources, the company significantly reduced its __carbon footprint__ and promoted a more sustainable business model.

2. Companies worldwide are increasingly recognizing the importance of ______________________, implementing practices that reduce their carbon footprint and promote green initiatives.

3. Effective ________________ requires meticulous attention to detail, from coordinating vendors to ensuring a seamless guest experience.

4. Expanding the city's __________________ system has significantly reduced traffic congestion and lowered air pollution levels.

5. The city council introduced several _________________ to reduce waste and promote recycling, transforming the community's approach to environmental conservation.

6. The city's _________________ includes initiatives to increase green spaces, improve air quality, and promote sustainable transportation options.

7. The government's investment in ______________________ aims to improve transportation networks and boost economic growth in the region.

8. The internship provided a __________________ for students to gain hands-on experience in cutting-edge research projects.

9. The startup set ________________ for its first year, aiming to double its customer base and expand into international markets.

10. Through the combined efforts of government policies and community action, we are working towards a __________________ for the next generation.

答案在本單元最後一頁。希望你已了解如何使用 **word partnerships**。

我們來細看本文中的文法，其中使用了一些介系詞 chunks 如下所示。

Task 4

請在文中找出下列介系詞 chunks，並注意看其用法。

· prepared to
· associated with
· features of
· reliance on
· precedent for

使用這些 chunks 時，請特別留意所搭配的介系詞。

Task 5

請用 Task 4 的正確介系詞填入下列空格。

1. The community's reliance __________ local agriculture has increased as people seek fresher and more sustainable food sources.

2. The features __________ the new software include enhanced security measures, a user-friendly interface, and faster processing speeds.

3. The health risks associated __________ smoking have led to widespread campaigns encouraging people to quit.

4. The landmark court ruling set a precedent __________ future cases involving digital privacy rights.

5. The team prepared __________ launch the new product by conducting thorough market research and finalizing the marketing strategy.

答案在本單元最後一頁。希望你有寫對。

Listening

現在我們來聽兩個人討論這篇文章。你會聽到許多相同的 word partnerships 和 chunks。這個練習將幫助你記住它們。

Task 6 1-2

請聽讀下列對話，你聽出了哪些前面 tasks 用到的詞彙？

A: Have you noticed how Paris is really pushing towards becoming Europe's greenest city by 2030? They're serious about environmental sustainability.

B: Yeah, I've read about that! They have some pretty innovative initiatives and ambitious goals. It's not just talk; they're actually taking steps to achieve it.

A: Exactly. Hosting the 2024 Olympics was a unique opportunity for them to showcase their dedication to sustainability on a global stage. They really prioritized eco-friendly practices in their event planning and infrastructure development.

B: I heard they're using renewable energy sources and promoting public transportation and cycling to minimize the carbon footprint associated with the games. They want to leave a positive environmental legacy.

A: One of the standout features of their green agenda is the underground cooling system they've implemented. As temperatures rise due to climate change, traditional cooling methods strain energy resources and increase environmental impact.

B: That system is brilliant. They've created an underground network of chilled water pipes that circulate cold water from the Seine River to cool buildings and public spaces. It reduces reliance on energy-intensive air conditioning and helps mitigate the urban heat island effect.

A: Right, and by leveraging the natural cooling properties of water and existing infrastructure, Paris has set a precedent for sustainable urban development. It's a groundbreaking approach.

B: Beyond the Olympics and cooling systems, they've also invested in expanding green spaces, improving air quality, and enhancing public transportation networks. Initiatives like "Paris Respire" have transformed certain neighborhoods into car-free zones on weekends.

A: That promotes walking, cycling, and community engagement. Plus, they're committed to phasing out fossil fuel-powered vehicles and transitioning to electric and alternative fuel vehicles. The incentives for electric vehicle adoption and expansion of charging infrastructure are impressive.

B: It's a comprehensive approach. Active citizen engagement and collaboration with businesses and organizations are also key. Grassroots movements, community gardens, and sustainability-focused events have really contributed to a culture of environmental awareness and action.

A: Partnerships with industry leaders have helped too. They're developing and implementing cutting-edge technologies and solutions. But looking ahead to 2030, there are still challenges like waste management, biodiversity loss, and equitable access to green spaces.

B: True, but with a clear vision, strong leadership, and a commitment to innovation, Paris is well-positioned to lead the way towards a more sustainable future. They're showing what can be done with dedication and collaboration.

A: I agree. It's inspiring to see a city so committed to a greener future. Let's hope other cities follow their example.

希望你能夠聽到或看到你在本單元中學習的所有語言。如果沒有，不妨多聽幾遍。

中譯

A：你有沒有注意到巴黎正在努力爭取 2030 年前成為歐洲最環保的城市？他們非常重視環境的永續性。

B：是的，我有讀過相關內容！他們有一些相當創新的舉措和遠大的目標，而且不是說說而已，是真的在行動。

A：沒錯。主辦 2024 年奧運對他們來說是一個獨特的機會，可以在全球舞台上展示他們對永續發展的投入。他們在活動策劃和基礎建設上都優先考慮了環保。

B：我聽說他們正在使用再生能源並推廣大衆運輸工具和自行車，以盡量減少與奧運相關的碳足跡。他們希望對環境留下正面的影響。

A：他們的綠色議程中最吸睛的就是地下冷卻系統。隨著氣候變遷導致氣溫上升，傳統的冷卻方式不但耗電，還會對環境造成更多負擔。

B：那個系統很厲害。他們創建了一個地下冷卻水管網路，將塞納河的冷水循環到建築物和公共空間。它減少了對高耗能空調的依賴，有助於緩解都市熱島效應。

A：嗯，透過利用水的自然冷卻特性和現有基礎設施，巴黎為永續城市發展樹立了先例。這是一種開創性的做法。

B：除了奧運和冷卻系統之外，他們還投資擴大綠地、改善空氣品質和加強大衆運輸網。「巴黎呼吸」等計畫已將某些街區變成週末無車區。

A：這鼓勵民衆多走路、騎自行車，還讓鄰里之間的互動更多。此外，他們也致力於逐步淘汰燃油車，改推廣電動車和替代燃料車。電動車和充電站的激勵政策非常吸引人。

B：這是一個全面性的方案。公民的積極參與以及和企業組織的合作也很關鍵。基層運動、社區花園和各種環保活動確實為環境意識的提升與落實做出了貢獻。

A：與產業領導者的合作也有幫助。他們正在研發高科技和解決方案並實際應用。不過，展望 2030 年，仍存在廢棄物管理、生物多樣性喪失和綠地公平分配等問題。

B：對啊，但憑藉著清晰的願景、強大的領導力和創新精神，巴黎有希望在永續未來的路上成為領頭羊，他們證明了只要有心和合作，就會有成果。

A：我同意。看到一座城市對環保如此投入，真是令人鼓舞。希望其他城市也能跟進巴黎的腳步。

在繼續往下學習之前，請先回到本單元開頭處確認那些學習目標自己是否已達成。

Answers

Task 1:

Q1: A Q2: B Q3: B Q4: A Q5: C

Task 2:

environmental	sustainability
innovative	initiatives
ambitious	goals
greener	future
unique	opportunity
event	planning
infrastructure	development
public	transportation
carbon	footprint
green	agenda

Task 3:

1. carbon footprint
2. environmental sustainability
3. event planning
4. public transportation
5. innovative initiatives
6. green agenda
7. infrastructure development
8. unique opportunity
9. ambitious goals
10. greener future

Task 5:

1. on 2. of 3. with 4. for 5. to

Unit 2

戈壁沙漠
The Gobi Desert

在本單元中，你將了解位於中國與蒙古國之間的世界最北沙漠。

研讀完你應達成的學習目標包括：

☐ 學到一些可用以談論本主題的 word partnerships
☐ 做了一些現在簡單式 (present simple tense) 練習

Reading

Task 1 2-1

請閱聽這篇文章並回答下面的問題。

Parts of northern and northwestern China, as well as southern Mongolia, are covered by the huge and rocky Gobi **Desert**. With a total size of over 1.3 million square kilometers, it is the fifth-largest desert in the world.

The Gobi Desert is distinguished by its **severe** and **extreme** climate, with wintertime lows of -40°C and summertime highs of 50°C. Strong winds and rare **precipitation** are further **characteristics** of the area, with summertime being the **primary** time for rain.

The Gobi Desert's **topography** is varied, with various elements such rocky mountains, lowlands covered with **gravel**, and stretches of naked sand. Southern portions of the deserts are a broad, flat plain, while the northern part is more mountainous, including the Altai Mountains.

The Bactrian camel, snow leopard, Gobi bear, and Gobi jerboa are just a few of the unusual and **endangered** animals that call the Gobi Desert home, in spite of its terrible environment. These **species** are well suited to live in this **harsh** environment, because they have **adapted** to the desert's severe temperature and lack of water.

The Gobi Desert has a long history of **nomadic** tribes and kingdoms residing there, giving it a rich cultural **heritage**. The Flaming Cliffs, a renowned paleontological site famous for its dinosaur fossils, the Mogao Caves, a collection of ancient Buddhist temples and art galleries, and the ruins of the ancient city of Karakorum, once the capital of the Mongol Empire, are just a few of the noteworthy **landmarks** in the area.

Moreover, the Gobi Desert has been a **crucial** location for scientific study, notably in the discipline of **paleontology**. Many dinosaur fossils have been found in the area, including some of the most complete and well-preserved examples ever found. The desert also makes an excellent setting for **astronomy** study due to its isolation and lack of light pollution.

VOCABULARY

desert [ˋdɛzɚt] *n.* 沙漠
severe [səˋvɪr] *adj.* 劇烈的
extreme [ɪkˋstrim] *adj.* 極端的
precipitation [prɪˏsɪpɪˋteʃən] *n.* 降雨
characteristic [ˏkærəktəˋrɪstɪk] *n.* 特徵
primary [ˋpraɪˏmɛrɪ] *adj.* 主要的
topography [təˋpɑgrəfɪ] *n.* 地形
gravel [ˋgrævl] *n.* 砂礫
endangered [ɪnˋdendʒɚd] *adj.* 瀕危的
species [ˋspiʃiz] *n.* 物種 (複數形)
harsh [harʃ] *adj.* 嚴酷的
adapt [əˋdæpt] *v.* 適應；改編
nomadic [noˋmædɪk] *adj.* 遊牧的
heritage [ˋhɛrətɪdʒ] *n.* 遺產
landmark [ˋlændˏmark] *n.* 地標
crucial [ˋkruʃəl] *adj.* 至關重要的
paleontology [ˏpelɪanˋtalədʒɪ] *n.* 古生物學
astronomy [əsˋtranəmɪ] *n.* 天文學

Comprehension questions

Q1: What is the main topic of the article?

A. north China

B. Mongolia

C. the Gobi Desert

Q2: What is the main topic of the second paragraph?

A. the climate of the Gobi desert

B. the wind in the Gobi Desert

C. the rainfall in the Gobi desert

Q3: What kind of animals live in the Gobi Desert?

A. bactrian camel, snow leopard

B. grizzly bears

C. birds

Q4: What tourist attractions are in the Gobi Desert?

A. the capital of the Chinese empire

B. the Mogao caves

C. nomadic tribes

Q5: What have scientists discovered in the Gobi Desert?

A. astronomy

B. light pollution

C. dinosaur fossils

答案在本單元最後一頁。如果答錯了，請再確認一次文章內容。

中譯

中國北方、西北方和蒙古南方有一大片區域被廣大的戈壁礫石荒漠覆蓋，總面積超過 130 萬平方公里，是世界第五大沙漠。

戈壁沙漠氣候嚴酷、極端，冬季最低溫可達攝氏零下 40 度，夏季最高溫可達攝氏 50 度。強風和罕見的降水是該地區的另一個特徵，夏季是降雨的主要時期。

戈壁沙漠的地形多樣，有石山、礫石低地、裸露沙丘等。南部地區多為寬闊的平原，而北部則多山，包括阿爾泰山脈。

儘管環境極其惡劣，雙峰駱駝、雪豹、戈壁熊和戈壁跳鼠等稀有瀕危動物仍以戈壁沙漠為家。這些物種之所以能夠在此生存，是因為牠們已適應了沙漠的極端溫差和缺水情況。

戈壁沙漠歷史悠久，過去遊牧部落和王國曾在此居住，使其擁有豐富的文化遺產，其中著名的地標包括：以恐龍化石聞名的古生物遺址火焰山、匯集古代佛教寺廟和藝術的莫高窟、曾為蒙古帝國首都的喀喇崑崙古城遺址等。

此外，戈壁沙漠一直是科學研究的重鎮，特別是在古生物學領域，該地區出土了許多非常完好的恐龍化石。由於與世隔絕且無光害，戈壁沙漠也為天文學研究提供了絕佳的環境。

現在，我們來研究 word partnerships。正如我在導論中所說，與其單獨記某個單字，以 word partnership 爲單位來學習效果更顯著。

文法甦活區

Task 2

請用上篇文章中的 word partnerships 完成下表。見範例。

severe	climate
wintertime	
	winds
rare	
	rainfall
	mountains
naked	
endangered	
	heritage
paleontological	

只要對照文章，便可輕鬆找出答案。

接下來，我們要利用上列 word partnerships 練習寫作。在下一個 task 中，你可能必須以不同的順序加以使用。

Task 3

請用 Task 2 表格中的 word partnerships 填入下列空格。見範例。

1. Conservation efforts are urgently needed to protect endangered animals such as the critically endangered rhinoceros and the elusive snow leopard, whose populations continue to decline due to habitat loss and poaching.

2. During the ____________________, temperatures often plummet to subzero levels, creating icy conditions and prompting residents to bundle up in layers to brave the cold.

3. Preserving the ____________________ of a community involves safeguarding its traditions, artifacts, and historic sites, ensuring that future generations can connect with and appreciate the rich tapestry of their collective identity.

4. The agricultural fields thrived as the region experienced bountiful ____________________, providing essential moisture to crops and fostering lush, green landscapes during the warmest months of the year.

5. The arid desert region typically sees ____________________, with infrequent and sporadic rainfall occurrences that are eagerly awaited by local communities for sustaining their scarce water resources.

6. The coastal areas experienced ____________________, whipping through the landscape with force, causing waves to crash against the shore.

7. The hikers marveled at the breathtaking scenery as they ascended the trail, surrounded by towering ____________________ that seemed to touch the sky.

8. The ____________________ revealed a treasure trove of fossilized remains, offering scientists a rare glimpse into the prehistoric world and unlocking mysteries about ancient life forms that once roamed the area.

9. The ____________________ in the region led to frequent heatwaves, intense storms, and prolonged droughts, posing significant challenges to agriculture and local ecosystems.

10. The vast desert stretched endlessly, with ____________________ shimmering under the scorching sun, creating an awe-inspiring but desolate landscape.

答案在本單元最後一頁。希望你已了解如何使用 **word partnerships**。

這篇文章使用的動詞時態是現在簡單式，因爲它描述的是事實。

Task 4

請再看一遍文章並在所有動詞下劃線。注意時態。

希望你能找到所有的現在式簡單動詞，請留意其中一些是被動的，並請注意看主動動詞字尾的「**s**」。

現在我們來練習在一些寫作中使用現在簡單式的動詞。

Task 5

下面是本單元主題文章的摘要，請使用框框內的動詞填入空格，並確保你使用的動詞是現在簡單式。

be	boast	feature	include	offer

The Gobi Desert, spanning parts of northern and northwestern China and southern Mongolia, 1. ____________ the world's fifth-largest desert, covering over 1.3 million square kilometers. It 2. ____________ a harsh climate with wintertime lows of -40°C and summertime highs of 50°C, along with strong winds and rare precipitation, primarily occurring in summer. The desert's diverse topography 3. ____________ rocky mountains, gravel-covered lowlands, and stretches of naked sand. Despite the challenging environment, the Gobi is home to unique and endangered species like the Bactrian camel and snow leopard. The region 4. ____________ a rich cultural heritage with historical sites such as the Flaming Cliffs and the ancient city of Karakorum. Additionally, the Gobi is a significant paleontological site, renowned for its dinosaur fossils, and 5. ____________ an ideal setting for scientific study in fields like astronomy due to its isolation and minimal light pollution.

答案在本單元最後一頁。希望你記得字尾要加「s」。

Listening

現在我們來聽兩個人討論這篇文章。你會聽到許多相同的 word partnerships 和動詞時態。這個練習將幫助你記住它們。

Task 6 2-2

請聽讀下列對話，你聽出了哪些前面 tasks 用到的詞彙？

A: Hey, have you ever heard about the Gobi Desert?

B: Yeah, it's that massive desert in northern and northwestern China, right? Covers over 1.3 million square kilometers.

A: Exactly! It's the fifth-largest desert in the world. Did you know it has a pretty extreme climate?

B: Oh, I've heard it can get crazy cold in winter, like -40°C, and scorching hot in summer, reaching up to 50°C.

A: Yeah, and the winds are strong, and precipitation is rare. Most of the rain happens during the summer.

B: That sounds harsh. What's the terrain like?

A: It's quite varied. Rocky mountains, gravel-covered lowlands, and stretches of naked sand. The southern part is a flat plain, while the northern part is more mountainous, with the Altai Mountains.

B: Wow, that's diverse. But I've heard some unique and endangered animals live there, like the Bactrian camel and the Gobi bear.

A: Absolutely! Despite the tough conditions, these animals have adapted to survive. The Gobi Desert is their home.

B: And there's a rich cultural history there too, right? Nomadic tribes and ancient kingdoms?

A: Yeah, the Gobi has a long history of nomadic tribes and kingdoms. There are even landmarks like the Flaming Cliffs, known for dinosaur fossils, the Mogao Caves, ancient Buddhist temples, and the ruins of Karakorum, the old Mongol Empire capital.

B: Speaking of dinosaurs, I've heard the Gobi Desert is a goldmine for paleontologists. Many well-preserved dinosaur fossils have been found there.

A: Absolutely! Some of the most complete examples ever discovered. The isolation and lack of light pollution also make it a great spot for astronomy studies.

B: That's fascinating. The Gobi Desert is not just a harsh environment; it's a hub for scientific research and has a rich cultural heritage.

A: Totally! It's a unique place with a lot more going on than just being a vast desert.

希望你能夠聽到或看到你在本單元中學習的所有語言。如果沒有，不妨多聽幾遍。

中譯

A：嘿，你聽過戈壁沙漠嗎？

B：嗯，就是橫跨中國北部和西北部的大沙漠，對吧？面積超過 130 萬平方公里。

A：沒錯！它是世界第五大沙漠。你知道嗎？那裡的氣候非常極端。

B：噢，我聽說冬天會很冷，大概零下 40 度，夏天又會熱到 50 度。

A：是啊，而且風很大，降水很少。大部分降雨都是在夏季。

B：聽起來氣候很嚴峻。那地形怎麼樣？

A：地形很多型態。有山、碎石低地和寸草不生的沙丘。南部是平坦的平原，北部多山，比如阿爾泰山脈。

B：哇，真的很不一樣。不過，我聽說那裡有一些獨特的瀕危動物，像是雙峰駱駝和戈壁熊。

A：對啊！儘管條件艱苦，這些動物還是適應了生存。戈壁沙漠就是牠們的家。

B：那裡也有豐富的文化歷史，對嗎？遊牧部落和古代王國之類的？

A：是的，戈壁有著悠久的遊牧部落和王國歷史，甚至還有一些地標，例如以恐龍化石聞名的火焰山、保存古代佛教寺廟的莫高窟和蒙古帝國舊都喀喇崑崙遺址。

B：說到恐龍，我聽說戈壁沙漠是古生物學家的寶庫，在那裡發現了許多保存完好的恐龍化石。

A：一點也沒錯！有些化石還是目前為止最完整的。而且，因為戈壁地處偏遠、光害少，所以那裡也是天文觀測的好據點。

B：真有趣。戈壁沙漠並非只有環境惡劣這個特點，它也是科學研究基地，並擁有豐富的文化遺產。

A：正是如此！戈壁是一個獨特的地方，除了廣闊的沙漠之外，還有好多值得探索的東西。

在繼續往下學習之前，請先回到本單元開頭處確認那些學習目標自己是否已達成。

Answers

Task 1:

Q1: C   Q2: A   Q3: A   Q4: B   Q5: C

Task 2:

severe	climate
wintertime	lows
strong	winds
rare	precipitation
summer	rainfall
rocky	mountains
naked	sand
endangered	animals
cultural	heritage
paleontological	site

Task 3:

1. endangered animals
2. wintertime lows
3. cultural heritage
4. summer rainfall
5. rare precipitation
6. strong winds
7. rocky mountains
8. paleontological site
9. severe climate
10. naked sand

Task 5:

1. is   2. features   3. includes   4. boasts   5. offers

Unit 3

馬尾藻海
The Sargasso Sea

在本單元中，你將了解大西洋中部的一個地方。

研讀完你應達成的學習目標包括：

☐ 學到一些可用以談論本主題的 word partnerships
☐ 練習了一些被動語態 (passive voice) 的介系詞 chunks

Reading

Task 1 3-1

請閱聽這篇文章並回答下面的問題。

An area of the Atlantic Ocean known as the Sargasso Sea is named for the **concentration** of a special kind of sargassum **seaweed** there. It is a part of the Atlantic Gyre, a **vast current** system that **revolves clockwise** and is generally centered between the West Indies and the Azores.

The Sargasso Sea is **distinctive** in that it is identified by the presence of sargassum rather than by **geographic boundaries**. The Atlantic Gyre's currents hold the seaweed in place, resulting in a unique area marked by floating mats of brownish-yellow seaweed.

The Sargasso Sea is renowned for its nutrient-rich waters that are crystal clear blue and home to a wide variety of **marine** life, including several fish species, crabs, jellyfish, and sea turtles. Several of these species are thought to be **endemic** to the Sargasso Sea since they cannot be found anywhere else in the world.

The Sargasso Sea has special **biological** value, but it also has cultural **significance**. It has a long history of being linked to **myths** and **tales**, such as the Bermuda Triangle tale, in which ships and airplanes are claimed to have **vanished** without a trace.

The Sargasso Sea, while being in a distant area, is **threatened** by a number of environmental issues, such as plastic pollution and the introduction of non-native species that might harm its sensitive **ecosystem**. The Sargasso Sea, which is regarded as one of the most significant marine environments in the world, and its distinctive **ecology** have recently been the subject of attempts to **conserve** and safeguard them.

VOCABULARY

concentration [ˌkansɛnˋtreʃən] *n.* 集中
seaweed [ˋsiˌwid] *n.* 海藻
vast [væst] *adj.* 巨大的
current [ˋkɝənt] *n.* 洋流
revolve [rɪˋvalv] *v.* 旋轉
clockwise [ˋklakˌwaɪz] *adv.* 順時針
distinctive [dɪˋstɪŋktɪv] *adj.* 特殊的
geographic [ʤɪəˋgræfɪk] *adj.* 地理學的
boundary [ˋbaʊndrɪ] *n.* 邊界
marine [məˋrin] *adj.* 海洋的
endemic [ɛnˋdɛmɪk] *adj.* 某地特有的
biological [ˌbaɪəˋlaʤɪkl] *adj.* 生物的
significance [sɪgˋnɪfəkəns] *n.* 意義
myth [mɪθ] *n.* 神話
tale [tel] *n.* 故事；傳說
vanish [ˋvænɪʃ] *v.* 消失
threaten [ˋθrɛtn] *v.* 威脅
ecosystem [ˋɛkoˌsɪstəm] *n.* 生態系統
ecology [ɪˋkaləʤɪ] *n.* 生態學
conserve [kənˋsɝv] *v.* 保護

Comprehension questions

Q1: What is the main topic of the article?

A. the Atlantic Ocean

B. the Sargasso Sea

C. seaweed

Q2: What is the main topic of the second paragraph?

A. the presence of seaweed in the ocean

B. the Atlantic Gyre

C. geographic boundaries

Q3: What kind of marine life lives in the Sargasso Sea?

A. octopus

B. several fish species

C. land turtles

Q4: What is the cultural significance of the Sargasso Sea?

A. many people have drowned there

B. many ships get lost there

C. it's linked to myths and tales

Q5: What threats does the Sargasso Sea face?

A. the seaweed is dying

B. plastic pollution

C. a sensitive ecosystem

答案在本單元最後一頁。如果答錯了，請再確認一次文章內容。

中譯

大西洋中有一個被稱為馬尾藻海的區域，因該地區集中生長一種特殊的馬尾藻而得名，屬大西洋環流的一部分。大西洋環流是一個順時針旋轉的巨大洋流系統，通常以西印度群島和亞速爾群島為中心。

馬尾藻海的獨特之處在於，它是透過馬尾藻的存在而不是地理邊界來識別的。大西洋環流的洋流將海藻固定在某個區域，形成了一個獨特的區域，其特徵是漂浮的棕黃色海藻層。

馬尾藻海以其營養豐富的海水而聞名，海水清澈見底，孕育了多種海洋生物，包括魚類、螃蟹、水母和海龜。其中一些物種被認為是馬尾藻海的特有種，在世界其他任何地方都找不到。

除了特殊的生物學價值之外，馬尾藻海域也具有文化意義，長久以來其與一些神秘故事相關聯，例如百慕達三角洲的傳說，據稱船隻和飛機在此地區消失得無影無蹤。

馬尾藻海雖然位於偏遠地區，卻面臨著許多環境問題的威脅，例如塑膠污染和可能破壞其敏感生態系統的外來物種入侵。馬尾藻海被認為是世界上最重要的海洋環境之一，其獨特的生態最近成為保護的重點對象。

接下來，我們往前繼續研究 word partnerships。容我再稍微提醒一遍，以 word partnership 爲單位來背單字永遠都比一個一個去硬記來得有效率。

文法甦活區

Task 2

請用上篇文章中的 word partnerships 完成下表。見範例。

current	system
geographic	
	mats
nutrient-rich	
	life
fish	
	species
environmental	
	pollution
sensitive	

只要對照文章，便可輕鬆找出答案。

現在，我們要利用上列 word partnerships 練習寫作。在下一個 task 中，你可能必須以不同的順序加以使用。

Task 3

請用 Task 2 表格中的 word partnerships 填入下列空格。見範例。

1. Addressing __environmental issues__ such as deforestation, pollution, and climate change requires global collaboration and a commitment to sustainable practices for the well-being of our planet.

2. All the oceans of the world are connected by a ________________.

3. Coastal cleanup efforts have intensified in response to the escalating problem of ________________, as discarded plastic items continue to pose a significant threat to marine ecosystems worldwide.

4. ________________ in the coral reef includes many colorful fish, intricate coral formations, and fascinating creatures that contribute to the biodiversity of the underwater ecosystem.

5. The city's expansion plans were limited by ____________________ such as mountains and rivers, influencing urban development in specific directions.

6. The conservation program aims to protect endangered ___________, ensuring the preservation of biodiversity and the sustainable management of aquatic ecosystems.

7. The construction project carefully navigated through the delicate wetland, recognizing it as a ________________, and implemented measures to minimize environmental impact.

8. The flourishing marine ecosystem in the coral reef is attributed to the ________________ that support diverse and vibrant marine life.

9. The lake was covered with ______________ of water lilies, creating a picturesque and serene scene for nature enthusiasts.

10. The lush rainforest is home to a variety of ___________________, found nowhere else on Earth, highlighting the unique biodiversity of this ecologically significant region.

答案在本單元最後一頁。希望你已了解如何使用 **word partnerships**。

這篇文章使用了大量帶有從屬介系詞的被動 chunks。

Task 4

請再看一遍文章，找出下列從屬介系詞 chunks 並劃底線。

- is named for
- is identified by
- is renowned for
- be endemic to
- is threatened by

希望你全部都能找到。請特別注意使用了哪些介系詞。

現在讓我們練習在寫作中使用這些從屬介系詞。

Task 5

請在下列句子中填入正確的介系詞。

1. Paris is renowned __________ its iconic landmarks, exquisite cuisine, and unparalleled art scene.

2. The city of New York is named __________ the Duke of York, who later became King James II of England.

3. The polar bear population is threatened __________ the rapid loss of Arctic sea ice, a crucial habitat for hunting and raising their young.

4. The red panda is endemic __________ the eastern Himalayas, where it inhabits bamboo forests in Nepal, Bhutan, and parts of China.

5. The species of bird is identified __________ its distinctive plumage and unique song patterns.

答案在本單元最後一頁。

Listening

現在我們來聽兩個人討論這篇文章。你會聽到許多相同的 word partnerships 和帶有從屬介系詞的被動 chunks。這個練習將幫助你記住它們。

Task 6 3-2

請聽讀下列對話，你聽出了哪些前面 tasks 用到的詞彙？

A: Have you ever heard of the Sargasso Sea in the Atlantic Ocean?

B: Yeah, isn't that the area with the special sargassum seaweed?

A: Exactly! It's this unique part of the Atlantic Gyre, marked by floating mats of brownish-yellow seaweed. The currents hold the seaweed in place, creating a distinctive area rather than being defined by geographic boundaries.

B: Wow, that sounds fascinating. What makes it so special?

A: Well, the Sargasso Sea is known for its crystal clear blue waters and is incredibly rich in nutrients. It's a haven for marine life, including various fish species, crabs, jellyfish, and sea turtles. Some of these species are even thought to be found only there.

B: That's amazing, but why is it culturally significant?

A: It has a long history tied to myths and tales, like the Bermuda Triangle story, where ships and airplanes are said to vanish mysteriously. The cultural significance adds to its allure.

B: It sounds like a delicate ecosystem. Is it facing any threats?

A: Unfortunately, yes. The Sargasso Sea is threatened by issues like plastic pollution and the introduction of non-native species, which could harm its sensitive ecology.

B: That's concerning. Is there anything being done to protect it?

A: Absolutely. Recently, there have been efforts to conserve and safeguard the Sargasso Sea. It's considered one of the most significant marine environments globally, so there's a push to address the environmental challenges it's facing.

B: Good to hear that steps are being taken. It's crucial to preserve such unique and important ecosystems.

希望你能掌握到你在本單元中學習的所有語言。如果沒有，多聽幾遍。

中譯

A：你有聽過大西洋的馬尾藻海嗎？

B：有啊，那裡有很特別的馬尾藻，對吧？

A：沒錯！那裡是大西洋環流的一部分，特點是漂浮著棕黃色海藻層。洋流將海藻固定住，形成一個獨特的區域，而不是由地理邊界界定。

B：哇，聽起來很神奇。它有什麼特別之處嗎？

A：馬尾藻海以其晶瑩剔透的藍色海水和豐富的營養著稱，是多種海洋生物的天堂，包括各種魚類、螃蟹、水母和海龜。其中有些物種據說是這裡特有的，世界上其他地方找不到。

B：真厲害，但為什麼它具有文化意義呢？

A：長久以來它與許多神秘故事有關，例如百慕達三角洲的傳說，據說有船隻和飛機在那裡神秘消失。這層文化意義增加了它的吸引力。

B：聽起來那裡的生態系統很脆弱。它有面臨什麼威脅嗎？

A：不幸的是，有。馬尾藻海面臨像塑膠污染和外來物種入侵等問題，這些問題可能會破壞它敏感的生態環境。馬尾藻海正面臨像塑膠污染和外來物種入侵等問題，這些問題可能會破壞它敏感的生態環境。

B：真令人擔憂。有什麼措施可以保護它嗎？

A：當然有。近年來，人們為保護馬尾藻海做出了努力，它被視為全球最重要的海洋環境之一，所以大家都在努力解決它面臨的環境挑戰。

B：聽到有措施正在進行真是太好了。保護這樣獨特且重要的生態系統真的很重要。

在繼續往下學習之前，請先回頭確認前面的學習目標是否已達成。

Answers

Task 1:

Q1: B Q2: A Q3: B Q4: C Q5: B

Task 2:

current	system
geographic	boundaries
floating	mats
nutrient-rich	waters
marine	life
fish	species
endemic	species
environmental	issues
plastic	pollution
sensitive	ecosystem

Task 3:

1. environmental issues
2. current system
3. plastic pollution
4. Marine life
5. geographic boundaries
6. fish species
7. sensitive ecosystem
8. nutrient-rich waters
9. floating mats
10. endemic species

Task 5:

1. for 2. for 3. by 4. to 5. by

Unit 4 加拉巴哥群島
The Galapagos Islands

本單元的閱讀文章比前兩篇稍長，也更具挑戰性。

研讀完你應達成的學習目標包括：

☐ 學到一些可用以談論本主題的 word partnerships
☐ 練習了一些描述目的與結果的 chunks

Reading

Task 1 4-1

請閱聽這篇文章並回答下面的問題。

In the vast expanse of the Pacific Ocean lies a group of enchanting **islands** that have **captured** the imagination of scientists, **conservationists**, and nature **enthusiasts** alike—the Galapagos Islands. Renowned for their unique biodiversity and critical role in shaping Charles Darwin's theory of evolution, these volcanic islands continue to be a **beacon** of natural **wonder** and a **testament** to the delicate balance of ecosystems.

The Galapagos Islands, located about 600 miles off the coast of Ecuador, consist of 18 main islands and **numerous** smaller **islets**. Their isolated location and varied geology have given rise to a stunning array of plant and animal species found nowhere else on Earth. Giant tortoises, marine iguanas, and blue-footed boobies are just a few examples of the **iconic fauna** that call the Galapagos home.

The islands' unique ecosystem played a **pivotal** role in shaping Charles Darwin's theory of evolution. During his famous voyage on HMS Beagle in 1835, Darwin **observed** distinct variations in species from island to island, leading to groundbreaking insights into the process of natural selection. Today, the Galapagos Islands continue to be a living laboratory for scientists studying evolution and ecology.

Despite their ecological significance, the Galapagos Islands face numerous challenges, primarily stemming from human activities. **Invasive** species, overfishing, and climate change threaten the delicate balance that has **evolved** over millennia. To **address** these **concerns**, the Ecuadorian government, in collaboration with international organizations, has implemented **stringent** conservation measures.

One of the remarkable success stories is the restoration of giant tortoise populations. Once on the brink of **extinction** due to overharvesting and invasive species, conservation efforts, including captive **breeding** programs and habitat restoration, have led to a significant rebound in tortoise numbers.

The Galapagos Islands attract thousands of visitors each year eager to **witness** the breathtaking **landscapes** and unique wildlife. However, the delicate nature of the ecosystem requires careful management to prevent the negative impacts of tourism. Strict **regulations** are in place to limit the number of visitors, control access to sensitive areas, and promote sustainable practices.

Local communities and tour **operators** actively participate in conservation initiatives, **fostering** a sense of responsibility and stewardship among residents and visitors alike. Education programs aim to raise awareness about the fragility of the ecosystem and the importance of preserving the islands' natural heritage.

As the world grapples with environmental challenges, the Galapagos Islands serve as a beacon of hope for conservation efforts. **Ongoing** research, community involvement, and international collaboration are crucial in ensuring the continued **resilience** of this extraordinary **archipelago**.

In the face of climate change and global biodiversity loss, the Galapagos Islands stand as a **reminder** of the **intricate** connections between species and their environments. Preserving this natural wonder requires a collective commitment to sustainable practices and a dedication to safeguarding the unique biodiversity that has fascinated scientists and nature enthusiasts for centuries.

VOCABULARY

island [ˋaɪlənd] *n.* 島
capture [ˋkæptʃɚ] *v.* 引起想像／關注
conservationist [ˌkansɚˋveʃənɪst] *n.* 保育人士
enthusiast [ɪnˋθjuzɪˌæst] *n.* 愛好者
beacon [ˋbikn] *n.* 燈塔
wonder [ˋwʌndɚ] *n./v.* 奇觀；想知道
testament [ˋtɛstəmənt] *n.* 證明
numerous [ˋnjumərəs] *adj.* 許多的
islet [ˋaɪlɪt] *n.* 小島
iconic [aɪˋkanɪk] *adj.* 代表性的
fauna [ˋfɔnə] *n.* 動物群
pivotal [ˋpɪvətl̩] *adj.* 重要的
observe [əbˋzɝv] *v.* 觀察；遵守（習俗等）
invasive [ɪnˋvesɪv] *adj.* 侵入的
evolve [ɪˋvalv] *v.* 逐步形成；發展
address [əˋdrɛs] *v.* 處理；解決
concern [kənˋsɝn] *n.* 擔憂；關注
stringent [ˋstrɪndʒənt] *adj.* 迫切的
extinction [ɪkˋstɪŋkʃən] *n.* 滅絕
breeding [ˋbridɪŋ] *n.* 繁殖
witness [ˋwɪtnɪs] *v.* 目擊；作證
landscape [ˋlændˌskep] *n.* 風景
regulation [ˌrɛgjəˋleʃən] *n.* 規則
operator [ˋapəˌretɚ] *n.* 經營者；公司
foster [ˋfɔstɚ] *v.* 培養
ongoing [ˋanˌgoɪŋ] *adj.* 持續的
resilience [rɪˋzɪlɪəns] *n.* 韌性；恢復力
archipelago [ˌarkəˋpɛləˌgo] *n.* 群島
reminder [rɪˋmaɪndɚ] *n.* 提醒
intricate [ˋɪntrəkɪt] *adj.* 複雜的

Comprehension questions

Q1: What is the main topic of the article?

A. the Pacific Ocean

B. the Galapagos Islands

C. Darwin's theory of evolution

Q2: What is the main topic of the second paragraph?

A. the fauna of the Galapagos Islands

B. tortoises

C. the isolated location of the Islands

Q3: What challenges do the Galapagos Islands face?

A. human activities

B. the animals are on the brink of extinction

C. environmental challenges

Q4: What are the local government doing about these problems?

A. they are preventing visitors from going there

B. they are encouraging local communities and tour operators to actively participate in conservation initiatives

C. they are seeking international cooperation

Q5: What does the Galapagos islands stand as a reminder of?

A. the importance of preserving natural wonders

B. the unique diversity found on our planet

C. the intricate connections between species and their environments

答案在本單元最後一頁。如果答錯了，請再確認一次文章內容。

中譯

在浩瀚的太平洋上，有一群迷人的島嶼吸引了科學家、自然資源保育人士和自然愛好者的目光——加拉巴哥群島。這些火山島因其獨特的生物多樣性聞名，並在塑造達爾文的進化論中扮演了重要角色，至今仍被視為自然奇觀的象徵，也是生態系統微妙平衡的證明。

加拉巴哥群島距離厄瓜多海岸約 600 英里，由 18 個主島和眾多小島組成。由於偏遠的地理位置和多樣的地質條件，這裡孕育了地球上獨一無二的動植物物種。像陸龜、海鬣蜥和藍腳鰹鳥，就是生活在加拉巴哥群島的代表性動物。

這些島嶼的獨特生態系統在達爾文進化論的形成中發揮了關鍵作用。1835 年，達爾文在英國皇家海軍小獵犬號 (HMS Beagle) 的著名航行中觀察到島嶼之間物種的明顯差異，從而對天擇過程產生了突破性的見解。如今，加拉巴哥群島仍是科學家研究演化和生態學的活生生的實驗室。

儘管具有重要的生態意義，加拉巴哥群島仍面臨許多挑戰，這些挑戰主要源自人類活動。入侵物種、過度捕撈和氣候變遷威脅著數千年來形成的微妙平衡。為了解決這些問題，厄瓜多政府與國際組織合作，推行了嚴格的保育措施。

其中一個顯著的成功案例是陸龜的復育。由於過度捕撈和入侵物種，陸龜一度瀕臨滅絕，但透過包括人工繁殖計畫和棲地恢復等保育努力，數量大幅回升。

每年有成千上萬的遊客前往加拉巴哥群島，渴望一睹壯麗的景觀和獨特的野生動物。然而，生態系統的脆弱性需要謹慎管理，以防止旅遊業的負面影響。相關單位制定了嚴格的規範限制遊客數、控制進入敏感區域並推廣永續的旅遊方式。

當地社區和旅行社也積極參與保育，培養居民和遊客的責任感和守護精神。此外，還透過教育計畫提高人們對生態系統脆弱性的認識，強調保護島嶼自然遺產的重要性。

在世界努力應對環境挑戰之際，加拉巴哥群島成為保育工作的希望燈塔。持續的研究、社區參與和國際合作對確保此群島的長期韌性至關重要。

面對氣候變遷和全球生物多樣性喪失，加拉巴哥群島提醒大家，物種與環境之間的連結是多麼錯綜複雜。保護這片自然奇觀需要對永續實踐的共同承諾，並致力於守護幾個世紀以來令科學家和自然愛好者著迷的奇妙生態。

接下來，我們往前繼續研究 word partnerships。別忘了，以 word partnership 爲單位來背單字是最有效率的記憶方式。

文法甦活區

Task 2

請用上篇文章中的 word partnerships 完成下表。見範例。

enchanting	islands
	biodiversity
critical	
delicate	
	location
iconic	
	laboratory
conservation	
	restoration
negative	

只要對照文章，便可輕鬆找出答案。

現在，我們要利用上列 word partnerships 練習寫作。在下一個 task 中，你可能必須以不同的順序加以使用。

Task 3

請用 Task 2 表格中的 word partnerships 填入下列空格。見範例。

1. Australia is renowned for its __iconic fauna__, with kangaroos and koalas representing just a fraction of the diverse and unique wildlife that calls the continent home.

2. Implementing effective ________________ is crucial to safeguarding endangered species and preserving the delicate balance of ecosystems for future generations.

3. In the business world, effective communication plays a __________ in fostering collaboration and driving innovation among team members.

4. Maintaining a _____________________ between work commitments and personal life is essential for overall well-being and sustained productivity.

5. The ambitious ____________________ project aims to revitalize the once-degraded wetlands, providing a renewed haven for diverse wildlife and promoting a healthier ecosystem.

6. The construction of the new highway had significant _____________ on the local environment, causing disruption to wildlife habitats and contributing to increased air and noise pollution.

7. The coral reefs of the Great Barrier Reef serve as a ____________, allowing scientists to study the intricate marine ecosystem and its responses to environmental changes.

8. The ___________________, with their pristine beaches and vibrant coral reefs, beckon travelers to a paradise of tranquility and natural beauty.

9. The rainforest's ___________________, teeming with rare species found nowhere else on Earth, highlights the importance of conservation efforts to protect these ecological treasures.

10. The small village, nestled in an ____________________ among the mountains, provided its residents with a peaceful escape from the hustle and bustle of city life.

答案在本單元最後一頁。希望你已了解如何使用 **word partnerships**。

我們來看看這篇文章中的一些文法，其中有很多篇幅在描述目的與結果。作完下列練習你就會了解這部分的細節。

Task 4

請再看一遍文章，找出下列描述目的或結果的 chunks 並劃底線。

- have given rise to
- have led to
- fostering
- leading to
- to limit

以上除了「to limit (to V)」是用來描述目的外，皆用以描述某事的結果。

Task 5

請從 Task 4 的 chunks 選出最適當者填入下列空格。

1. The community center plays a crucial role, ____________ a sense of belonging and collaboration among residents through various cultural events and social activities.
2. The ongoing global pandemic and its widespread impact on economies and healthcare systems ____________ unprecedented changes in how societies function and prioritize public health.
3. The persistent drought conditions ____________ a critical water shortage in the region, necessitating urgent conservation measures.
4. The rapid advancements in technology ____________ a myriad of opportunities and challenges in our interconnected world.
5. The company has implemented strict guidelines on waste disposal and adopted eco-friendly practices in its manufacturing processes ____________ the environmental impact.

答案在本單元最後一頁。

Listening

現在我們來聽兩個人討論這篇文章。你會聽到許多相同的 word partnerships 和描述目的與結果的 chunks。

Task 6 4-2

請聽讀下列對話，你聽出了哪些前面 tasks 用到的詞彙？

A: Hey, have you ever heard about the Galapagos Islands?

B: Yeah, aren't those the islands that Charles Darwin visited during his famous voyage on the HMS Beagle?

A: Exactly! They're a group of enchanting islands in the Pacific Ocean, about 600 miles off the coast of Ecuador. They're known for their unique biodiversity and played a critical role in shaping Darwin's theory of evolution.

B: Oh, right! Giant tortoises, marine iguanas, and those blue-footed boobies—those are some of the iconic fauna found there, aren't they?

A: Spot on! The islands' isolated location and delicate balance of the ecosystem have given rise to a stunning array of plant and animal species found nowhere else on Earth.

B: Darwin's observations on the variations in species from island to island really changed the game in understanding evolution, didn't they?

A: Absolutely. His groundbreaking insights into natural selection were a result of studying the distinct variations in species across the islands. And guess what? The Galapagos Islands are still a living laboratory for scientists studying evolution and ecology.

B: That's fascinating! But I've heard there are challenges the islands are facing, right?

A: Unfortunately, yes. Human activities like invasive species, overfishing, and climate change pose significant threats to the delicate balance of the ecosystems there.

B: That's sad. What's being done to address these issues?

A: Well, the Ecuadorian government, along with international organizations, has implemented strict conservation measures. They've had remarkable success stories, like the restoration of giant tortoise populations that were once on the brink of extinction.

B: That's a relief to hear. With all the beauty and uniqueness, I can imagine the islands attract a lot of visitors.

A: Indeed, thousands of visitors each year. But the delicate nature of the ecosystem requires careful management to prevent negative impacts. There are strict regulations in place to control access to sensitive areas and promote sustainable practices.

B: It's great that there's a focus on responsible tourism. Are the local communities involved in conservation efforts?

A: Absolutely! Local communities and tour operators actively participate in conservation initiatives. There are education programs to raise awareness about the fragility of the ecosystem and the importance of preserving the natural heritage of the islands.

B: It sounds like a collective effort. In the face of global environmental challenges, the Galapagos Islands seem to be a beacon of hope for conservation.

A: Definitely. Ongoing research, community involvement, and international collaboration are crucial to ensuring the continued resilience of this extraordinary archipelago.

B: It's inspiring to see how such a unique place can be a reminder of the intricate connections between species and their environments.

A: Absolutely. Preserving the Galapagos Islands requires a collective commitment to sustainable practices and habitat restoration that has fascinated scientists and nature enthusiasts for centuries.

中譯

A：嘿，你聽過加拉巴哥群島嗎？

B：有啊，那不是達爾文在他著名的小獵犬號航行時造訪的群島嗎？

A：沒錯！它們是太平洋上的一群迷人島嶼，距離厄瓜多海岸約 600 英里。這些島嶼因為獨特的生物多樣性聞名，並且對於達爾文進化論有關鍵的影響。

B：噢，沒錯！像陸龜、海鬣蜥和藍腳鰹鳥，這些都是在那裡發現的代表性動物，對吧？

A：完全正確！這些島嶼的孤立位置和生態系統的微妙平衡孕育出許多其他地方找不到的動植物物種。

B：達爾文對島嶼間物種差異的觀察確實改變了我們對進化的理解，是不是？

A：確實如此。他對天擇的劃時代見解就是來自研究這些群島上不同物種之間的明顯差異。你知道嗎？加拉巴哥群島至今仍是科學家研究進化與生態的活實驗室。

B：真是太有趣了！但我聽說這些島嶼正面臨一些挑戰，對吧？

A：很遺憾的是，對。入侵物種、過度捕撈和氣候變遷等人類活動對那裡生態系統的微妙平衡構成了重大威脅。

B：真可惜。那有什麼辦法在解決這些問題嗎？

A：厄瓜多政府與國際組織實施了嚴格的保育措施，並取得一些了不起的成果，例如曾瀕臨滅絕的巨龜種群已成功復育。

B：太好了。那麼美麗和獨特的地方，我可以想像會吸引很多遊客吧。

A：對啊，每年有數千名遊客造訪。不過，因為生態系統非常脆弱，所以需要小心管理以避免負面影響。相關當局制定了嚴格的規範來管控遊客進入敏感區域，並推廣永續的做法。

B：看到他們注重負責任的旅遊管理真好。當地社區有參與保育工作嗎？

A：當然！當地社區和旅遊業者積極參與保育行動。他們還有教育計畫來提高人們對生態系統脆弱性和保護島嶼自然遺產重要性的認識。

B：聽起來得靠集體努力才能達成呢。面對全球環境挑戰，加拉巴哥群島似乎成為保育工作的希望燈塔。

A：你說得很對。持續的研究、社區參與和國際合作對於確保此非凡群島的韌性至關重要。

B：這真是鼓舞人心。如此獨特的地方提醒我們，物種與環境之間的關聯有多複雜。

A：沒錯。保護加拉巴哥群島需要大家一起投入永續做法和棲地復育。幾百年來這裡一直吸引著科學家和大自然愛好者的關注。

在繼續往下學習之前，請先回頭確認前面的學習目標是否已達成。

Answers

Task 1:

Q1: B   Q2: A   Q3: A   Q4: B   Q5: C

Task 2:

enchanting	islands
unique	biodiversity
critical	role
delicate	balance
isolated	location
iconic	fauna
living	laboratory
conservation	measures
habitat	restoration
negative	impacts

Task 3:

1. iconic fauna
2. conservation measures
3. critical role
4. delicate balance
5. habitat restoration
6. negative impacts
7. living laboratory
8. enchanting islands
9. unique biodiversity
10. isolated location

Task 5:

1. leading to / fostering
2. have led to
3. are leading to
4. have given rise to
5. to limit

Unit 5 蒙塞拉特修道院
Escolania de Montserrat

在本單元中，你將了解西班牙的一個地方。

研讀完你應達成的學習目標包括：

□ 學到一些可用以談論本主題的 word partnerships
□ 使用 which 作了一些關係子句 (relative clause) 練習

Reading

Task 1 5-1

請閱聽這篇文章並回答下面的問題。

One of the most known **choirs** in the world is at Montserrat Monastery, which is a **monastery** perched atop a mountain in Catalonia, Spain. Escolania de Montserrat, the monastery choir, has a long history and has been singing there since the 14th century. Over 50 boys at the Escolania de Montserrat reside and learn at the monastery, ranging in age from 9 to 14. They participate in the daily **liturgies** at the **abbey** as the choir while also receiving a **rigorous** education in music, academics, and **religion**. The choir has become well-known all over the world for its **renditions** of polyphonic, Catalan, and Gregorian **chant**.

The Salve Regina, which is performed at the conclusion of each day at Vespers, is one of the **centerpieces** of the abbey performances. The choir has been singing the Salve Regina, which is a **hymn** to the Virgin Mary, every day for more than 700 years. One of the oldest constantly sung pieces of music in the world, the **custom** has been passed down from choirboy to choirboy.

The choir performs daily liturgies as well as concerts and travels all over the world. They have given worldwide performances at the Royal Albert Hall in London and Carnegie Hall in New York, all of which are **illustrious** locations. Famous musicians including Plácido Domingo, José Carreras, and Montserrat Caballé have all worked with the choir.

Many medals and decorations have been **bestowed** upon the Escolania de Montserrat, including the Cross of Sant Jordi, which is one of Catalonia's greatest **distinctions**. The choir is a part of the UNESCO World Heritage List.

The monastery decided to let girls into its choir in recent years, which is a great innovation. This choice was taken in consideration of the times' shifting trends and to give boys and girls the same chances. The choir accepted its first cohort of female members in 2011.

The girls in the choir receive the same **demanding** instruction and training as the boys. They **supplement** their normal **academic** courses with music instruction. Along with taking part in regular **liturgical** services, they also provide performances at events and on tours.

The addition of female singers to the Montserrat choir has been highly appreciated and has improved the monastery. Also, it has assisted in bringing more guests and tourists to the monastery, who come to experience the distinctive sound of the mixed choir.

The Escolania de Montserrat is a jewel of Catalonia and Spain, and its regular concerts at the Montserrat Monastery are a **monument** to the beauty and power of music. They serve as a reminder of the value of history and culture in our lives via their **devotion** to preserving and playing centuries-old music.

VOCABULARY

choir [kwaɪr] *n.* 唱詩班
monastery [ˋmɑnəs͵tɛrɪ] *n.* 修道院
liturgy [ˋlɪtɚdʒɪ] *n.* 禮拜儀式
abbey [ˋæbɪ] *n.* 大修道院
rigorous [ˋrɪgərəs] *adj.* 嚴格的
religion [rɪˋlɪdʒən] *n.* 宗教
rendition [rɛnˋdɪʃən] *n.* 演繹
chant [tʃænt] *n.* 聖歌
centerpiece [ˋsɛntɚ͵pis] *n.* 最重要的部分
hymn [ˋhɪm] *n.* 聖歌
custom [ˋkʌstəm] *n.* 習俗；慣例
illustrious [ɪˋlʌstrɪəs] *adj.* 著名的
bestow [bɪˋsto] *v.* 贈與
distinction [dɪˋstɪŋkʃən] *n.* 榮譽
demanding [dɪˋmændɪŋ] *adj.* 要求高的
supplement [ˋsʌpləmənt] *v.* 補充
academic [ækəˋdɛmɪk] *adj.* 學術的
liturgical [lɪˋtɝdʒɪkl] *adj.* 禮拜儀式的
monument [ˋmɑnjəmənt] *n.* 紀念碑
devotion [dɪˋvoʃən] *n.* 奉獻；致力

Comprehension questions

Q1: What is the article about?

A. the Monastery of Montserrat in Spain

B. a famous boys choir

C. Spanish culture

Q2: What is the main topic of the second paragraph?

A. the virgin Mary

B. one of the oldest constantly sung pieces of music in the world

C. the choir's performances

Q3: What is part of the UNESCO World Heritage list?

A. the Cross of Sant Jordi

B. the choir

C. the monastery

Q4: What happened in 2011?

A. the music stopped

B. the times changed

C. girls were admitted into the choir for the first time

Q5: What kind of education do the girls and boys of the choir receive?

A. a normal education with musical instruction

B. a normal education

C. musical instruction only

答案在本單元最後一頁。如果答錯了，請再確認一次文章內容。

中譯

世界上最著名的合唱團之一位於蒙塞拉特修道院，這是一座坐落於西班牙加泰隆尼亞山頂的修道院。蒙塞拉特男童合唱團 (Escolania de Montserrat) 歷史悠久，自 14 世紀以來一直在此歌唱。蒙塞拉特男童合唱團的 50 多名男孩在修道院居住和學習，年齡介於 9 到 14 歲之間。他們作為合唱團參加修道院的每日禮拜，同時接受嚴格的音樂、學術和宗教教育，並以其對複調聖歌、加泰隆尼亞聖歌和格里高利聖歌的演繹而聞名於世。

《Salve Regina》是合唱團表演的核心曲目，每天晚禱結束時都會演唱。七百多年來，合唱團日日演唱這首獻給聖母瑪利亞的讚美詩——世界上持續演唱時間最久的音樂作品之一，這個傳統代代相傳，由歷代男童合唱團成員承接下來。

合唱團除了每日參加禮拜外，也會到世界各地巡迴演出。他們曾在倫敦皇家阿爾伯特音樂廳和紐約卡內基音樂廳等大場地演出。普拉西多．多明哥、何塞．卡雷拉斯、蒙塞拉特．卡巴耶等名音樂家都曾與其合作。

蒙塞拉特男童合唱團曾獲得許多獎章和榮譽，其中包括加泰隆尼亞最高榮譽之一的聖喬治十字勳章。該合唱團也被登載於聯合國教科文組織世界遺產名錄內。

近年來，蒙塞拉特修道院決定讓女孩加入合唱團，這是一個重大的創新。此舉是考慮到時代的變遷，希望不分性別給予同樣的機會。合唱團於 2011 年接納了第一批女性團員。

合唱團中的女孩接受與男孩相同的嚴格指導和訓練。她們在正常學術課程的基礎上，還接受音樂教育。除了參加定期的禮拜儀式外，她們也會在各種活動和巡演中表演。

女性歌手加入蒙塞拉特合唱團受到了高度讚賞，並讓修道院變得更好。同時，這也幫助吸引了更多訪客前來修道院，體驗混聲合唱團的獨特音色。

蒙塞拉特男童合唱團是加泰隆尼亞和西班牙的瑰寶，其於蒙塞拉特修道院定期舉辦的音樂會是音樂之美和力量的紀念碑。他們致力於保存和演奏數百年歷史的音樂，提醒我們歷史與文化在日常生活中的價值。

讓我們繼續做更多練習，熟悉更多文法與詞組。

文法甦活區

Task 2

請用上篇文章中的 word partnerships 完成下表。見範例。

monastery	choir
daily	
rigorous	
	performances
	performances
music	
	services
	sound
mixed	
centuries-old	

只要對照文章，便可輕鬆找出答案。

現在，我們要利用上列 word partnerships 練習寫作。

Task 3

請用 Task 2 表格中的 word partnerships 填入下列空格。見範例。

1. The ___monastery choir___ filled the sacred halls with harmonious chants, creating an atmosphere of tranquility and spiritual reverence.

PART 1
Unit 1
Unit 2
Unit 3
Unit 4
Unit 5
PART 2
PART 3
PART 4
PART 5
PART 6

2. His success in the challenging field was a testament to his ________ ________________, which prepared him for the complexities of his profession.

3. The cathedral was adorned with candlelight as the community gathered for the solemn and meaningful ________________________, creating an atmosphere of spiritual reflection and devotion.

4. The beauty of the concert transported the audience to another era, as the musicians skillfully performed ________________________ that resonated with timeless melodies.

5. The monks diligently observed their ____________________, engaging in prayer, contemplation, and communal worship.

6. The ____________________ of the vintage vinyl record playing on the turntable filled the room, evoking a sense of nostalgia and warmth.

7. The _____________________________, characterized by their ethereal acoustics and soul-stirring melodies, captivated audiences and provided a unique blend of spiritual and artistic experiences.

8. The __________________, composed of sopranos, altos, tenors, and basses, harmonized flawlessly, creating a rich tapestry of sound that resonated through the concert hall.

9. The renowned orchestra embarked on a tour, showcasing their musical prowess through __________________________________ that captivated audiences across continents.

10. The ____________________ provided by the experienced teacher not only imparted technical skills but also fostered a deep appreciation for the art, shaping students into well-rounded musicians.

答案在本單元最後一頁。希望你已了解如何使用 **word partnerships**。

本文使用了一些帶有 which 這一字的關係子句。馬上來看看。

Task 4

請找出文中寫著下列 which 關係子句的部分，並劃底線。

· which is performed
· which is a hymn to the Virgin Mary
· all of which are illustrious locations
· which is one of Catalonia's greatest distinctions
· which is a great innovation

若想要爲句子添加額外資訊時，可使用 which 關係子句。接下來讓我們練習在一些寫作中實際運用看看吧。在這裡我們將討論略爲不同的主題。

Task 5

請從 Task 4 的 chunks 選出最適當者填入下列空格。

1. She shared her travel stories, highlighting the picturesque landscapes and vibrant cultures of her journey, ______________________ that left a lasting impression on her.
2. The architectural marvel of Sagrada Familia, ______________________, draws visitors from around the world to admire its unique beauty and historical significance.
3. The choral composition, ______________________, is sung with reverence and devotion during special religious ceremonies.
4. The new smartphone model, ______________________, incorporates cutting-edge technology and features that redefine the user experience.
5. The orchestral masterpiece, ______________________ annually during the cultural festival, has become a cherished tradition in the community.

答案在本單元最後一頁。

Listening

現在我們來聽兩個人討論這篇文章。你會聽到許多相同的 word partnerships 和文法 chunks。

Task 6 5-2

請聽讀下列對話，你聽出了哪些前面 tasks 用到的詞彙？

A: Have you ever heard of the monastery choir at Montserrat Monastery in Catalonia, Spain?

B: Oh, you mean Escolania de Montserrat? Absolutely! They're amazing, enchanting audiences with their timeless renditions of polyphonic, Catalan, and Gregorian chant.

A: Exactly! Their performances really showcase the rich musical heritage of the monastery. Have you had the chance to see them live?

B: Not yet, but I've heard they've given performances at the Royal Albert Hall, which is very prestigious.

A: Yes, and Carnegie Hall.

B: Must be an incredible experience.

A: Indeed, it's on my bucket list! The monastery choir is truly a gem, preserving centuries-old music and adding so much cultural value to the region.

B: And didn't they recently include girls in the choir?

A: Yes, they did! The addition of female singers has brought a wonderful dynamic.

B: It's great to see them embracing diversity while maintaining their devotion to tradition.

希望你能掌握到本單元的所有學習內容。如果沒有，多聽幾遍。

中譯

A：你聽過西班牙加泰隆尼亞的蒙塞拉特修道院合唱團嗎？

B：噢，你是說蒙塞拉特男童合唱團？當然知道！他們用永恆的複調、加泰隆尼亞語和格里高利聖歌的詮釋令人驚嘆，讓觀眾著迷。

A：沒錯！他們的表演充分展示了修道院豐富的音樂傳統。你有親眼目睹過他們的現場表演嗎？

B：還沒有，但我聽說他們在皇家阿爾伯特音樂廳演出過，那是非常有聲望的場地。

A：對，還有卡內基音樂廳。

B：那是很了不起的經驗。

A：確實，它在我的願望清單上！這個修道院合唱團真的是一顆寶石，保存了數百年的音樂，並為該地區增添如此多的文化價值。

B：他們最近不是還納入女性成員嗎？

A：是的！女性歌手的加入帶來了精彩的活力。

B：真高興看到他們在堅守傳統的同時也擁抱多樣性。

在繼續往下學習之前，請先回頭確認前面的學習目標是否已達成。

Answers

Task 1:

Q1: A Q2: B Q3: B Q4: C Q5: A

Task 2:

monastery	choir
daily	liturgies
rigorous	education
abbey	performances
worldwide	performances
music	instruction
liturgical	services
distinctive	sound
mixed	choir
centuries-old	music

Task 3:

1. monastery choir
2. rigorous education
3. liturgical services
4. centuries-old music
5. daily liturgies
6. distinctive sound
7. abbey performances
8. mixed choir
9. worldwide performances
10. music instruction

Task 5:

1. all of which are illustrious locations
2. which is one of Catalonia's greatest distinctions
3. which is a hymn to the Virgin Mary
4. which is a great innovation
5. which is performed

Part 2

Photo by Giovana Miketen on Unsplash

人物

PEOPLE

Unit 6

阿嘉莎・克莉絲蒂

Agatha Christie

在本單元中，你將了解一位著名推理小說作家的故事。

研讀完你應達成的學習目標包括：

☐ 學到一些可用以談論本主題的 word partnerships

☐ 完成一些動詞時態的練習

Reading

Task 1 6-1

請閱聽這篇文章並回答下面的問題。

In the **realm** of **detective** fiction, one name stands out as a beacon of **brilliance** and creativity—Agatha Christie. Born on September 15, 1890, in Torquay, England, Christie would go on to become the best-selling novelist of all time, enchanting readers with her captivating **mysteries** and unforgettable **characters**.

Agatha Mary Clarissa Miller, later known as Agatha Christie, spent her early years surrounded by a world of books and storytelling. Raised in a **well-to-do** family, she received an education at home and developed an early passion for **literature**. Her childhood was marked by an avid interest in a variety of **genres**, but it was the works of Wilkie Collins, Arthur Conan Doyle, and E. Phillips Oppenheim that fuelled her fascination with **crime** and mystery. Christie's life took a turn towards adventure during World War I when she worked as a nurse and pharmacist. Her experiences during this time would later influence her writing, adding a layer of realism and depth to her detective stories.

Agatha Christie's literary career took off with her **debut** novel, "The **Mysterious** Affair at Styles," introducing the iconic Hercule Poirot to the world. Published in 1920, this novel laid the foundation for Christie's **reputation** as the "Queen of Crime." Poirot, along with other recurring characters like Miss Marple, became beloved figures in the literary landscape.

The hallmark of Christie's writing was her ability to craft intricate **plots** filled with **red herrings** and unexpected twists. From the **exotic** settings of "Death on the Nile" to the **claustrophobic atmosphere** of "**Murder** on the Orient Express," her novels transported readers to a world of **suspense** and **intrigue**.

Agatha Christie's impact on the mystery genre is immeasurable. With a career spanning over five **decades**, she penned 66 detective novels, 14 short story collections, and the world's longest-running play, "The Mousetrap." Her works have been translated into numerous languages and adapted into countless films, TV series, and stage productions.

What sets Christie apart is not just her **prolific** output but also the sheer brilliance of her storytelling. Her ability to keep readers guessing until the final pages, combined with her keen understanding of human psychology, **cemented** her status as a literary giant.

Agatha Christie's own life took a mysterious turn in 1926 when she disappeared for 11 days, sparking a nationwide manhunt. The circumstances surrounding her vanishing remain a topic of speculation and intrigue to this day. Her reappearance, claiming **amnesia**, only added to the **mystique** surrounding the famous author.

Agatha Christie's influence on the mystery genre persists long after her passing in 1976. Her works continue to **captivate** new generations of readers, and her legacy is celebrated annually through events like the Agatha Christie **Festival**. Her impact on popular culture is evident in the countless adaptations and references in literature, film, and television.

As we reflect on the life and work of Agatha Christie, it is clear that her **contributions** to literature extend far beyond the pages of her books. She not only entertained millions but also left an **indelible** mark on the art of storytelling, reminding us that, in the world of mystery, she will forever be the unrivaled Queen.

VOCABULARY

realm [rɛlm] *n.* 領域
detective [dɪˋtɛktɪv] *adj.* 偵探的
brilliance [ˋbrɪljəns] *n.* 才華
mystery [ˋmɪstərɪ] *n.* 謎案
character [ˋkærɪktɚ] *n.* 角色
well-to-do [ˋwɛltəˋdu] *adj.* 富裕的
literature [ˋlɪtərətʃɚ] *n.* 文學
genre [ˋʒanrə] *n.* 類型
crime [kraɪm] *n.* 犯罪
debut [ˋdɛbˏju] *n.* 首次亮相
mysterious [mɪsˋtɪrɪəs] *adj.* 神秘的
reputation [ˏrɛpjəˋteʃən] *n.* 聲望
plot [plat] *n.* 情節
red herring 轉移注意力的事情
exotic [ɛgˋzatɪk] *adj.* 異國情調的
claustrophobic [ˏklɔstrəˋfobɪk] *adj.* 導致幽閉恐懼症的
atmosphere [ˋætməsˏfɪr] *n.* 氣氛
murder [ˋmɝdɚ] *n.* 謀殺
suspense [səˋspɛns] *n.* 懸疑
intrigue [ɪnˋtrig] *n.* 陰謀
decade [ˋdɛked] *n.* 十年
prolific [prəˋlɪfɪk] *adj.* 多產的
cement [sɪˋmɛnt] *v.* 鞏固
amnesia [æmˋniʒɪə] *n.* 失憶症
mystique [mɪsˋtik] *n.* 神秘感
captivate [ˋkæptəˏvet] *v.* 使著迷
festival [ˋfɛstəvl] *n.* 節日
contribution [ˏkantrəˋbjuʃən] *n.* 貢獻
indelible [ɪnˋdɛləbl] *adj.* 難以磨滅的

Comprehension questions

Q1: What is the main topic of the article?

A. crime fiction

B. the life and work of a crime writer

C. some crime novels

Q2: What is the main topic of the second paragraph?

A. Arthur Conan Doyle

B. her early life and literary influences

C. World War I

Q3: Who is Agatha Christie's most famous character?

A. the Mysterious Affair at Styles

B. Sherlock Holmes

C. Hercule Poirot

Q4: What happened in 1926?

A. she had amnesia

B. Agatha Christie disappeared

C. she started a nationwide manhunt

Q5: How many detective novels did she write?

A. 11

B. 14

C. 66

答案在本單元最後一頁。如果答錯了，請再確認一次文章內容。

中譯

在偵探小說領域，有個才華洋溢的名字堪稱創造力的燈塔——阿嘉莎．克莉絲蒂。她於 1890 年 9 月 15 日出生於英國托奇，最終成為有史以來最暢銷的小說家，以其引人入勝的懸疑故事和難忘的角色吸引了無數讀者。

阿嘉莎．瑪麗．克萊麗莎．米勒，後稱阿嘉莎．克莉絲蒂，童年時便生活在書籍與故事的世界裡。她生長在一個富裕的家庭，接受家庭教育，從小就對文學充滿熱情。小時候對各種文學體裁抱有濃厚興趣，但正是威爾基．柯林斯、亞瑟．柯南．道爾和 E. 菲力浦斯．奧本海姆的作品激發了她對犯罪故事和謎案的迷戀。克莉絲蒂的生活在第一次世界大戰期間變得充滿冒險，當時她擔任護理師和藥劑師的經歷為她日後的寫作增添了現實主義與深度。

阿嘉莎．克莉絲蒂的文學生涯始於其處女作《史岱爾莊謀殺案》，向世界介紹了著名的赫丘勒．白羅。這部小說出版於 1920 年，為克莉絲蒂「犯罪女王」的聲譽奠定了基礎。白羅和瑪波小姐等其他經常出現的角色一起成為文學界的經典人物。

克莉絲蒂寫作的標誌是她能夠精心編織出充滿偽裝線索和出乎意料的複雜情節。從《尼羅河謀殺案》的異國情調到《東方快車謀殺案》的壓迫氛圍，其小說將讀者帶入一個充滿懸念和陰謀的世界。

阿嘉莎．克莉絲蒂對懸疑小說的影響無法估量，其職業生涯長達 50 多年，創作了 66 部偵探小說、14 部短篇故事集，以及全球最長壽的舞台劇《捕鼠器》，作品被翻譯成多種語言並改編成無數的電影、電視劇和舞台劇。

克莉絲蒂的與衆不同之處不僅在於她相當多產，也包括其敘事才華。她能夠讓讀者在最後一頁之前都無法猜測到結局，再加上她對人類心理的敏銳洞察，鞏固了她成為文學巨擘的地位。

1926 年，阿嘉莎．克莉絲蒂的生活發生了神秘的轉變，她失蹤了 11 天，引發了全國性的搜索。她失蹤的原因至今仍是衆人好奇的話題，而她聲稱失憶後重新出現，為這位名作家增添了神秘色彩。

即使在 1976 年辭世後，阿嘉莎．克莉絲蒂對懸疑小說的影響依然存在，其作品仍舊吸引著新一代讀者，每年透過阿嘉莎．克莉絲蒂節等活動來紀念她。無論是在文學、電影或電視劇中，都能看到對她作品無數的改編與致敬，顯示出她對流行文化的深遠影響。

當我們回顧阿嘉莎．克莉絲蒂的一生與作品時，顯然她對文學的貢獻遠超出其書籍。她不僅娛樂了數百萬人，還在故事敘述的藝術上留下了不可磨滅的印記，提醒我們，在懸疑小說的世界裡，她將永遠是無與倫比的女王。

文法甦活區

Task 2

請用上篇文章中的 word partnerships 完成下表。見範例。

detective	fiction
best-selling	
	mysteries
unforgettable	
	novel
recurring	
	plots
red	
	twists
prolific	

只要對照文章，便可輕鬆找出答案。

現在，我們要利用上列 word partnerships 練習寫作。

Task 3

請用 Task 2 表格中的 word partnerships 填入下列空格。見範例。

1. As the gripping narrative unfolded, the author masterfully incorporated __unexpected twists__ that not only kept readers on the edge of their seats but also reshaped the entire storyline, leaving them in awe of the storytelling finesse.

2. Her bookshelf was filled with classic ____________________ novels, showcasing a fascination with thrilling whodunits and cunning sleuths solving perplexing mysteries.

3. In the author's latest work of fiction, she introduces a cast of ____________________ whose unique personalities and compelling journeys resonate long after the final chapter has been read.

4. The author skillfully weaved a tapestry of ____________________, leaving readers on the edge of their seats as they eagerly turned each page to uncover the secrets hidden within the pages of the suspenseful novel.

5. The author's series of detective novels features a set of ____________________, each with their own distinct personalities and quirks, creating a rich and interconnected world that keeps readers eagerly anticipating the next installment.

6. The best-selling author amazed literary enthusiasts with her ____________________, consistently delivering a diverse range of novels that spanned multiple genres, showcasing her versatility and dedication to the craft.

7. The best-selling author is known for crafting ____________________ that intricately interweave unexpected twists and turns, keeping readers guessing until the final, satisfying resolution.

8. The ____________________ captivated readers worldwide with her gripping storytelling and intricate character development, earning her a devoted fan base eagerly awaiting each new literary masterpiece.

9. The clever detective deliberately scattered ____________________ throughout the investigation, leading both the characters and readers down misleading paths before revealing the true, unsuspected culprit in a brilliant plot twist.

10. The young writer garnered critical acclaim with her ______________, a poignant and beautifully crafted exploration of love and loss set against the backdrop of a small seaside town.

答案在本單元最後一頁。

Task 4

請再讀一遍文章，並在所有動詞劃底線。注意所使用的動詞時態和原因。

本文主要使用過去簡單式來描述阿嘉莎的生活，因為她已去世；使用現在簡單式以描述其工作和成就，則是因為這兩項是事實，與時間無關。

Task 5

下面是主題文章的摘要，請使用框框內的動詞填入空格。

add	captivate	emerge	ensure	influence	mark	set

Agatha Christie, born in 1890 in Torquay, England, 1. ______________ as the unparalleled Queen of Crime and the best-selling novelist of all time. Her early passion for literature, 2. ______________ by authors like Wilkie Collins and Arthur Conan Doyle, 3. ______________ the stage for her iconic detective stories featuring Hercule Poirot and Miss Marple. Christie's experiences as a nurse during World War I 4. ______________ depth to her writing, and her debut novel, "The Mysterious Affair at Styles," 5. ______________ the beginning of a prolific career spanning over five decades. With 66 detective novels, 14 short story collections, and the world's longest-running play, "The Mousetrap," Christie's storytelling brilliance, intricate plots, and unexpected twists 6. ______________ readers worldwide. Her mysterious 1926 disappearance and the enduring legacy of her works 7. ______________ her impact on the mystery genre, celebrated through events like the Agatha Christie Festival, ensuring her place as the unrivaled Queen of Mystery.

答案在本單元最後一頁。希望你動詞時態都有寫對。

Listening

現在我們來聽兩個人討論這篇文章。你會聽到許多相同的 word partnerships 和文法 chunks。

Task 6 6-2

請聽讀下列對話，你聽出了哪些前面 tasks 用到的詞彙？

A: Have you ever read any detective fiction? There's this author, Agatha Christie, who's an absolute beacon of brilliance and creativity.

B: Agatha Christie, you say? I've heard the name but never really explored her works. When did she live?

A: She was born on September 15, 1890, in Torquay, England, and she went on to become the best-selling novelist of all time. Her captivating mysteries and unforgettable characters have enchanted readers for generations.

B: Interesting. How did she get into writing detective stories?

A: Well, her childhood was filled with books and storytelling. She developed a passion for literature, especially crime and mystery, inspired by authors like Wilkie Collins and Arthur Conan Doyle. During World War I, she worked as a nurse and pharmacist, and those experiences influenced her writing, adding realism to her detective stories.

B: That's quite a unique background. Tell me more about her debut novel.

A: Her literary career took off with her debut novel "The Mysterious Affair at Styles," published in 1920. That introduced Hercule Poirot, an iconic detective who, along with other recurring characters like Miss Marple, became beloved figures in detective fiction.

B: Sounds intriguing. What's the hallmark of her writing?

A: Agatha Christie was known for crafting intricate plots filled with red herrings and unexpected twists. Her novels, from "Death on the Nile" to "Murder on the Orient Express," transport readers to a world of suspense and intrigue.

B: Impressive. Did she write a lot?

A: Oh, definitely. Over five decades, she penned 66 detective novels, 14 short story collections, and even the world's longest-running play, "The Mousetrap." Her impact on the mystery genre is immeasurable.

B: Wow, that's a prolific output. What sets her apart, though?

A: It's not just the quantity; it's the sheer brilliance of her storytelling. Her ability to keep readers guessing and her understanding of human psychology cemented her status as a literary giant.

B: I read something about her mysterious disappearance in 1926. What happened there?

A: Yes, she vanished for 11 days, sparking a nationwide manhunt. The circumstances remain a topic of speculation and intrigue. When she reappeared, claiming amnesia, it only added to the mystique surrounding her.

B: Intriguing indeed. How about her legacy?

A: Well, even after her passing in 1976, Agatha Christie's influence on the mystery genre persists. Her works continue to captivate new generations, celebrated through events like the Agatha Christie Festival. She's left an indelible mark on storytelling.

B: It sounds like her contributions extend far beyond her books. In the world of mystery, she's the unrivaled Queen.

A: Absolutely. Her impact on popular culture is evident in countless adaptations and references in literature, film, and television. Agatha Christie is a true legend.

希望你能掌握到本單元的所有學習內容。如果沒有，多聽幾遍。

中譯

A：你讀過偵探小說嗎？有個作家叫阿嘉莎．克莉絲蒂，她才華橫溢，而且超有創意。

B：你說阿嘉莎．克莉絲蒂？名字我聽過，但從來沒有深入了解過她的作品。她是什麼時候的作家？

A：她 1890 年 9 月 15 日出生在英國托奇，後來成為有史以來最暢銷的小說家。她引人入勝的謎案和令人難忘的角色讓好幾個世代的讀者著迷。

B：哇，那她是怎麼開始寫偵探小說的？

A：嗯，她的童年充滿了書籍和故事。受到威爾基．柯林斯、亞瑟．柯南．道爾等作家的啓發，她對文學產生了濃厚的興趣，尤其是犯罪和懸疑小說。第一次世界大戰期間，她曾是護理師和藥劑師，這些經歷為她的偵探小說增添了真實感。

B：這樣的背景真特別。告訴我更多關於她的出道作品吧。

A：她的文學生涯從 1920 年出版的小說《史岱爾莊謀殺案》開始，在這本書當中赫丘勒．白羅這位經典偵探角色首度登場。他與另一位經常出現的角色瑪波小姐一樣，成為了偵探小說中的經典人物。

B：聽起來很有趣。她的寫作有什麼特色？

A：阿嘉莎以構建錯綜複雜的情節著稱，其中處處是轉移注意力和意想不到的反轉。從《尼羅河謀殺案》到《東方快車謀殺案》，她的小說將讀者帶入一個充滿懸念和陰謀的世界。

B：感覺很精彩。她的作品很多嗎？

A：噢，很多。五十年多來，她創作了 66 部偵探小說、14 部短篇故事集，甚至還有全球最長壽的舞台劇《捕鼠器》。她對懸疑類小說的影響是無法估量的。

B：哇，真是多產。那她最厲害的地方是什麼？

A：不只是數量多，她講故事的功力一流。她善於讓讀者猜不到結局，加上對人性心理的洞察，讓她成為文學界的大師。

B：我聽說她在 1926 年神秘失蹤過。那是怎麼回事？

A：對，她失蹤了 11 天，引發了全國大搜索。她失蹤的原因至今仍是謎團。她重新出現後聲稱自己失憶，這更加深了她的神秘色彩。

B：也太神秘了吧。那她有什麼影響嗎？

A：嗯，即使在 1976 年去世後，阿嘉莎對懸疑小說的影響依舊不減。她的作品吸引著新一代的讀者，每年都有阿嘉莎．克莉絲蒂節這樣的活動來紀念她。她在敘事藝術上的貢獻是不可磨滅的。

B：感覺她的影響力遠超出了她的書籍。在推理的世界裡，她是無與倫比的女王。

A：沒錯。她對流行文化的影響也顯而易見，無論是文學、電影還是電視劇，都有無數的改編和致敬。阿嘉莎．克莉絲蒂真的是一個傳奇人物。

在繼續往下學習之前，不妨回顧確認一下開頭的學習目標是否已達成。

Answers

Task 1:

Q1: B   Q2: B   Q3: C   Q4: B   Q5: C

Task 2:

detective	fiction
best-selling	novelist
captivating	mysteries
unforgettable	characters
debut	novel
recurring	characters
intricate	plots
red	herrings
unexpected	twists
prolific	output

Task 3:

1. unexpected twists
2. detective fiction
3. unforgettable characters
4. captivating mysteries
5. recurring characters
6. prolific output
7. intricate plots
8. best-selling novelist
9. red herrings
10. debut novel

Task 5:

1. emerged
2. influenced
3. set
4. added
5. marked
6. captivated
7. ensured

德瑞克·賈曼
Derek Jarman

在本單元中，你將了解一位著名畫家、園丁和電影導演的故事。

研讀完你應達成的學習目標包括：

- ☐ 學到一些可用以談論本主題的 word partnerships
- ☐ 完成一些動詞時態的練習

Reading

Task 1 7-1

請閱聽這篇文章並回答下面的問題。

Derek Jarman, the pioneering **filmmaker**, artist, and writer, left an indelible mark on British culture with his vivid imagination, political **activism**, and **unapologetic queerness**. His legacy continues to inspire and challenge us.

Jarman was born in 1942 in Northwood, Middlesex, and studied painting and stage design at the Slade School of Fine Art in London. He burst onto the film scene in the late 1970s with his **provocative** and experimental feature films, such as "Sebastiane" (1976), "Jubilee" (1978), and "The Tempest" (1979), which challenged **conventional** storytelling and sexuality.

But it was his later works, such as “Caravaggio” (1986) and “Blue” (1993), that cemented his reputation as a **visionary** artist who tackled social and political issues with a bold and poetic style. In “Blue”, which was made after he was **diagnosed** with HIV/AIDS, Jarman explored his own **mortality** and the **stigma** surrounding the disease, using a single blue screen and a powerful **voiceover** to convey his personal journey and message of hope.

Jarman’s artistic vision was intimately connected to his sense of place and **identity**. In 1986, he purchased a **derelict** fisherman’s **cottage** at Dungeness, a **remote** and windswept landscape on the coast of Kent, and transformed it into a unique and enchanting home and garden. The cottage, which he called Prospect Cottage, became a **haven** for his creativity and a symbol of his connection to nature and the sea.

But Jarman was not just an artist and a gardener. He was also a passionate **activist** who used his platform to **advocate** for social justice and LGBTQ+ rights, and to challenge the government’s **inadequate** response to the AIDS **crisis**. In 1987, he co-founded the pressure group AIDS Coalition to Unleash Power (ACT UP), which **staged protests** and direct actions to demand better treatment and care for people living with HIV/AIDS. Jarman himself was diagnosed with the disease in 1986, and he documented his experiences in his diary “Modern Nature” (1991), which combined personal reflections, political commentary, and lyrical descriptions of his garden and the changing seasons.

Jarman died on February 19, 1994, at the age of 52, but his spirit lives on in his art, his activism, and his legacy of **queer** creativity and resilience. Prospect Cottage, which he **bequeathed** to his partner Keith Collins, has become a **pilgrimage** site for fans and admirers, and a symbol of hope and inspiration for a new generation of LGBTQ+ artists and activists.

As we remember Derek Jarman today, we honor his life and his vision, and we continue to fight for the causes he **championed**: equality, justice, and the right to love and live without fear or shame.

PART 1
PART 2
Unit 6
Unit 7
Unit 8
Unit 9
Unit 10
PART 3
PART 4
PART 5
PART 6

VOCABULARY

filmmaker [ˋfɪlm͵mekɚ] *n.* 導演
activism [ˋæktəvɪzəm] *n.* 行動主義
unapologetic [͵ʌnə͵pɑləˋdʒɛtɪk] *adj.* 不認錯的
queerness [ˋkwɪrnɪs] *n.* 酷兒傾向
provocative [prəˋvɑkətɪv] *adj.* 啓發性的
conventional [kənˋvɛnʃənl̩] *adj.* 傳統的
visionary [ˋvɪʒə͵nɛrɪ] *adj./n.* 有遠見的（人）
diagnose [͵daɪəgˋnoz] *v.* 診斷
mortality [mɔrˋtælətɪ] *n.* 死亡
stigma [ˋstɪgmə] *n.* 污名
voiceover [ˋvɔɪs͵ovɚ] *n.* 旁白
identity [aɪˋdɛntətɪ] *n.* 身分
derelict [ˋdɛrə͵lɪkt] *adj.* 荒廢的
cottage [ˋkɑtɪdʒ] *n.* 小屋
remote [rɪˋmot] *adj.* 遙遠的；偏僻的
haven [ˋhevən] *n.* 避風港
activist [ˋæktəvɪst] *n.* 活動家
advocate [ˋædvə͵ket] *v.* 提倡
inadequate [ɪnˋædəkwɪt] *adj.* 不充分的
crisis [ˋkraɪsɪs] *n.* 危機
stage [stedʒ] *v.* 籌劃
protest [ˋprotɛst] *n.* 抗議
queer [kwɪr] *adj.* 同性戀的
bequeath [bɪˋkwið] *v.* 遺留
pilgrimage [ˋpɪlgrəmɪdʒ] *n.* 朝聖
champion [ˋtʃæmpɪən] *v.* 擁護

Comprehension questions

Q1: What is the main idea of the article?

A. LGTBQ+ activism

B. feature films

C. the life and work of a filmmaker

Q2: What is the main topic of the third paragraph?

A. some of Jarman's later movies

B. his HIV diagnosis

C. voiceovers

Q3: What did Jarman do in 1986?

A. he visited Dungeness

B. he bought Prospect Cottage

C. he built a cottage

Q4: What is his book "Modern Nature" about?

A. personal reflections, political commentary, and lyrical descriptions

B. gardening

C. LGBTQ+ politics

Q5: In addition to painting, directing movies and gardening, what other activities did Jarman do?

A. he campaigned for gardeners

B. HIV activism

C. he joined the government

答案在本單元最後一頁。如果答錯了，請再確認一次文章內容。

中譯

德里克·賈曼是一位電影導演先鋒、藝術家和作家，以其豐富的想像力、政治活動和無畏的酷兒身分，在英國文化中留下了不可磨滅的印記。他的藝術遺產至今仍激勵和挑戰著我們。

1942 年，賈曼出生於英國米德爾塞克斯郡的諾斯伍德，在倫敦斯萊德美術學院學習繪畫和舞台設計。1970 年代末，他憑藉如《塞巴斯提安》(1976)、《慶典》(1978) 和《暴風雨》(1979) 等充滿挑釁和實驗性的長片在電影界嶄露頭角，顛覆了傳統的敘事方式和性別觀念。

然而，真正奠定他作為一位具遠見藝術家之聲譽的是其後期作品，如《浮世繪》(1986) 和《藍》(1993)，他以大膽而富有詩意的風格處理社會和政治問題。在確診患有愛滋病後執導的《藍》中，賈曼以單一的藍色畫面和強烈的旁白，探索了其本身的死亡和圍繞此疾病的污名，傳遞了個人經歷和希望的訊息。

賈曼的藝術視野與他的歸屬感和身分認同密切相關。1986 年，他在肯特郡海岸偏僻且多風的鄧傑內斯購買了一間廢棄的漁民小屋，並將其改造成獨特而迷人的住宅和花園。這間小屋被他稱為「願景屋」，成為他創作的避風港，也是他與自然和海洋連結的象徵。

但賈曼不僅僅是一位藝術家和園丁，他也是一位充滿熱情的社會活動家，利用自己的平台倡導社會正義和 LGBTQ+ 權利，並批判政府對愛滋病危機應對不力。1987 年，他共同創立了壓力團體「愛滋病聯合行動組織 (ACT UP)」，透過抗議和直接行動，要求對感染 HIV/AIDS 的病患提供更好的治療和照顧。賈曼本人於 1986 年被診斷出患有此疾病，他在日記《現代自然》(1991) 中記錄了自己的經歷，日記結合了個人反思、政治評論，以及對花園和季節變化的抒情描述。

賈曼於 1994 年 2 月 19 日去世，享年 52 歲，但他的精神依然存續於其藝術、行動主義以及酷兒創造力與韌性的影響中。他將「願景屋」遺贈給伴侶基斯·柯林斯，該小屋如今成為了粉絲和崇拜者的朝聖地，也為新一代 LGBTQ+ 藝術家和活動家帶來希望與啟發。

今日，我們緬懷德瑞克·賈曼，向他的生命和願景致敬，並繼續捍衛他所倡導的價值：平等、正義，以及不再懼怕或羞恥地去愛與生活的權利。

文法甦活區

Task 2

請用上篇文章中的 word partnerships 完成下表。見範例。

vivid	imagination
political	
	queerness
visionary	
	journey
artistic	
	activist
AIDS	
	protests
personal	

只要對照文章，便可輕鬆找出答案。

Task 3

請用 Task 2 表格中的 word partnerships 填入下列空格。見範例。

1. With a vivid imagination, he transformed the ordinary backyard into a fantastical jungle where talking squirrels and rainbow-colored butterflies coexisted in a whimsical harmony.

2. Her passion for social justice fuelled her commitment to __________ __________, leading her to organize grassroots campaigns and advocate for change in her community.

3. With an __________, Alex fearlessly navigated the world, proudly embracing his identity and challenging societal norms with a radiant authenticity.

4. The gallery featured a captivating exhibition by the __________, whose innovative use of mixed media and thought-provoking concepts left visitors in awe of the boundless creativity on display.

5. The filmmaker translated his unique __________ onto the screen, creating a visually stunning and emotionally resonant masterpiece that captivated audiences around the world.

6. As a __________, Maya dedicated her life to championing human rights, tirelessly advocating for marginalized communities and sparking meaningful change through her unwavering commitment.

7. In response to the unjust policies, citizens organized and __________ __________ in the city center, demanding change and drawing attention to their collective call for social justice.

8. In her intimate diary, she delved into the depths of __________, unraveling the tapestry of her thoughts and emotions as she navigated the complexities of life's journey.

9. Embarking on a __________ of self-discovery, Sarah explored new horizons, confronted challenges, and celebrated victories that ultimately shaped her into a resilient and enlightened individual.

10. During the height of the __________ in the 1980s, communities came together to raise awareness, provide support, and push for medical advancements to combat the devastating impact of the disease.

答案在本單元最後一頁。

Task 4

請再讀一遍文章，並在所有動詞劃底線。注意所使用的動詞時態和原因。

🗝 與上一單元一樣，本文主要使用過去簡單式描述賈曼的生平，因為他已離世，而使用現在簡單式描述其成就，因為成就是事實，與時間無關。

Task 5

下面是主題文章的摘要，請使用框框內的動詞填入空格。

create	gain	leave	live	showcase	use

Derek Jarman, the influential filmmaker, artist, and writer, 1. ________ an enduring impact on British culture with his bold creativity, political activism, and unapologetic queerness. Born in 1942, Jarman 2. ________ recognition in the late 1970s for experimental films like "Sebastiane" and "Jubilee," challenging conventional storytelling and sexuality. His later works, including "Caravaggio" and "Blue," 3. ________ his visionary approach to addressing social and political issues. Diagnosed with HIV/AIDS, Jarman 4. ________ "Blue" to explore mortality and challenge stigma. Beyond his art, he was a passionate activist, co-founding ACT UP to advocate for HIV/AIDS awareness. Purchasing a cottage in Dungeness, he 5. ________ Prospect Cottage, reflecting his intimate connection to place and identity. Despite his death in 1994, Jarman's legacy 6. ________ on through his art, activism, and the symbolic Prospect Cottage, inspiring LGBTQ+ artists and activists to continue his fight for equality and justice.

🗝 答案在本單元最後一頁。希望你動詞時態都有寫對。

Listening

現在我們來聽兩個人討論這篇文章。你會聽到許多相同的 word partnerships 和文法 chunks。

Task 6 7-2

請聽讀下列對話，你聽出了哪些前面 tasks 用到的詞彙？

A: Have you ever heard of Derek Jarman?

B: Oh, absolutely! Derek Jarman was a groundbreaking filmmaker, artist, and writer who left a lasting impact on British culture. His vivid imagination, political activism, and unapologetic queerness really set him apart.

A: Right? He was born in 1942 in Northwood, Middlesex, and did you know he studied painting and stage design at the Slade School of Fine Art in London? His films like "Sebastiane," "Jubilee," and "The Tempest" in the late '70s challenged conventional storytelling and sexuality.

B: Yeah, but it's his later works, especially "Caravaggio" and "Blue," that solidified his reputation as a visionary artist. "Blue," made after his HIV/AIDS diagnosis, is a powerful exploration of his mortality and the stigma around the disease, using just a single blue screen and a poignant voiceover.

A: It's such a powerful artistic vision!

B: Exactly. And his connection to place and identity was so intimate. In 1986, he transformed a derelict fisherman's cottage in Dungeness into Prospect Cottage, a unique home and garden reflecting his creativity and connection to nature.

A: And let's not forget that he was a passionate activist. In 1987, he co-founded ACT UP, a pressure group which staged protests for better treatment and care for people with HIV/AIDS during the AIDS crisis. His diary "Modern Nature" documented his personal journey, blending personal reflections, political commentary, and poetic descriptions of his garden.

B: Sadly, he passed away in 1994 at 52, but his spirit lives on. Prospect Cottage, bequeathed to his partner Keith Collins, has become a pilgrimage site, symbolizing hope for a new generation of LGBTQ+ artists and activists.

A: Absolutely. Derek Jarman's legacy is all about equality, justice, and the right to love and live without fear or shame.

B: A great man, then.

A: Yes.

希望你能夠聽到或看到你在本單元中學習的所有語言。如果沒有，不妨多聽幾遍。

中譯

A：你聽過德瑞克・賈曼嗎？

B：當然！德瑞克・賈曼是一個創新的電影導演、藝術家和作家，對英國文化留下了深遠的影響。他生動的想像力、政治行動和毫不掩飾的酷兒身分使他與眾不同。

A：對吧？他 1942 年出生在米德爾塞克斯郡的諾斯伍德。你知道他曾在倫敦斯萊德美術學院學習繪畫和舞台設計嗎？他在 70 年代末拍攝的《塞巴斯提安》、《慶典》和《暴風雨》等電影挑戰了傳統敘事和性別觀念。

B：是啊，但更重要的是他後期的作品，特別是《浮世繪》和《藍》，確立了他作為有遠見的藝術家的地位。《藍》是在他確診愛滋病後拍攝的，透過藍色畫面和令人心酸的畫外音，強烈探索了他的死亡和關於這個疾病的污名。

A：真的很震撼！

B：沒錯。而且他與地方歸屬感和身分的連結非常密切。1986 年，他將鄧傑內斯的一間廢棄的小漁屋改造成「願景屋」，這座獨特的家和花園體現了他的創造力和他與自然的聯繫。

A：別忘了他還是一位充滿熱情的活動家。1987 年，他共同創立了「ACT UP」，這是一個壓力團體，在愛滋病危機期間發起抗議活動，要求為 HIV/AIDS 患者提供更好的醫療和照顧。他的日記《現代自然》記錄了他的心路歷程，融合了個人反思、政治評論和對花園的詩意描述。

B：可惜他在 1994 年 52 歲時去世了，但他的精神永遠存在。「願景屋」遺贈給他的伴侶基思．柯林斯，現在已成為一個朝聖景點，象徵著新一代 LGBTQ+ 藝術家和活動家的希望。

A：完全同意。德瑞克．賈曼遺留下關於平等、正義，以及無須感到恐懼或羞恥地愛與生活的權利。

B：他是個了不起的人。

A：對。

在繼續往下學習之前，請先回到本單元開頭處確認那些學習目標自己是否已達成。

Answers

Task 1:

Q1: C Q2: A Q3: B Q4: A Q5: B

Task 2:

vivid	imagination
political	activism
unapologetic	queerness
visionary	artist
personal	journey
artistic	vision
passionate	activist
AIDS	crisis
staged	protests
personal	reflections

Task 3:

1. vivid imagination
2. political activism
3. unapologetic queerness
4. visionary artist
5. artistic vision
6. passionate activist
7. staged protests
8. personal reflections
9. personal journey
10. AIDS crisis

Task 5:

1. left
2. gained
3. showcased
4. used
5. created
6. lives

Unit 8 約翰・米爾頓 John Milton

在本單元中，你將了解一位著名詩人的故事。

研讀完你應達成的學習目標包括：

- ☐ 學到一些可用以談論本主題的 word partnerships
- ☐ 完成一些動詞時態的練習

Reading

Task 1 8-1

請閱聽這篇文章並回答下面的問題。

The world of literature **owes** much of its **grandeur** to the works of John Milton, and at the **pinnacle** of his literary achievements stands the **epic** poem, "Paradise Lost." This magnum opus, first published in 1667, has left an indelible mark on English literature, exploring **profound theological** and **philosophical** themes while showcasing Milton's extraordinary talent as a **poet**.

Before we look in more detail at "Paradise Lost," it is essential to understand the life of the man behind the **masterpiece**. John Milton, born in London on December 9, 1608, lived through a **tumultuous** period in English history. He witnessed the English Civil War, the **execution** of King Charles I, and the establishment of the Commonwealth of England under Oliver Cromwell.

Milton, a **staunch** supporter of the Commonwealth, penned numerous political essays during this time. However, his true brilliance lay in **poetry**, and he dedicated his later years to creating his most significant work, "Paradise Lost."

"Paradise Lost" is a **sprawling** epic in blank verse consisting of twelve books. It **recounts** the biblical story of the fall of man, from the **rebellion** of Satan and his angels to the expulsion of Adam and Eve from the Garden of Eden. The **poem** explores complex theological questions, such as the nature of good and evil, the concept of free will, and the relationship between **humanity** and God.

Milton's **portrayal** of Satan as a tragic, charismatic figure challenges traditional religious **notions** and raises profound philosophical questions. The poem's exploration of these themes has made it a subject of intense scholarly analysis and **debate** for centuries.

"Paradise Lost" not only marked a pinnacle in Milton's career but also had a lasting influence on English literature. Its **majestic** style, rich language, and deep philosophical themes laid the **groundwork** for later Romantic poets like William Blake and John Keats. The poem's exploration of the human condition and the struggle between good and evil continue to **resonate** with readers today.

Moreover, Milton's use of blank verse in "Paradise Lost" played a crucial role in the development of the English epic tradition. His skillful use of language and rhythm set a high standard for future poets to **emulate**.

John Milton's "Paradise Lost" remains a literary treasure, admired not only for its **poetic** beauty but also for its exploration of profound questions about humanity and the **divine**. It has been adapted into various art forms, including theater, film, and even graphic novels, demonstrating its enduring relevance.

As readers continue to be captivated by the timeless themes and **eloquent** verses of "Paradise Lost," John Milton's legacy as one of the greatest poets in the English language lives on. His work reminds us that even in the face of **adversity**, the power of creativity and expression can **transcend** time and leave an indelible mark on the world.

VOCABULARY

owe [o] *v.* 歸功於
grandeur [ˋgrændʒɚ] *n.* 宏偉
pinnacle [ˋpɪnəkḷ] *n.* 頂峰
epic [ˋɛpɪk] *n.* 史詩（般的作品）
profound [prəˋfaʊnd] *adj.* 深刻的
theological [ˌθiəˋlɑdʒɪkḷ] *adj.* 神學的
philosophical [ˌfɪləˋsɑfɪkḷ] *adj.* 哲學的
poet [ˋpoɪt] *n.* 詩人
masterpiece [ˋmæstɚˌpis] *n.* 傑作
tumultuous [tjuˋmʌltʃʊəs] *adj.* 紛亂的
execution [ˌɛksɪˋkjuʃən] *n.* 處決
staunch [stɔntʃ] *adj.* 堅定的
poetry [ˋpoɪtrɪ] *n.*（總稱）詩
sprawling [ˋsprɔlɪŋ] *adj.* 龐大的
recount [ˌriˋkaʊnt] *v.* 講述
rebellion [rɪˋbɛljən] *n.* 反叛；反抗
poem [ˋpoɪm] *n.*（一首）詩
humanity [hjuˋmænətɪ] *n.* 人類
portrayal [porˋtreəl] *n.* 描繪
notion [ˋnoʃən] *n.* 觀念
debate [dɪˋbet] *n.* 辯論
majestic [məˋdʒɛstɪk] *adj.* 雄偉的
groundwork [ˋgraʊndˌwɝk] *n.* 基礎
resonate [ˋrɛzəˌnet] *v.* 引起共鳴
emulate [ˋɛmjəˌlet] *v.* 效仿
poetic [poˋɛtɪk] *adj.* 詩的
divine [dəˋvaɪn] *adj.* 神的
eloquent [ˋɛləkwənt] *adj.* 富表現力的
adversity [ədˋvɝsətɪ] *n.* 逆境
transcend [trænˋsɛnd] *v.* 超越

Comprehension questions

Q1: What is the main topic of the article?

A. English literature

B. an epic poem called 'Paradise Lost'

C. the life and work of an English poet

Q2: What tumultuous period of English history did Milton live through?

A. World War I

B. the Commonwealth

C. the execution of King Charles II

Q3: What is the main topic of the fourth paragraph?

A. the relationship between humanity and God

B. 'Paradise Lost'

C. the story of Adam and Eve

Q4: What is the main topic of the sixth paragraph?

A. the influence of 'Paradise Lost' on subsequent poets and writers

B. the Romantics

C. William Blake

Q5: Why is 'Paradise Lost' still famous?

A. it's the only work of its kind in English

B. it's a very long epic

C. the timeless themes and eloquent verses

答案在本單元最後一頁。如果答錯了，請再確認一次文章內容。

中譯

文學世界的輝煌很大一部分要歸功於約翰·米爾頓的作品，他的文學成就巔峰就是史詩《失樂園》。這部鉅作於 1667 年首次出版，對英國文學產生了深遠的影響，不僅探索了深刻的神學和哲學主題，同時展示了米爾頓作為詩人的非凡才華。

在詳細探討《失樂園》之前，有必要了解這部傑作的創作者的生平。約翰·米爾頓 1608 年 12 月 9 日出生於倫敦，經歷了英國史上的一個動盪時期。他目睹了英國內戰、國王查理一世的處決，以及奧利弗·克倫威爾領導下英格蘭聯邦的建立。

米爾頓是英格蘭聯邦的堅定支持者，在此期間寫下了許多政治文章。然而，他真正的才華體現於詩歌創作，他將晚年奉獻給了他最重要的作品《失樂園》。

《失樂園》是一部龐大的無韻詩史詩，由十二卷組成。它講述了聖經中人類墮落的故事，從撒旦及其天使的叛亂到亞當與夏娃被逐出伊甸園。這首詩探討了複雜的神學問題，例如善與惡的本質、自由意志的概念，以及人與上帝之間的關係。

米爾頓將撒旦描繪成一個具有悲劇色彩且富有魅力的形象，挑戰了傳統的宗教觀念，並提出了深刻的哲學問題。幾個世紀以來，學者們對詩中這些主題的探討一直是激烈爭論的焦點。

《失樂園》不僅是米爾頓事業的巔峰，而且對英國文學產生了持久的影響。它雄偉的風格、豐富的語言和深刻的哲學主題為後來的浪漫主義詩人如威廉·布萊克和約翰·濟慈奠定了基礎，詩中對人類處境和善惡鬥爭的探索至今仍引起讀者的共鳴。

此外，米爾頓在《失樂園》中運用的無韻詩形式對英國史詩傳統的發展起到了至關重要的作用。他對語言和節奏的掌握為後來的詩人樹立了效仿的高標準。

約翰·米爾頓的《失樂園》至今仍是一部文學瑰寶，無論是因其詩歌之美，還是其對人類與神性問題的深刻探索，都備受推崇。它已被改編成各種藝術形式，包括戲劇、電影，甚至圖像小說，在在顯示了其不朽的魅力。

隨著讀者持續被《失樂園》永恆的主題和富表現力的詩句所吸引，約翰·米爾頓作為最偉大英文詩人之一的地位依然長存。他的作品提醒我們，即使面對逆境，創造力和表達的力量也能超越時間，在世界上留下不可磨滅的印記。

文法甦活區

Task 2

請用上篇文章中的 word partnerships 完成下表。見範例。

epic	poem
indelible	
	themes
extraordinary	
	supporter
political	
	story
majestic	
	language
enduring	

只要對照文章，便可輕鬆找出答案。

Task 3

請用 Task 2 表格中的 word partnerships 填入下列空格。見範例。

1. Her extraordinary talent for painting brought life to the canvas, capturing the attention and admiration of art enthusiasts worldwide.

2. Her profound kindness left an ________________ on everyone she met, forever influencing their perspectives and hearts.

3. In her literature class, the teacher encouraged students to explore the profound symbolism embedded in a ____________________, prompting insightful discussions about its cultural and moral significance.

4. Shakespeare's plays continue to captivate audiences worldwide, showcasing their ____________________ as they explore timeless themes of love, power, and the complexities of the human condition.

5. The architect designed the palace with a ____________________, featuring grand archways, towering columns, and intricate details that exuded regal splendor.

6. The author's novel was praised for its ________________, weaving together vibrant descriptions and eloquent prose that brought the story's world to life in the minds of readers.

7. The novel delves into ____________________ of love, loss, and the intricate tapestry of human relationships, leaving readers with a deep and introspective understanding of life.

8. The poet spent years crafting an ____________________ that vividly depicted the hero's journey through mythical realms and trials.

9. The professor assigned a series of thought-provoking ____________________, challenging students to critically analyze and engage with diverse perspectives on current societal issues.

10. Throughout his political career, he remained a ________________ of environmental conservation, consistently advocating for sustainable policies and initiatives.

答案在本單元最後一頁。

Task 4

請再讀一遍文章，並在所有動詞劃底線。注意所使用的動詞時態和原因。

這篇文章主要使用過去簡單式描述米爾頓的一生，因為他已不在人間；使用現在簡單式描述其成就，因為成就是事實，與時間無關。

Task 5

下面是主題文章的摘要，請使用框框內的動詞填入空格。

become	challenge	explore	influence	mark	set

The article delves into the life and literary legacy of John Milton, focusing on his magnum opus, “Paradise Lost.” Born in 1608 and living through the tumultuous English Civil War, Milton, a dedicated supporter of the Commonwealth, 1. __________ renowned for his political essays. However, it was in poetry that he truly shone, dedicating his later years to crafting the epic poem “Paradise Lost,” published in 1667. This sprawling work, comprising twelve books in blank verse, 2. __________ profound theological and philosophical themes surrounding the fall of man. Milton’s portrayal of Satan as a tragic figure 3. __________ traditional beliefs, sparking centuries of scholarly analysis. “Paradise Lost” not only 4. __________ the zenith of Milton’s career but also 5. __________ later Romantic poets and 6. __________ a standard for the English epic tradition. The poem’s enduring relevance is evident in its adaptations across various art forms, attesting to Milton’s status as one of the greatest English poets, leaving an indelible mark on literature and prompting reflection on the enduring power of creativity and expression.

答案在本單元最後一頁。希望你動詞時態都有寫對。

Listening

現在我們來聽兩個人討論這篇文章。你會聽到許多相同的 word partnerships 和文法 chunks。

Task 6 8-2

請聽讀下列對話，你聽出了哪些前面 tasks 用到的詞彙？

A: Hey, have you ever looked into the world of John Milton and his masterpiece, "Paradise Lost"?

B: Oh, absolutely! Milton's life was quite a rollercoaster during the English Civil War and the Commonwealth era, wasn't it?

A: Totally! Born in 1608, he witnessed some tumultuous times. He was a staunch supporter of the Commonwealth, writing loads of political essays, but it's his poetry that truly stands out.

B: Ah, "Paradise Lost," right? Published in 1667? That's quite a literary treasure.

A: Exactly! It's an epic poem in twelve books, written in blank verse. It tells the biblical story of the fall of man, from Satan's rebellion to Adam and Eve getting booted out of Eden.

B: That sounds intense. What's so special about it?

A: Well, Milton delves into theology and philosophy, profound themes—good and evil, free will, the relationship between humans and God. And get this, he paints Satan as a tragic, charismatic figure, challenging traditional religious ideas.

B: Whoa, that's interesting. No wonder it's been debated for centuries.

A: Oh, for sure. And it's not just a historical relic. "Paradise Lost" left an indelible mark and influenced later poets like Blake and Keats. Milton's use of blank verse set a high standard for English epic tradition.

B: Impressive. Does it still resonate today?

A: Absolutely. It's been adapted into theater, film, graphic novels—you name it. The majestic style and rich language keep captivating readers. Milton's legacy as an extraordinary talent and one of the greatest English poets lives on, reminding us of the enduring relevance of creativity and expression.

B: Sounds like I need to dive into "Paradise Lost" soon. Thanks for the mini-tour of Milton's world!

希望你能夠聽到或看到你在本單元中學習的所有語言。如果沒有，不妨多聽幾遍。

中譯

A：嘿，你有沒有研究過約翰・米爾頓和他的傑作《失樂園》？

B：噢，當然有！米爾頓的生活在英國內戰和英聯邦時期真的是大起大落，不是嗎？

A：完全沒錯！他出生於 1608 年，見證了動盪的時代。他是英聯邦的堅定支持者，寫了大量的政治文章，但真正讓他出名的還是他的詩作。

B：啊，你是說《失樂園》，對吧？ 1667 年出版？那真的是經典啊。

A：正是！它是一部由十二卷組成的史詩，用無韻詩寫成，講述了聖經中人類墮落的故事，從撒旦的反叛到亞當和夏娃被趕出伊甸園。

B：聽起來很震撼。它有什麼特別之處？

A：嗯，米爾頓深入探討了神學和哲學的主題，例如善與惡、自由意志、人與神的關係。他把撒旦描繪成一個悲劇性的、有魅力的人物，挑戰了傳統的宗教觀念。

B：哇，真有意思。難怪它幾個世紀以來備受爭論。

A：是啊。不僅僅是歷史地位，《失樂園》對後來的詩人，像布萊克和濟慈，都有深遠的影響。米爾頓對無韻詩的使用為英國史詩傳統樹立了高標準。

B：真了不起。那它在今天仍能引起共鳴嗎？

A：當然。它被改編成戲劇、電影、圖像小說——各種形式。那種大器的文風、豐富的語言仍吸引著讀者。米爾頓作為一位非凡的天才和最偉大的英國詩人之一的貢獻繼續存在，提醒我們創造力和表達的力量是永恆的。

B：聽起來我得好好讀一讀《失樂園》了。謝謝你帶我走了一趟米爾頓迷你之旅！

在繼續往下學習之前，請先回到本單元開頭處確認那些學習目標自己是否已達成。

Answers

Task 1:

Q1: C   Q2: B   Q3: B   Q4: A   Q5: C

Task 2:

epic	poem
indelible	mark
profound	themes
extraordinary	talent
staunch	supporter
political	essays
biblical	story
majestic	style
rich	language
enduring	relevance

Task 3:

1. extraordinary talent
2. indelible mark
3. biblical story
4. enduring relevance
5. majestic style
6. rich language
7. profound themes
8. epic poem
9. political essays
10. staunch supporter

Task 5:

1. became
2. explores
3. challenges
4. marked
5. influenced
6. set

Unit 9 戴安娜．奈德
Diana Nyad

在本單元中，你將了解一位著名運動員的故事。

研讀完你應達成的學習目標包括：

- ☐ 學到一些可用以談論本主題的 word partnerships
- ☐ 針對現在完成式 (present perfect tense) 進行一些練習

Reading

Task 1 9-1

請閱聽這篇文章並回答下面的問題。

In the realm of remarkable **feats** of human endurance and determination, few stories shine as brightly as that of Diana Nyad. A name **synonymous** with resilience and unwavering commitment, Nyad's remarkable journey has captured the hearts and minds of people worldwide. Her **triumphant** achievement in long-distance swimming stands as a testament to the power of the human spirit.

Born on August 22, 1949, in New York City, Diana Nyad's passion for swimming was **ignited** at a young age. With an early **aptitude** for the water, she soon began setting records and gaining recognition as a **formidable** swimmer. However, it wasn't until 1978 that Nyad's name became etched in the **annals** of history, as she attempted to swim the **treacherous** 103-mile stretch from Cuba to Florida with a shark cage.

Although she didn't succeed in her first attempt, the journey ignited a burning desire within Nyad to conquer the seemingly **insurmountable** challenge. Her determination remained unshaken, and she made further attempts in the coming years, including in 2011 and 2012. While these efforts **fell short** of her goal, Nyad's **indefatigable** spirit only seemed to grow stronger.

It was on September 2, 2013, that Nyad's name would become synonymous with **triumph**. At the age of 64, she successfully completed the epic swim from Cuba to Florida, a **grueling** 110-mile journey, without the use of a shark cage. Nyad's success was not without its challenges. She faced treacherous currents, jellyfish stings, and extreme exhaustion throughout the journey, but her unyielding determination and unwavering spirit **carried her through**. Her accomplishment was celebrated worldwide, and she quickly became an inspiration to people of all ages.

Nyad's remarkable story resonates far beyond the world of sports. It serves as a symbol of resilience and **perseverance** in the face of adversity. In interviews and public appearances, she has often emphasized the importance of pursuing one's dreams, no matter the obstacles.

Since her historic swim, Diana Nyad has continued to be an advocate for her sport and a source of inspiration. She has also become a motivational speaker and authored a **memoir**, "Find a Way," in which she shares her personal journey and the lessons she learned along the way.

Nyad's legacy extends far beyond her achievements in the water. She has become an **emblem** of human potential, reminding us all that with determination, **grit**, and an unshakeable belief in our dreams, we can overcome the seemingly insurmountable. Her story is a testament to the **indomitable** human spirit and a source of inspiration for generations to come.

Comprehension questions

Q1: What is the main topic of the article?

A. long distance swimming

B. the life and achievements of a long distance swimmer

C. swimming

Q2: When did Nyad start swimming?

A. 1949　　B. at an early age　　C. 1978

Q3: When did she succeed in swimming to Cuba?

A. 1978　　B. 2011　　C. 2013

Q4: What were some of the challenges she faced during her epic swim?

A. boredom

B. sharks and jellyfish

C. loneliness

Q5: What has she done since her epic swim?

A. she is a public speaker

B. she still swims every day

C. she swam the English Channel

答案在本單元最後一頁。如果答錯了，請再確認一次文章內容。

VOCABULARY

feat [fit] *n.* 英勇事蹟
synonymous [sɪˋnɑnəməs] *adj.* 同義的
triumphant [traɪˋʌmfənt] *adj.* 勝利的
ignite [ɪgˋnaɪt] *v.* 點燃
aptitude [ˋæptəˏtjud] *n.* 天資
formidable [ˋfɔrmɪdəbl̩] *adj.* 傑出的
annals [ˋænl̩z] *n.* 編年史 (複數形)
treacherous [ˋtrɛtʃərəs] *adj.* 危險的
insurmountable [ˏɪnsɚˋmaʊntəbl̩] *adj.* 無法克服的
fall short 未達成
indefatigable [ˏɪndɪˋfætɪgəbl̩] *adj.* 不屈不撓的
triumph [ˋtraɪəmf] *n.* 勝利
grueling [ˋgruəlɪŋ] *adj.* 使人精疲力盡的
carry through 使度過困難
perseverance [ˏpɝsəˋvɪrəns] *n.* 毅力
memoir [ˋmɛmwɑr] *n.* 回憶錄
emblem [ˋɛmbləm] *n.* 象徵
grit [grɪt] *n.* 毅力
indomitable [ɪnˋdɑmətəbl̩] *adj.* 不屈不撓的

中譯

在人類毅力和決心的卓越事蹟中，很少有故事像戴安娜・奈德的那樣閃閃發光。奈德是「韌性」與「堅持到底」的代名詞，其非凡旅程擄獲了全世界人們的心。她在長距離游泳中的輝煌成就是人類精神力量的見證。

1949 年 8 月 22 日，戴安娜・奈德出生於紐約市，她對游泳的熱情從年輕時就被點燃。憑藉早期的游泳天賦，她很快就開始創造紀錄並獲得認可，成為一名令人敬畏的游泳運動員。然而，直到 1978 年，奈德的名字才被載入史冊，當時她嘗試用防鯊籠游過古巴到佛羅里達之間那段危險的 103 英里海域。

儘管她的初次嘗試沒有成功，這趟旅程在她心中燃起了不服輸的念頭，想要征服這項艱鉅的挑戰。她的決心並未動搖，在接下來的幾年裡繼續嘗試，包括 2011 年和 2012 年。雖然這些努力未能實現目標，但奈德不屈不撓的精神卻愈加堅定。

2013 年 9 月 2 日，奈德的名字終於成為勝利的象徵。64 歲時，她在沒有使用鯊魚籠的情況下成功完成了從古巴到佛羅里達 110 英里的史詩級泳程。這段艱苦旅程一路上充滿挑戰。她不僅要面對洶湧的洋流和水母的叮咬，還要克服極度疲勞，但她不屈的決心和堅定不移的精神支撐著她度過了難關。她的成就迅速傳遍全球，並成為各年齡層人們的啓發。

奈德的非凡故事在體育界之外也引起了廣泛的共鳴，成為面對逆境時堅韌和毅力的象徵。在採訪和公開露面中，她經常強調追求夢想的重要性，無論遇到什麼障礙。

自從那次歷史性的游泳壯舉，奈德持續為游泳運動發聲，同時也成為一名勵志演說家，並撰寫了一本回憶錄《泳不放棄》(Find a Way)，在書中分享了她的心路歷程和人生體悟。

奈德的歷史定位遠遠超出了她在水中的成就。她已成為人類潛力的象徵，提醒我們所有人，只要有決心、勇氣和對夢想不可動搖的信念，我們就能克服看似無法逾越的困難。她的故事就是堅定意志的最佳典範，並將繼續激勵未來世代。

文法甦活區

Task 2

請用上篇文章中的 word partnerships 完成下表。見範例。

remarkable	feats
human	
	achievement
long-distance	
	records
shark	
insurmountable	
	determination
	spirit
grueling	

只要對照文章，便可輕鬆找出答案。

Task 3

請用 Task 2 表格中的 word partnerships 填入下列空格。見範例。

1. After years of dedicated research and tireless effort, the scientist celebrated a ___triumphant achievement___ when her ground-breaking discovery was acknowledged and applauded by the scientific community.

2. Despite facing numerous challenges and exhausting conditions, the hikers' incredible display of ____________________ allowed them to complete the grueling trek across the rugged terrain.

3. Despite facing numerous setbacks and challenges, Maria approached her ambitious project with ____________________, demonstrating resilience and unwavering commitment to achieving her goals.

4. Despite facing numerous setbacks, Emily's ____________________ propelled her forward, inspiring those around her with unwavering enthusiasm and resilience in the pursuit of their dreams.

5. Equipped with a sturdy ____________________, the adventurous divers descended into the deep blue ocean to witness the majestic creatures up close, ensuring a thrilling and safe underwater experience.

6. The athlete trained rigorously for months to prepare for the upcoming competition, where they aimed to showcase their prowess in ____________________ by tackling challenging open-water courses.

7. The athlete's ____________________ on the track not only broke records but also captivated the world with their extraordinary speed and endurance.

8. The exceptional sprinter astonished the crowd by ________________ in multiple track and field events, leaving an indelible mark on the sport's history with their unparalleled speed and skill.

9. The team considered the steep mountain range ahead as an ________________, but their shared determination and innovative approach ultimately led them to conquer the seemingly impossible climb.

10. Undeterred by the ________________ through rugged terrain and adverse weather conditions, the determined explorers pressed on, driven by the promise of reaching the remote, untouched destination.

答案在本單元最後一頁。

Task 4

請再讀一遍文章，並在所有動詞劃底線。注意所使用的動詞時態和原因。

本文有些地方使用過去簡單式來描述戴安娜．奈德的生平，並使用現在簡單式來描述她的成就。文中也使用了現在完成式，因為奈德至今仍活著。當某人還活著時，我們用現在完成式來談論他們的成就。

Task 5

下面是主題文章的摘要，請使用框框內的動詞填入空格。

become	complete	emerge	leave	reach	stand

Diana Nyad, born in 1949, 1. ________________ as an enduring symbol of human resilience and determination. From her early records as a swimmer, Nyad's journey 2. ________________ a historic milestone in 2013 when, at the age of 64, she successfully **3.** ________________ a grueling 110-mile swim from Cuba to Florida without a shark cage. Her numerous attempts prior to this achievement showcased an unshaken commitment to conquering the seemingly insurmountable challenge. Nyad's triumph, marked by treacherous conditions and physical strains, **4.** ________________ an indelible mark, making her an inspiration to people worldwide. Beyond her swimming accomplishments, Nyad **5.** ________________ a motivational speaker and author, emphasizing the importance of pursuing dreams despite obstacles. Her legacy **6.** ________________ as a testament to the indomitable human spirit and continues to inspire generations.

答案在本單元最後一頁。記得，現在完成式中助動詞應使用「**has/have**」，而現在簡單式的第三人稱動詞字尾要加上「**s**」。

Listening

現在我們來聽兩個人討論這篇文章。你會聽到許多相同的 word partnerships 和文法 chunks。

Task 6 9-2

請聽讀下列對話，你聽出了哪些前面 tasks 用到的詞彙？

A: Have you ever heard of Diana Nyad?

B: Oh, absolutely! She's that incredible swimmer, right?

A: Right! Diana Nyad's story is truly remarkable. Born in 1949, her passion for swimming started early on, and she gained recognition for setting records. In 2013, at the age of 64, she accomplished an extraordinary feat by swimming 110 miles from Cuba to Florida without a shark cage.

B: Wow, that's impressive! What led her to attempt such a grueling journey?

A: Well, in 1978, she initially tried it with a shark cage but didn't succeed. However, that experience ignited a strong desire within her to conquer the seemingly insurmountable challenge. She made several attempts over the years, facing obstacles like currents, jellyfish stings, and exhaustion.

B: That's some serious determination! Did she eventually succeed?

A: Yes, on September 2, 2013, she completed the triumphant achievement. Her success was celebrated globally, and she became an inspiration to people of all ages. Nyad's story goes beyond sports—it symbolizes unshaken determination in the face of adversity.

B: Incredible! What has she been up to since then?

A: Well, she's become an advocate for long-distance swimming, a motivational speaker, and even authored a memoir called "Find a Way," sharing her personal journey and the lessons she learned.

B: Her story sounds like a testament to human endurance. It's amazing how she continues to inspire generations.

A: Absolutely. Diana Nyad's legacy serves as a reminder that with an indefatigable spirit and an unshakeable belief in one's dreams, we can achieve the most remarkable feats.

希望你能夠聽到或看出本單元的重點內容。如果沒有，不妨多聽幾遍。

中譯

A：你聽過戴安娜．奈德嗎？

B：噢，當然啊！她是那個了不起的游泳運動員，對吧？

A：對啊！戴安娜．奈德的故事真的很不一般。出生於 1949 年的她從小就對游泳充滿熱情，並以打破紀錄而聞名。2013 年，64 歲的她完成了一項驚人的壯舉，從古巴游到佛羅里達，長達 110 英里，而且沒有使用防鯊籠。

B：哇，太強了吧！她怎麼會想挑戰這麼辛苦的事？

A：嗯，1978 年，她曾經嘗試過一次，當時用了防鯊籠，但沒有成功。然而，那次經歷激起了她內心的強烈渴望，想要征服這個看似無法達成的挑戰。多年來，她多次嘗試，但遇到了洋流、水母螫傷和極度疲憊等障礙。

B：真是毅力十足！她最終成功了嗎？

A：是的，2013 年 9 月 2 日，她完成了這項壯舉。這次成功讓她受到全球矚目，成為各年齡層人們的榜樣。奈德的故事超越了體育範疇，它象徵著在逆境中堅定不移的決心。

B：好厲害！她後來在做什麼呢？

A：她成為了長泳的倡導者、勵志演說家，甚至寫了一本名為《泳不放棄》的回憶錄，分享她的心路歷程和所學到的生命智慧。

B：她的故事就像是人類毅力的證明。真令人驚嘆，她一直在激勵著一代又一代的人。

A：沒錯。戴安娜．奈德的傳奇提醒我們，只要有不服輸的精神和對夢想的堅定信念，我們就能實現非凡的成就。

在繼續往下學習之前，不妨回顧確認一下開頭的學習目標是否已達成。

Answers

Task 1:

Q1: B   Q2: B   Q3: C   Q4: B   Q5: A

Task 2:

remarkable	feats
human	endurance
triumphant	achievement
long-distance	swimming
setting	records
shark	cage
insurmountable	challenge
unshaken	determination
indefatigable	spirit
grueling	journey

Task 3:

1. triumphant achievement
2. human endurance
3. unshaken determination
4. indefatigable spirit
5. shark cage
6. long-distance swimming
7. remarkable feats
8. setting records
9. insurmountable challenge
10. grueling journey

Task 5:

1. has emerged
2. reached
3. completed
4. has left
5. has become
6. stands

Unit 10 羅伯特・奧本海默
Robert Oppenheimer

在本單元中，你將了解一位著名科學家的故事。

研讀完你應達成的學習目標包括：

- ☐ 學到一些可用以談論本主題的 word partnerships
- ☐ 完成一些動詞時態的練習

Reading

Task 1 10-1

請閱聽這篇文章並回答下面的問題。

In the realm of scientific brilliance and intellectual **curiosity**, few names stand as tall as that of Robert Oppenheimer, the brilliant **physicist** and scientific visionary, who played a pivotal role in shaping the course of history through his work on the Manhattan Project.

Born on April 22, 1904, in New York City, Oppenheimer displayed an exceptional **intellect** from an early age. His **insatiable** thirst for knowledge led him to excel in his academic **pursuits**, ultimately leading him to earn a PhD in **physics** from the University of Göttingen in Germany. Oppenheimer's contributions to science extended far beyond the **confines** of **academia**. However, it was his pivotal role in the development of the **atomic bomb** during World War II that would make him famous. As the director of the

Manhattan Project's Los Alamos Laboratory, Oppenheimer led a team of brilliant scientists, engineers, and technicians who worked tirelessly to harness the power of the **atom**.

Under Oppenheimer's guidance, the Los Alamos Laboratory became a **hotbed** of scientific innovation. His ability to cultivate an environment that nurtured collaboration and creativity was instrumental in the successful development of the world's first atomic bomb. Despite the **immense** pressure and **ethical dilemmas** surrounding the project, Oppenheimer's leadership ensured its completion. On July 16, 1945, in the **desolate** New Mexico desert, Oppenheimer's work reached its climax. Codenamed Trinity, the first-ever atomic bomb was **detonated**, forever changing the course of warfare and the world's understanding of scientific possibilities. Oppenheimer himself famously quoted the "Bhagavad Gita," an ancient Indian text, saying, "Now I am become Death, the destroyer of worlds," reflecting the profound impact of his creation.

However, Oppenheimer's involvement with the atomic bomb came at a personal cost. Following the **bombings** of Hiroshima and Nagasaki in 1945, he became a vocal advocate for **nuclear disarmament**. Oppenheimer's **moral** convictions **clashed** with the escalating Cold War tensions, and his security clearance was eventually **revoked** due to concerns about his loyalty. Despite this **setback**, Oppenheimer's unwavering commitment to the pursuit of knowledge remained undiminished.

In the aftermath of the Manhattan Project, Oppenheimer continued his influential career in academia, focusing on **theoretical** physics and serving as the director of the Institute for Advanced Study at Princeton. His contributions to science were recognized with numerous awards and honors, including the Enrico Fermi Award and the Albert Einstein Award.

Beyond his scientific achievements, Oppenheimer's legacy also lies in his profound impact on shaping the scientific community. His dedication to education and mentoring young scientists inspired generations of researchers to push the boundaries of knowledge and to **approach** scientific inquiry with an unwavering curiosity.

VOCABULARY

curiosity [ˌkjʊrɪˋɑsətɪ] *n.* 好奇心；求知欲
physicist [ˋfɪzɪsɪst] *n.* 物理學家
intellect [ˋɪntḷˌɛkt] *n.* 智力
insatiable [ɪnˋseʃɪəbḷ] *adj.* 永不滿足的
pursuit [pɚˋsut] *n.* 追求；從事
physics [ˋfɪzɪks] *n.* 物理學
confines [kənˋfaɪnz] *n.* 範圍 (複數形)
academia [ˌækəˋdimɪə] *n.* 學術界
atomic [əˋtɑmɪk] *adj.* 原子的
bomb [bɑm] *n.* 炸彈
atom [ˋætəm] *n.* 原子
hotbed [ˋhɑtˌbɛd] *n.* 溫床
immense [ɪˋmɛns] *adj.* 巨大的
ethical [ˋɛθɪkḷ] *adj.* 道德的
dilemma [dəˋlɛmə] *n.* 困境
desolate [ˋdɛsḷɪt] *adj.* 荒蕪的
detonate [ˋdɛtəˌnet] *v.*（使）爆炸
bombing [ˋbɑmˌɪŋ] *n.* 轟炸
nuclear [ˋnjuklɪɚ] *adj.* 核能的
disarmament [dɪsˋɑrməmənt] *n.* 裁軍
moral [ˋmɔrəl] *adj.* 道德的
clash [klæʃ] *v.* 發生衝突
revoke [rɪˋvok] *v.* 撤銷
setback [ˋsɛtˌbæk] *n.* 挫折
theoretical [ˌθiəˋrɛtɪkḷ] *adj.* 理論的
approach [əˋprotʃ] *v./n.* 應對；方法

Comprehension questions

Q1: What is the main topic of the article?

A. Robert Oppenheimer

B. Manhattan

C. the atomic bomb

Q2: Where did he get his PhD from?

A. Gottingen in Germany

B. in New Mexico

C. Manhattan

Q3: What was the Manhattan Project?

A. an urban renewal program

B. a project to develop an atomic bomb

C. a project to win WWII

Q4: After the bomb was dropped on Nagasaki and Hiroshima, what did Oppenheimer do?

A. he celebrated victory over the Japanese

B. he celebrated the end of WWII

C. he campaigned for nuclear disarmament

Q5: What is Oppenheimer's legacy?

A. his impact on the scientific community

B. he won the Nobel Prize

C. he changed the way we do science

答案在本單元最後一頁。如果答錯了，請再確認一次文章內容。

中譯

在科學才華和求知欲領域，很少有人能像羅伯特・奧本海默一樣令人矚目，他是一位傑出的物理學家和科學遠見者，憑藉在曼哈頓計畫中的重要角色，深刻地改變了歷史進程。

奧本海默於 1904 年 4 月 22 日出生於紐約市，從小便展現出非凡的智力。他對知識的無盡渴望使他在學術上表現優異，最終獲得了德國哥廷根大學的物理學博士學位。然而，奧本海默對科學的貢獻遠超出學術範疇。二戰期間，他身為曼哈頓計畫洛斯阿拉莫斯實驗室的主任，致力於研發原子彈而聲名大噪。奧本海默領導了一支由頂尖科學家、工程師和技術人員組成的團隊，孜孜不倦地開發原子能的力量。

在奧本海默的指導下，洛斯阿拉莫斯實驗室成為科學創新的基地。他能夠創造一個培養協作與創造力的環境，這對成功研發世界上第一顆原子彈至關重要。儘管該計畫面臨龐大的壓力和道德困境，奧本海默的領導能力使其順利完成。1945 年 7 月 16 日，在荒涼的新墨西哥州沙漠中，奧本海默的工作達到了巔峰。代號為「三位一體 (Trinity)」的第一顆原子彈引爆，徹底改變了戰爭型態和世界對科學可能性的理解。奧本海默引用了古印度典籍《薄伽梵歌》的一句話：「現在我變成死亡，世界的毀滅者」，反映出他對自己創造物的複雜心情。

然而，奧本海默參與原子彈研製也付出了沉重的代價。1945 年廣島和長崎遭到原子彈轟炸後，他成為核裁軍的積極倡導者。奧本海默的道德信念與不斷升級的冷戰緊張局勢發生衝突，由於當局對其忠誠度的質疑，他的安全許可最終被撤銷。儘管遭遇此挫折，奧本海默追求知識的熱忱從未消退。

曼哈頓計畫結束後，奧本海默繼續活躍於學術界，專注於理論物理學的研究，並擔任普林斯頓大學高級研究所所長。他對科學的貢獻獲得了無數獎項與榮譽，包括恩里科・費米獎和阿爾伯特・愛因斯坦獎。

除了科學成就之外，奧本海默在科學界的發展上也具有深遠影響。他對培育年輕科學家的奉獻精神激勵了一代又一代的研究者突破知識的界限，並以不滅的好奇心來探索科學。

文法甦活區

Task 2

請用上篇文章中的 word partnerships 完成下表。見範例。

scientific	brilliance
intellectual	
	role
atomic	
	innovation
personal	
	clearance
unwavering	
	physics
numerous	

只要對照文章，便可輕鬆找出答案。

Task 3

請用 Task 2 表格中的 word partnerships 填入下列空格。見範例。

1. The dropping of the ___atomic bomb___ on Hiroshima and Nagasaki during World War II had profound and lasting consequences, altering the course of history and sparking debates about the ethics of nuclear weapons.

2. His dedication to his work came at a ________________, as he often sacrificed time with his family and personal pursuits to meet the demands of his career.

3. The dedicated team played a ________________ in the success of the project, contributing their expertise and commitment to overcoming challenges and achieving milestones.

4. The classified nature of the project required employees to undergo a rigorous background check to obtain the necessary ______________, ensuring that sensitive information remained protected.

5. Her insatiable ______________________________ drove her to explore diverse fields of study, leading to a rich and multidimensional understanding of the world.

6. The ground-breaking discovery showcased the scientist's __________ __________________, revealing a profound understanding of complex phenomena in the realm of quantum physics.

7. Albert Einstein made significant contributions to _________________, revolutionizing our understanding of space, time, and gravity with his ground-breaking theories.

8. The constant pursuit of ______________________________ has led to remarkable advancements in technology and medicine, revolutionizing the way we live and shaping the future of human progress.

9. Throughout her distinguished career, the accomplished scientist has received ______________________, recognizing her outstanding contributions to the field of environmental research and sustainability.

10. Despite facing numerous challenges, the team demonstrated an _______________________ to the project, working tirelessly to achieve their goals and deliver exceptional results.

答案在本單元最後一頁。

Task 4

請再讀一遍文章，並在所有動詞劃底線。注意所使用的動詞時態和原因。

> 與前面的單元類似，有時文章使用過去式來描述奧本海默的生平事件，有時則使用現在式來描述他的成就。

Task 5

下面是主題文章的摘要，請使用框框內的動詞填入空格。

become	clash	continue	extend	lead	make

Robert Oppenheimer, born in 1904, was a brilliant physicist known for his exceptional intellect and academic achievements, earning a PhD in physics from the University of Göttingen. While his contributions to science were extensive, it was his role as the director of the Los Alamos Laboratory during the Manhattan Project that 1. ________________ him famous. Oppenheimer's leadership and ability to foster collaboration 2. ____________ to the successful development of the first atomic bomb, codenamed Trinity, in 1945. Despite the ethical dilemmas and personal costs associated with the project, Oppenheimer later 3. ____________ an advocate for nuclear disarmament. His moral convictions 4. ____________ with Cold War tensions, leading to the revocation of his security clearance. Nevertheless, Oppenheimer 5. ____________ his influential career in academia, contributing to theoretical physics and serving as the director of the Institute for Advanced Study at Princeton. His legacy 6. ____________ beyond scientific achievements, as his dedication to education and mentorship inspired generations of researchers to approach scientific inquiry with unwavering curiosity.

> 答案在本單元最後一頁。請別忘了，現在簡單式的第三人稱動詞字尾要加上「s」。

Listening

現在我們來聽兩個人討論這篇文章。

Task 6 10-2

請聽讀下列對話，你聽出了哪些前面 tasks 用到的詞彙？

A: Hey, have you ever heard of Robert Oppenheimer? That guy was a brilliant physicist and played a major role in shaping history.

B: Oh yeah, Oppenheimer, the physicist, right? Born in 1904 in New York City, he was stimulated by real intellectual curiosity. Earned his PhD in physics from the University of Göttingen in Germany.

A: Exactly! And it's not just his scientific brilliance; he played a pivotal role in the Los Alamos Laboratory during the Manhattan Project. Under his guidance, they developed the world's first atomic bomb.

B: Ah, the Trinity test in the New Mexico desert in 1945, right? Oppenheimer famously quoted the "Bhagavad Gita" at that moment, saying, "Now I am become Death, the destroyer of worlds." It's wild how that creation changed the course of warfare.

A: Yeah, but it came with a personal cost. After the bombings of Hiroshima and Nagasaki, he displayed unwavering commitment for nuclear disarmament, which didn't sit well with the Cold War tensions. His security clearance was even revoked.

B: That's tough. But you know what's fascinating? Despite all that, Oppenheimer continued his career in academia, focusing on theoretical physics and even becoming the director of the Institute for Advanced Study at Princeton.

A: Absolutely! He received numerous awards for his contributions to science, like the Enrico Fermi Award and the Albert Einstein Award.

And let's not forget his impact on shaping the scientific community, inspiring generations with his dedication to education and mentorship.

B: Wow, Oppenheimer's life is like a rollercoaster of brilliance, ethics, and scientific innovation. It's impressive how he managed to leave such a lasting legacy.

希望你能夠聽到或看出本單元的重點內容。如果沒有，不妨多聽幾遍。

中譯

A：嘿，你聽過羅伯特．奧本海默嗎？他是個天才物理學家，對歷史有重大影響。

B：噢，奧本海默，物理學家，對吧？1904 年他出生於紐約市，對知識有著強烈的好奇心，在德國哥廷根大學獲得物理學博士學位。

A：沒錯！而且不僅是他的科學才華，他在曼哈頓計畫中的洛斯阿拉莫斯實驗室也發揮了關鍵作用。在他的指導下，他們研發出世界上第一顆原子彈。

B：啊，1945 年在新墨西哥州沙漠進行的「三位一體」測試，對吧？奧本海默當時還引用了《薄伽梵歌》的名言：「現在我變成死亡，世界的毀滅者。」那個發明徹底改變了戰爭的進程。

A：是啊，但這也給他個人帶來了沉重的代價。廣島和長崎被轟炸後，他堅定不移地支持核裁軍，這與冷戰的緊張局勢格格不入，所以最終他的安全許可被撤銷了。

B：那真是艱難。不過你知道嗎？儘管經歷了這些，奧本海默依然繼續他的學術生涯，專注於理論物理學，甚至成為普林斯頓大學高級研究所所長。

A：確實如此！他因為對科學的貢獻獲得了許多獎項，例如恩里科．費米獎和阿爾伯特．愛因斯坦獎。而且別忘了，他對科學界的影響力不容忽視，他致力於教育和指導後進，啓發了一代又一代的人。

B：哇，奧本海默的一生就像雲霄飛車一樣，充滿才華、道德考驗和科學創新。他能留下如此深遠的影響，真是令人欽佩。

在繼續往下學習之前，請先回到本單元開頭處確認那些學習目標自己是否已達成。

Answers

Task 1:

Q1: A Q2: A Q3: B Q4: C Q5: A

Task 2:

scientific	brilliance
intellectual	curiosity
pivotal	role
atomic	bomb
scientific	innovation
personal	cost
security	clearance
unwavering	commitment
theoretical	physics
numerous	awards

Task 3:

1. atomic bomb
2. personal cost
3. pivotal role
4. security clearance
5. intellectual curiosity
6. scientific brilliance
7. theoretical physics
8. scientific innovation
9. numerous awards
10. unwavering commitment

Task 5:

1. made
2. led
3. became
4. clashed
5. continued
6. extends

NOTES

Part 3

Designed by Freepik

節慶

EVENTS

Unit 11

世界地球日
Earth Day

本單元的學習目標包括：

- □ 學到一些可用以談論本主題的 word partnerships
- □ 練習一些介系詞 chunks

Reading

Task 1 11-1

請閱聽這篇文章並回答下面的問題。

Every year on April 22, millions of people around the globe come together to celebrate Earth Day. This annual event, dedicated to environmental protection and awareness, has its roots in a tragic event and the vision of a determined leader. Understanding the **origin** of Earth Day and what we can do to honor it provides a powerful reminder of our responsibility to protect our planet.

The **inception** of Earth Day is **intertwined** with a significant environmental **disaster**: the 1969 Santa Barbara **oil spill**. On January 28, 1969, a **blowout** occurred on a Union Oil drilling platform off the coast of Santa Barbara, California, releasing over three million gallons of crude oil into the Pacific Ocean. The spill **devastated** local wildlife, blackened beaches, and drew national attention to the dangers of **offshore** drilling and the broader environmental issues facing the United States.

Witnessing this **catastrophe**, **Senator** Gaylord Nelson from Wisconsin was **galvanized** into action. Nelson, a long-time advocate for environmental conservation, saw an opportunity to channel the growing public concern about pollution and ecological degradation into a political **movement**. Inspired by the student anti-war movement, he **envisioned** a "national **teach-in** on the environment." With the help of activist Denis Hayes, Nelson organized the first Earth Day on April 22, 1970.

The response was **overwhelming**. On that day, an **estimated** 20 million Americans took to the streets, parks, and auditoriums to **demonstrate** for a healthier, more sustainable environment. It marked the birth of the modern environmental movement, leading to significant **legislative** achievements, including the establishment of the Environmental Protection Agency (EPA) and the passage of the Clean Air **Act**, Clean Water Act, and Endangered Species Act.

Earth Day serves as a crucial reminder that the fight for a cleaner, healthier planet is far from over. Here are several ways individuals can promote environmental awareness and contribute to the cause:

Reduce, Reuse, Recycle:
One of the simplest yet most effective ways to reduce waste is by following the three R's. Reducing **consumption**, reusing items when possible, and recycling **materials** helps decrease the amount of waste that ends up in **landfills** and oceans.

Conserve Energy and Water:
Simple actions like turning off lights when not in use, using energy-efficient **appliances**, and fixing leaks can significantly reduce energy and water consumption. Adopting renewable energy sources like solar and wind power is also a powerful step towards sustainability.

Support Sustainable Practices:

Choosing products made from sustainable materials, supporting companies with eco-friendly practices, and eating a plant-based diet can all reduce one's environmental footprint. Buying locally produced goods also cuts down on the carbon **emissions** associated with transportation.

Plant Trees and Gardens:

Trees **absorb** carbon dioxide and provide oxygen, making them vital to combating climate change. Gardening, whether in backyards or community spaces, supports local ecosystems and promotes biodiversity.

Educate and Advocate:

Spreading awareness about environmental issues and advocating for policy changes can have a broad impact. Engaging with community initiatives, supporting environmental organizations, and participating in local clean-up efforts are ways to inspire others and push for **systemic** change.

VOCABULARY

origin [ˋɔrədʒɪn] *n.* 起源；由來
inception [ɪnˋsɛpʃən] *n.* 開端
intertwine [ˏɪntɚˋtwaɪn] *v.* 使緊密關聯
disaster [dɪˋzæstɚ] *n.* 災難
oil spill 漏油
blowout [ˋbloˋaʊt] *v.* 爆裂噴出
devastate [ˋdɛvəsˏtet] *v.* 摧毀
offshore [ˋɔfˋʃor] *adj.* 離岸的；近海的
catastrophe [kəˋtæstrəfɪ] *n.* 災難
senator [ˋsɛnətɚ] *n.* 參議員
galvanize [ˋgælvəˏnaɪz] *v.* 使振奮
movement [ˋmuvmənt] *n.* 運動
envision [ɪnˋvɪʒən] *v.* 設想
teach-in [ˋtitʃˏɪn] *n.* 座談會
overwhelming [ˏovɚˋhwɛlmɪŋ] *adj.* 勢不可擋的
estimate [ˋɛstəˏmet] *v./n.* 估計
demonstrate [ˋdɛmənˏstret] *v.* 示威
legislative [ˋlɛdʒɪsˏletɪv] *adj.* 立法的
act [ækt] *n.* (常大寫) 法案；行爲
consumption [kənˋsʌmpʃən] *n.* 消耗
material [məˋtɪrɪəl] *n.* 材料
landfill [ˋlændfɪl] *n.* 垃圾填埋場
appliance [əˋplaɪəns] *n.* 器具；設備
emission [ɪˋmɪʃən] *v.* 排放
absorb [əbˋsɔrb] *v.* 吸收
systemic [sɪsˋtɛmɪk] *adj.* 系統性的

Comprehension questions

Q1: What is the main topic of the article?

A. environmental protection

B. Earth Day and its origins

C. the 1969 Santa Barbara oil spill

Q2: What is the main topic of the third paragraph?

A. a catastrophe

B. Senator Nelson's decision to take action on environmental pollution

C. the student anti-war movement

Q3: What happened on the first Earth Day in 1970?

A. the birth of the modern environmental movement

B. police arrested protestors

C. 20 million people around the world demonstrated

Q4: How can people promote environmental awareness?

A. by reducing waste

B. by protesting

C. by using landfills

Q5: Why does planting trees and gardens help the environment?

A. they make cities look better

B. trees absorb oxygen

C. it supports local ecosystems

答案在本單元最後一頁。如果答錯了，請再確認一次文章內容。

中譯

每年 4 月 22 日，全球數百萬人齊聚一堂慶祝世界地球日。這個一年一度的活動旨在提高環保意識，其起源與一場悲劇和一位堅定的領袖息息相關。了解地球日的由來以及如何紀念它這件事提醒我們，愛護地球，人人有責。

地球日的開始與 1969 年的一次重大環境災難——聖塔芭芭拉漏油事件有關。1969 年 1 月 28 日，加州聖塔芭芭拉海岸附近的聯合石油公司鑽井平台發生油井爆炸，釋放了超過三百萬加侖的原油流入太平洋。這次漏油摧毀了當地的野生動物，污染了海灘，並引起大眾關注到離岸鑽油風險和更廣泛的環境問題。

目睹這場災難後，威斯康辛州參議員蓋洛德．尼爾森採取了行動。尼爾森長期倡導環境保護，他看到了一個機會，將公眾對污染和生態退化日益增長的關注轉化為政治運動。受到學生反戰運動啓發，他策劃了一場「全國環境宣講會」。在活動家丹尼斯．海斯的協助下，尼爾森於 1970 年 4 月 22 日組織了第一次的地球日活動。

這次活動的反應非常熱烈。當天，估計有兩千萬美國人走上街頭、公園和禮堂示威，要求建立更健康、更永續的環境。這標誌著現代環保運動的誕生，並帶來了重大的立法成就，包括成立環保局 (EPA)、通過《潔淨空氣法》、《潔淨水法》和《瀕危物種法》。

地球日提醒我們，為了更乾淨、更健康的地球，還有好長一段路要奮鬥。每個人可透過以下幾種方式提高環保意識並做出貢獻：

減少、重複使用、回收：
遵循三 R 原則是減少浪費最簡單但最有效的方法之一。減少消耗、盡可能重複使用物品，以及回收材料皆有助於減少最終進入垃圾掩埋場和海洋的廢棄物量。

節省能源和水：
不使用時關燈、使用節能電器和修理漏水等簡單的行動可顯著減少能源和水的消耗。採用太陽能和風能等再生能源也是邁向永續發展的重要一步。

支持永續實踐：
選擇由永續材料製成的產品、支持環保實踐的公司和攝取植物性飲食都能減少環境足跡。購買當地生產的商品也能減少運輸中的碳排放。

種植樹木和花園：
樹木吸收二氧化碳並釋放氧氣，對抗氣候變遷至關重要。無論是在自家後院或社區空間種植花園，都能支持當地的生態系統，促進生物多樣性。

教育與倡導：
宣傳環保議題並提倡政策改革能產生廣泛的影響。參與社區倡議、支持環保組織，以及參加當地的清潔行動都是很好的方式來鼓勵大家一起行動，推動制度上的改變。

文法甦活區

Task 2

請用上篇文章中的 word partnerships 完成下表。見範例。

tragic	event
	leader
environmental	
	spill
local	
	attention
public	
	movement
legislative	
	planet

只要對照文章，便可輕鬆找出答案。

接下來，我們要利用上列 word partnerships 練習寫作。

Task 3

請用 Task 2 表格中的 word partnerships 填入下列空格。見範例。

1. Adopting renewable energy sources and reducing plastic waste are crucial steps toward a __cleaner planet__ for future generations.

2. Conservation efforts in the region have significantly improved the habitat and increased the population of the ________________.

3. The civil rights era was marked by a powerful ________________ that sought to end racial segregation and achieve equality for all citizens.

4. The community came together to support one another after the ________________ of the devastating earthquake.

5. The ________________ inspired her team to overcome numerous obstacles and achieve their ambitious goals.

6. The ____________________ caused by the chemical spill had long-lasting effects on the local wildlife and water supply.

7. The groundbreaking research on climate change quickly garnered ________________, leading to widespread media coverage and policy discussions.

8. The ________________ polluted miles of pristine coastline, causing severe damage to marine life and local economies dependent on tourism and fishing.

9. The proposed industrial project was halted due to overwhelming ________________ about its potential environmental impact.

10. The senator's time in office was distinguished by significant ________________, including the passage of several key environmental protection laws.

答案在本單元最後一頁。

我們來細看本文中的文法，其中使用了一些介系詞 chunks，如下所示。

Task 4

請在文中找出下列介系詞 chunks，並注意看其用法。

· dedicated to
· vision of
· advocate for
· concern about
· inspired by
· serves as

使用這些 **chunks** 時，請特別留意所搭配的介系詞。

接著是寫作練習，請利用上列介系詞片語實際寫寫看。（主題略有不同）

Task 5

請用 Task 4 的正確介系詞填入下列空格。

1. As a passionate environmentalist, she continues to advocate _______ stronger conservation policies and sustainable practices.
2. Her vision ___________ a more inclusive and equitable society has inspired many to join the movement for social justice.
3. Inspired ___________ the resilience of the local community, the artist created a mural celebrating their strength and unity.
4. The growing concern ___________ air pollution has led many cities to implement stricter emissions regulations.
5. The historic landmark serves ___________ a reminder of the town's rich cultural heritage and enduring legacy.
6. The new community center is dedicated ___________ providing educational resources and support services to underprivileged families.

答案在本單元最後一頁。

Listening

現在我們透過「聽」來複習主題文章。這組對話比較長，請務必先完整聽過一遍，不要急著看翻譯。

Task 6 11-2

請聽讀下列對話，你聽出了哪些前面 tasks 用到的詞彙？

A: Hey Jamie, did you know that every year on April 22, millions of people around the globe come together to celebrate Earth Day?

B: Yeah, I've heard about it. It's that annual event dedicated to environmental protection and awareness, right?

A: Exactly. It's interesting because the origin of Earth Day is tied to a tragic event and the vision of a determined leader.

B: Really? What tragic event are you talking about?

A: It all started with the 1969 Santa Barbara oil spill. On January 28, a blowout occurred on a Union Oil drilling platform off the coast of Santa Barbara, California, releasing over three million gallons of crude oil into the Pacific Ocean.

B: Wow, that sounds devastating. What happened next?

A: The spill devastated local wildlife, blackened beaches, and drew national attention to the dangers of offshore drilling and broader environmental issues facing the United States.

B: I can imagine that must have been a wake-up call for many people.

A: Absolutely. Witnessing this environmental disaster, Senator Gaylord Nelson from Wisconsin was galvanized into action. Nelson, a long-time advocate for environmental conservation, saw an opportunity to channel the growing public concern about pollution and ecological degradation into a political movement.

B: That's inspiring. What did he do?

A: Inspired by the student anti-war movement, he envisioned a "national teach-in on the environment." With the help of activist Denis Hayes, Nelson organized the first Earth Day on April 22, 1970 to draw national attention to the issue.

B: How did people respond to it?

A: The response was overwhelming. On that day, an estimated 20 million Americans took to the streets, parks, and auditoriums to demonstrate for a healthier, more sustainable environment. It marked the birth of the modern environmental movement and led to significant legislative achievements.

B: Like what?

A: It led to the establishment of the Environmental Protection Agency (EPA) and the passage of the Clean Air Act, Clean Water Act, and Endangered Species Act.

B: That's impressive. Earth Day really made a difference.

A: It did, and it serves as a crucial reminder that the fight for a cleaner planet is far from over.

B: So, what can we do to honor Earth Day and contribute to environmental awareness?

A: There are several ways. For starters, we can follow the three R's: Reduce, Reuse, Recycle. Reducing consumption, reusing items when possible, and recycling materials help decrease the amount of waste that ends up in landfills and oceans.

B: Makes sense. What else?

A: We can conserve energy and water. Simple actions like turning off lights when not in use, using energy-efficient appliances, and fixing leaks can significantly reduce energy and water consumption. Adopting renewable energy sources like solar and wind power is also a powerful step towards sustainability.

B: I've heard supporting sustainable practices is important too.

A: Definitely. Choosing products made from sustainable materials, supporting companies with eco-friendly practices, and eating a plant-based diet can all reduce our environmental footprint. Buying locally produced goods also cuts down on the carbon emissions associated with transportation.

B: What about planting trees and gardens?

A: That's a great idea. Trees absorb carbon dioxide and provide oxygen, making them vital to combating climate change. Gardening, whether in backyards or community spaces, supports local ecosystems and promotes biodiversity.

B: And how can we educate and advocate for these causes?

A: Spreading awareness about environmental issues and advocating for policy changes can have a broad impact. Engaging with community initiatives, supporting environmental organizations, and participating in local clean-up efforts are ways to increase public concern and push for systemic change.

B: Thanks for the info, Alex. This conversation really opened my eyes to the importance of Earth Day and what we can do to help the environment.

A: Glad to hear that, Jamie. Every little bit helps, and together we can make a big difference.

希望你能夠聽到或看到本單元的學習重點。如果沒有，不妨多聽幾遍。

中譯

A：嘿，Jamie，妳知道每年 4 月 22 日全球有數百萬人都在慶祝地球日嗎？

B：嗯，我聽過。那是致力於提升環保意識的年度活動，對吧？

A：沒錯。特別的是，地球日的由來和一個悲劇和堅定領袖的遠見有關。

B：真的嗎？你說的是什麼悲劇？

A：一切始於 1969 年的聖塔芭芭拉漏油事件。1 月 28 日，加州聖塔芭芭拉海岸附近的聯合石油公司鑽井平台發生油井爆炸，導致超過三百萬加侖的原油流入太平洋。

B：哇，這聽起來很糟。接下來發生了什麼事？

A：漏油事件摧毀了當地野生動物，污染了海灘，並引起全國對離岸鑽油和更廣泛的環境問題的關注。

B：我想這對很多人來說一定是個警鐘。

A：當然。目睹這場環境災難，威斯康辛州參議員蓋洛德．尼爾森採取了行動。他長期在提倡環保，認為這是一個把公眾對污染和生態退化的關注轉化為政治運動的機會。

B：這很鼓舞人心。他做了什麼？

A：在學生反戰運動的啓發下，他策劃了一場「全國環境宣講會」。在活動家丹尼斯．海斯的幫助下，尼爾森於 1970 年 4 月 22 日組織了第一次的地球日，吸引全國關注。

B：人們的反應怎麼樣？

A：反應超熱烈。當天大概共有兩千萬美國人走上街頭、公園和禮堂，示威要求更健康、更永續的環境。這象徵現代環保運動的誕生，也帶來了重大的立法成就。

B：例如？

A：像是環境保護局 (EPA) 的成立，還有《潔淨空氣法》、《潔淨水法》和《瀕危物種法》都因此通過了。

B：好厲害。地球日確實發揮了重要作用。

A：沒錯，它提醒我們，為了更乾淨的地球而努力的責任遠遠還沒有結束。

B：那我們該怎麼做來紀念地球日並為提高環保意識做出貢獻呢？

A：有幾種方法。首先，我們可以遵循三個 R：Reduce（減少）、Reuse（重複使用）、Recycle（回收）。減少消費、盡可能重複使用物品，以及回收材料皆有助於減少最終進入垃圾掩埋場和海洋的廢棄物量。

B：有道理。還有什麼？

A：我們可以節約能源和水。隨手關燈、使用節能電器和修理漏水等簡單的行動可大幅減少能源和水的消耗。採用太陽能和風能等再生能源也是邁向永續發展的重要一步。

B：我聽說支持永續實踐也很重要。

A：的確。選擇由永續材料製成的產品、支持採用環保做法的公司，以及多吃植物性飲食都能減少我們的環境足跡。購買當地生產的商品也能減少運輸過程中的碳排放。

B：那種樹和花園呢？

A：很棒。樹木吸收二氧化碳、釋放氧氣，對抗氣候變遷上很重要。在後院或社區空間進行園藝有助於支持當地生態系統並促進生物多樣性。

B：要怎麼教育和倡導這些事情呢？

A：宣導環境議題並提倡政策改革可產生廣泛的影響。參與社區倡議、支持環保團體、加入清潔行動都能鼓勵更多人關注環保並推動制度上的改變。

B：謝謝你的分享，Alex。聽你這麼說，讓我更了解地球日的重要性，還有我們能做些什麼來幫助環境。

A：不客氣，Jamie。一點一滴都有幫助，只要我們齊心協力，就能做出巨大的改變。

在繼續往下學習之前，請先回到本單元開頭處確認那些學習目標自己是否已達成。

Answers

Task 1:

Q1: B Q2: B Q3: A Q4: A Q5: C

Task 2:

tragic	event
determined	leader
environmental	disaster
oil	spill
local	wildlife
national	attention
public	concern
political	movement
legislative	achievements
cleaner	planet

Task 3:

1. cleaner planet
2. local wildlife
3. political movement
4. tragic event
5. determined leader
6. environmental disaster
7. national attention
8. oil spill
9. public concern
10. legislative achievements

Task 5:

1. for 2. of 3. by 4. about 5. as 6. to

Unit 12

查爾斯三世加冕典禮

The Coronation of Charles III

本單元的學習目標包括：

☐ 學到一些可用以談論本主題的 word partnerships
☐ 練習用動詞描述事件並留意注意事項

Reading

Task 1 12-1

請閱聽這篇文章並回答下面的問題。

In a grand display of tradition and **regality**, Charles III was **crowned** this week as the King of the United Kingdom in a splendid **coronation ceremony** held at Westminster Abbey. The historic event witnessed the **culmination** of a centuries-old **ritual**, with the **monarch** assuming the responsibilities of the crown amid the awe-inspiring presence of **sacred** objects.

The coronation of Charles III commenced with a **procession** through the streets of London, as thousands of well-wishers lined the route to catch a glimpse of their new **sovereign**. The **vibrant** display of **pomp** and **pageantry** set the stage for a **momentous** occasion that would resonate throughout the nation.

As the ceremony unfolded within the hallowed halls of Westminster Abbey, the ancient rituals that have accompanied coronations for generations were faithfully observed. The Archbishop of Canterbury **officiated** the proceedings, adding a **spiritual** dimension to the majestic event.

One of the **highlights** of the coronation was the use of sacred objects, each imbued with profound historical and religious significance. The St Edward's Crown, adorned with precious gemstones, took center stage as it was placed upon the head of Charles III. This iconic symbol of the British monarchy, traditionally used for coronations, represents the weight of responsibility and the authority **vested** in the new monarch.

Another sacred object that played a pivotal role in the ceremony was the Sovereign's Orb. Crafted from gold and adorned with **exquisite** jewels, the orb **symbolizes** the monarch's role as the defender of the Christian faith. Its presence serves as a constant reminder of the spiritual and moral **obligations** bestowed upon the new sovereign.

The ancient Coronation Chair, built under the orders of King Edward I in 1296, played a crucial part in the ceremony. Housing the legendary Stone of Scone, this **magnificent** chair has witnessed the crowning of British monarchs for centuries. The Stone of Scone, also known as the Stone of Destiny, is believed to have once been used in the coronation ceremonies of Scottish kings, symbolizing the union of the realms.

As Charles III assumed the **throne**, he **pledged** his commitment to the service of the nation and its people. In his coronation address, he emphasized his dedication to **upholding** the values that define the United Kingdom, promising to work tirelessly for the betterment of the country and its citizens.

The coronation of Charles III marks a significant **milestone** in British history. Steeped in centuries-old traditions and observed with the utmost reverence, this ceremonial event has united the nation in **celebration**. As the new monarch takes up the mantle, the world eagerly watches, filled with anticipation for the next chapter of the United Kingdom under the **reign** of King Charles III.

VOCABULARY

regality [riˋgælətɪ] *n.* 君權；王位
crown [kraʊn] *n./v.* 王冠；爲……加冕
coronation [ˏkɔrəˋneʃən] *n.* 加冕典禮
ceremony [ˋsɛrəˏmonɪ] *n.* 儀式；典禮
culmination [ˏkʌlməˋneʃən] *n.* 最高點
ritual [ˋrɪtʃʊəl] *n.* 儀式；典禮
monarch [ˋmanək] *n.* 君主
sacred [ˋsekrɪd] *adj.* 神聖的
procession [prəˋsɛʃən] *n.* 行列；隊伍
sovereign [ˋsavrɪn] *n.* 君主
vibrant [ˋvaɪbrənt] *adj.* 充滿活力的
pomp [pamp] *n.* 盛況
pageantry [ˋpædʒəntrɪ] *n.* 壯觀
momentous [moˋmɛntəs] *adj.* 重大的
officiate [əˋfɪʃɪˏet] *v.* 主持（儀式）
spiritual [ˋspɪrɪtʃʊəl] *adj.* 精神的；宗教的
highlight [ˋhaɪˏlaɪt] *n./v.* 亮點；突顯
vest [vɛst] *v.* 賦予（權力、財產等）
exquisite [ˋɛkskwɪzɪt] *adj.* 精美的
symbolize [ˋsɪmbḷˏaɪz] *v.* 象徵
obligation [ˏabləˋgeʃən] *n.* 義務
magnificent [mægˋnɪfəsənt] *adj.* 華麗的
throne [θron] *n.* 王座；王位
pledge [plɛdʒ] *v.* 許諾；發誓
uphold [ʌpˋhold] *v.* 維護
milestone [ˋmaɪlˏston] *n.* 里程碑
celebration [ˏsɛləˋbreʃən] *n.* 慶祝
reign [ren] *n.* 統治

Comprehension questions

Q1: What is the main topic of the article?

A. the crown of Saint Edward

B. the Sovereign's Orb

C. the coronation of Charles III

Q2: What is the fourth paragraph about?

A. precious gemstones

B. all the sacred objects used in the coronation

C. the Saint Edward's Crown

Q3: What is the Sovereign's Orb?

A. it is a symbol of the monarch's role as the defender of Christianity

B. it has a famous gemstone

C. a key part of the ceremony

Q4: What is the Stone of Scone?

A. a magic stone

B. a stone from Scotland used in the coronation of Scottish kings

C. a type of bread

Q5: Why is the Coronation of Charles III important?

A. many people attended the Coronation

B. it marks an important moment in British history

C. things will never be the same again

答案在本單元最後一頁。如果答錯了，請再確認一次文章內容。

中譯

在展現傳統與王室威儀的盛大儀式中，查爾斯三世於本週在西敏寺加冕成為英國國王。這場歷史性的加冕典禮延續了數百年以來的傳統，君主在令人敬畏的聖物前承擔了王冠的責任。

查爾斯三世的加冕典禮以遊行揭開序幕，王室隊伍穿梭於倫敦街道，沿途都是成千上萬的祝福者，只為一睹新君主的風采。壯觀的場面讓這個舉國矚目的重要時刻顯得格外隆重。

加冕典禮在西敏寺神聖的殿堂內進行，遵循著世代傳承的古老儀式。坎特伯里大主教主持了整個儀式，為這場盛典增添了宗教氛圍。

加冕典禮的亮點之一是聖物的使用，每件都具有深刻的歷史和宗教意義。鑲有珍貴寶石的聖愛德華王冠在查爾斯三世的頭上閃耀著光芒，是歷代英國君王加冕象徵，代表新君主所承擔的責任和權力。

另一件重要聖物是「君主權杖」。這件以黃金製成並鑲嵌精美珠寶的權杖象徵著君主作為基督教信仰守護者的角色，其存在時刻提醒著新君主肩負的精神和道德責任。

古老而華麗的加冕椅也是典禮的焦點之一，該椅由愛德華一世於 1296 年下令建造，椅座內嵌有傳奇的「司康石」，幾個世紀以來見證了英國君主的加冕。司康石，又稱「命運之石」，相傳曾用於蘇格蘭國王的加冕禮，象徵著王國的統一。

當查爾斯三世登基時，他承諾全心全意為國家和人民服務。在加冕致詞中，他強調自己致力於維護英國的核心價值，並承諾將努力不懈為國家和全體國民謀求福祉。

查爾斯三世的加冕是英國歷史上一個重要的里程碑。這場儀式秉承了數百年的傳統，並以最崇高的敬意舉行，全國上下團結一致慶祝。隨著新君主即位，全球熱切地關注著，對國王查爾斯三世統治下的英國新篇章充滿期待。

文法甦活區

Task 2

請用上篇文章中的 word partnerships 完成下表。見範例。

grand	display
coronation	
	event
centuries-old	
	objects
new	
	display
momentous	
	observed
new	

只要對照文章，便可輕鬆找出答案。

接下來，我們要利用上列 word partnerships 練習寫作。

Task 3

請用 Task 2 表格中的 word partnerships 填入下列空格。見範例。

1. As the country welcomed its __new sovereign__, the air was filled with a sense of anticipation and hope for a bright and prosperous future under the reign of the young monarch.

PART 1
PART 2
PART 3
Unit 11
Unit 12
Unit 13
Unit 14
Unit 15
PART 4
PART 5
PART 6

2. Graduation day was a ________________________ for the students, their families, and the entire school community, marking the culmination of years of hard work and academic achievement.

3. The ________________________, passed down through generations, added a sense of profound significance and cultural richness to the annual harvest festival.

4. The coronation of Charles III was marked by a __________________ of tradition and regality, capturing the essence of centuries-old ceremonial splendor.

5. The coronation of the ______________________ brought a sense of excitement and optimism, as the people eagerly anticipated the fresh perspective and leadership that would define this era.

6. The garden came alive in a ____________________ of colors as the flowers bloomed in a breathtaking array, creating a scene of natural beauty that captivated all who visited.

7. The grandeur of the ___________________ left spectators in awe as the newly crowned monarch ascended the throne with regal grace.

8. The moon landing in 1969 was a ___________________ that marked a giant leap for humanity in the exploration of outer space.

9. The temple's inner sanctum housed an array of _________________, each imbued with spiritual significance and revered by the devout worshippers.

10. The traditional ceremony was ______________________ each year, honoring the customs and rituals that had been passed down through generations.

答案在本單元最後一頁。

再作一個文法練習吧！透過練習，你會更清楚本單元的文法重點。

Task 4

請再讀一遍文章，並在下列單字劃底線。從這些詞組中你注意到什麼？

- commenced with
- set the stage for
- unfolded
- were observed
- played a pivotal role
- played a crucial part

這些詞組都是用來描述事件的動詞或片語。「commenced with」和「set the stage for」用以描述事件的開始；「played a pivotal role」和「played a crucial role」用以描述事件的重要階段。

Task 5

請用 Task 4 的詞組填入下列空格。

1. Her innovative ideas and strategic planning ____________________ in the company's successful expansion into new markets.

2. The conference ____________________ a thought-provoking keynote address, setting the tone for the insightful discussions and collaboration that would follow.

3. The dedicated team of scientists ____________________ in the success of the mission, contributing their expertise and determination to overcome challenges and achieve groundbreaking results.

4. The events of that fateful day ____________________ slowly, revealing a series of unforeseen challenges that would reshape the course of their lives.

5. The groundbreaking scientific discovery ________________ a new era of advancements, inspiring researchers worldwide to explore uncharted territories in their quest for knowledge.

6. The laboratory protocols ________________ meticulously, ensuring that every step of the experiment was conducted with precision and accuracy.

答案在本單元最後一頁。

Listening

Task 6 12-2

請聽讀下列對話，你聽出了哪些前面 tasks 用到的詞彙？

A: Did you catch the news about Charles III's coronation this week?

B: Absolutely! It was quite a grand display of tradition and regality. The coronation ceremony at Westminster Abbey was splendid.

A: I heard it was a historic event with centuries-old rituals. Must have been quite a sight.

B: Indeed! The whole thing commenced with a procession through London. Thousands of people lined the streets to see their new sovereign.

A: The vibrant display and pageantry set the stage for a momentous occasion, didn't it?

B: Absolutely. And as the ceremony unfolded at Westminster Abbey, the Archbishop of Canterbury faithfully observed all the rituals, adding a spiritual touch to the whole event.

A: I read about the sacred objects being used. The St Edward's Crown and the Sovereign's Orb, they hold so much historical and religious significance.

B: The St Edward's Crown, especially, is iconic. It represents the weight of responsibility and authority vested in the new sovereign.

A: And what about the Coronation Chair and the Stone of Scone? Such ancient artifacts with centuries of history.

B: They played a crucial part in the ceremony. The Stone of Scone, also known as the Stone of Destiny, has a fascinating history tied to the coronations of Scottish kings.

A: Charles III pledged his commitment to the nation during the ceremony, right?

B: Exactly. In his coronation address, he emphasized his dedication to upholding the values of the United Kingdom and working tirelessly for the betterment of the country.

A: It's a momentous occasion in British history. The whole world is watching as Charles III takes up the mantle.

B: Indeed. The coronation has united the nation in celebration, and there's a sense of anticipation for the next chapter of the United Kingdom under the new monarch King Charles III.

能夠進步的練習方式：先聽到至少大致了解的程度後再看翻譯。

中譯

A：你有看到這禮拜查爾斯三世的加冕新聞嗎？

B：當然！真是一場充滿傳統與王室威儀的盛典。西敏寺的加冕典禮好壯觀。

A：我聽說那是一個有數百年歷史的儀式，現場一定很震撼吧。

B：確實如此！整個活動從倫敦的遊行開始，成千上萬的人站在街道兩旁，想一睹新君主的風采。

A：華麗的排場真是令人印象深刻。

B：沒錯。隨著典禮在西敏寺進行，坎特伯里大主教忠實地主持了所有儀式，為整個活動增添了神聖的氛圍。

A：我讀到典禮使用了很多聖物，像是聖愛德華王冠和君主權杖，這些都有深刻的歷史和宗教意義。

B：尤其是聖愛德華王冠，非常具有代表性，象徵著新君主的責任和權力。

A：那加冕椅和司康石呢？這些古老文物已有數百年的歷史。

B：它們在典禮中扮演了重要角色。司康石，又叫命運之石，有著與蘇格蘭國王加冕相關的歷史，意義非凡。

A：查爾斯三世在儀式上許下了他對國家的承諾，對嗎？

B：沒錯。在加冕致詞中，他強調了自己將致力於維護英國的核心價值，並將為國家的進步努力不懈。

A：這是英國歷史上的重要時刻，全世界都在關注查爾斯三世即位。

B：確實如此。加冕典禮凝聚了全國一同慶祝，也讓人們對查爾斯三世統治下的英國未來充滿期待。

在繼續往下學習之前，請先回到本單元開頭處確認那些學習目標自己是否已達成。

Answers

Task 1:

Q1: C Q2: C Q3: A Q4: B Q5: B

Task 2:

grand	display
coronation	ceremony
historic	event
centuries-old	ritual
sacred	objects
new	sovereign
vibrant	display
momentous	occasion
faithfully	observed
new	monarch

Task 3:

1. new sovereign
2. momentous occasion
3. centuries-old ritual
4. grand display
5. new monarch
6. vibrant display
7. coronation ceremony
8. historic event
9. sacred objects
10. faithfully observed

Task 5:

1. played a crucial part / pivotal role in
2. commenced with
3. played a crucial part / pivotal role in
4. unfolded
5. set the stage for
6. were observed

Unit 13 同志驕傲月
June Pride

本單元的學習目標包括：

- ☐ 認識一些與 LGBTQ+ 相關的慶祝活動與其由來
- ☐ 練習一些用以描述抗議和訴求政治改革的搭配詞

Reading

Task 1 13-1

請閱聽這篇文章並回答下面的問題。

As rainbow flags adorn city streets and vibrant celebrations fill the air, the month of June takes on a special significance worldwide. Recognized as Pride Month, June is a time to **commemorate** the **progress**, resilience, and ongoing struggle for equality of the LGBTQ+ community. With a rich history rooted in activism, this month serves as a powerful reminder of the ongoing fight for **inclusivity** and acceptance.

The origins of Pride Month can be traced back to the pivotal Stonewall Uprising in June 1969. The Stonewall Inn, a gay bar in New York City's Greenwich Village, became the **epicenter** of a rebellion against the discriminatory treatment and **raids** by the police targeting the LGBTQ+ community. The brave individuals who took a stand that night, **predominantly** queer people of color and transgender activists, ignited a movement that would shape the fight for LGBTQ+ rights for generations to come.

Following the Stonewall Uprising, LGBTQ+ activists organized the first Pride **march** in New York City on June 28, 1970, marking the one-year anniversary of the historic event. This march, known as the Christopher Street Liberation Day March, brought together thousands of individuals who proudly celebrated their identities and demanded equality. The spirit of this **inaugural** march quickly spread, inspiring similar Pride **parades** and events in cities around the world.

Over the years, Pride Month has evolved into a global celebration of diversity and a platform for advocacy. It serves as a rallying point for LGBTQ+ individuals and **allies** to raise awareness, promote acceptance, and push for legislative changes that protect and uphold their rights. Pride events, ranging from parades and festivals to educational **panels** and art exhibitions, provide spaces for the community to express their **authentic** selves while fostering a sense of belonging and the **unity**.

Pride Month also serves as a **somber** reminder of the struggles faced by LGBTQ+ individuals. It is a time to honor the courage of those who have fought for equality, as well as remember the lives lost due to hate, **discrimination**, and **prejudice**. It is a call to action to address ongoing challenges, such as systemic **homophobia**, **transphobia**, and the fight for **comprehensive** LGBTQ+ rights worldwide.

While significant progress has been made, there is still much work to be done. Pride Month serves as a reminder that equality is an ongoing pursuit and that everyone has a role to play in creating a more inclusive society. It encourages individuals and institutions to examine their own **biases**, challenge discriminatory practices, and actively support LGBTQ+ rights.

Comprehension questions

Q1: What is the main topic of the article?

A. why June is Pride month

B. gay pride

C. the Stonewall Uprising

Q2: What happened in June 1969?

A. Pride Month started

B. the Stonewall Uprising

C. a gay bar opened in Greenwich Village

Q3: When and where was the first Pride march?

A. Stonewall June 1969

B. New York City June 1970

C. the article doesn't say

Q4: What has Pride Month come to mean?

A. a global celebration of diversity and a platform for advocacy

B. an occasion for a great parade

C. equal rights for all LGBTQ+

Q5: What does Pride Month serve as a reminder of?

A. those who died of AIDS in the 1980s

B. it marks an important moment in American history

C. equality is an ongoing pursuit

答案在本單元最後一頁。如果答錯了，請再確認一次文章內容。

VOCABULARY

commemorate [kəˋmɛməˌret] *v.* 慶祝
progress [ˋpragrɛs] *n.* 進展
inclusivity [ˌɪnkluˋsɪvɪtɪ] *n.* 包容
epicenter [ˋɛpɪˌsɛntɚ] *n.* 中心
raid [red] *n.* 襲擊
predominantly [prɪˋdamɪnəntlɪ] *adv.* 主要地
march [martʃ] *n.* 遊行
inaugural [ɪnˋɔgjərəl] *adj.* 首次的
parade [pəˋred] *n.* 遊行
ally [ˋælaɪ] *n.* 盟友；支持者

中譯

當彩虹旗飄揚在城市街道上，繽紛的慶祝活動「遍地開花」時，六月在全世界都具有特殊的意義。六月是「同志驕傲月」，是紀念 LGBTQ+ 群體的進步、堅韌和為平等而持續奮鬥的時刻。根植於社運行動的豐富歷史，這個月強烈提醒人們，開闢包容與接納之路仍在進行中。

同志驕傲月的起源可追溯至 1969 年 6 月的石牆事件。位於紐約市格林威治村的石牆酒吧是當時對抗警方針對 LGBTQ+ 社群的歧視和突襲的起點。那晚勇敢站出來的人主要是有色人種的酷兒和跨性別活動家，他們的反抗點燃了這場運動，改變了未來 LGBTQ+ 權利的奮鬥歷程。

石牆事件後，1970 年 6 月 28 日，LGBTQ+ 活動家於紐約市組織了第一次驕傲遊行，紀念這歷史性事件一週年。這場遊行稱為「克里斯多夫街解放日遊行」，吸引了數千勇敢展示身分、爭取平等的人參加。該次遊行的精神迅速傳播開來，激勵了世界各地城市舉辦類似的遊行和活動。

多年來，同志驕傲月已演變為全球支持多元的慶典和倡議平台。它是 LGBTQ+ 個人和盟友的一個集結點，旨在提高意識、促進接納，並推動立法改革以維護他們的權利。從遊行、節慶到教育座談和藝術展覽，各種活動為酷兒群體提供表達真實自我並增進歸屬感和團結的空間。

同志驕傲月也沉重地提醒著人們 LGBTQ+ 個體的處境艱難。這是向那些為平等奮鬥的人致敬的時刻，也是在悼念因仇恨、歧視、偏見而逝去的生命。它呼籲大家關注一直存在的問題，例如體制性恐同、恐跨，並持續為全球 LGBTQ+ 的全面權利努力。

儘管取得了重大進展，但仍有許多工作要做。同志驕傲月提醒大家，平等是一個不斷追求的目標，每個人都有責任為創造更包容的社會貢獻一份力量。它鼓勵個人和機構審視自己的偏見，挑戰歧視性的行為，並積極支持 LGBTQ+ 權利。

VOCABULARY

panel [ˋpænḷ] *n.* 專家座談會；板
authentic [ɔˋθɛntɪk] *adj.* 真實的
unity [ˋjunətɪ] *n.* 團結
somber [ˋsambɚ] *adj.* 嚴肅的
discrimination [dɪˌskrɪməˋneʃən] *n.* 歧視
prejudice [ˋprɛdʒədɪs] *n.* 偏見
homophobia [ˌhoməˋfobɪə] *n.* 同性戀恐懼症
transphobia [ˌtrænzˋfobɪə] *n.* 跨性別恐懼症
comprehensive [ˌkamprɪˋhɛnsɪv] *adj.* 全面的
bias [ˋbaɪəs] *n.* 偏見；偏愛

文法甦活區

Task 2

請用上篇文章中的 word partnerships 完成下表。見範例。

rainbow	flags
city	
	celebrations
special	
	history
ongoing	
	treatment
brave	
	march
lives	

只要對照文章，便可輕鬆找出答案。

接下來，我們要利用上列 word partnerships 練習寫作。

Task 3

請用 Task 2 表格中的 word partnerships 填入下列空格。見範例。

1. As the sun dipped below the horizon, the bustling city streets came alive with the glow of neon signs and the rhythmic hum of traffic.

2. Despite numerous efforts, the community continues to face an ________________ with poverty and inequality.

3. In the face of adversity, ________________ stepped forward to champion equality and justice for all.

4. The ancient castle atop the hill boasts a ________________, filled with tales of kings, battles, and centuries of tradition.

5. The city streets were filled with energy and solidarity during the annual ________________, as thousands of LGBTQ+ individuals and allies came together to celebrate love and acceptance.

6. The company's policy of ________________ toward minority employees sparked widespread outrage and calls for reform.

7. The memorial stands as a somber reminder of the ________________ to the tragic event, a testament to the resilience of those left behind.

8. The old oak tree in the backyard held ________________ for the family, serving as a symbol of resilience and generations past.

9. The parade was a vibrant display of inclusion and acceptance, with ________________ fluttering joyously in the breeze.

10. The town square was alive with ________________, as people danced to the beat of drums and colorful streamers filled the air.

答案在本單元最後一頁。

再作一個文法練習吧！透過練習，你會更清楚本單元的文法重點。

Task 4

請再讀一遍文章，並在下列 word partnerships 劃底線。注意看其用法。

- took a stand
- ignited a movement
- demanded equality
- promote acceptance
- push for legislative changes

這些詞組都是用來描述抗議或訴求政治改革的搭配詞，皆由動詞和名詞組成；有些動詞是過去簡單式，有些動詞是現在簡單式。請記住，我們使用過去簡單式來指稱已完成的過去事件；使用現在簡單式以指稱當前的事實。

Task 5

請用 Task 4 的詞組填入下列空格。

1. Citizens rallied together to ____________________, advocating for policies that would better protect the rights of marginalized communities.

2. Despite the risks, she courageously ____________________ against injustice, inspiring others to join her in the fight for equality.

3. Educational programs and community events are essential to ____________________ and understanding among diverse groups.

4. The grassroots campaign ____________________ for environmental awareness, mobilizing communities around the world to take action against climate change.

5. The protesters marched through the streets, chanting slogans that ____________________ and justice for all marginalized communities.

答案在本單元最後一頁。這些句子都是關於抗議或尋求改變的，請注意其中不同的動詞時態。

Listening

Task 6 13-2

請聽讀下列對話，你聽出了哪些前面 tasks 用到的詞彙？

A: Hey, have you noticed all the rainbow flags lining the city streets lately?

B: Yeah, it's Pride Month! June holds a special significance for the LGBTQ+ community worldwide.

A: Right, it's a time to commemorate their progress and ongoing struggle for equality, isn't it?

B: Absolutely. Did you know it all started with the Stonewall Uprising back in 1969?

A: Yeah, at the Stonewall Inn in New York City. Brave individuals took a stand against discriminatory treatment by the police.

B: Exactly. That event ignited a movement that led to the first Pride march in 1970, marking the one-year anniversary of Stonewall.

A: And now, Pride events happen all over the world, promoting acceptance and advocating for legislative changes.

B: Yeah, they're not just vibrant celebrations, but platforms for raising awareness and demanding equality.

A: It's incredible how far they've come, but there's still so much work to do, right?

B: Definitely. Pride Month reminds us of the ongoing struggles faced by LGBTQ+ individuals, their rich history, and the need for everyone to support their rights.

A: Absolutely. It's also a reminder of the lives lost to AIDS in the mid-1980s.

B: Exactly. We can all play a part in promoting equality and acceptance.

請先確實聆聽音檔，大致了解後再看翻譯。

中譯

A：嘿，你有沒有注意到最近街上都掛滿了彩虹旗？

B：有啊，現在是同志驕傲月嘛！六月對全球 LGBTQ+ 族群來說具有特殊的意義。

A：對，這是紀念他們的進步和為平等而持續奮鬥的時刻，對吧？

B：沒錯。你知道這一切是從 1969 年的石牆事件開始的嗎？

A：我知道，在紐約市的石牆酒吧。勇敢的人們站出來反抗警方的歧視待遇。

B：沒錯。那次事件引發了一場運動，促成了 1970 年第一次的驕傲遊行，紀念石牆一週年。

A：現在，驕傲活動在全球「遍地開花」，推動接納共融和倡導立法改革。

B：是啊，這些活動不僅是色彩繽紛的慶典，更是提高意識和爭取平等的平台。

A：他們走到今天真的很不容易，但還有很多工作要做，對吧？

B：確實如此。驕傲月提醒我們 LGBTQ+ 群體所面臨的挑戰、他們豐富的歷史，以及每個人支持自己權利的必要性。

A：沒錯。這也讓我們想起 1980 年代中期因愛滋病逝去的生命。

B：真的。我們都能為促進平等和接納出一份力。

在繼續往下學習之前，請先回到本單元開頭處確認那些學習目標自己是否已達成。

Answers

Task 1:

Q1: A Q2: B Q3: B Q4: A Q5: C

Task 2:

rainbow	flags
city	streets
vibrant	celebrations
special	significance
rich	history
ongoing	struggle
discriminatory	treatment
brave	individuals
Pride	march
lives	lost

Task 3:

1. city streets
2. ongoing struggle
3. brave individuals
4. rich history
5. Pride march
6. discriminatory treatment
7. lives lost
8. special significance
9. rainbow flags
10. vibrant celebrations

Task 5:

1. push for legislative changes
2. took a stand
3. promote acceptance
4. ignited a movement
5. demanded equality

Unit 14 冬至
The Winter Solstice

本單元的學習目標包括：

□ 認識一些世界各地在冬至時節的習俗
□ 運用複數語塊 (plural chunks) 做一些練習

Reading

Task 1 14-1

請閱聽這篇文章並回答下面的問題。

As the winter **solstice** graces the Northern **Hemisphere** with its longest night and the Southern Hemisphere with its longest day, **diverse** cultures worldwide come together in some unique and vibrant celebrations that honor the changing seasons and the triumph of light over darkness.

In the Northern Hemisphere, the winter solstice falls around December 21, marking the official **onset** of winter. Communities across Europe, Asia, and North America commemorate this **celestial** event with a variety of customs deeply rooted in history and tradition.

In Scandinavia, the ancient festival of Yule takes center stage. Celebrated for several days, Yule marks the rebirth of the sun and the promise of longer days to come. **Festivities** include the lighting of candles and the Yule log, symbolizing the triumph of light over darkness.

In China, the Dongzhi Festival, also known as the Winter Solstice Festival, is a time for family **reunions**. Many traditional dishes like tangyuan (sweet rice dumplings) are prepared, symbolizing family unity and the return of longer, brighter days.

The ancient Romans celebrated the winter solstice with Saturnalia, a festival dedicated to the god Saturn. During this time, social **norms** were temporarily overturned, and **revelers** engaged in **feasting**, gift-giving, and **merriment**.

In the Southern Hemisphere, where the winter solstice occurs around June 21, communities in South America, Africa, and Australia celebrate the triumph of light and the promise of warmer days.

In Peru, the Incan festival of Inti Raymi celebrates the sun god Inti. The historic ceremony involves colorful processions, music, and dance as participants express gratitude for the sun's life-giving energy.

Indigenous communities in Australia mark the winter solstice with traditional **corroborees**. These ceremonies, involving song, dance, and storytelling, connect participants with the land and the natural rhythms of the seasons.

Kwanzaa, celebrated in late December, **incorporates** elements of various African harvest festivals and emphasizes unity, creativity, and self-determination. The lighting of the Kinara, a candle holder, symbolizes the principles of Kwanzaa.

While the specific customs and traditions may vary, the **essence** of winter solstice celebrations remains universal—a time to reflect on the cycles of nature, express gratitude, and come together as communities. In an increasingly interconnected world, these diverse celebrations remind us of the common **thread** that unites humanity in the shared experience of the changing seasons and the **perennial** hope for light, warmth, and **renewal**.

Comprehension questions

Q1: What is the main topic of the article?

A. celebrations around the world

B. the Winter solstice

C. how the winter solstice is celebrated around the world

Q2: How do they celebrate the winter solstice in Scandinavia?

A. with social norms being overturned

B. with family reunions

C. with a Yule log

Q3: In the Southern hemisphere, when is the winter solstice celebrated?

A. December 21

B. June 21

C. Christmas

Q4: What is the 5th paragraph about?

A. how the ancient Romans celebrated the solstice

B. revelers

C. the god Saturn

Q5: How do they celebrate the solstice in Africa?

A. by celebrating Kwanzaa

B. with harvest festivals

C. with the lighting of the Kinara

答案在本單元最後一頁。如果答錯了，請再確認一次文章內容。

VOCABULARY

solstice [ˋsalstɪs] *n.*【天】至點
hemisphere [ˋhɛməs͵fɪr] *n.*（地球的）半球
diverse [daɪˋvɝs] *adj.* 多樣的
onset [ˋan͵sɛt] *n.* 開始
celestial [sɪˋlɛstʃəl] *adj.* 天空的
festivity [fɛsˋtɪvətɪ] *n.* 慶祝活動
reunion [riˋjunjən] *n.* 團聚
norm [nɔrm] *n.* 規範

中譯

冬至為北半球帶來最長的夜晚，為南半球帶來最長的白晝，世界各地的不同文化各自以獨特而充滿活力的方式來慶祝這個季節變換，讚頌光明戰勝黑暗的力量。

在北半球，冬至大約在 12 月 21 日，標誌著冬季正式到來。歐洲、亞洲和北美洲的社區以各種深植於歷史和傳統的習俗來紀念這一個天文現象。

在斯堪地那維亞，古老的耶魯節 (Yule) 是備受重視的慶典。耶魯節為期不只一天，象徵太陽的重生和白晝將盛。節日活動包括點燃蠟燭和焚燒冬至木 (Yule log)，象徵光明戰勝黑暗。

在中國，冬至是家人團聚的時刻。人們準備許多如湯圓等傳統菜餚，象徵家庭團圓和長日光明的回歸。

古羅馬人以農神節 (Saturnalia) 慶祝冬至，這是一個獻給農業之神的節日。在此期間，社會規範暫時被顛覆，人們互贈禮物並盡情享受宴會和歡樂時光。

在南半球，冬至大約在 6 月 21 日，南美洲、非洲和澳洲的社區以慶祝光明和期待回暖的日子為主題舉辦各種活動。

在秘魯，印加的太陽祭 (Inti Raymi) 是為了敬奉太陽神印帝 (Inti)。歷史悠久的慶祝儀式包括色彩繽紛的遊行、音樂和舞蹈，參與者藉此表達對太陽賜予生命能量的感恩之情。

澳洲的原住民社區透過傳統的歌舞儀式來迎接冬至，這些儀式包括歌唱、舞蹈和講故事，讓參加者與土地以及自然季節的節奏產生連結。

而在 12 月底舉行的寬扎節 (Kwanzaa)，融合了多種非洲豐收節的元素，強調團結、創造力和自我決心。節日中點燃的燭台 (Kinara) 象徵寬扎節的基本價值。

儘管各地的慶典習俗不盡相同，但冬至慶祝的核心精神卻是相通的——這是一個反思自然週期、感恩生命，並與社群一同慶祝的時刻。在這個日益緊密相連的世界中，這些多樣化的慶祝活動提醒我們，人類共享這段季節變化的體驗，以及對光明、溫暖與重生的共同渴望與期盼。

VOCABULARY

reveler [ˋrɛvələ] *n.* 狂歡者
feast [fist] *v.* 盡情飲食
merriment [ˋmɛrɪmənt] *n.* 歡樂
indigenous [ɪnˋdɪdʒɪnəs] *adj.* 原住民的
corroboree [kəˋrabərɪ] *n.* 歌舞宴會
incorporate [ɪnˋkɔrpə͵ret] *v.* 融合
essence [ˋɛsns] *n.* 本質
thread [θrɛd] *n.* 線
perennial [pəˋrɛnɪəl] *adj.* 長期存在的
renewal [rɪˋnjuəl] *n.* 更新；復興

文法甦活區

Task 2

請用上篇文章中的 word partnerships 完成下表。見範例。

longest	night
changing	
	festival
family	
	dishes
family	
	norms
colorful	
	communities
diverse	

只要對照文章，便可輕鬆找出答案。

接下來，我們要利用上列 word partnerships 練習寫作。

Task 3

請用 Task 2 表格中的 word partnerships 填入下列空格。見範例。

1. As the leaves turned golden and the air grew crisper, the __changing__ __seasons__ signaled the arrival of autumn in all its vibrant glory.

2. Challenging societal expectations and questioning traditional ________________, she embarked on a journey of self-discovery to forge her own path in life.

3. During the holiday feast, the dining table was adorned with an array of ________________, each carefully prepared to honor cherished family recipes passed down through generations.

4. Efforts to preserve the unique heritage of ________________ involve promoting sustainable practices that respect their deep connection to the land and cultural traditions.

5. ________________ are always filled with laughter, shared memories, and the joy of reconnecting with loved ones after long periods of separation.

6. On the ________________ of the year, the village gathered around the bonfire, sharing stories and warmth to celebrate the winter solstice.

7. The challenges they faced only strengthened their bond, showcasing the resilience of ________________ as they navigated through life's ups and downs together.

8. The city's calendar was filled with ________________, reflecting the multicultural tapestry that wove together various traditions and joyous festivities throughout the year.

9. The small town revived an ________________, bringing together generations to celebrate traditions that had been passed down through centuries.

10. The streets came alive with vibrant energy as ________________ paraded through the city, celebrating a rich tapestry of cultures and traditions.

答案在本單元最後一頁。

再作一個文法練習吧！透過練習，你會更清楚本單元的文法重點。

Task 4

請再讀一遍文章，並在下列單字劃底線。它們有什麼共通點？

· some · several · many · various · diverse

這些字我稱之為複數語塊 **(plural chunks)**。如果你仔細觀察，你會發現這些字後面的名詞總是複數。

Task 5

請改正下列句子中的錯誤。

1. She carefully examined the antique shop, hoping to find some hidden treasure among the shelves of old books and dusty artifacts.

2. After exploring the bustling marketplace, she purchased several vibrant fabric to create a patchwork quilt that would capture the essence of her travels.

3. In the library, many student were engrossed in their studies, creating a quiet yet bustling atmosphere of focused academic pursuits.

4. The art gallery showcased various style and medium, offering a diverse and eclectic range of creative expressions for visitors to appreciate.

5. The conference featured diverse perspective from various industry, sparking insightful discussions among professionals from different sectors.

答案在本單元最後一頁。希望你有發現複數語塊後的許多名詞字尾都沒有加上「**s**」，這樣是錯誤的。

Listening

現在我們來聽兩個人討論這篇文章。

Task 6 14-2

請聽讀下列對話，你聽出了哪些前面 tasks 用到的詞彙？

A: Have you ever thought about how different cultures celebrate the longest night?

B: Oh, absolutely! It's fascinating how diverse the celebrations for this ancient festival are around the world.

A: Right? In the Northern Hemisphere, like Europe and Asia, they have traditions like the Yule festival in Scandinavia, where they light candles and the Yule log to symbolize the changing seasons and the triumph of light over darkness.

B: And in China, during the Dongzhi Festival, it's all about family reunions and preparing traditional dishes like tangyuan to symbolize family unity and the return of longer, brighter days.

A: Exactly! And did you know that the ancient Romans had Saturnalia during the winter solstice? It was a time of feasting, gift-giving, and a temporary overturning of social norms.

B: That's intriguing! Meanwhile, in the Southern Hemisphere, places like Peru celebrate the sun god Inti with the Incan festival of Inti Raymi. Colorful processions, music, and dance are part of the festivities.

A: And in Australia, indigenous communities mark the winter solstice with corroborees, connecting with the land and the natural rhythms of the seasons through song, dance, and storytelling.

B: It's amazing how each culture has its unique way of celebrating the changing seasons. Have you heard of Kwanzaa? It incorporates African harvest festival elements and is celebrated in late December with principles like unity, creativity, and self-determination.

A: Yes, I have! The lighting of the Kinara during Kwanzaa symbolizes those principles. It's a great example of how diverse cultures emphasize similar values during this time.

B: Definitely. Regardless of the specific customs, there's a universal theme—reflecting on nature's cycles, expressing gratitude, and coming together as communities.

A: Absolutely! In an interconnected world, these diverse celebrations remind us of our shared experiences and the perennial hope for light, warmth, and renewal.

請先確實聆聽音檔，大致了解後再看翻譯。

中譯

A：你有想過不同文化是怎麼慶祝一年中最長的夜晚嗎？

B：噢，當然有啊！世界各地對這個古老節日的慶祝方式非常多樣，讓人想知道更多。

A：是不是？在北半球，比如歐洲和亞洲，有像斯堪地那維亞的耶魯節那樣的傳統，人們點燃蠟燭和冬至木來象徵季節變換和光明戰勝黑暗。

B：在中國，冬至期間，人們都會和家人團聚，準備湯圓等傳統菜餚，象徵著家庭團圓和白晝逐漸回歸，變得更長、更明亮。

A：沒錯！你知道嗎？古羅馬人在冬至時期也有一個節日叫農神節。他們會舉行盛宴、互相贈送禮物，並且暫時打破社會規範，讓整個社會進入狂歡模式。

B：真有趣！而在南半球，比如秘魯，他們藉由印加的太陽祭來慶祝太陽神印帝。節日期間有色彩繽紛的遊行、音樂和舞蹈。

A：在澳洲，原住民社區則有一個叫作科羅伯的傳統儀式來迎接冬至。這些儀式包括歌唱、舞蹈和講故事，透過這些活動來與土地和自然節奏產生連結。

B：真的很有意思！每個文化都有自己的獨特方式來慶祝季節的變化。你聽過寬扎節嗎？它結合了非洲豐收節的元素，在十二月底舉行，強調團結、創造力和自我決心。

A：聽過！寬扎節點燃的 Kinara 燭台代表了這些原則。這也說明了不同文化在這段時間強調相似的價值觀。

B：沒錯。無論具體的習俗有多不同，大家都有一個共同的主題，也就是反思自然循環、感恩、團結。

A：完全同意！在這個相互連結的世界中，這些不同的慶祝活動提醒我們，人們共享著相似的體驗以及對光明、溫暖和重生的渴望。

在繼續往下學習之前，請先回到本單元開頭處確認那些學習目標自己是否已達成。

PART 1
PART 2
PART 3
Unit 11
Unit 12
Unit 13
Unit 14
Unit 15
PART 4
PART 5
PART 6

Answers

Task 1:

Q1: B   Q2: C   Q3: B   Q4: A   Q5: C

Task 2:

longest	night
changing	seasons
ancient	festival
family	reunions
traditional	dishes
family	unity
social	norms
colorful	processions
indigenous	communities
diverse	celebrations

Task 3:

1. changing seasons
2. social norms
3. traditional dishes
4. indigenous communities
5. Family reunions
6. longest night
7. family unity
8. diverse celebrations
9. ancient festival
10. colorful processions

Task 5:

1. She carefully examined the antique shop, hoping to find some hidden **treasures** among the shelves of old books and dusty artifacts.
2. After exploring the bustling marketplace, she purchased several vibrant **fabrics** to create a patchwork quilt that would capture the essence of her travels.

3. In the library, many **students** were engrossed in their studies, creating a quiet yet bustling atmosphere of focused academic pursuits.
4. The art gallery showcased various **styles** and **mediums**, offering a diverse and eclectic range of creative expressions for visitors to appreciate.
5. The conference featured diverse **perspectives** from various **industries**, sparking insightful discussions among professionals from different sectors.

Unit 15 國際婦女節 International Women's Day

本單元的學習目標包括：

- □ 認識一個與婦女權利相關的節日與其由來
- □ 練習一些用以描述抗議的動詞語塊和搭配詞

Reading

Task 1 15-1

請閱聽這篇文章並回答下面的問題。

Every year on March 8, people all around the world observe International Women's Day (IWD) to honor the social, economic, cultural, and political accomplishments of women. Also, it serves to emphasize the continuous fight for gender equality, advocate for women's rights and **gender** justice, and increase awareness of gender inequality.

The origins of International Women's Day may be traced to revolutionary activities among working-class women and their **sympathizers**. The first International Women's Day was observed in early 1900, when women in Europe and North America were fighting for the right to vote and improved working conditions. Tens of thousands of women marched through New York City in 1908 to generate **momentum** for better pay and working conditions, which is said to be the origin of the day. A year later, the Socialist Party of America declared a day in honor of women.

The idea for a global day came to Clara Zetkin, the leader of the "women's office" of the German Social Democratic Party, in 1910 while she was in Copenhagen for a meeting. She **proposed** having a celebration on the same day every year to press for requests.

On March 8, 1914, a march in support of women's **suffrage** was held in London, and on March 8, 1917, the Russian Revolution was officially **launched** when tens of thousands of Russian women **rallied** for peace and food. The **tsar** was **compelled** to step down. The United States celebrated the inaugural International Women's Day in 1909, and the United Nations later declared it a worldwide holiday in 1975.

International Women's Day has a different topic every year and emphasizes a certain problem or a problem for women. Chose to Challenge, Women in Leadership: Creating an Equal Future in a COVID-19 World, and Think Equal, Build Smart, Innovate for Change were some of the more recent topics.

Across the world, the day is observed in a variety of ways, including rallies, marches, and other occasions that highlight women's challenges and accomplishments. It is also a time to recognize the contributions that women have made to society at large and to their communities.

International Women's Day, in general, acts as a reminder of the continuous battle for gender **parity** and the need for cooperation in order to build a more fair and just world for all women.

VOCABULARY

gender [ˋdʒɛndɚ] *n.* 性別
sympathizer [ˋsɪmpəˌθaɪzɚ] *n.* 支持者
momentum [moˋmɛntəm] *n.* 氣勢
propose [prəˋpoz] *v.* 提議
suffrage [ˋsʌfrɪdʒ] *n.* 投票權
launch [lɔntʃ] *v.* 發動；提出
rally [ˋrælɪ] *v.* 集結
tsar [tsɑr] *n.* 沙皇
compel [kəmˋpɛl] *v.* 強迫
parity [ˋpærətɪ] *n.* 平等

Comprehension questions

Q1: What is the main idea of the article?

A. the Russian Revolution

B. International Women's Day

C. the Suffragette movement

Q2: When did the first International Woman's Day march happen?

A. in the last century

B. in 1908

C. in 1900

Q3: What happened on March 8 1914?

A. the First World War broke out

B. women in the UK marched for the right to vote

C. people demonstrated against World War I in London

Q4: Who was Clara Zetkin?

A. the leader of the "women's office" of the German Social Democratic Party

B. the inventor of the International Women's Day

C. a citizen of Copenhagen

Q5: What are some of the topics of International Women's Day?

A. Chose to Challenge

B. rallies and marches

C. the continuous battle for gender parity

答案在本單元最後一頁。如果答錯了，請再確認一次文章內容。

中譯

每年 3 月 8 日，世界各地的人們都會慶祝國際婦女節 (IWD)，以表彰女性在社會、經濟、文化和政治方面的成就。此外，這一天也是提醒大家性別平等的持續努力，呼籲重視女性權益和性別正義，並提高對性別不平等的認識。

國際婦女節的起源可追溯至工人階級女性與其支持者的革命行動。最早的國際婦女節活動出現在 20 世紀初，當時歐美的女性們正在爭取投票權和較好的工作條件。1908 年，數以萬計的女性在紐約市遊行，為爭取更高工資和改善工作環境發聲，據說這就是這個節日的由來。一年後，美國社會黨宣布設立一個致敬女性的日子。

1910 年，德國社會民主黨「婦女辦公室」領袖克拉拉 · 蔡特金 (Clara Zetkin) 在哥本哈根參加會議時，提出要有一個全球性的婦女節，每年在同一天舉辦慶祝活動，來推動各種訴求。

1914 年 3 月 8 日，倫敦舉行了一場支持女性投票權的遊行；1917 年 3 月 8 日，俄羅斯革命正式爆發，成千上萬的俄羅斯女性為和平與糧食問題走上街頭，最終迫使沙皇退位。美國則在 1909 年舉行了第一次國際婦女節活動，而聯合國直到 1975 年才正式將這一天定為全球性節日。

國際婦女節每年都有不同的主題，聚焦某個特定的女性議題。近幾年的主題包括「挑戰不平等」、「女性領導：在 COVID-19 時代創造平等的未來」，以及「提倡平等、建設智慧、創新改變」等。

世界各地以多種方式紀念這一天，包括集會、遊行和其他活動，藉以突顯女性所面臨的挑戰和取得的成就。這天也是表彰女性對整個社會及其社區貢獻的時刻。

總體而言，國際婦女節提醒人們，追求性別平等仍在進行中，且需要大家共同努力，才能為所有女性創造一個更加公平和公正的世界。

文法甦活區

Task 2

請用上篇文章中的 word partnerships 完成下表。見範例。

gender	equality
	rights
working-class	
better	
	conditions
Socialist	
	suffrage
worldwide	
	future
women's	

只要對照文章，便可輕鬆找出答案。

接下來，我們要利用上列 word partnerships 練習寫作。

Task 3

請用 Task 2 表格中的 word partnerships 填入下列空格。見範例。

1. An equal future is a collective aspiration where individuals of all backgrounds have equitable opportunities to thrive, unencumbered by discrimination or systemic barriers.

2. ________________ is crucial for ensuring that individuals are fairly compensated for their work and can achieve financial stability and security.

3. ________________ is essential for creating a fair and just society where everyone has equal opportunities and rights regardless of their gender.

4. Improving ________________________ is vital for safeguarding the well-being and productivity of employees, fostering a positive and sustainable work environment.

5. International Women's Day is celebrated as a ________________, honoring the social, economic, cultural, and political achievements of women while advocating for gender equality.

6. The ongoing struggle for ________________ continues to demand recognition and action towards achieving gender equality in all aspects of society.

7. The __________________ advocates for policies aimed at reducing income inequality and ensuring social justice for all members of society.

8. ____________________________, from scientific breakthroughs to social advancements, have profoundly shaped history and continue to inspire progress towards gender equality and empowerment worldwide.

9. _________________________, the hard-fought battle for women's right to vote, marked a significant milestone in the journey towards gender equality and political empowerment.

10. _____________________ often face unique challenges in balancing their jobs, family responsibilities, and societal expectations.

答案在本單元最後一頁。

再作一個文法練習吧！透過練習，你會更清楚本單元的文法重點。

Task 4

請再讀一遍文章，並在下列 word partnerships 劃底線。它們有什麼共通點？

- emphasize the continuous fight for
- advocate for
- increase awareness of
- fighting for
- generate momentum for

這些字詞是動詞語塊 (verb chunks)，用以描述抗議。在本文中，你會發現它們都與描述抗議目的的搭配詞一起使用。

Task 5

請用 Task 4 的詞組填入下列空格。注意動詞時態的寫法。

1. ______________________________ gender equality underscores the ongoing efforts needed to address systemic injustices and ensure a fair and inclusive society for all.

2. Many activists around the globe are _______________ environmental justice, aiming to protect our planet and ensure a sustainable future for generations to come.

3. She has been a passionate ______________________ gender equality, tirelessly working to promote opportunities and rights for women around the world.

4. Social media campaigns play a vital role in ______________________ important issues like climate change, helping to educate and mobilize communities for collective action.

5. The recent protests have helped ________________________ social change, sparking conversations and actions aimed at addressing systemic inequalities.

答案在本單元最後一頁。這些句子都是關於抗議或尋求改變的。

Listening

Task 6 15-2

請聽讀下列對話，你聽出了哪些前面 tasks 用到的詞彙？

A: Did you know that International Women's Day has its roots in the early 20th century when women were fighting for their rights?

B: Really? I didn't know that. What were they fighting for exactly?

A: Well, back then, women in Europe and North America were advocating for things like the right to vote and better working conditions. In fact, the first International Women's Day was observed in 1908 when thousands of working-class women marched in New York City for better pay and working conditions.

B: That's fascinating. So, how did it become a global celebration?

A: Clara Zetkin, a leader in the German Socialist Party, proposed the idea of a global day to celebrate women's achievements and advocate for their rights. In 1910, while she was in Copenhagen for a meeting, she suggested having a celebration on the same day every year.

B: And then it spread from there?

A: Yes, exactly. In 1914, there was a march in London in support of women's suffrage, and in 1917, during the Russian Revolution, thousands of Russian women rallied for peace, food, and women's rights which eventually led to the tsar stepping down.

B: Is that right?

A: Yes. The United States celebrated the first International Women's Day in 1909, and it became a worldwide holiday declared by the United Nations in 1975.

B: It's incredible how it all started from local movements and eventually became a global phenomenon.

A: Absolutely. And each year, International Women's Day focuses on a different theme to highlight specific challenges women face. For example, recent themes include Women in Leadership: Creating an Equal Future in a COVID-19 World and Think Equal, Build Smart, Innovate for Change.

B: It's important to keep raising awareness and advocating for gender equality. How do people usually celebrate the day?

A: There are various ways people observe it, from rallies and marches to events that highlight women's accomplishments and challenges. It's also a time to recognize the contributions women make to society and their communities.

B: Well, it's definitely a reminder of the ongoing struggle for an equal future and the need for cooperation to build a more just world for everyone.

A: Exactly. And it's heartening to see how far we've come, but there's still a lot of work to be done.

B: Absolutely. Let's hope that each International Women's Day brings us closer to that goal.

請先確實聆聽音檔，大致了解後再看翻譯。

中譯

A：你知道國際婦女節起源於 20 世紀初嗎？那時候女性正在為自己的權利而奮鬥。

B：真的嗎？我不知道欸。她們究竟在爭取什麼？

A：嗯，當時歐美的女性主要是在爭取投票權和更好的工作條件。事實上，1908 年人們第一次慶祝國際婦女節，當時成千上萬的工人階級女性在紐約市遊行，要求更高的工資和改善工作環境。

B：有意思。那它是怎麼變成全球性節慶的？

A：德國社會黨領袖克拉拉．蔡特金提出了設立全球婦女日的想法，以表彰女性的成就並倡導她們的權利。1910 年，當在哥本哈根參加會議時，她建議每年在同一天舉辦慶祝活動。

B：然後就這樣傳開了嗎？

A：沒錯。1914 年，倫敦舉行了支持女性選舉權的遊行；1917 年，在俄羅斯革命期間，數千名俄羅斯女性為和平、糧食和女性權利而集結，最終迫使沙皇下台。

B：真的嗎？

A：是的。美國在 1909 年慶祝了第一個國際婦女節，而聯合國則在 1975 年正式將它定為全球性的節日。

B：真是不可思議，這一切從地方性運動開始，最終變成了全球性的現象。

A：對啊。而且每年的國際婦女節都有不同的主題，聚焦女性面臨的特定挑戰。例如，近幾年的主題包括「女性領導：在 COVID-19 時代創造平等的未來」和「提倡平等、建設智慧、創新改變」。

B：不斷提升意識和推動性別平等非常重要。那大家通常是怎麼慶祝這一天的？

A：從集會遊行到強調女性成就與挑戰的活動，慶祝的方式有很多種。這一天也用來感謝女性對社會和社區做出的貢獻。

B：嗯，這正提醒著我們，平等的未來仍須努力爭取，而且需要大家合作來建立一個更公正的世界。

A：沒錯。看到這麼多進展真的很令人振奮，但還有很多需要改進的地方。

B：真的。希望每一年的國際婦女節都能讓我們更接近這個目標。

在繼續往下學習之前，請先回到本單元開頭處確認那些學習目標自己是否已達成。

Answers

Task 1:

Q1: B Q2: C Q3: B Q4: A Q5: A

Task 2:

gender	equality
women's	rights
working-class	women
better	pay
working	conditions
Socialist	Party
women's	suffrage
worldwide	holiday
equal	future
women's	accomplishments

Task 3:

1. equal future
2. Better pay
3. Gender equality
4. working conditions
5. worldwide holiday
6. women's rights
7. Socialist Party
8. Women's accomplishments
9. Women's suffrage
10. Working-class women

Task 5:

1. Emphasizing the continuous fight for
2. fighting for
3. advocate for
4. increasing awareness of
5. generate momentum for

NOTES

Part 4

Internet

Designed by Freepik

事物

THINGS

Unit 16

網路
The Internet

本單元的學習目標包括：

- ☐ 學到一些可用以談論本主題的 word partnerships
- ☐ 針對描述發明起源和科學突破的詞組作一些練習

Reading

Task 1 16-1

請閱聽這篇文章並回答下面的問題。

In the annals of human history, few **inventions** have had as profound an impact on society as the Internet. Born out of the visionary minds of brilliant individuals, the Internet has evolved from a **modest** idea into a global network that has reshaped communication, **commerce**, and culture.

The roots of the Internet can be traced back to the 1960s when the US Department of Defense sought a way to create a **robust** communication network that could **withstand** a nuclear attack. The result was ARPANET, the **precursor** to the modern Internet, which made its first successful connection on October 29, 1969. UCLA and the Stanford Research Institute communicated through two computers, marking the birth of a revolutionary concept.

Fast forward to 1989, when British computer scientist Sir Tim Berners-Lee introduced the concept of the World Wide Web (WWW). His proposal **outlined** a system that used hypertext to enable users to **navigate** and share information easily. Berners-Lee's invention laid the groundwork for the user-friendly Internet experience we know today.

The 1990s witnessed the rise of the dot-com boom, as **entrepreneurs** and **investors** seized the potential of the Internet for commercial purposes. Companies like Amazon, eBay, and Yahoo emerged, transforming the digital landscape and paving the way for e-commerce.

Advancements in technology, particularly the widespread adoption of **broadband** in the late 1990s and early 2000s, fuelled the Internet's **expansion**. Faster and more reliable connections enabled richer multimedia content, streaming services, and a **surge** in online collaboration.

The 21st century ushered in the era of Web 2.0, characterized by user-generated content and social media. Platforms like Facebook, Twitter, and YouTube transformed the Internet into a **dynamic** space for sharing ideas, opinions, and personal experiences on a global **scale**.

The **advent** of smartphones in the late 2000s further **revolutionized** Internet usage. Mobile devices brought the Internet into the hands of billions, enabling instant communication, access to information, and the development of mobile **applications** that have become an **integral** part of modern life.

While the Internet has brought about incredible advancements, it has also presented challenges such as cybersecurity threats, privacy concerns, and issues related to misinformation. Innovations, including **blockchain** technology and artificial intelligence, continue to shape the Internet's future, promising new solutions and possibilities.

As we reflect on the invention and development of the Internet, it becomes clear that its impact on society is immeasurable. The Internet has connected people across **continents**, transformed industries, and **democratized** access to information. As we navigate the ever-evolving digital landscape, the story of the Internet serves as a testament to human **ingenuity**, innovation, and the **boundless** possibilities that technology can unlock for the future.

Vocabulary

invention [ɪnˋvɛnʃən] *n.* 發明
modest [ˋmɑdɪst] *adj.* 不大（或不多）的
commerce [ˋkɑmɝs] *n.* 商業
robust [rəˋbʌst] *adj.* 堅固耐用的
withstand [wɪðˋstænd] *v.* 抵擋
precursor [priˋkɝsɚ] *n.* 前身
outline [ˋaʊtˏlaɪn] *v.* 概述
navigate [ˋnævəˏget] *v.* 導航；瀏覽
entrepreneur [ˏɑntrəprəˋnɝ] *n.* 企業家
investor [ɪnˋvɛstɚ] *n.* 投資者
broadband [ˋbrɔdˋbænd] *adj.* 寬頻的
expansion [ɪkˋspænʃən] *n.* 擴展
surge [sɝdʒ] *n.* 激增
dynamic [daɪˋnæmɪk] *adj.* 動態的
scale [skel] *n.* 刻度；規模
advent [ˋædvɛnt] *n.* 出現
revolutionize [ˏrɛvəˋluʃəˏnaɪz] *v.* 徹底改變
application [ˏæpləˋkeʃən] *n.* 應用（程式）
integral [ˋɪntəgrəl] *adj.* 不可或缺的
blockchain [ˋblɑkˏtʃen] *n.* 區塊鏈
continent [ˋkɑntənənt] *n.* 大陸；洲
democratize [dɪˋmɑkrəˏtaɪz] *v.* 使大眾化
ingenuity [ˏɪndʒəˋnuətɪ] *n.* 智慧
boundless [ˋbaʊndlɪs] *adj.* 無限的

Comprehension questions

Q1: What is the main topic of the article?

A. the invention and history of the Internet

B. the inventor of the Internet

C. what life was like before the Internet

Q2: What was ARPANET?

A. an early form of the Internet

B. an early type of computer

C. a nuclear attack

Q3: What happened in the late 1990s?

A. 5G was invented

B. mobile devices were invented

C. people began to use broadband

Q4: What happened in the early 2000s?

A. streaming services were invented

B. broadband was invented

C. mobile phones were invented

Q5: What are some of the challenges the Internet has brought?

A. people are looking at their phones all the time

B. energy use has gone up

C. the rise of misinformation

答案在本單元最後一頁。如果答錯了，請再確認一次文章內容。

中譯

在人類歷史上，很少有發明能像網路一樣對社會產生如此深遠的影響。網路源於一群有遠見的傑出人物的智慧發想，從一個不起眼的構思發展成全球網絡，並徹底改變了人們的通訊方式、商業運作和文化交流。

網路的起源可追溯至 1960 年代，當時美國國防部尋求一種方法來創建能夠抵禦核攻擊的強大通訊網路。結果，阿帕網 (ARPANET) 應運而生，它是現代網路技術的前身，並於 1969 年 10 月 29 日成功完成首次連接。加州大學洛杉磯分校 (UCLA) 和史丹佛研究所透過兩台電腦進行通訊，這標誌著一個革命性概念的誕生。

時間快轉至 1989 年，英國電腦科學家提姆．伯納斯李爵士提出了全球資訊網（World Wide Web，簡稱 WWW）的概念，其構想描述了一個使用超文本 (hypertext) 來方便使用者瀏覽和分享資訊的系統。伯納斯李的發明為今日所知的使用者友善網路體驗奠定了基礎。

1990 年代見證了網路熱潮的興起，企業家和投資者抓住了網路於商業用途上的潛力。亞馬遜、eBay 和雅虎等公司相繼崛起，改變了數位格局，並引領了電子商務的興盛。

技術的進步，尤其是 1990 年代末和 2000 年代初寬頻網路的普及，進一步促進了網路的擴展。更快、更穩定的連線促使多媒體內容豐富化、串流服務興起、線上協作激增。

進入 21 世紀後，網路 2.0時代來臨，其特徵是使用者創建的內容和社群媒體。Facebook、Twitter 和 YouTube 等平台將網路轉變為在全球分享想法、觀點和個人經驗的動態空間。

2000 年代後期智慧型手機的問世進一步徹底改變了網路的使用模式。行動裝置將網路帶入數十億人的手中，實現了即時通訊、資訊取得和行動應用程式的開發，這些已成為現代生活中不可或缺的一部分。

儘管網路帶來了巨大的進步，但也帶來了諸如網路安全威脅、隱私問題和錯誤資訊等挑戰。區塊鏈技術和人工智慧等創新繼續塑造著網路的未來，並提供了新的解決方案與可能性。

回顧網路的發明和發展，不難看出它對社會的影響是無法估量的。網路將各大洲的人們串聯在一起，改變了產業，並使資訊變得更加普及。在這個不斷變化的數位世界中，網路的故事成為人類智慧、創新和科技開創未來無限可能性的最佳見證。

文法甦活區

Task 2

請用上篇文章中的 word partnerships 完成下表。見範例。

communication	network
successful	
	concept
share	
	boom
commercial	
	adoption
multimedia	
	services
online	

只要對照文章，便可輕鬆找出答案。

接下來，我們要利用上列 word partnerships 練習寫作。

Task 3

請用 Task 2 表格中的 word partnerships 填入下列空格。見範例。

1. It's crucial to __share information__ transparently within the team to ensure everyone is on the same page and can collaborate effectively.

PART 1
PART 2
PART 3
PART 4
Unit 16
Unit 17
Unit 18
Unit 19
Unit 20
PART 5
PART 6

2. ____________________ facilitates seamless teamwork among remote employees, allowing them to share ideas, documents, and feedback in real-time regardless of geographical locations.

3. ____________________ have transformed the entertainment industry, offering a vast library of movies, TV shows, and original content accessible anytime, anywhere.

4. The ____________________ enabled seamless interaction between users across the globe.

5. The development of artificial intelligence has expanded rapidly, with applications ranging from healthcare to finance, all driven by ____________________ seeking efficiency and innovation.

6. The ________________ of the late 1990s saw a rapid rise in Internet-based businesses and investments, leading to both unprecedented growth and eventual market volatility.

7. The smartphone's user-friendly interface and versatility led to its ____________________, revolutionizing how people communicate and access information globally.

8. The startup introduced a ____________________ in renewable energy storage, promising to reshape the industry landscape.

9. The team celebrated their ________________________ to the satellite, ensuring uninterrupted data transmission from remote locations.

10. The website features an array of ____________________, including videos, podcasts, and interactive graphics, to engage users across various platforms.

答案在本單元最後一頁。

再作一個文法練習吧！透過練習，你會更清楚本單元的文法重點。

Task 4

請再看一遍文章，並在下列 word partnerships 劃底線。注意看其用法。

· be traced back to
· the precursor to
· laid the groundwork for
· seized the potential of
· paving the way for

這些詞組在討論科技或某種突破的起源時都能派上用場。

Task 5

請用 Task 4 的詞組填入下列空格。

1. The company's innovative approach ________________ emerging technologies, propelling them to the forefront of their industry.
2. The early experiments in electricity conducted by Benjamin Franklin ________________ the development of modern electrical engineering principles.
3. The invention of the printing press by Johannes Gutenberg revolutionized communication and literacy, ________________ the spread of knowledge and ideas during the Renaissance.
4. The origins of the tradition can ________________ ancient civilizations such as the Egyptians and Mesopotamians.
5. The steam engine is considered ________________ modern trains.

答案在本單元最後一頁。請注意其中不同的動詞時態。

Listening

Task 6 16-2

請聽讀下列對話，你聽出了哪些前面 tasks 用到的詞彙？

A: You know, when you think about it, the Internet has completely changed the world as we know it.

B: Absolutely! It's incredible how something that started as a defence project turned into this global communication network that we rely on for almost everything.

A: And it's not just about communication anymore. The Internet has transformed how we shop, how we learn, even how we socialize.

B: Yeah, remember when it all began with ARPANET? That was back in the 1960s. Just a couple of scientists who managed to create a successful connection between two computers.

A: It's amazing how far we've come since then. And Tim Berners-Lee's idea of the World Wide Web was such a revolutionary concept and really laid the groundwork for what we have today.

B: Totally. And then the dot-com boom of the '90s was wild. Everyone saw the potential for commercial purposes, and companies like Amazon and eBay changed the game.

A: Right, and with the advent of broadband, things really took off. Suddenly, we could do so much more with the Internet—sharing information, streaming services, online collaboration, you name it.

B: And let's not forget about multimedia content. Web 2.0 social media completely changed the way we interact online. It's like a whole new world of communication opened up.

A: True, and the widespread adoption of smartphones made it even more accessible. Now, everyone has the Internet in their pocket, wherever they go. Online collaboration is so much easier now too.

B: But it's not all sunshine and rainbows. Cybersecurity, privacy concerns, misinformation—these are all big challenges we face with the Internet.

A: Definitely. But with advancements like blockchain and AI, there's hope for addressing those issues and shaping a better future for the Internet.

B: Absolutely. When you look at the journey of the Internet, it's a testament to human innovation and the power of technology to transform our world.

請先確實聆聽音檔，了解後再看翻譯喔。

中譯

A：你知道嗎，仔細想想，網路真的徹底改變了我們的世界。

B：超同意！很難想像它原本只是個國防計畫，結果演變成現在這個我們幾乎所有事情都依賴的全球網路。

A：而且現在也不僅僅只是通訊用途了。網路改變了我們的購物方式、學習方式，甚至社交方式。

B：對啊，還記得一開始的 ARPANET 嗎？那是 1960 年代的事了，當時就幾個科學家成功連上兩台電腦而已。

A：想不到科技的進展能走到如今這個地步。提姆．伯納斯李想出來的全球資訊網 (World Wide Web) 真是個超創新的概念，為我們今天所擁有的一切奠定了基礎。

B：沒錯，然後 90 年代的網路熱潮超瘋狂！大家都發現它的商業潛力，像 Amazon 和 eBay 這些公司顛覆了遊戲規則。

A：對啊，特別是寬頻技術出現之後，網路就開始起飛了。突然之間，我們能在網路上做更多的事情——分享資訊、看串流影片、線上協作等。

B：還有，別忘了多媒體內容的出現。Web 2.0 時代的社群媒體更是改變了我們在線上互動的方式，就像打開了一個全新的溝通世界。

A：沒錯，而且智慧型手機的普及更讓網路變得隨手可得。現在每個人幾乎隨時隨地都能上網，做什麼都方便多了，線上協作也變得更簡單。

B：但也不是完全美好的，像是網路安全、隱私問題、假新聞等，這些都是我們現在面對的挑戰。

A：的確。不過隨著區塊鏈和人工智慧等技術的進步，我們有望解決這些問題，並塑造一個更美好的網路未來。

B：完全同意。當你回顧網路的發展歷程時，你會發現它無疑是人類創新的見證，也是科技改變世界的力量。

Answers

Task 1:

Q1: A Q2: A Q3: C Q4: B Q5: C

Task 2:

communication	network
successful	connection
revolutionary	concept
share	information
dot-com	boom
commercial	purposes
widespread	adoption
multimedia	content
streaming	services
online	collaboration

Task 3:

1. share information
2. Online collaboration
3. Streaming services
4. communication network
5. commercial purposes
6. dot-com boom
7. widespread adoption
8. revolutionary concept
9. successful connection
10. multimedia content

Task 5:

1. seized the potential of
2. laid the groundwork for
3. paving the way for
4. be traced back to
5. the precursor to

Unit 17

塑膠的發明
The Invention of Plastic

本單元的學習目標包括：

□ 學到一些可用以談論本主題的 word partnerships
□ 練習一些討論發明起源和科學突破的詞組

Reading

Task 1 17-1

請閱聽這篇文章並回答下面的問題。

In the early 20th century, a groundbreaking invention emerged from the laboratories of scientific innovation, forever **altering** the course of human history. Plastic, a **versatile** and **synthetic** material, burst onto the scene, revolutionizing industries, changing lifestyles, and leaving an indelible mark on the world.

The **dawn** of the 20th century saw an escalating demand for alternatives to natural materials such as ivory, **shellac**, and rubber. The **breakthrough** came in 1907, when Belgian-born American Leo Hendrik Baekeland introduced Bakelite, the world's first fully synthetic plastic. Bakelite, derived from **phenol** and **formaldehyde**, exhibited exceptional heat resistance, electrical **insulating** properties, and **durability**. This "material of a thousand uses" marked the advent of a new era in material science.

The introduction of Bakelite paved the way for a surge of research and innovation in the field of plastics. Engineers and chemists across the globe began to explore and **manipulate** various polymers, giving rise to an array of plastic varieties **tailored** for specific applications. Nylon, introduced in the 1930s, revolutionized **textiles** and brought **affordable** and durable clothing to the masses. Polyethylene, developed in the 1940s, found its way into packaging, transforming the way products were transported and stored.

The aftermath of World War II witnessed an explosive growth in plastic production. Plastics' **lightweight** nature, coupled with their **moldability** and affordability, **aligned** perfectly with the post-war consumer culture and the demand for convenience. **Disposable** items, once made from traditional materials, were now mass-produced using plastics. The advent of Tupperware, introduced in the 1940s, highlighted the material's convenience and **versatility**, becoming a **household** name.

While plastics brought unparalleled convenience and innovation, they also brought unforeseen challenges. The durability that made plastics so desirable also led to their **persistence** in the environment. Plastic waste, especially single-use items, began **accumulating** in landfills and oceans, giving rise to an urgent environmental crisis. The widespread use of non-biodegradable plastics raised concerns about long-term ecological **consequences**.

In recent decades, the **adverse** environmental impact of plastic pollution has **spurred** awareness and efforts towards sustainability. Researchers, entrepreneurs, and activists have joined forces to develop **biodegradable** plastics, recycling technologies, and alternative materials. Governments and industries are **enacting** policies to reduce single-use plastics and promote **circular** economy models.

The invention of plastic stands as a testament to human ingenuity and the power of innovation. Its impact on modern life is undeniable, transforming industries and everyday experiences alike. As we navigate the challenges posed by plastic waste, we are reminded of the **dual** nature of this synthetic **marvel**—a material that has brought immense progress, yet demands responsible management to ensure a cleaner, more sustainable future for generations to come.

VOCABULARY

alter [ˋɔltɚ] *v.* 改變
versatile [ˋvɜsətl̩] *adj.* 多功能的
synthetic [sɪnˋθɛtɪk] *adj.* 合成的
dawn [dɔn] *n.* 開端
shellac [ʃəˋlæk] *n.* 蟲膠
breakthrough [ˋbrekˌθru] *n.* 突破
phenol [ˋfinɔl] *n.* 酚
formaldehyde [fɔrˋmældəˌhaɪd] *n.* 甲醛
insulate [ˋɪnsəˌlet] *v.* 使絕緣
durability [ˌdjurəˋbɪlətɪ] *n.* 耐用性
manipulate [məˋnɪpjəˌlet] *v.* 運用
tailor [ˋtelɚ] *v.* 使適應特定需要
textile [ˋtɛkstaɪl] *n.* 織物
affordable [əˋfɔrdəbl̩] *adj.* 負擔得起的
lightweight [ˋlaɪtˋwet] *adj.* 輕便的
moldability [ˌmoldəˋbɪlətɪ] *n.* 可塑性
be aligned with 與……一致
disposable [dɪˋspozəbl̩] *adj.* 一次性的
versatility [ˌvɜsəˋtɪlətɪ] *n.* 多用途
household [ˋhaʊsˌhold] *adj.* 家喻戶曉的
persistence [pɚˋsɪstəns] *n.* 持久
accumulate [əˋkjumjəˌlet] *v.* 累積
consequence [ˋkɑnsəˌkwɛns] *n.* 後果
adverse [ædˋvɜs] *adj.* 負面的
spur [spɜ] *v.* 促進
biodegradable [ˌbaɪodɪˋgredəbl̩] *adj.* 可生物分解的
enact [ɪnˋækt] *v.* 制定
circular [ˋsɜkjəlɚ] *adj.* 循環的
dual [ˋdjuəl] *adj.* 雙重的
marvel [ˋmɑrvl̩] *n./v.* 驚奇事物；驚嘆

Comprehension questions

Q1: What is the main topic of the article?

A. the invention of Tupperware

B. the invention of Bakelite

C. the invention of plastic

Q2: What is Bakelite?

A. something you can bake

B. an early form of plastic

C. a durable substance

Q3: What does the text say about nylon?

A. it was invented during the 1930s

B. it was an early form of plastic

C. it was very good for tailoring

Q4: What are the challenges of plastics?

A. they persist in the environment

B. they are hard to make

C. they are expensive to produce

Q5: What are biodegradable plastics?

A. an alternative type of plastic

B. they do not last forever

C. a recycling technology

答案在本單元最後一頁。如果答錯了，請再確認一次文章內容。

中譯

20 世紀初，一個改變人類歷史的重要發明在科學家的實驗室中誕生了——塑膠。這種多用途的合成材料橫空出世，迅速改變了各個產業、生活方式，並在全球留下了深遠的影響。

在那年代，人們對象牙、蟲膠和橡膠等天然材料替代品的需求日益增加。1907 年出現了轉捩點，比利時裔美國人利奧．亨德里克．貝克蘭發明了全球首款完全合成的塑膠——酚醛塑料 (Bakelite)。由酚和甲醛製成，具有超強的耐熱性、絕緣性和耐用性，因而被稱為「千用之材」的酚醛塑料開啓了材料科學的新紀元。

酚醛塑料的誕生為塑膠領域的研究與創新掀開了序幕。全球的工程師和化學家開始探索和運用各種聚合物，研發出一系列適合不同用途的塑膠材料。例如，1930 年代問世的尼龍改變了紡織業，讓大家都能買到經濟實惠又耐穿的衣物。1940 年代開發的聚乙烯則被廣泛應用於包裝，改變了產品運輸和儲存的方式。

第二次世界大戰後，塑膠生產出現爆炸性成長。塑膠的輕便性、可塑性和經濟性與戰後消費文化的需求非常契合。原本使用傳統材料製作的一次性用品，如今都改用塑膠進行大規模生產。1940 年代推出的特百惠 (Tupperware) 更是突顯了塑膠材料的便利性和多用途性，成為家喻戶曉的品牌。

塑膠帶來了無與倫比的便利性和創新的同時，也帶來了許多始料未及的問題。塑膠的耐用性使其備受歡迎，但也導致它們在環境中持久存在。塑膠廢棄物，尤其是一次性用品，開始在垃圾掩埋場和海洋中堆積，引發了緊迫的環境危機。非生物可分解的塑膠隨處可見，讓人擔憂它對生態系統的長期影響。

近幾十年來，塑膠污染的嚴重性讓人們意識到環保的重要性。研究人員、企業家和環保人士聯手研發生物可分解塑膠、回收技術和替代材料。各國政府和產業正在制定政策，減少使用一次性塑膠並推廣循環經濟模式。

塑膠的發明證明了人類的聰明才智和創新的力量。塑膠對現代生活的影響無庸置疑，它改變了產業發展和日常生活體驗。當我們應對塑膠廢棄物帶來的挑戰時，其「兩面性」也變得更加明顯——這種材料帶來了巨大的進步，但同時也需要負責任的管理，以確保子孫後代擁有一個更乾淨、更永續的未來。

文法甦活區

Task 2

請用上篇文章中的 word partnerships 完成下表。見範例。

groundbreaking	invention
scientific	
	material
indelible	
	demand
natural	
	resistance
electrical insulating	
	growth
lightweight	

只要對照文章，便可輕鬆找出答案。

接下來，我們要利用上列 word partnerships 練習寫作。

Task 3

請用 Task 2 表格中的 word partnerships 填入下列空格。見範例。

1. Artisans prefer using __natural materials__ like wood and clay due to their timeless beauty, sustainability, and unique textures.

2. The aerospace industry increasingly relies on carbon fiber composites due to their ________________, enabling aircraft to achieve greater fuel efficiency and extended flight ranges.

3. The discovery of penicillin by Alexander Fleming in 1928 marked a pivotal ________________ that revolutionized medicine by introducing the first antibiotic, saving countless lives and shaping modern healthcare practices.

4. The moon landing of 1969 left an ________________ on human history, inspiring generations and showcasing the boundless possibilities of exploration and technological advancement.

5. The newly developed ceramic coating boasts exceptional ________________, making it ideal for protecting surfaces in high-temperature environments such as industrial furnaces and aerospace applications.

6. The rapid growth of electric vehicles has led to an ________________ for lithium-ion batteries, driving innovation in battery technology and sustainable energy solutions.

7. The silicone rubber used in electrical cables exhibits outstanding ________________, ensuring safe and efficient transmission of power without the risk of electrical leakage or short circuits.

8. The smartphone was a ________________ that revolutionized communication and access to information worldwide.

9. The startup experienced ________________ in its first year, quickly expanding its customer base and market reach, solidifying its position as a disruptive force in the tech industry.

10. The widespread use of ________________________ like polyester and nylon in clothing manufacturing has led to increased durability and affordability, transforming the fashion industry and consumer preferences worldwide.

答案在本單元最後一頁。

再作一個文法練習吧！透過練習，你會更清楚本單元的文法重點。

Task 4

請再看一遍文章，並在下列 word partnerships 劃底線。注意看其用法。

- groundbreaking invention
- burst onto the scene
- revolutionizing industries
- leaving an indelible mark
- breakthrough

這些詞組在討論科技突破或某種創新時很有用。

Task 5

請用 Task 4 的詞組填入下列空格。

1. Marie Curie's groundbreaking research on radioactivity ____________ ____________________ on the field of science, earning her two Nobel Prizes and shaping the course of modern physics and medicine.

2. The development of quantum computing represents a ____________ in computer science, promising unprecedented processing power and capabilities beyond the limitations of classical computing.

3. The electric car manufacturer ________________, swiftly capturing the attention of consumers worldwide with its innovative technology and commitment to sustainability.

4. The implementation of artificial intelligence and machine learning algorithms is ____________________ such as healthcare, finance, and transportation, drastically improving efficiency, accuracy, and decision-making processes.

5. The invention of the Internet is often hailed as a ________________ that has transformed nearly every aspect of modern life, from communication and commerce to education and entertainment.

答案在本單元最後一頁。請注意其中不同的動詞時態。

Listening

Task 6 17-2

請聽讀下列對話，你聽出了哪些前面 tasks 用到的詞彙？

A: Hey, have you ever thought about how much plastic has changed the world?

B: Absolutely! It really was a groundbreaking invention. It's incredible how something as simple as plastic has had such a massive impact on our lives.

A: I was reading about its history the other day. It really was a great scientific innovation. Did you know it all started with Bakelite in 1907?

B: Yeah, Bakelite was the pioneer. A synthetic material that revolutionized so many industries with its versatility and durability.

A: It really left an indelible mark on the world.

B: Yes. And then came nylon and polyethylene, transforming textiles and packaging. After that there was an escalating demand for plastic.

A: Especially after World War II. Natural materials were replaced with plastic, largely because of its electrical insulating properties.

B: The demand for convenience skyrocketed, and suddenly there was explosive growth in plastic.

A: Tupperware was a game-changer, wasn't it? Suddenly, everything was in plastic containers.

B: True, because of its heat resistance and lightweight nature. But with all the convenience came a downside. Plastic waste started piling up everywhere.

A: Exactly. It's shocking how durable it is, yet that's also what makes it such a problem in the environment.

B: Thankfully, there's been a growing awareness about plastic pollution. People are really pushing for more sustainable solutions.

A: Absolutely. Biodegradable plastics and recycling technologies are making strides, and governments are starting to take action too.

B: It's a reminder that while plastic has brought us so much progress, we need to manage it responsibly for a cleaner future.

A: Definitely! It's all about finding that balance between innovation and sustainability.

請先確實聆聽音檔，了解後再看翻譯喔。

中譯

A：嘿，你有沒有想過塑膠對世界的改變有多大？

B：當然有！真是一個劃時代的發明。很難想像塑膠這樣簡單的東西對我們的生活產生了這麼巨大的影響。

A：前幾天我讀到有關它的歷史。這確實是一項偉大的科學創新。你知道這一切都始於 1907 年的酚醛塑料 (Bakelite) 嗎？

B：知道啊，酚醛塑料是塑膠的先驅。它是一種合成材料，耐用、用途多，不僅改變了工業生產，還影響了很多行業。

A：塑膠真的讓世界大不同啊。

B：嗯。接著出現了尼龍和聚乙烯，徹底改變了紡織業和包裝業。從那以後，對塑膠的需求不斷增加。

A：尤其是二戰後。許多天然材料被塑膠取代，主要因為它具有良好的電絕緣性。

B：沒錯，那時候大家都在追求便利，結果塑膠的生產量瞬間暴增。

A：然後特百惠這個品牌的崛起帶來了顛覆性的改變呢！突然間，所有東西都裝在塑膠容器裡了。

B：是啊，因為塑膠耐用又輕便。但問題也隨之而來。塑膠垃圾開始在各地堆積。

A：沒錯。塑膠的耐久性很驚人，但這也是為什麼它在環境中成為大問題的原因。

B：還好現在大家對塑膠污染的意識愈來愈強，很多人在推動更環保的解決方案。

A：沒錯。可生物分解塑膠和回收技術都有了進展，政府也開始採取行動了。

B：這提醒我們，雖然塑膠帶來了很多進步，但人們必須負責任地加以管理，才能擁有更乾淨的未來。

A：真的！在創新與永續之間找到平衡非常重要。

Answers

Task 1:

Q1: C   Q2: B   Q3: A   Q4: A   Q5: B

Task 2:

groundbreaking	invention
scientific	innovation
synthetic	material
indelible	mark
escalating	demand
natural	materials
heat	resistance
electrical insulating	properties
explosive	growth
lightweight	nature

Task 3:

1. natural materials
2. lightweight nature
3. scientific innovation
4. indelible mark
5. heat resistance
6. escalating demand
7. electrical insulating properties
8. groundbreaking invention
9. explosive growth
10. synthetic materials

Task 5:

1. left an indelible mark
2. breakthrough
3. burst onto the scene
4. revolutionizing industries
5. groundbreaking invention

Unit 18

泰迪熊

The Teddy Bear

本單元的學習目標包括：

☐ 學到一些可用以談論本主題的 word partnerships
☐ 針對過去簡單式 (past simple tense) 進行一些練習

Reading

Task 1 18-1

請閱聽這篇文章並回答下面的問題。

In the world of **stuffed** animals, few have captured the hearts of young and old alike quite like the Teddy bear. These **cuddly companions** have been **cherished** for generations, but have you ever wondered how the Teddy bear got its name and came into **existence**?

The origin story of the Teddy bear takes us back over a century to a rather unlikely place and time—a hunting trip in November 1902. It was during one of President Theodore "Teddy" Roosevelt's hunting **expeditions** in Mississippi that the iconic toy was born.

The story begins with President Roosevelt, a man known for his love of hunting. On this particular trip, Roosevelt and his companions were **tracking** a black bear. After a long and unsuccessful day, the hunters managed to corner a bear and tie it to a tree, intending to give the President the opportunity to take the final shot.

However, President Roosevelt found the situation **unsportsmanlike** and refused to kill the helpless bear. He ordered the bear to be set free, and the incident was documented in a cartoon drawn by Clifford Berryman and published in The Washington Post. This political cartoon, titled "Drawing the Line in Mississippi," **depicted** Roosevelt's **compassionate** act.

The cartoon, which featured a **diminutive**, lovable bear, caught the attention of a Brooklyn shopkeeper named Morris Michtom. Michtom and his wife, Rose, were toy makers who had been producing stuffed animals. Inspired by the cartoon, they created a stuffed bear and displayed it in their shop window with a sign that read "Teddy's Bear." The bear was an instant hit, and customers soon began asking for their own "Teddy bears."

The Michtoms' creation, the "Teddy bear," quickly gained **popularity**, and they sought **permission** from President Roosevelt to use his name. Roosevelt, who appreciated the **gesture** and the positive association with the bear, **consented**. The Teddy bear **craze** swept the nation, and it wasn't long before other toy manufacturers started producing their own versions.

The Teddy bear has since become an enduring symbol of **comfort**, love, and childhood **innocence**. From the smallest pocket-sized bears to giant **plush** companions, Teddy bears have a special place in the hearts of people of all ages.

The story of how the Teddy bear got its name is a testament to the power of **compassion** and the enduring impact of a simple act of kindness. Today, these cuddly **creatures** continue to bring joy and warmth to countless homes around the world, proving that the legacy of a single bear saved by President Roosevelt lives on in the form of the beloved Teddy bear.

Comprehension questions

Q1: What is the main topic of the article?

A. President Roosevelt

B. a bear hunt

C. the origin of the Teddy bear

Q2: Where did the Teddy bear get its name?

A. it was the name of the bear President Roosevelt didn't shoot

B. it was the name of the President

C. it was the name of the president's child

Q3: Who produced the first Teddy bear?

A. President Roosevelt

B. a toymaker

C. Clifford Berryman

Q4: What is 'drawing the line in Mississippi'?

A. the name of a cartoon

B. President Roosevelt refused to shoot a bear

C. a political movement

Q5: Who were the Michtoms?

A. friends of the President's

B. toymakers

C. cartoon artists

答案在本單元最後一頁。如果答錯了，請再確認一次文章內容。

VOCABULARY

stuffed [stʌft] *adj.* 填製的
cuddly [ˋkʌdlɪ] *adj.* 令人想抱的
companion [kəmˋpænjən] *n.* 同伴；陪伴
cherish [ˋtʃɛrɪʃ] *v.* 珍愛
existence [ɪgˋzɪstəns] *n.* 存在
expedition [ˏɛkspɪˋdɪʃən] *n.* 遠征
track [træk] *v.* 追蹤
unsportsmanlike [ʌnˋsportsmənˏlaɪk] *adj.* 沒有運動家精神的
depict [dɪˋpɪkt] *v.* 描繪

中譯

在絨毛玩具的世界裡，很少有角色能像泰迪熊一樣不分老少擄獲人們的心。這些可愛的玩偶陪伴了無數個世代，但你有沒有想過，泰迪熊到底是怎麼來的？它的名字又是從哪裡來的呢？

泰迪熊的起源可追溯至一百多年前一個頗為意外的時間和地點：1902 年 11 月的密西西比州狩獵之旅。就在這次狩獵探險期間，這件極具代表性的玩具誕生了。

故事始於老羅斯福總統，他以熱愛狩獵聞名。在一次旅行中，老羅斯福和他的夥伴正在追捕一隻黑熊。經過漫長而失敗的一天後，獵人們設法困住這隻黑熊，並將其綁在樹上，打算讓總統開最後一槍。

然而，老羅斯福總統認為這樣做違反體育精神，拒絕殺死這隻無助的熊，他下令將熊釋放。這則軼事被插畫家克利福德．貝瑞曼記錄下來，並刊登在《華盛頓郵報》上。這幅政治漫畫題為《在密西西比劃界 (Drawing the Line in Mississippi)》，描繪了老羅斯福總統慈悲為懷的行為。

這幅漫畫以一隻可愛的小熊為主角，吸引了布魯克林一位名叫莫里斯．米赫頓的店主的注意。米赫頓和他的妻子蘿絲是做絨毛玩偶的玩具製造商，看到漫畫後靈機一動，做了一隻絨毛熊放在店內櫥窗展示，還掛了一個牌子寫著「泰迪的熊 (Teddy's Bear)」。結果這隻熊一炮而紅，顧客們紛紛來店要求訂製屬於自己的「泰迪熊」。

米赫頓夫婦的創作「泰迪熊」迅速流行起來，他們尋求老羅斯福總統的許可使用其名字。老羅斯福覺得這個玩偶與他的「熊故事」有正面連結，於是欣然同意。隨著泰迪熊熱潮席捲全國，很快其他玩具製造商也跟著推出各種版本的泰迪熊。

自此之後，泰迪熊成為療癒、愛與童年純真的永恆象徵。無論是口袋大小的小熊，還是巨大的絨毛熊，泰迪熊在不同年齡層的人心中佔有特殊的地位。

泰迪熊名字的由來，見證了慈悲之心與一個簡單善行的力量。時至今日，這些可愛的玩偶依舊為無數家庭帶來歡樂與溫馨，也讓我們知道，那隻老羅斯福救下的熊的故事，透過泰迪熊永流傳。

VOCABULARY

compassionate [kəm`pæʃənɪt] *adj.* 慈悲的
diminutive [də`mɪnjətɪv] *adj.* 小的
popularity [͵papjə`lærətɪ] *n.* 受歡迎
permission [pɚ`mɪʃən] *n.* 允許
gesture [`dʒɛstʃɚ] *n.* 手勢；行動
consent [kən`sɛnt] *v.* 同意
craze [krez] *n.* 狂熱
comfort [`kʌmfɚt] *n.* 舒適；慰藉
innocence [`ɪnəsns] *n.* 純真
plush [plʌʃ] *adj.* 毛茸茸的
compassion [kəm`pæʃən] *n.* 憐憫
creature [`kritʃɚ] *n.* 生物（含有憐愛之意）

文法甦活區

Task 2

請用上篇文章中的 word partnerships 完成下表。見範例。

stuffed	animals
origin	
	trip
unsportsmanlike	
	act
political	
	hit
enduring	
	bears
beloved	

只要對照文章，便可輕鬆找出答案。

接下來，我們要利用上列 word partnerships 練習寫作。

Task 3

請用 Task 2 表格中的 word partnerships 填入下列空格。見範例。

1. After witnessing the elderly woman struggling to carry her groceries, the teenager performed a __compassionate act__ by offering to help her carry them home.

2. As she entered the nursery, she was greeted by shelves lined with colorful ________________, each one holding a story of its own.

3. Children clutched their ________________ tightly as they explored the amusement park, finding comfort in their tiny companions amidst the excitement of the rides.

4. During the ________________, they eagerly scanned the forest for signs of wildlife, hoping for a successful day of tracking and adventure.

5. The ancient oak tree stood tall in the town square, its gnarled branches serving as an ________________ of strength and resilience for generations to come.

6. The ________________, passed down through generations, sat proudly on the shelf, a cherished symbol of childhood memories and unconditional love.

7. The new song became an ________________, soaring to the top of the charts within hours of its release.

8. The newspaper's front page featured a biting ________________, depicting the candidates as circus performers juggling promises while the electorate looked on in skepticism.

9. The referee quickly intervened when tempers flared, deeming the aggressive behavior on the field an ________________ that needed immediate resolution.

10. The superhero's ________________ revealed the tragic event that ignited his journey to justice and redemption.

答案在本單元最後一頁。

再作一個文法練習吧！透過練習，你會更清楚本單元的文法重點。

Task 4

請再看一遍文章，並在文中過去簡單式動詞劃底線。

這篇文章使用了許多過去簡單式動詞，因為故事發生的時間已結束。

Task 5

下面是主題文章的摘要，請使用框框內的動詞填入空格。

become	capture	display	refuse	spark

The article recounts the origin story of the beloved Teddy bear, tracing back to a hunting trip involving President Roosevelt. After Roosevelt 1. ______________ to kill a cornered bear in an unsportsmanlike situation, a political cartoon 2. ________________ his compassionate act, inspiring a Brooklyn shopkeeper named Morris Michtom to create a stuffed bear. 3. ________________ as "Teddy's Bear" in their shop window, it quickly 4. ________________ an instant hit, leading to the widespread popularity of the Teddy bear across the nation. With Roosevelt's permission, the Michtoms' creation 5. ________________ a Teddy bear craze, eventually prompting other toy manufacturers to produce their own versions of the iconic stuffed animal.

答案在本單元最後一頁。請注意動詞時態的寫法。

Listening

現在我們來聽兩個人討論這篇文章。你會聽到許多相同的 word partnerships 和文法 chunks。這個練習將幫助你記住它們。

Task 6 18-2

請聽讀下列對話，你聽出了哪些前面 tasks 用到的詞彙？

A: Do you know how the Teddy bear came to be?

B: No, I don't think so. What's the origin story behind it?

A: Well, it all started with President Roosevelt on a hunting trip. He refused to shoot a bear because he found the situation unsportsmanlike.

B: Really? What happened next?

A: Roosevelt's compassionate act was captured in a political cartoon, which inspired a maker of stuffed animals named Morris Michtom to create a stuffed bear.

B: That's fascinating! What did Michtom do with it?

A: He displayed it in his shop window as "Teddy's Bear," and it became an instant hit. People started asking for their own "Teddy bears."

B: So, that's how the Teddy bear craze began?

A: Exactly. And with Roosevelt's permission, the Michtoms' creation sparked a nationwide trend, leading other toy manufacturers to produce their own versions, such as pocket-sized bears. The Teddy bear is now an enduring symbol of childhood.

B: Wow, I had no idea the beloved Teddy bear all started with a hunting trip and a compassionate act. Thanks for sharing!

請先確實聆聽音檔，了解後再看翻譯喔。

中譯

A：你知道泰迪熊是怎麼來的嗎？

B：不知道欸，它是怎麼誕生的？

A：嗯，這要追溯到老羅斯福總統的一次狩獵旅行。當時他拒絕射殺一隻熊，因為他覺得那樣做不符合運動家精神。

B：真的嗎？後來發生了什麼事？

A：老羅斯福這個富有同情心的行為被畫成了一幅政治漫畫，並啓發了絨毛玩偶製造商莫里斯．米赫頓做了一隻絨毛熊。

B：好酷！那米赫頓用它做了什麼？

A：他把這隻熊放在店裡展示，還標上「泰迪熊」的牌子，結果超多人來詢問，大家都想買一隻。

B：原來泰迪熊熱潮就是這樣開始的？

A：沒錯。在老羅斯福的許可下，米赫頓夫婦的創作引發了全國性的潮流，其他玩具製造商也紛紛推出自己的版本，例如袖珍熊。如今，泰迪熊已成為童年永恆的象徵。

B：哇，我都不知道這麼受人喜愛的泰迪熊居然是因為一次狩獵旅行和一個善良的舉動而誕生的。感謝分享！

Answers

Task 1:

Q1: C Q2: B Q3: B Q4: A Q5: B

Task 2:

stuffed	animals
origin	story
hunting	trip
unsportsmanlike	situation
compassionate	act
political	cartoon
instant	hit
enduring	symbol
pocket-sized	bears
beloved	Teddy bear

Task 3:

1. compassionate act
2. stuffed animals
3. pocket-sized bears
4. hunting trip
5. enduring symbol
6. beloved Teddy bear
7. instant hit
8. political cartoon
9. unsportsmanlike situation
10. origin story

Task 5:

1. refused
2. captured
3. displayed
4. became
5. sparked

Unit 19

巧克力
Chocolate

本單元的學習目標包括：

☐ 學到一些可用以談論本主題的 word partnerships
☐ 針對動詞的被動語態 (passive voice) 做一些練習

Reading

Task 1 19-1

請閱聽這篇文章並回答下面的問題。

Chocolate, the **indulgent delight** cherished by millions worldwide, has a dark side that often remains hidden behind its **delectable facade**. Beyond the **allure** of its rich flavor lies a story **tainted** by **deforestation**, child **labor**, and the **exploitation** of **vulnerable** communities, particularly in the cocoa-growing regions of Cote D'Ivoire and Ghana.

Cote D'Ivoire and Ghana collectively produce more than half of the world's cocoa, making them vital players in the global chocolate industry. However, this production comes at a significant environmental cost. The **relentless** demand for cocoa has led to extensive deforestation in these countries, as forests are cleared to make way for cocoa plantations. This **rampant** deforestation not only destroys precious ecosystems but also contributes to climate change, exacerbating the global environmental crisis.

Moreover, the production of cocoa in Cote D'Ivoire and Ghana is **marred** by the **pervasive** issue of child labor. According to estimates by the International Labor Organization (ILO), hundreds of thousands of children are engaged in **hazardous** work on cocoa farms, often subjected to grueling conditions and deprived of their basic rights. These children, many of whom are **trafficked** from neighboring countries or **exploited** within their own communities, are forced to **toil** long hours in the fields, exposed to harmful **pesticides** and **machinery**, and denied access to education and **healthcare**.

The Harkin-Engel Protocol, also known as the Cocoa Protocol, was established in 2001 as an international framework aimed at addressing the issue of child labor in the cocoa industry. Signed by major chocolate companies, governments, and civil society organizations, the **protocol** sought to **eliminate** the worst forms of child labor in cocoa production by 2005. However, despite initial efforts, progress has been slow and the prevalence of child labor persists, casting doubts on the effectiveness of voluntary initiatives in tackling such complex systemic issues.

While some **strides** have been made to combat deforestation and child labor in the cocoa supply chain, much remains to be done. The responsibility lies not only with chocolate companies but also with consumers, who have the power to drive change through their purchasing decisions. By supporting ethically sourced chocolate brands that **prioritize** environmental sustainability and fair labor practices, consumers can send a powerful message to the industry and help create a more equitable and sustainable cocoa sector.

In conclusion, the story of chocolate is not just one of sweetness and indulgence but also of **hardship** and **exploitation**. The deforestation of cocoa-growing regions, coupled with the **prevalence** of child labor, highlights the urgent need for systemic change within the chocolate industry. Only through collaborative efforts involving governments, corporations, and civil society can we address these pressing issues and ensure that the production of chocolate is both environmentally sustainable and socially responsible.

VOCABULARY

indulgent [ɪn`dʌldʒənt] *adj.* 放縱的
delight [dɪ`laɪt] *n.* 愉悅
delectable [dɪ`lɛktəbḷ] *adj.* 美味的
facade [fə`sɑd] *n.* 表面
allure [ə`lɪʊr] *n.* 誘惑
taint [tent] *v.* 污染
deforestation [ˌdifɔrəs`teʃən] *n.* 森林砍伐
labor [`lebɚ] *n.* 勞工
exploitation [ˌɛksplɔɪ`teʃən] *n.* 開發
vulnerable [`vʌlnərəbḷ] *adj.* 弱勢的
relentless [rɪ`lɛntlɪs] *adj.* 不間斷的
rampant [`ræmpənt] *adj.* 猖獗的
mar [mɑr] *v.* 損傷；玷污
pervasive [pɚ`vesɪv] *adj.* 普遍存在的
hazardous [`hæzɚdəs] *adj.* 危險的
traffic [`træfɪk] *v.* 非法交易
exploit [ɪk`splɔɪt] *v.* 剝削；利用
toil [tɔɪl] *v.* 做苦工
pesticide [`pɛstɪˌsaɪd] *n.* 殺蟲劑
machinery [mə`ʃinərɪ] *n.* 機械
healthcare [`hɛlθˌkɛr] *n.* 醫療保健
protocol [`protəˌkɑl] *n.* 協議；草案
eliminate [ɪ`lɪməˌnet] *v.* 消除
stride [straɪd] *n.* 進展
prioritize [praɪ`ɔrəˌtaɪz] *v.* 優先考慮
hardship [`hɑrdʃɪp] *n.* 艱困
exploitation [ˌɛksplɔɪ`teʃən] *n.* 剝削；利用
prevalence [`prɛvələns] *n.* 盛行

Comprehension questions

Q1: What is the main topic of the article?

A. chocolate

B. some countries in Africa

C. child slavery

Q2: What is the main topic of the second paragraph?

A. deforestation

B. where cocoa is produced

C. ecosystems

Q3: What does the International Labor Organization estimate?

A. most of the world's chocolate is produced in the Cote D'Ivoire and Ghana

B. children are engaged in chocolate production

C. many children in the world are trafficked

Q4: What is the Harkin-Engel Protocol?

A. a chocolate manufacturing company

B. an agreement between chocolate manufacturers to stop child labor

C. a labor organization

Q5: Who is to blame for child labor in the chocolate industry?

A. the chocolate manufacturing companies

B. the consumer

C. the chocolate manufacturing companies and consumers

答案在本單元最後一頁。如果答錯了，請再確認一次文章內容。

中譯

巧克力，這種讓全球數百萬人愛不釋手的美味甜點，其實背後有著不為人知的黑暗面。在它誘人的濃郁風味背後，隱藏著一個受砍伐森林、童工和剝削弱勢社區所污染的故事，尤其是在象牙海岸和加納的可可種植地區。

象牙海岸和加納的可可豆產量佔世界總量的一半以上，可說是全球巧克力產業的重鎮。然而，這樣的生產要付出巨大的環境代價。為滿足不斷增長的可可需求，這些國家的森林被大量砍伐，以便騰出土地來種植可可。猖獗的森林砍伐不僅破壞了珍貴的生態系統，也加劇了氣候變遷，讓全球的環境問題變得更加嚴重。

此外，象牙海岸和加納的可可生產還被普遍存在的童工問題所玷污。根據國際勞工組織 (ILO) 估計，數十萬名兒童在可可農場從事危險工作，經常在艱苦的條件下勞動，基本權利被剝奪。這些孩子中，許多人是從鄰國被拐賣來的，或在當地社區中遭到剝削，被迫在田裡長時間工作，接觸有害的農藥和機械設備，且無法接受教育或享有醫療服務。

《哈金安格議定書》，又稱《可可議定書》，成立於 2001 年，是一個旨在解決可可產業童工問題的國際框架。這項協議由主要巧克力公司、各國政府和公民社會組織簽署，目標是在 2005 年前消除可可生產中最嚴重的童工問題。然而，儘管起初做出了努力，但進展緩慢，童工現象依舊普遍存在，讓人質疑自願性倡議是否真的能解決如此複雜的系統性問題。

雖然至今在打擊可可供應鏈中的毀林和童工問題上取得了一些進展，但仍有很大的改善空間。這不僅是巧克力公司的責任，消費者也有能力藉由購買決策來促進改變。透過支持優先考慮環境永續性和落實公平勞動的良心品牌，消費者就能向產業發出強而有力的訊息，並幫助創造一個更公平和永續的可可產業。

總而言之，巧克力的故事並不只是甜美的享受，它還涉及許多艱辛和剝削。可可種植區的森林砍伐，加上童工的盛行，突顯了巧克力產業急需系統性改革。唯有在政府、企業與民間社會的共同努力下，我們才能解決這些迫切問題，確保巧克力生產能兼顧環境永續性和社會責任。

文法甦活區

Task 2

請用上篇文章中的 word partnerships 完成下表。見範例。

indulgent	delight
	side
rich	
	players
relentless	
	issue
child	
	work
grueling	
	rights

只要對照文章，便可輕鬆找出答案。

接下來，我們要利用上列 word partnerships 練習寫作。

Task 3

請用 Task 2 表格中的 word partnerships 填入下列空格。見範例。

1. Access to clean water is a ___basic right___ that should be afforded to every individual, regardless of their socio-economic status or geographic location.

2. Beneath the company's glossy exterior lay a ________________, filled with unethical business practices and a toxic work environment.

3. Despite various efforts to address it, poverty remains a __________ ____________ affecting millions of people worldwide.

4. In the battle against climate change, renewable energy sources like solar and wind power have become ______________ in the global effort to reduce carbon emissions.

5. The homemade stew simmered for hours, resulting in a dish with a ______________ that delighted everyone at the dinner table.

6. The international community continues to grapple with the challenge of eradicating ______________, which deprives millions of children of their education and childhood.

7. The marathon runners pushed through ____________________, battling extreme heat and fatigue to reach the finish line.

8. The ____________________ for the latest smartphones has led to rapid advancements in technology and increased competition among manufacturers.

9. The spa weekend was an ________________, offering a perfect escape from the stresses of everyday life with its soothing massages and tranquil surroundings.

10. Workers in the construction industry often do ________________, including exposure to dangerous machinery and materials.

答案在本單元最後一頁。

現在我們來看看這篇文章中的一些文法，其中使用了一些被動語塊。

Task 4

請在文中找出下列被動語塊 (be chunks) ，並留意其用法。

· are cleared
· is marred
· are engaged
· are trafficked
· are forced
· was established

當句中未提及執行動作的主詞，或者要描述過程時，使用被動語態會更合適。

Task 5

請用 Task 4 的詞組填入下列空格。

1. Children as young as six ______________ across borders and forced into labor on cocoa farms, a tragic reality that demands urgent attention from the international community.

2. In conflict zones, sometimes civilians ________________ to flee their homes, leaving behind everything they hold dear in search of safety and refuge.

3. Large swathes of forest ____________ every year to make room for agricultural expansion, contributing to the loss of biodiversity and habitat destruction.

4. Many young students ___________ in volunteer work, demonstrating their commitment to making a positive impact in their communities.

5. The nonprofit organization ____________________ with the noble goal of providing educational opportunities to underprivileged children in rural areas.

6. The otherwise picturesque landscape ________________ by the scars of industrial pollution, a reminder of the environmental degradation caused by human activity.

答案在本單元最後一頁。

Listening

Task 6 19-2

請聽讀下列對話，你聽出了哪些前面 tasks 用到的詞彙？

A: You know, chocolate is such a beloved treat worldwide, but there's a dark side to its production that many people overlook.

B: Yeah, I've heard about that. It's pretty concerning how cocoa production contributes to deforestation and environmental degradation in places like Cote D'Ivoire and Ghana.

A: Exactly. It's shocking how much forest is cleared just to make way for cocoa plantations. And the impact on ecosystems and climate change is significant.

B: And let's not forget about the issue of child labor in cocoa farming. It's heartbreaking to think about all those children being forced to do hazardous work in grueling conditions, deprived of their basic rights.

A: Absolutely. The numbers are staggering, with hundreds of thousands of children affected. It's a pervasive issue that needs urgent attention.

B: That's why initiatives like the Harkin-Engel Protocol were established, right? To address child labor in the cocoa industry?

A: Yes, exactly. But unfortunately, progress has been slow, and the problem persists. It makes you question the effectiveness of voluntary initiatives in tackling such deep-rooted issues.

B: It's not just up to chocolate companies to solve these problems, though, although they are vital players in the problem. Consumers also play a crucial role in driving change through their purchasing decisions and relentless demand for the rich flavor of chocolate.

A: Absolutely. By supporting ethically sourced chocolate brands that prioritize environmental sustainability and fair labor practices, consumers can send a powerful message to the industry.

B: Definitely. It's about being informed and making conscious choices to support a more equitable and sustainable cocoa sector.

A: In the end, chocolate isn't just about sweetness and indulgent delight. It's also about confronting the hardships and exploitation in its production and working together to create positive change.

B: Couldn't agree more. It's time for collaborative efforts involving governments, corporations, and civil society to address these pressing issues and ensure a better future for cocoa farmers and the environment.

請先確實聆聽音檔，了解後再看翻譯喔。

中譯

A：你知道嗎，巧克力是全球超受歡迎的零食，但其實它的生產過程背後有一個被許多人忽視的黑暗面。

B：對啊，我有聽過，像是可可生產會造成象牙海岸和加納等地方的森林砍伐，還會破壞環境，真的很令人擔心。

A：沒錯。為了種植可可樹，被砍伐的森林面積令人震驚。這對生態系統和氣候變遷造成的影響很巨大。

B：而且別忘了可可種植業的童工問題。想到那些孩子被迫在惡劣的環境中從事危險工作，無法享有基本權利，真的很難過。

A：真的。受到影響的孩子多達數十萬，這是一個普遍存在的問題，急待解決。

B：這就是為什麼像《哈金安格議定書》這類倡議被提出來的原因，對吧？目的是為了解決可可產業中的童工問題？

A：沒錯。但遺憾的是，進展緩慢，問題依然存在。這讓人不禁懷疑，這類自願性倡議真能有效解決這麼根深蒂固的問題嗎？

B：但這不只是巧克力公司單方面的責任，雖然他們很關鍵，但消費者也有很大的影響力。消費者的購買選擇也很重要，畢竟需求高才會引發這些問題。

A：沒錯。如果消費者願意支持那些重視環保和公平交易的巧克力品牌，就能向這個產業傳遞一個強烈的訊號。

B：完全同意。重點就是了解真相，然後做出更負責任的選擇，支持一個更公平、更永續的可可產業。

A：說到底，巧克力不僅僅是甜味和令人愉悅的享受，它同時也代表著我們必須正視其生產過程中的艱困與剝削，並共同努力帶來正面的改變。

B：非常認同你。現在是時候讓政府、企業和民間社會攜手合作，解決這些迫切問題，為可可農民和環境創造美好的未來。

Answers

Task 1:

Q1: A   Q2: B   Q3: B   Q4: B   Q5: C

Task 2:

indulgent	delight
dark	side
rich	flavor
vital	players
relentless	demand
pervasive	issue
child	labor
hazardous	work
grueling	conditions
basic	rights

Task 3:

1. basic right
2. dark side
3. pervasive issue
4. vital players
5. rich flavor
6. child labor
7. grueling conditions
8. relentless demand
9. indulgent delight
10. hazardous work

Task 5:

1. are trafficked
2. are forced
3. are cleared
4. are engaged
5. was established
6. is marred

Unit 20 太空探索發明

Space Exploration Inventions

本單元的學習目標包括：

- ☐ 學到一些可用以談論本主題的詞組
- ☐ 針對描述起源的片語做一些練習

Reading

Task 1 20-1

請閱聽這篇文章並回答下面的問題。

Space **exploration**, with its boundless **frontiers** and relentless pursuit of knowledge, has not only expanded our understanding of the **universe** but has also **sparked** innovations that have transformed life here on Earth. Many of the technologies that we now consider normal had their origins in the challenges and demands of space travel. Here are four remarkable inventions that were born out of space exploration.

Memory foam, renowned for its ability to conform to pressure and then **regain** its original shape, was initially developed for NASA's **spaceflight** comfort. Created in the 1960s as a response to the need for more comfortable and safer seating in **spacecraft**, memory foam's unique properties quickly **garnered** attention. Today, this innovation is **ubiquitous** in mattresses, pillows, footwear, and even medical **equipment**, enhancing comfort and support for people around the world.

Global Positioning System (GPS) technology has revolutionized navigation and location-based services. Originally devised for **military** applications and space exploration, GPS allows precise **positioning** of objects on Earth's surface by **utilizing** signals from a network of **satellites**. This technology found its way into **civilian** use, transforming how we navigate cities, explore new places, and even track fitness activities. From turn-by-turn directions to ride-sharing apps, GPS has become an essential part of modern life.

The **durable** lenses that protect our eyes from the sun's glare and dust owe their existence to space exploration. NASA collaborated with a company to develop scratch-resistant **coatings** for **astronauts**' helmet visors in the 1970s. This innovation not only improved astronaut safety by maintaining clear visibility but also had practical applications on Earth. Today, scratch-resistant coatings are used in eyeglasses, sunglasses, camera lenses, and more, extending the **lifespan** of these essential **optical** devices.

Cordless power tools can also be traced back to the Apollo program of the 1960s and 70s. NASA engineers faced a unique challenge: how to design compact, lightweight tools that astronauts could use during **extravehicular** activities on the Moon. Traditional tools with cords proved impractical in the **vacuum** of space, as cords could become **tangled**, restrict movement, and pose a safety **hazard**.

In response, NASA developed cordless tools that could operate efficiently in a zero-gravity environment. The result was the first cordless drill, which accompanied astronauts on lunar missions. This innovative tool not only assisted astronauts in collecting samples and conducting experiments on the Moon's surface but also paved the way for a revolutionary leap in Earthly technology.

The spirit of exploration and the quest for solutions to the challenges of space travel have yielded remarkable inventions that continue to shape our lives on Earth. From memory foam providing us with comfort and restful sleep to GPS guiding us through uncharted **territories** and scratch-resistant lenses enhancing our vision, to the convenience of cordless power tools, these innovations **underscore** the far-reaching impact of space exploration. As we look to the future, it's a testament to human ingenuity that the pursuit of the **cosmos** has led to such practical and transformative advancements in our everyday lives.

VOCABULARY

exploration [ˌɛkspləˋreʃən] *n.* 探索
frontier [frʌnˋtɪr] *n.* 邊界
universe [ˋjunəˌvɝs] *n.* 宇宙
spark [spɑrk] *v.* 激勵
regain [rɪˋgen] *v.* 恢復
spaceflight [ˋspesˌflaɪt] *n.* 太空飛行
spacecraft [ˋspesˌkræft] *n.* 太空船
garner [ˋgɑrnɚ] *v.* 獲得
ubiquitous [juˋbɪkwətəs] *adj.* 無所不在的
equipment [ɪˋkwɪpmənt] *n.* 設備
military [ˋmɪləˌtɛrɪ] *adj.* 軍用的
positioning [pəˋzɪʃənɪŋ] *n.* 定位
utilize [ˋjutḷˌaɪz] *v.* 利用
satellite [ˋsætḷˌaɪt] *n.* 衛星
civilian [sɪˋvɪljən] *adj.* 民用的
durable [ˋdjʊrəbḷ] *adj.* 耐用的
coating [ˋkotɪŋ] *n.* 塗層
astronaut [ˋæstrəˌnɔt] *n.* 太空人
lifespan [ˋlaɪfˋspæn] *n.* 使用期限
optical [ˋɑptɪkḷ] *adj.* 光學的
cordless [ˋkɔrdlɪs] *adj.* 無線的
extravehicular [ˌɛkstrəviˋhɪkjəlɚ] *adj.* 太空船外的
vacuum [ˋvækjuəm] *n.* 真空
tangled [ˋtæŋgḷd] *adj.* 纏在一起的
hazard [ˋhæzɚd] *n.* 危險
territory [ˋtɛrəˌtorɪ] *n.* 領土；領域
underscore [ʌndɚˋskor] *v.* 強調
cosmos [ˋkɑzməs] *n.* 宇宙

Comprehension questions

Q1: What is the main topic of the article?

A. the origin of memory foam

B. the origin of GPS

C. some inventions that developed from space exploration

Q2: What is the origin of memory foam?

A. comfortable sleeping for astronauts

B. comfortable seating for astronauts

C. medical equipment for astronauts

Q3: What is the origin of scratch-resistant coatings?

A. sunglasses

B. camera lenses

C. helmet visors

Q4: What is the origin of GPS?

A. ride-sharing apps

B. military applications

C. fitness-tracking apps

Q5: What is the origin of cordless power tools?

A. compact lightweight tools

B. tools for use outside the spacecraft

C. a revolutionary leap in Earthly technology

答案在本單元最後一頁。如果答錯了，請再確認一次文章內容。

中譯

太空探索憑藉其無限的邊界和對知識的不懈追求，不僅擴大了我們對宇宙的了解，也激發出改變地球生活的創新。許多現在看似稀鬆平常的技術，其實最初都是為了應對太空旅行中的各種挑戰而誕生的。以下是四個因太空探索而誕生的有趣發明。

記憶泡棉以其能夠回應壓力並恢復原狀的能力而聞名，最初是為了提升 NASA 太空飛行舒適度而研發的。該技術於 1960 年代誕生，旨在解決太空船中更舒適、更安全的座椅需求，其獨特特性很快便引起了關注。如今，這項創新在床墊、枕頭、鞋類甚至醫療設備中無所不在，為世界各地的人們提高了舒適度和支撐力。

全球定位系統 (GPS) 技術徹底改變了導航和基於位置的服務。GPS 最初是為軍事應用和太空探索而設計的，利用衛星網路的訊號對地球表面的物體進行精確定位。這項技術逐漸應用於民用，改變了我們在城市中導航、探索新地點，甚至追蹤健身活動的方式。從路線導航到共乘應用程式，GPS 已成為現代生活中不可或缺的一部分。

保護眼睛免受太陽眩光和灰塵侵害的耐用鏡片，其技術同樣源自太空探索。1970 年代，NASA 與一家公司合作開發太空人頭盔護目鏡的防刮塗層。這項創新不僅透過保持清晰的能見度提升了太空人的安全性，而且在地球上也有實際應用。如今，防刮塗層廣泛應用於眼鏡、太陽眼鏡、相機鏡頭等產品上，延長了這些重要光學設備的使用壽命。

無線電動工具的起源可追溯到 1960 至 1970 年代的阿波羅計畫。NASA 工程師面臨著一個獨特的挑戰：如何設計出太空人在月球艙外活動期間使用的小巧、輕便的工具。傳統的有線工具在太空真空環境中並不實用，因為電線可能會纏繞、限制活動，甚至成為安全隱患。

為此，NASA 開發了能在零重力環境中高效運作的無線工具。於是，第一款無線電鑽隨太空人登上了月球，幫助他們在月球表面收集樣本並進行實驗。這項創新工具不僅協助太空人完成任務，也為地球上的技術進步奠定了基礎，開創了無線工具的革命性發展。

太空探索的精神和對解決太空旅行挑戰的追求，孕育了眾多卓越的發明，這些發明至今仍在地球上改變著我們的生活。從記憶泡棉為我們帶來舒適睡眠，到 GPS 指引我們穿越未知領域、再到防刮鏡片提升我們的視覺體驗，以及無線電動工具的便利性，這些創新都彰顯了太空探索的廣泛影響。展望未來，這些來自探索宇宙的智慧結晶，證明了人類在過程中，如何催生出顛覆日常生活的實用發明。

文法甦活區

Task 2

請用上篇文章中的 word partnerships 完成下表。見範例。

space	exploration
boundless	
	pursuit
remarkable	
	shape
spaceflight	
	properties
military	
	use
scratch-resistant	

只要對照文章，便可輕鬆找出答案。

接下來，我們要利用上列 word partnerships 練習寫作。

Task 3

請用 Task 2 表格中的 word partnerships 填入下列空格。見範例。

1. ___Space exploration___ has opened up vast new horizons for humanity, revealing the wonders of the cosmos and inspiring future generations to reach for the stars.

2. Space exploration continues to push the boundaries of human knowledge, leading us into ______________________ of discovery and understanding.

3. The 21st century has witnessed __________________________ that have revolutionized industries, from the smartphone to renewable energy technologies.

4. The architect's design featured an ________________, seamlessly blending modern aesthetics with functional practicality.

5. ____________________ is a critical consideration for long-duration missions, prompting engineers to develop innovative solutions to ensure astronauts' well-being in the harsh environment of space.

6. The material exhibits ____________________, making it invaluable for applications ranging from aerospace engineering to medical technology.

7. The technology's versatility extends to ______________________, where it enhances strategic capabilities and safeguards national security interests.

8. The new smartphone model boasts _________________________, ensuring durability and maintaining its pristine appearance even after prolonged use.

9. In his ___________________ of excellence, he dedicated countless hours to perfecting his craft, achieving remarkable success in his field.

10. Drones have found ______________________ in various industries, from agriculture to filmmaking, revolutionizing the way tasks are accomplished and data is collected.

答案在本單元最後一頁。

現在我們來看看這篇文章中的一些文法。

Task 4

請再看一遍文章，並在文中找出下列片語並劃底線。

- had their origins in
- was initially developed for
- originally devised for
- owe their existence to
- be traced back to

這些片語都是關於起源。當我們想要強調某物的起源時，便可派上用場。

Task 5

請用 Task 4 的詞組填入下列空格。

1. Many modern technologies, such as the Internet and GPS, ____________________________ in government-funded research projects aimed at solving complex challenges.
2. Many of today's medical breakthroughs ____________________ to decades of tireless research and collaboration among scientists, clinicians, and engineers.
3. The computer mouse ____________________ for use with the revolutionary Xerox Alto computer in the 1970s.
4. The encryption algorithm ____________________ for securing military communications but has since found widespread application in safeguarding sensitive data across various industries.
5. The origins of modern computing can ____________________ to the groundbreaking work of visionaries like Alan Turing and Charles Babbage in the early 20th century.

答案在本單元最後一頁。

Listening

Task 6 20-2

請聽讀下列對話，你聽出了哪些前面 tasks 用到的詞彙？

A: Hey, have you ever thought about how space exploration has impacted our everyday lives?

B: Not really, but I guess it has led to some remarkable inventions and technologies, right?

A: Absolutely! Take memory foam, for example. Did you know it was originally developed for NASA's spaceflight comfort?

B: No way! I always thought memory foam was just for mattresses.

A: Yeah, it was created in the 1960s to ensure spaceflight comfort because it maintains its original shape. Now it's everywhere, from mattresses to footwear.

B: Yes, that's one of its unique properties. That's fascinating! What else?

A: Well, GPS technology was also born out of space exploration. It first had military applications but now we rely on it for everything from navigation to tracking our fitness activities.

B: I had no idea GPS had such humble beginnings. What about those scratch-resistant coatings we use in glasses and sunglasses?

A: Those actually came from NASA too! They needed durable lenses for astronaut helmet visors, and now we benefit from them here on Earth.

B: Wow, it's amazing how space exploration has led to so many practical inventions for civilian use. What about cordless power tools?

A: Yep, those originated from the Apollo program. NASA needed tools that astronauts could use on the Moon without cords getting in the way, so they developed the first cordless drill.

B: Incredible! It's mind-blowing to think about how our everyday technologies have roots in the boundless frontiers of space exploration.

A: Definitely. It just goes to show the far-reaching impact of human ingenuity and the relentless pursuit of the unknown.

B: Absolutely. I'll definitely think about space exploration differently from now on. Thanks for sharing all this!

A: No problem! It's always fascinating to learn about the connections between space and our daily lives.

請先確實聆聽音檔，了解後再看翻譯喔。

中譯

A：嘿，你有沒有想過太空探索對我們日常生活影響很大？

B：還真沒有，但我猜應該有一些很厲害的發明跟技術是因為太空探索而來的吧？

A：沒錯！像記憶泡棉就是個例子。你知道它最早其實是為了 NASA 太空飛行的舒適度而研發的嗎？

B：不會吧！我一直以為記憶泡棉只是用在床墊上的東西。

A：對啊，它在 1960 年代被研發出來，就是為了提升太空船座椅的舒適度，因為它能保持原本的形狀。現在不只床墊，連鞋子和醫療器材上都看得到它的蹤影。

B：沒錯，那就是它的特性。真有意思！還有什麼？

A：嗯，GPS 技術也是從太空探索中誕生的。它最初是為了軍事用途，但現在我們從導航到健身追蹤都離不開它。

B：沒想到 GPS 的起源竟然這麼低調！那我們眼鏡和太陽眼鏡上的防刮塗層呢？

A：那也是 NASA 研發的！他們當年為了讓太空人的頭盔能在太空中保持清晰視野，才發明了防刮塗層，結果我們現在在地球上也能享受到這個技術的好處。

B：哇，太酷了！沒想到這麼多實用的東西都跟太空探索有關，那無線電動工具呢？

A：對！無線電動工具的技術源自阿波羅登月計畫。當時他們需要能在月球上用的工具，但傳統的有線工具在太空中不方便，電線容易纏繞而且會妨礙行動，所以他們就設計了第一款無線電鑽。

B：太不可思議了！真難想像我們日常用的這些科技竟然都和遙遠的太空探索有關。

A：是啊，這就是人類智慧和對未知世界不懈追求的最佳見證。

B：絕對是。以後我會用不同的眼光看待太空探索。謝謝你分享這些資訊！

A：不客氣！聊聊太空與我們日常生活之間的關聯很有趣。

Answers

Task 1:

Q1: C Q2: B Q3: C Q4: B Q5: B

Task 2:

space	exploration
boundless	frontiers
relentless	pursuit
remarkable	inventions
original	shape
spaceflight	comfort
unique	properties
military	applications
civilian	use
scratch-resistant	coatings

Task 3:

1. Space exploration
2. boundless frontiers
3. remarkable inventions
4. original shape
5. Spaceflight comfort
6. unique properties
7. military applications
8. scratch-resistant coatings
9. relentless pursuit
10. civilian use

Task 5:

1. had their origins
2. owe their existence / can be traced back
3. was initially developed / was originally devised
4. was originally devised / was initially developed
5. be traced back / owe their existence

NOTES

Part 5

Designed by イラストAC

科技

TECHNOLOGY

Unit 21

AI 浪潮下的影響

Industries Effected by AI

本單元的學習目標包括：

- □ 學到一些可用以談論本主題的 word partnerships
- □ 練習一些 chunks 以描述某項技術的重要性

Reading

Task 1 21-1

請閱聽這篇文章並回答下面的問題。

In an era characterized by rapid technological advancements, one particular innovation has emerged as a **game-changer** across industries worldwide: artificial intelligence (AI). With its ability to process vast amounts of data, learn from patterns, and make **autonomous** decisions, AI is transforming the way businesses operate. While its potential impact spans multiple sectors, several industries are set to experience significant **disruptions** as AI takes center stage.

The healthcare and medicine industry stands at the **forefront** of AI-driven **transformations**. From **diagnostics** and drug discovery to patient care and administrative tasks, AI technologies are revolutionizing healthcare in numerous ways. AI-powered **algorithms** can analyze medical images with **unprecedented** accuracy, aiding **radiologists** in **detecting** early signs of diseases. **Virtual** assistants equipped with natural language processing

capabilities are improving patient **interactions** and **streamlining** administrative processes. Additionally, AI is playing a crucial role in developing personalized treatments, leveraging vast amounts of patient data to identify effective **therapies** and **predict** disease outcomes.

The **finance** and banking sector is undergoing a profound AI-driven revolution. Intelligent algorithms are being employed for **fraud** detection, risk **assessment**, and **algorithmic** trading. AI-powered chatbots and virtual assistants are enhancing customer service by providing personalized recommendations and addressing **inquiries** promptly. Advanced data **analytics** algorithms are assisting **financial** institutions in detecting patterns and making data-driven decisions, leading to improved efficiency and reduced costs. Moreover, AI-based robo-advisors are becoming increasingly popular, providing automated and personalized **investment** advice to individuals.

AI is reshaping the transportation and **logistics** industry, bringing significant advancements in areas such as autonomous vehicles, route **optimization**, and supply chain management. Self-driving cars and trucks are being developed and tested by major companies, aiming to **enhance** safety and efficiency while reducing human errors. AI algorithms are helping logistics companies **optimize** delivery routes, minimize fuel consumption, and streamline operations through predictive **maintenance**. With the **integration** of AI, transportation networks are becoming smarter, more reliable, and better equipped to handle the demands of the modern world.

VOCABULARY

game-changer [ˋgem.tʃendʒɚ] *n.* 影響力極大的創新事物
autonomous [ɔˋtanəməs] *adj.* 自主的
disruption [dɪsˋrʌpʃən] *n.* 顛覆
forefront [ˋfor.frʌnt] *n.* 最前線
transformation [.trænsfɚˋmeʃən] *n.* 轉型
diagnostics [.daɪəgˋnastɪks] *n.* 診斷法
algorithm [ˋælgə.rɪðm] *n.* 演算法
unprecedented [ʌnˋprɛsə.dɛntɪd] *adj.* 前所未有的
radiologist [.redɪˋalədʒɪst] *n.* 放射科醫師
detect [dɪˋtɛkt] *v.* 偵測

Comprehension questions

Q1: What is the main topic of the article?

A. healthcare and medicine

B. transportation and logistics

C. the industries must likely to be impacted by AI

Q2: How will AI impact healthcare?

A. AI can help radiologists

B. AI will invent new drugs

C. AI will replace doctors

Q3: How will AI impact the logistics industry?

A. AI will drive trucks

B. AI will make routes shorter and more efficient

C. AI will replace computers

Q4: How will AI impact finance and banking?

A. it will lead to improved efficiency and reduced costs

B. it will make everyone richer

C. it will make everyone poorer

Q5: How will AI impact driving?

A. there will be self-driving cars

B. human errors will be a thing of the past

C. the modern world will be more demanding

答案在本單元最後一頁。如果答錯了，請再確認一次文章內容。

VOCABULARY

virtual [ˋvɜtʃuəl] *adj.* 虛擬的
capability [ˌkepəˋbɪlətɪ] *n.* 能力
interaction [ˌɪntəˋrækʃən] *n.* 互動
streamline [ˋstrimˌlaɪn] *v.* 簡化
therapy [ˋθɛrəpɪ] *n.* 療法
predict [prɪˋdɪkt] *v.* 預測
finance [faɪˋnæns] *n.* 財政；金融
fraud [frɔd] *n.* 詐騙
assessment [əˋsɛsmənt] *n.* 評估
algorithmic [ˌælgɚˋrɪðmɪk] *adj.* 演算法的

中譯

在這個科技進步日新月異的時代，有一項技術成為了顛覆各行各業的關鍵，那就是人工智慧 (AI)。AI 具備處理大量數據、學習模式、自主決策的能力，正在改寫企業的運作方式。雖然其影響力已滲透到很多領域，但有幾個產業將在 AI 成為主導力量時，面臨巨大衝擊。

醫療保健與醫藥產業處於 AI 革命的最前線。從診斷疾病到研發新藥，再到患者護理和行政管理，AI 幾乎無所不在。AI 驅動的演算法能以前所未有的準確度分析醫學影像，幫助放射科醫師及時發現疾病的早期徵兆。具備自然語言處理能力的虛擬助手改善了患者互動體驗，並簡化了醫院的行政流程。此外，AI 還能根據大量病患數據制定個性化治療方案，甚至能預測疾病的發展結果，讓醫療變得更有效率。

金融業和銀行業也正被 AI 顛覆。智慧演算法被用於詐欺偵測、風險評估和程式交易。AI 聊天機器人和虛擬助手成了銀行的新寵，提供個性化的建議並且快速解決客戶疑問。先進的數據分析演算法幫助金融機構檢測模式並做出數據驅動的決策，從而提高效率並降低成本。此外，AI 理財機器人愈來愈受歡迎，它們能自動提供個人化的投資建議。

AI 同樣在重塑交通業和物流業。從自駕車輛、路線優化到供應鏈管理，AI 技術帶來了相當顯著的進展。許多大企業都在研發和測試自駕汽車和卡車，希望藉此提升安全性和效率，減少人為錯誤。另一方面，AI 演算法能幫助物流公司優化配送路線、降低燃料消耗，並透過預測性維護讓整體營運更流暢。隨著 AI 技術的整合，交通網路變得更智慧、更可靠，也更能應對現代社會的需求。

VOCABULARY

inquiry [ɪnˋkwaɪrɪ] *n.* 詢問
analytics [ænḷˋɪtɪks] *n.* 分析法
financial [faɪˋnænʃəl] *adj.* 財政的；金融的
investment [ɪnˋvɛstmənt] *n.* 投資
logistics [loˋdʒɪstɪks] *n.* 物流
optimization [ˌɑptɪmaɪˋzeʃən] *n.* 優化
enhance [ɪnˋhæns] *v.* 提升；增加
optimize [ˋɑptəˌmaɪz] *v.* 優化
maintenance [ˋmentənəns] *n.* 維護；保養
integration [ˌɪntəˋgreʃən] *n.* 整合

文法甦活區

Task 2

請用上篇文章中的 word partnerships 完成下表。見範例。

rapid technological	advancements
artificial	
	decisions
potential	
	disruptions
healthcare	
	discovery
patient	
	tasks
intelligent	

只要對照文章，便可輕鬆找出答案。

接下來，我們要利用上列 word partnerships 練習寫作。

Task 3

請用 Task 2 表格中的 word partnerships 填入下列空格。見範例。

1. Artificial intelligence is revolutionizing industries by automating tasks, analyzing vast amounts of data, and enabling machines to learn and adapt autonomously.

2. Autonomous vehicles rely on advanced algorithms to make split-second ______________________________, navigating complex roadways with precision and safety.

3. ___________________ relies heavily on cutting-edge technologies such as artificial intelligence and high-throughput screening to accelerate the identification and development of novel treatments for various diseases.

4. Effective ________________ encompasses not only medical treatment but also holistic support, personalized attention, and empathy to promote healing and well-being.

5. The _____________________________ continues to innovate, leveraging advancements in technology and medical research to improve patient care and outcomes worldwide.

6. ___________________ are revolutionizing industries by rapidly analyzing vast datasets, identifying patterns, and providing valuable insights to inform decision-making processes and drive innovation forward.

7. _________________________________ have transformed our daily lives, revolutionizing how we communicate, work, and interact with the world around us.

8. Streamlining _________________ through automation and digitalization frees up valuable time for healthcare professionals to focus on delivering high-quality patient care and improving overall efficiency in medical facilities.

9. The ____________________ of renewable energy technologies extends far beyond environmental benefits, promising to reshape economies, mitigate climate change, and foster sustainable development worldwide.

10. The rise of e-commerce has brought ______________________________ to traditional brick-and-mortar retail, prompting retailers to adapt their strategies to stay competitive in the digital age.

答案在本單元最後一頁。

再作一個文法練習吧！透過練習，你會更清楚本單元的文法重點。

Task 4

請再看一遍文章，找出下列 chunks 並劃底線。

- has emerged as
- is transforming
- stands at the forefront of
- are revolutionizing
- is playing a crucial role in

這些詞組皆用於描述某項技術的重要性，其中的動詞時態各異。我們使用現在進行式描述現正發生的趨勢，使用現在完成式描述持續至現在的結果。

Task 5

請用 Task 4 的詞組填入下列空格。

1. Electric vehicles ___________________ the automotive industry, offering environmentally friendly alternatives to traditional gasoline-powered cars and reshaping transportation norms worldwide.

2. Renowned for its groundbreaking research and innovative technologies, the institution ___________________________ of scientific advancement, shaping the future of countless fields.

3. The concept of self-driving cars ____________________ a potential solution to transportation challenges, promising safer and more efficient travel in the future.

4. The integration of artificial intelligence into various sectors ________ ______________ industries, enhancing efficiency, and revolutionizing traditional methods of operation.

5. The integration of renewable energy sources like solar and wind power ___________________ in reducing carbon emissions and combating climate change on a global scale.

答案在本單元最後一頁。

Listening

Task 6 21-2

請聽讀下列對話，你聽出了哪些前面 tasks 用到的詞彙？

A: Have you noticed all the new rapid technological advancements nowadays?

B: Absolutely, it's incredible how much innovation is happening across different industries. One particular innovation that's been making waves lately is artificial intelligence.

A: Oh yeah, AI seems to be everywhere these days. How exactly is it changing things?

B: Well, AI can process huge amounts of data, learn from patterns, and even make autonomous decisions. It's basically leading to significant disruptions in the way businesses operate.

A: That sounds like the potential impact could be huge. Which industries do you think will be most affected?

B: Definitely healthcare industries and medicine. AI is already revolutionizing things like diagnostics, drug discovery, and even patient care and administrative tasks.

A: That's fascinating. How does it work in healthcare?

B: AI-powered algorithms can analyze medical images with incredible accuracy, helping doctors detect diseases earlier. And virtual assistants are streamlining administrative processes and improving patient interactions.

A: Wow, that could really make a difference in people's lives. What about other industries?

B: Well, finance and banking are also undergoing a major transformation thanks to AI. Intelligent algorithms are being used for fraud detection, risk assessment, and even personalized investment advice.

A: It's amazing how versatile AI is. What about transportation and logistics?

B: AI is making big strides there too. Think self-driving cars and trucks, optimized delivery routes, and smarter supply chain management.

A: It's impressive how AI is reshaping so many different aspects of our world.

B: Absolutely. It's exciting to think about what the future holds with all these advancements.

請先確實聆聽音檔，了解後再看翻譯喔。

中譯

A：你有沒有注意到，現在科技進步得好快？

B：當然有啊，各行各業的創新速度真是驚人。最近特別引人注目的技術就是 AI。

A：噢，對啊，AI 現在似乎無所不在。它到底是怎麼影響各產業的？

B：嗯，AI 能處理大量數據、從中學習模式，甚至能自動決定。基本上，要是說 AI 正在顛覆企業運作的方式也不為過。

A：聽起來影響很大呢。你覺得哪個產業受影響最大？

B：肯定是醫藥相關產業。AI 在診斷、藥物研發、患者照護，甚至行政管理上都帶來了很大的變革。

A：好酷喔！那 AI 在醫療領域是怎麼運作的？

B：AI 驅動的演算法能以驚人的準確度分析醫學影像，幫助醫生更早發現疾病。而且，虛擬助手還能簡化行政流程，提升患者互動的體驗。

A：哇，這真的能大大改善人們的生活欸。那其他行業呢？

B：金融業和銀行業也因為 AI 發生了很大的變化。智慧演算法現在被用來防詐騙、做風險評估，甚至提供個人化的投資建議。

A：AI 太萬能了。那交通和物流方面呢？

B：這兩個領域的進展也很快。像是自駕汽車和卡車、優化配送路線，以及更智慧的供應鏈管理。

A：真是太厲害了，AI 幾乎在改變我們生活的各個層面。

B：沒錯。想想未來有這些科技進展的生活，真是令人興奮！

Answers

Task 1:

Q1: C   Q2: A   Q3: B   Q4: A   Q5: A

Task 2:

rapid technological	advancements
artificial	intelligence
autonomous	decisions
potential	impact
significant	disruptions
healthcare	industry
drug	discovery
patient	care
administrative	tasks
intelligent	algorithms

Task 3:

1. Artificial intelligence
2. autonomous decisions
3. Drug discovery
4. patient care
5. healthcare industry
6. Intelligent algorithms
7. Rapid technological advancements
8. administrative tasks
9. potential impact
10. significant disruptions

Task 5:

1. are revolutionizing
2. stands at the forefront
3. has emerged as
4. is transforming
5. is playing a crucial role

Unit 22

電力之前的照明

Lighting Before Electricity

本單元的學習目標包括：

- ☐ 學到一些可用以談論本主題的詞組
- ☐ 進一步熟悉從屬介系詞 chunks

Reading

Task 1 22-1

請閱聽這篇文章並回答下面的問題。

In an age when the flip of a **switch** instantly bathes our homes in light, it's easy to take **electricity** for granted. However, the history of how people **illuminated** their homes before the invention of electricity is a **fascinating** journey through ingenuity and innovation that reminds us of the immense importance of this groundbreaking development.

Before electricity, candles were a common source of **illumination**. Candle making dates back to ancient **civilizations**, and over time, they evolved from tallow or beeswax to more affordable options like stearin and paraffin. Although candles provided soft, warm light, they had their limitations. They were **prone** to **drips**, smoke, and had a limited burn time.

Oil **lamps** were another **prevalent** method of lighting in pre-electricity times. These lamps, fuelled by various oils such as whale oil, kerosene, and vegetable oil, offered a more consistent and brighter light compared to candles. Their design allowed for adjustable **wicks**, enabling users to control the **intensity** of the flame.

The 19th century saw the advent of gas lighting, a significant advancement in home illumination. Gas lamps were fuelled by coal gas or later, natural gas. They provided a more intense and steady light, significantly improving visibility in homes and streets. This innovation brought about significant improvements in urban living conditions.

The late 19th and early 20th centuries brought the most transformative development in home lighting: electricity. With Thomas Edison's invention of the practical **incandescent** light **bulb** in 1879, homes, streets, and cities were suddenly illuminated in ways previously thought impossible.

Electric lighting brought several key advantages. It was more reliable and safer than open **flames**, it could be easily controlled with switches, and it eliminated the need for constant maintenance, as required by oil lamps and candles. Furthermore, it allowed for the development of various types of lighting **fixtures**, making it possible to design well-lit and comfortable spaces.

The widespread adoption of electricity had a profound impact on society. It extended working hours, allowing for more economic **productivity**, and transformed the way people lived. The **availability** of electric lighting in homes revolutionized daily **routines**, enhancing comfort and quality of life.

Additionally, electricity played a crucial role in the development of new industries and technologies, laying the foundation for the modern world. It allowed for the creation of electrical appliances, from refrigerators to washing machines, and powered the second industrial revolution.

While electricity has become an indispensable part of modern living, it's important to remember and appreciate the **ingenious** methods people employed to light their homes before its advent. From the **humble** candle to the **sophisticated** gas lamp, these historical lighting sources offer valuable lessons in resourcefulness and the human drive for innovation.

The development of electricity marked a turning point in human history, significantly improving living conditions, productivity, and quality of life. As we **bask** in the convenience of electric lighting today, let us not forget the remarkable journey that brought us to this point, and the **tremendous** impact it continues to have on our world.

VOCABULARY

switch [swɪtʃ] *n.* 開關
electricity [ˌilɛkˋtrɪsətɪ] *n.* 電
illuminate [ɪˋluməˌnet] *v.* 照亮
fascinating [ˋfæsnˌetɪŋ] *adj.* 極有趣的
illumination [ɪˌljuməˋneʃən] *n.* 照明
civilization [ˌsɪvl̩əˋzeʃən] *n.* 文明
prone [pron] *adj.* 易於……的
drip [drɪp] *n.* 滴下
lamp [læmp] *n.* 燈
prevalent [ˋprɛvələnt] *adj.* 普遍的
wick [wɪk] *n.* 燭芯；燈芯
intensity [ɪnˋtɛnsətɪ] *n.* 強度
incandescent [ˌɪnkænˋdɛsnt] *adj.* 白熾的
bulb [bʌlb] *n.* 電燈泡
flame [flem] *n.* 火焰
fixture [ˋfɪkstʃɚ] *n.*（屋內的）固定裝置
productivity [ˌprodʌkˋtɪvətɪ] *n.* 生產力
availability [əˌveləˋbɪlətɪ] *n.* 可用度
routine [ruˋtin] *n.* 例行公事
ingenious [ɪnˋdʒinjəs] *adj.* 巧妙的
humble [ˋhʌmbl̩] *adj.* 普通的；不起眼的
sophisticated [səˋfɪstɪˌketɪd] *adj.* 複雜的
bask [bæsk] *v.* 取暖
tremendous [trɪˋmɛndəs] *adj.* 巨大的

Comprehension questions

Q1: What is the main topic of the article?

A. candles

B. electricity

C. domestic lighting

Q2: Before the 19th century, how did people illuminate their homes?

A. gas light

B. candles

C. light bulbs

Q3: How did people illuminate their homes in the early 19th century?

A. candles

B. gas lights

C. electric light

Q4: Who invented the electric light bulb?

A. Thomas Edison

B. an electrician

C. Nikola Tesla

Q5: What was the impact of electric lighting on society?

A. it made things safer

B. it revolutionized daily routines

C. there were many types of lighting fixtures

答案在本單元最後一頁。如果答錯了，請再確認一次文章內容。

中譯

在如今這個按下開關就能瞬間照亮家中的時代，我們很容易認為電是理所當然的。然而，在電力發明之前，人們如何照亮家園的歷史是一段充滿智慧與創新的旅程，提醒我們這項突破性發展的重要性。

在電力出現之前，蠟燭是常見的照明來源。蠟燭的製作可追溯至古代文明，隨著時間的推移，從早期的動物脂肪或蜂蠟，演變為更經濟實惠的材料，如硬脂酸和石蠟。儘管蠟燭能提供柔和、溫暖的光線，但也有局限性：易滴蠟、產生煙霧，且燃燒時間有限。

油燈是電力發明前另一種普遍的照明方式。油燈以鯨油、煤油和植物油等各種油為燃料，與蠟燭相比，能提供更穩定、更明亮的光源。油燈的設計還配有可調節的燈芯，使用者可控制火焰的亮度。

19 世紀時，煤氣燈的出現成為家庭照明的一大進步。煤氣燈以煤氣或後來的天然氣為燃料，能提供更強烈且穩定的光線，大大提升了家庭和街道的能見度。這項創新顯著改善了城市生活條件。

真正徹底改變家庭照明方式的是 19 世紀末和 20 世紀初的電力發展。1879 年，湯瑪斯・愛迪生發明了實用的白熾燈泡，讓家庭、街道和城市能以前所未有的方式被照亮。

電燈帶來了許多關鍵優勢。與明火相比，它更可靠、更安全，還能透過開關輕鬆控制，且不需要像油燈和蠟燭那樣頻繁維護。此外，電燈的出現讓燈具的設計變得多樣化，從而使人們能打造出光線充足、舒適的空間。

電力普及對社會產生了深遠的影響。它延長了工作時間，提高了經濟生產力，並改變了人們的生活方式。家裡有了電燈後，我們的日常作息也被徹底改變，生活變得更方便、更舒適。

更棒的是，電力的發展也催生了許多新產業和新技術，為現代世界的進步打下了基礎。電力讓冰箱、洗衣機等家用電器得以誕生，推動了第二次工業革命的進程。

雖然電力已成為現代生活中不可或缺的一部分，但我們也不應忘記在電力出現之前，人們用來照明的巧妙方法。從簡單的蠟燭到複雜的煤氣燈，這些歷史悠久的照明方式展現出人類在資源利用與創新上的智慧。

電力的發明無疑是人類歷史上的重大轉折點，它大幅改善了生活品質、提升了工作效率，也改變了我們的生活方式。今日，當我們享受電力帶來的便利時，也別忘了這段充滿創新與努力的歷程，以及它對世界產生的巨大且持續的影響。

文法甦活區

Task 2

請用上篇文章中的 word partnerships 完成下表。見範例。

candle	making
oil	
	oils
adjustable	
	lighting
transformative	
	light bulb
widespread	
	productivity
daily	

只要對照文章，便可輕鬆找出答案。

接下來，我們要利用上列 word partnerships 練習寫作。

Task 3

請用 Task 2 表格中的 word partnerships 填入下列空格。見範例。

1. After researching various techniques, Sarah embarked on her candle making journey, blending fragrances to create unique and captivating scents.

2. As the power went out during the storm, the family relied on ________ ________ to illuminate their home, casting a warm and nostalgic glow throughout the room.

3. Establishing consistent ________________ can enhance productivity, improve time management, and promote overall well-being.

4. ______________ was once a common method of illumination in urban areas before electricity, casting an eerie glow on the cobblestone streets of Victorian London.

5. In her aromatherapy practice, Maria carefully curated a collection of ______________, each possessing its own therapeutic properties to promote relaxation and wellbeing.

6. Investments in technology and infrastructure can significantly boost ______________________ by streamlining processes and increasing output efficiency.

7. The ______________________ in the lantern allowed Henry to control the intensity of the light, providing just the right amount of illumination for his evening reading sessions.

8. The construction of the new community center sparked a _________ ___________________ in the neighborhood, revitalizing the area and bringing together residents in a newfound sense of community pride.

9. The introduction of smartphones led to their ____________________, fundamentally changing how people communicate and access information on a global scale.

10. Thomas Edison's invention of the ______________________________ revolutionized the way we illuminate our homes, paving the way for modern lighting technology.

答案在本單元最後一頁。

再作一個文法練習吧！透過練習，你會更清楚本單元的文法重點。

Task 4

請再看一遍文章，找出下列 chunks 並劃底線。

· were prone to
· compared with/to
· the advent of
· development in
· the need for

這些都是帶有從屬介系詞的語塊，所搭配的介系詞是固定的。

Task 5

連連看：請將左右兩邊的句子合理地連在一起。注意必要的標點符號。見範例。

1	Children who consume excessive amounts of sugary snacks are prone	● ●	with its predecessors, showcasing significant advancements in technology and efficiency
2	The increasing frequency of natural disasters highlights the urgent need	● ●	in renewable energy technology promises to revolutionize the way we generate and utilize power, leading to a more sustainable future
3	The performance of the new model was outstanding compared	● ●	of the Internet, information became more accessible than ever before, transforming the way we communicate, learn, and conduct business on a global scale
4	The recent development	● ●	for stronger infrastructure and better disaster preparedness measures to protect vulnerable communities
5	With the advent	● ●	to developing dental cavities and other oral health issues

答案在本單元最後一頁。注意其中所搭配的介系詞。

Listening

Task 6 22-2

請聽讀下列對話，你聽出了哪些前面 tasks 用到的詞彙？

A: You know, it's remarkable how easily we overlook the significance of electricity in our lives.

B: Absolutely. In this age of instant light with the flick of a switch, we tend to take it for granted. But have you ever stopped to think about how people illuminated their homes before electricity?

A: Actually, not really. I guess they used candles, right?

B: Yes, candles were indeed a common source of light. Candle making was a common household activity. They've been around since ancient times, made from various materials like tallow or beeswax.

A: Oh, like those scented candles we use for ambiance?

B: Exactly. But candles had their limitations, like dripping wax and limited burn time.

A: So, what did people use before candles?

B: Well, oil lamps were another popular option. They burned various oils like whale oil or kerosene, offering a steadier and brighter light compared to candles. Plus, they had adjustable wicks for intensity.

A: Ah, I see. But didn't that produce a lot of smoke?

B: Some did, but advancements were made, especially with gas lighting in the 19th century. Gas lamps fueled by coal or natural gas provided even brighter and more consistent light.

A: Wow, I had no idea. So, when did electricity come into play?

B: It wasn't until the late 19th century when Thomas Edison invented the incandescent light bulb. That was transformative development.

A: No kidding. I can't imagine life without electric lighting now.

B: It's true. Electric lighting made everything so much safer, reliable, and convenient. Its widespread adoption revolutionized daily routines and even extended working hours, boosting economic productivity.

A: And it paved the way for so many other inventions, like electrical appliances.

B: Absolutely. The impact of electricity on society has been immense, shaping the modern world as we know it.

A: It's incredible how something as simple as lighting has such a profound effect on our lives.

B: Definitely. It's a reminder of the ingenuity and innovation of humanity throughout history.

請先確實聆聽音檔，了解後再看翻譯喔。

中譯

A：你有沒有發現，我們很容易忽略電在我們生活中的重要性。

B：真的。在這個只須輕按開關就能瞬間點亮燈光的時代，我們常常視電力為理所當然。但你有沒有想過，在電力出現之前，人們是怎麼照明的？

A：嗯，還真沒仔細想過欸，我猜他們用蠟燭吧？

B：對，蠟燭確實是當時最常見的光源。做蠟燭是一種很普遍的家庭活動，從古代開始，蠟燭就以多種材料製成，例如動物脂肪或蜂蠟。

A：噢，就像現在我們用來營造氣氛的香氛蠟燭一樣？

B：沒錯。不過蠟燭也有它的局限性，像是容易滴蠟和燃燒時間短。

A：那在蠟燭出現之前呢？大家用什麼？

B：其實，油燈也是當時很受歡迎的選擇。油燈是用鯨油、煤油或植物油來點燃，光線比蠟燭更穩定也更亮。而且，油燈配有調節燈芯，可控制光亮的強度。

A：原來如此。但這樣不是會產生很多煙霧嗎？

B：確實有些油燈會產生煙霧，但隨著技術的進步，尤其是 19 世紀的煤氣燈出現後，這種情況得到了很大的改善。煤氣燈使用煤氣或天然氣作為燃料，提供更穩定、更亮的光源。

A：哇，真是長知識了！那電力是什麼時候普及的？

B：要到 19 世紀末，愛迪生發明了白熾燈泡之後，電燈才開始進入普通人的生活。那真是一個劃時代的發明。

A：沒錯，我現在根本無法想像沒有電燈的日子。

B：確實如此。電燈讓一切變得更安全、穩定、方便，它的普及改變了人們的日常作息，甚至延長了工作時間，提升了經濟生產力。

A：而且它促進了各種家電的發明。

B：對啊。電力對社會的影響超級大，它塑造了現代生活。

A：想不到看似簡單的照明發展，居然對我們的生活有如此深遠的影響。

B：沒錯，這正提醒我們，歷史上人類的智慧與創新精神是多麼值得敬佩。

Answers

Task 1:

Q1: C　Q2: B　Q3: B　Q4: A　Q5: B

Task 2:

candle	making
oil	lamps
various	oils
adjustable	wicks
gas	lighting
transformative	development
incandescent	light bulb
widespread	adoption
economic	productivity
daily	routines

Task 3:

1. candle making
2. oil lamps
3. daily routines
4. Gas lighting
5. various oils
6. economic productivity
7. adjustable wicks
8. transformative development
9. widespread adoption
10. incandescent light bulb

Task 5:

1. Children who consume excessive amounts of sugary snacks **are prone to** developing dental cavities and other oral health issues.
2. The increasing frequency of natural disasters highlights **the urgent need for** stronger infrastructure and better disaster preparedness measures to protect vulnerable communities.
3. The performance of the new model was outstanding **compared with/to** its predecessors, showcasing significant advancements in technology and efficiency.
4. The recent **development in** renewable energy technology promises to revolutionize the way we generate and utilize power, leading to a more sustainable future.
5. With **the advent of** the Internet, information became more accessible than ever before, transforming the way we communicate, learn, and conduct business on a global scale.

Unit 23 冷藏技術
Refrigeration

本單元的學習目標包括：

□ 學到一些可用以談論本主題的 word partnerships
□ 熟悉一些 chunks 以討論某技術在各階段的發展

Reading

Task 1　23-1

請閱聽這篇文章並回答下面的問題。

In the **sweltering** heat of summer or the dead of winter, the convenience of **refrigeration** is often taken for granted in our daily lives. However, the story of refrigeration is a fascinating journey that **spans** centuries, from the earliest **icehouses** to the cutting-edge smart **fridges** of today.

The roots of refrigeration can be traced back to ancient civilizations. Early cultures, including the Chinese and Persians, discovered the cooling properties of ice and snow and used various techniques to **preserve** food. However, it wasn't until the 18th century that the concept of artificial refrigeration began to take shape.

The 19th century witnessed significant strides in refrigeration technology. **Pioneers** like Oliver Evans and Jacob Perkins developed early mechanical refrigeration systems, laying the groundwork for the icebox era. These early systems used **compression** and **evaporation** principles, but they were often large and impractical for widespread use.

The breakthrough came in 1876 when Carl von Linde, a German engineer, invented the first practical and **compact refrigerator** using ammonia as a **refrigerant**. This marked the birth of household refrigeration, allowing families to preserve food more effectively and reduce dependency on ice deliveries.

The early 20th century saw the transition from gas-powered to electric refrigerators. General Electric introduced the first electrically powered household refrigerator in 1911, revolutionizing kitchens across America. The development of Freon as a safer refrigerant in the 1920s further **propelled** the growth of refrigeration technology.

Advancements in refrigeration continued to **soar** in the latter half of the 20th century. The Space Race indirectly contributed to improvements in **insulation** materials, benefiting the efficiency of refrigerators. In the 21st century, smart fridges equipped with Internet connectivity, temperature control apps, and energy-saving features have become commonplace, reflecting the constant innovation in the field.

As society became more aware of environmental issues, the refrigeration industry faced challenges related to the use of synthetic refrigerants with high global warming potential. Efforts are **underway** to develop more sustainable alternatives, emphasizing eco-friendly refrigeration solutions to mitigate environmental impact.

From the icehouses of ancient civilizations to the smart fridges of today, the history of refrigeration is a testament to human ingenuity. As we celebrate the convenience it brings to our lives, the ongoing quest for sustainability ensures that the cool journey of refrigeration will continue to evolve, promising a future that is both efficient and environmentally responsible.

Comprehension questions

Q1: What is the main topic of the article?

A. modern fridges

B. the inventor of the fridge

C. refrigeration

Q2: How did early cultures keep their food cold?

A. they put it outdoors

B. they had ice houses

C. they used ice and snow

Q3: What did refrigeration look like in the 19th century?

A. there were early machine refrigeration systems

B. there were iceboxes

C. artificial refrigeration began to take shape

Q4: What did Carl von Linde do?

A. he invented the first practical fridge

B. he developed Freon

C. he invented the first electrically-powered fridge

Q5: What did General Electric do?

A. they invented insulation materials

B. they introduced the first electric fridge

C. they designed kitchens

答案在本單元最後一頁。如果答錯了，請再確認一次文章內容。

VOCABULARY

sweltering [ˋswɛltərɪŋ] *adj.* 悶熱的
refrigeration [rɪˏfrɪdʒəˋreʃən] *n.* 冷藏
span [spæn] *v.*（時間）持續；跨越
icehouse [ˋaɪsˏhaʊs] *n.* 冰庫
fridge [frɪdʒ] *n.* 冰箱
preserve [prɪˋzɜv] *v.* 保存
pioneer [ˏpaɪəˋnɪr] *n.* 先驅；開拓者
compression [kəmˋprɛʃən] *n.* 壓縮

中譯

無論在炎熱的夏天或寒冷的冬天，冷藏設備的便利性在日常生活中經常被視為理所當然。然而，冷藏技術的發展歷程是一段橫跨數世紀的迷人旅程，從最早的冰窖到當今最先進的智慧冰箱。

冷藏技術的根源可追溯至古代文明。像中國和波斯這些古老的文化，早就發現了冰和雪的冷卻特性，並利用各種方法來保存食物。不過，一直到 18 世紀，人工冷藏的概念才開始成形。

19 世紀見證了冷藏技術的重大進展。奧利弗．埃文斯和雅各．帕金斯等先驅者開發了早期的機械製冷系統，為冰箱時代奠定了基礎。這些早期的系統使用壓縮和蒸發原理，但通常體積龐大，不利於廣泛使用。

真正的突破是在 1876 年，德國工程師卡爾．馮林德發明了首款使用氨作為冷媒的小型實用冰箱。這標誌著家用冷藏技術的誕生，使家庭能更有效地保存食物，減少對送冰服務的依賴。

20 世紀初期，冰箱技術開始從燃氣驅動轉向電力驅動。奇異公司 (GE) 於 1911 年推出了第一台家用電冰箱，徹底改變了美國的廚房。1920 年代氟利昂 (Freon) 這種更安全的冷媒出現，進一步推動了冰箱技術的發展。

20 世紀後半期，冷藏技術持續突飛猛進。太空競賽間接促進了隔熱材料的改良，提升了冰箱的效能。進入 21 世紀後，配備網路連線、溫度控制應用程式和節能功能的智慧冰箱已變得相當普遍，反映出該領域的不斷創新。

隨著大家對環境問題愈來愈重視，冷藏業也面臨了合成冷媒的挑戰，因為這種冷媒是全球暖化潛勢較高的化學物質。各方正在積極研發更永續的替代品，強調以環保冷藏方案來減少環境影響。

從古代的冰窖到今天的智慧冰箱，冷藏技術的歷史真是人類智慧的最佳見證。當我們享受冷藏技術帶來的便利時，追求永續發展的努力仍在持續推進，確保這段「涼爽之旅」能不斷進化，為未來帶來更高效、更環保的解決方案。

VOCABULARY

evaporation [ɪˏvæpəˋreʃən] *n.* 蒸發
compact [ˋkamˏpækt] *adj.* 小巧的
refrigerator [rɪˋfrɪdʒəˏretɚ] *n.* 冰箱
refrigerant [rɪˋfrɪdʒərənt] *n.* 冷媒
propel [prəˋpɛl] *v.* 推進
soar [sor] *v.* 暴增
insulation [ˏɪnsəˋleʃən] *n.* 隔熱；絕緣
underway [ˏʌndɚˋwe] *adj.* 進行中的

文法甦活區

Task 2

請用上篇文章中的 word partnerships 完成下表。見範例。

sweltering	heat
mechanical	
icebox	
ice	
	refrigerators
	refrigerant
	alternatives
environmental	
	ingenuity
ongoing	

只要對照文章，便可輕鬆找出答案。

接下來，我們要利用上列 word partnerships 練習寫作。

Task 3

請用 Task 2 表格中的 word partnerships 填入下列空格。見範例。

1. As society becomes more environmentally conscious, there is a growing demand for __sustainable alternatives__ to traditional energy sources, driving innovation in renewable energy technologies.

2. During the ________________, households relied on blocks of ice to keep food cool before the widespread adoption of electric refrigerators.

3. ___________________________ have become a staple appliance in modern households, offering convenient and efficient cooling solutions for preserving food and beverages.

4. ____________________ knows no limits, as evidenced by the myriad of inventions and innovations that have shaped our world and propelled us forward into the future.

5. In the early 20th century, __________________ were a common sight as horse-drawn carts clattered through neighborhoods, providing households with blocks of ice to keep their iceboxes cool before the advent of electric refrigeration.

6. The adoption of _____________________ in air conditioning units has significantly reduced environmental impact and mitigated potential health hazards associated with older, ozone-depleting substances.

7. The construction of the new industrial plant is under scrutiny due to its potential ___________________ on the surrounding ecosystem.

8. The invention of ___________________________ revolutionized food preservation, allowing perishable goods to be transported over long distances without spoiling.

9. The __________________ for knowledge and understanding drives scientists and researchers to explore new frontiers and push the boundaries of human understanding.

10. The __________________ of the midday sun beat down mercilessly on the parched desert landscape.

答案在本單元最後一頁。

再作一個文法練習吧！透過練習，你會更清楚本單元的文法重點。

Task 4

請再看一遍文章，找出下列 chunks 並劃底線。

- began to take shape
- laying the groundwork for
- the breakthrough
- the birth of
- propelled the growth

若要說明某技術從開始到後期的發展，上列語塊都是很好的選擇。

Task 5

請用 Task 4 的詞組填入下列空格。

1. The initial meetings and brainstorming sessions were crucial in ______________________________ the ambitious research project ahead, setting the stage for future progress and innovation.

2. ____________________________ in renewable energy technology promises to revolutionize the way we power our world, offering a sustainable alternative to fossil fuels.

3. _________________________ the Internet marked a paradigm shift in global communication, forever altering the way information is accessed and shared across the world.

4. The introduction of smartphones ________________________ of the mobile app industry, transforming the way people interact with technology on a daily basis.

5. As the plans were finalized and the details ironed out, the project ______________________, offering a glimpse of the ambitious endeavor ahead.

答案在本單元最後一頁。

Listening

Task 6 23-2

請聽讀下列對話，你聽出了哪些前面 tasks 用到的詞彙？

A: You know, it's funny how we hardly ever think about refrigeration, even though it's such a big part of our lives.

B: Yeah, you're right. Refrigeration has come a long way, hasn't it? I mean, imagine living without it, especially during the sweltering heat of summer!

A: Absolutely. Did you know that the idea of refrigeration dates back to ancient civilizations? They used ice and snow to preserve food.

B: Really? I had no idea it went back that far. So, when did artificial refrigeration start becoming a thing?

A: Well, it wasn't until the 18th century that people started experimenting with it. Mechanical refrigeration systems started popping up, but they were pretty bulky and not very practical.

B: Ah, got it. So, when did things start to change for the better?

A: It wasn't until 1876 when Carl von Linde invented the first practical refrigerator using ammonia. That really revolutionized things, making household refrigeration a reality.

B: Wow, that's quite a breakthrough. And then, I suppose electric refrigerators came into play?

A: Exactly. Before that, though, there was the icebox era, when ice deliveries were made to people's houses.

B: No kidding!

A: General Electric introduced the first electrically powered household refrigerator in 1911, and from there, it just kept getting better. They even developed safer refrigerants like Freon in the 1920s.

B: It's amazing how far refrigeration technology has come. I mean, now we have smart fridges with Internet connectivity and all sorts of fancy features.

A: Oh, absolutely. And with the growing concern for the environment, there's a big push for more sustainable alternatives too.

B: That's good to hear. It's important that we keep innovating while also being mindful of the environmental impact.

A: Definitely. The journey of refrigeration has been quite a cool one, hasn't it?

B: Absolutely! And it's reassuring to know that it's an ongoing quest with a focus on making it even more efficient and environmentally responsible.

請先確實聆聽音檔，了解後再看翻譯喔。

中譯

A：說來挺有趣的，我們平常幾乎不會去想冷藏這件事，雖然它已經是生活中不可或缺的一部分。

B：對啊，你說得沒錯。冷藏技術發展到現在真的不簡單。我的意思是，你想喔，如果沒有冷藏技術，尤其是在夏天炎熱的時候，日子會有多難過！

A：完全同意。而且你知道嗎？其實冷藏的概念可以追溯到很久以前，古代人就會用冰和雪來保存食物。

B：真的嗎？我還真不知道它的歷史這麼悠久。那人工冷藏又是什麼時候開始的？

A：嗯，一直到 18 世紀，人們才開始研究人工冷藏技術。當時雖然有一些機械冷藏系統，但又大又笨重，不太實用。

B：噢，原來如此。那是從什麼時候才開始有改變的呢？

A：1876 年，有個叫卡爾．馮林德的人發明了第一台實用的製冷機，裡面用了氨作為冷媒。這才讓家庭冷藏成為可能。

B：哇，那真是劃時代的發明啊！接著應該就是電冰箱的時代了吧？

A：沒錯。但在那之前，還有一段「冰塊箱」時代。那時候大家是靠送冰塊到家裡來保存食物。

B：真的假的！

A：1911 年，奇異公司推出了第一台家用電冰箱，之後技術就愈來愈成熟了。到了 1920 年代，他們還研發出更安全的冷媒，比如氟利昂。

B：冷藏技術的進步真令人驚嘆。現在的智慧冰箱還能連上網路，功能五花八門。

A：噢，對啊。而且隨著環保意識抬頭，現在還有很多更永續的技術在發展。

B：這樣很好。創新固然重要，但也要顧及環境影響才行。

A：對啊，冷藏技術這一路走來還真是很「酷」呢！

B：一點也沒錯！而且讓人安心的是，技術不斷進步中，未來的冰箱會更高效、更環保。

Answers

Task 1:

Q1: C   Q2: C   Q3: A   Q4: A   Q5: B

Task 2:

sweltering	heat
mechanical	refrigeration
icebox	era
ice	deliveries
electric	refrigerators
safer	refrigerant
sustainable	alternatives
environmental	impact
human	ingenuity
ongoing	quest

Task 3:

1. sustainable alternatives
2. icebox era
3. Electric refrigerators
4. Human ingenuity
5. ice deliveries
6. safer refrigerants
7. environmental impact
8. mechanical refrigeration
9. ongoing quest
10. sweltering heat

Task 5:

1. laying the groundwork for
2. The breakthrough
3. The birth of
4. propelled the growth
5. began to take shape

Unit 24 奈米科技的應用
Nanotechnology

本單元的學習目標包括：

- □ 學到一些可用以談論本主題的詞組
- □ 練習一系列描述創造或製作某物的動詞

Reading

Task 1 24-1

請閱聽這篇文章並回答下面的問題。

In the realm of science and technology, there exists a magical world too small for the naked eye to see—nanotechnology. While the **term** might sound like something out of a sci-fi movie, it's a real scientific field that's making huge strides in various industries. Today, let's **embark** on a journey to understand the basics of nanotechnology.

Nanotechnology deals with the incredibly **tiny**, the **minuscule**, the world of **nanometers**. A nanometer is one billionth of a meter, and to put that into perspective, a single human hair is about 80,000 to 100,000 nanometers wide. It's like working with building blocks on an atomic scale.

Nanotechnology offers endless possibilities, and it's already making a big impact in our lives. Here are a few key areas where nanotech shines:

Medicine:

Doctors can use nanoparticles to deliver drugs to specific **cells**, treat cancer more effectively, and even repair damaged **tissue**.

Electronics:

The ultra-small **transistors** in your smartphone and computer chips are made using nanotechnology, allowing for faster and more powerful devices.

Energy:

Nanotech materials are helping us create better and more efficient solar cells and batteries, which can store more energy and last longer.

Environment:

Scientists are developing nanomaterials that can help clean polluted water and air, making the world a greener place.

Nanotechnology involves working with and manipulating tiny **structures**. Here are some basic concepts:

Nanoparticles:

These are incredibly small **particles** that can be engineered for specific tasks. Think of them as miniature workers who can perform tasks at the **molecular** level.

Nanomaterials:

These are **substances** with structures at the nanoscale. They can have unique properties that regular materials don't possess. For example, carbon nanotubes are stronger than steel and very light.

Top-Down vs. Bottom-Up:

Scientists can either "**carve**" or "build" things at the nanoscale. Top-down involves **shrinking** existing materials, while bottom-up is about **assembling** from individual atoms or molecules.

The future of nanotechnology holds promise and some challenges. As we continue to unlock the secrets of the nanoscale world, here are a few things to look forward to:

Smaller, Faster **Electronics**:

Our **gadgets** will become even more powerful and energy-efficient.

Medical Breakthroughs:

Nanotechnology will revolutionize healthcare, from diagnosing diseases to **curing** them.

Cleaner Environment:

Solutions for tackling pollution and conserving resources will come from nanotech innovations.

Ethical and Safety Concerns:

We'll need to address ethical and safety issues, such as environmental impacts and the potential **misuse** of nanotechnology.

In conclusion, while nanotechnology might seem like something from the distant future, it's already here, changing our lives in **subtle** but profound ways. It's an exciting field, where science fiction becomes science fact, and it promises to keep pushing the boundaries of what we can achieve. So, the next time you marvel at your sleek smartphone or hear about a groundbreaking medical discovery, remember that nanotechnology is the small wonder making it all possible.

Vocabulary

term [tɝm] *n.* 名稱
embark [ɪm`bark] *v.* 登上；開始
tiny [`taɪnɪ] *adj.* 極小的
minuscule [mɪ`nʌskjul] *adj.* 微小的
nanometer [`nænoˏmitɚ] *n.* 奈米
cell [sɛl] *n.* 細胞；電池
tissue [`tɪʃʊ] *n.* 細胞組織
transistor [træn`zɪstɚ] *n.* 電晶體
structure [`strʌktʃɚ] *n.* 構造
particle [`partɪkḷ] *n.* 微粒
molecular [mə`lɛkjəlɚ] *adj.* 分子的
substance [`sʌbstəns] *n.* 物質
carve [karv] *v.* 雕刻
shrink [ʃrɪŋk] *v.* 使縮小
assemble [ə`sɛmbḷ] *v.* 組裝
electronics [ɪlɛk`tranɪks] *n.* 電子產品
gadget [`gædʒɪt] *n.* 小器具
cure [kjʊr] *v.* 治癒
misuse [mɪs`juz] *n.* 濫用
subtle [`sʌtḷ] *adj.* 隱約的

Comprehension questions

Q1: What is the main topic of the article?

A. nanotechnology

B. very small things

C. new technologies

Q2: How wide is a human hair?

A. one nano

B. more than 80,000 nanos

C. one atom

Q3: What are some of the uses of nanotechnology?

A. to purify water

B. to make smaller smartphones

C. to cure cancer

Q4: How will nanotechnology impact medicine?

A. it will be able to help diagnose illnesses

B. it will cure cancer

C. it will replace doctors

Q5: What are the ethical and safety concerns around nanotechnology?

A. there could be negative environmental impacts

B. people might not understand it

C. it could be used to spread disinformation

答案在本單元最後一頁。

中譯

在科技領域中，存在著一個肉眼看不見的神奇世界——奈米科技。雖然這個詞聽起來像是科幻電影中的概念，但它是一個真實的科學領域，在各行各業中都取得了巨大的進步。今天，讓我們踏上了解奈米技術基礎知識的旅程。

奈米技術與極其微小的奈米世界有關。一奈米是十億分之一公尺，為幫助理解可以這麼說：一根人類頭髮的寬度約為 80,000 到 100,000 奈米。這相當於在原子的尺度上堆積木。

奈米技術有無限的可能性，現在已經在我們的日常生活中發揮了很大的作用。以下是幾個奈米技術應用的重要領域：

醫療
醫生可使用奈米顆粒將藥物精確地送達特定細胞，從而更有效地治療癌症，甚至修復受損的組織。
電子產品
智慧型手機和電腦晶片中的超小型電晶體就是利用奈米技術製作的，這讓裝置運行更快、性能更強大。
能源
奈米技術材料正在幫助我們創造更好、更高效的太陽能電池和電池，它們可以儲存更多能量，使用壽命更長。
環境
科學家正在研發能淨化受污染水源和空氣的奈米材料，讓世界變得更環保。

奈米技術涉及處理和操作微小結構。以下是一些基本概念：

奈米粒子
極其微小的顆粒，能被設計用來完成特定任務，可將它們想像成在分子層級工作的迷你工人。
奈米材料
具有奈米級結構的物質，擁有普通材料所沒有的獨特特性。例如，碳奈米管比鋼更堅固，而且非常輕。
自上而下與自下而上
科學家可以在奈米尺度上「雕刻」或「建造」事物。自上而下是將現有的材料縮小，而自下而上則是從個別原子或分子開始組裝。

奈米科技的未來充滿了希望，但也面臨一些挑戰。隨著我們不斷解鎖奈米世界的奧秘，以下是一些值得期待的事情：

更小、更快的電子產品
裝置將變得更強大、更節能。

醫學突破

奈米技術將徹底改變醫療保健，從疾病診斷到治療。

更乾淨的環境

解決污染和節約資源的解決方案將來自奈米技術的創新。

道德與安全問題

道德與安全問題有待解決，例如環境影響和奈米技術的潛在濫用。

總而言之，雖然奈米技術似乎來自遙遠的未來，但它早已進入我們的生活，悄悄地改變著我們的世界。這是一個振奮人心的領域，科幻小說正成為科學事實，它將繼續推動人類挑戰極限。因此，下次當你對著手中輕巧時尚的智能手機讚歎，或聽到令人驚奇的醫學突破時，別忘了，那就是奈米技術這個「小」奇蹟帶來的成果。

文法甦活區

Task 2

請用上篇文章中的 word partnerships 完成下表。見範例。

miniscule	world
building	
	scale
treat	
	damaged tissue
computer	
	cells
tiny	
	breakthroughs
cleaner	

只要對照文章，便可輕鬆找出答案。

接下來，我們要利用上列 word partnerships 練習寫作。

Task 3

請用 Task 2 表格中的 word partnerships 填入下列空格。見範例。

1. At the ___atomic scale___, matter behaves in ways that defy classical intuition, revealing a fascinating realm governed by quantum mechanics.

PART 1
PART 2
PART 3
PART 4
PART 5
Unit 21
Unit 22
Unit 23
Unit 24
Unit 25
PART 6

2. Implementing sustainable practices and renewable energy sources is essential for achieving a ________________ and safeguarding the health of our planet for future generations.

3. In the vast expanse of the universe, Earth appears as a __________ __________, yet its significance to humanity is immeasurable.

4. Nanotechnology enables the creation of __________________ with remarkable precision, paving the way for groundbreaking innovations in fields ranging from medicine to electronics.

5. Recent ______________________ in gene editing technology offer unprecedented potential for targeted treatments, promising to revolutionize the way we approach and manage various genetic disorders.

6. Researchers are tirelessly working to develop innovative treatments that target cancer cells while minimizing harm to healthy tissues, aiming to revolutionize the way we _____________.

7. _____________ harness the abundant energy of the sun to provide clean and renewable electricity, offering a sustainable solution to power the world's growing energy needs.

8. Stem cell therapy holds immense promise in the field of regenerative medicine, offering the potential to ______________________ and restore function in a myriad of medical conditions.

9. The rapid advancement in technology continues to push the boundaries of innovation, resulting in ever-smaller and more powerful ________ ________ that revolutionize the way we interact with digital devices.

10. Understanding basic arithmetic operations is crucial as they serve as the _______________ for more advanced mathematical concepts.

答案在本單元最後一頁。

再作一個文法練習吧！透過練習，你會更清楚本單元的文法重點。

Task 4

請再看一遍文章並在所有動詞下劃線。

- create
- developing
- working with
- manipulating
- address
- achieve

小提示：這些動詞用以描述創造／開發新事物、解決問題或達成目標。

Task 5

請用 Task 4 的單字填入下列空格。

1. Scientists are ______________ new methods to combat climate change and protect the planet's delicate ecosystems.
2. Scientists are ________________ genetic sequences to enhance crop resilience and increase yields in changing environmental conditions.
3. The government is implementing policies to ________________ the socioeconomic disparities and improve access to education and healthcare for marginalized communities.
4. The team of researchers is ________________ local communities to implement sustainable farming practices and improve agricultural productivity.
5. Through collaboration and innovation, scientists and engineers strive to ______________ transformative solutions to address pressing global challenges.
6. Through dedication and perseverance, individuals can ____________ their goals and make meaningful contributions to society.

答案在本單元最後一頁。

Listening

Task 6 24-2

請聽讀下列對話，你聽出了哪些前面 tasks 用到的詞彙？

A: Hey, have you ever heard of nanotechnology?

B: Yeah, I've heard the term before, but I'm not exactly sure what it's all about.

A: Well, it's this fascinating field that deals with the miniscule world, like on the atomic scale and molecules, which are the building blocks of our world.

B: Wow, that sounds mind-blowingly small. What kind of things do they do with it?

A: Oh, all sorts of things! Like in medicine, they use nanoparticles to achieve medical breakthroughs, such as delivering drugs right to specific cells, which can be super helpful for treating cancer, or repairing damaged tissue.

B: That's incredible! And what about in other areas?

A: Well, in electronics, they make these really tiny components for things like computer chips, which makes our devices faster and more powerful.

B: Amazing!

A: Yeah. They are also using the technology to create solar cells.

B: So, how do they actually work with stuff that small?

A: It's pretty wild. They can manipulate these tiny structures, like building things atom by atom. It's kind of like working with LEGO bricks, but way, way smaller.

B: That's so cool. But are there any downsides or challenges?

A: Yeah, definitely. There are concerns about the environmental impact and safety of some nanomaterials, so researchers are working hard to address those issues. But they think nanoparticles could help to create a cleaner environment.

B: Makes sense. But it sounds like nanotechnology has a lot of potential to do some really amazing things.

A: Absolutely! It's already changing our lives in so many ways, and the possibilities for the future are endless.

B: Well, thanks for explaining it to me. I'll definitely have to look into it more.

A: No problem! It's a pretty fascinating topic. Let me know if you have any more questions!

請先確實聆聽音檔，了解後再看翻譯喔。

中譯

A：嘿，你有聽過奈米科技嗎？

B：有啊，我聽過，但我不太清楚它到底是什麼。

A：嗯，它是一個很酷的領域，主要是研究非常小的東西，像原子、分子這些東西，這些是構成我們世界的基本單位。

B：哇，聽起來超級小！那他們用這技術做什麼啊？

A：噢，各種各樣的事情！像在醫療方面，他們利用奈米顆粒來實現醫療突破，比如把藥物精準送達特定的細胞，這對治療癌症或修復受損組織非常有幫助。

B：這也太厲害了吧！那其他領域呢？

A：嗯，在電子領域，他們製造非常微小的元件，像電腦晶片之類的，這讓我們的設備運行更快、更強大。

B：太驚人了！

A：是啊。他們還用這技術來製作太陽能電池。

B：那他們怎麼處理這麼小的東西呢？

A：這真的很神奇。他們可以精準操控這些微小的結構，像堆積木一樣，一個原子一個原子地「拼」出來，但小到不行。

B：超酷的！但這技術有什麼壞處或挑戰嗎？

A：有啊，當然有。一些奈米材料的環境影響和安全性讓人擔心，所以研究人員正在努力解決這些問題。不過，他們也認為奈米顆粒可能有助於創造更乾淨的環境。

B：有道理。但聽起來奈米技術的潛力非常大，能做出很多驚人的事情。

A：沒錯！它已經在很多方面改變了我們的生活，未來的可能性更是無限。

B：嗯，謝謝你跟我解釋這些。我得多了解了解。

A：不客氣！這話題很有趣，有問題隨時問我吧！

Answers

Task 1:

Q1: A Q2: B Q3: A Q4: A Q5: A

Task 2:

miniscule	world
building	blocks
atomic	scale
treat	cancer
repair	damaged tissue
computer	chips
solar	cells
tiny	structures
medical	breakthroughs
cleaner	environment

Task 3:

1. atomic scale
2. cleaner environment
3. minuscule world
4. tiny structures
5. medical breakthroughs
6. treat cancer
7. Solar cells
8. repair damaged tissue
9. computer chips
10. building blocks

Task 5:

1. developing
2. manipulating
3. address
4. working with
5. create
6. achieve

Unit 25

內燃機奇蹟
Internal Combustion Engine

本單元的學習目標包括：

☐ 學到一些可用以談論本主題的詞組
☐ 練習一些描述事物特徵的動詞和語塊

Reading

Task 1 25-1

請閱聽這篇文章並回答下面的問題。

In the heart of every car, boat, motorcycle, and **aircraft** lies a marvel of **engineering**—the **internal combustion** engine. This iconic invention has revolutionized transportation since its inception, propelling humanity into an era of unprecedented **mobility** and progress. But how does this ingenious **contraption** work? Let's delve into the intricate **mechanics** that drive the internal combustion engine.

At its core, the internal combustion engine operates on the principles of **converting** chemical energy from fuel into **mechanical** energy. It accomplishes this feat through a series of controlled **explosions** within a confined space, known as the combustion **chamber**.

The process begins with the introduction of a mixture of air and fuel into the combustion chamber. In most **gasoline** engines, this mixture consists of

vaporized gasoline and air. In **diesel** engines, however, only air is initially drawn into the chamber, with fuel injected directly into the compressed air.

Once the air-fuel mixture is present, the next step involves compressing it within the combustion chamber. This compression increases the pressure and temperature of the mixture, making it more **reactive** and **conducive** to combustion. It's important to note that this compression is achieved by the movement of **pistons** within the engine.

As the piston reaches the top of its stroke, a spark plug ignites the compressed air-fuel mixture in gasoline engines. The spark ignites the mixture, causing it to rapidly expand and generate high-pressure gases. This sudden increase in pressure forces the piston back down, converting the chemical energy of the fuel into mechanical energy.

In diesel engines, combustion occurs differently. The high temperature and pressure within the combustion chamber cause the diesel fuel to ignite spontaneously, without the need for a spark plug. This process is known as compression ignition and is a defining characteristic of diesel engines.

Regardless of the ignition method, the resulting downward motion of the piston creates rotational motion in the engine's **crankshaft**. This rotational energy is then transmitted through the **transmission** and **drivetrain**, ultimately propelling the vehicle forward. But the process doesn't end there. After each combustion event, the **exhaust** gases produced during the combustion process are **expelled** from the combustion chamber through the exhaust system. This expulsion allows for fresh air to enter the chamber for the next cycle, ensuring the continuous operation of the engine.

The internal combustion engine's ability to efficiently convert fuel into mechanical energy has made it the cornerstone of modern transportation. From the roar of a V8 engine to the hum of a turbocharged four-cylinder, the principles underlying its operation remain consistent across a wide range of applications.

In conclusion, the internal combustion engine stands as a testament to human ingenuity and innovation. Its elegant design and remarkable efficiency continue to drive technological advancements in transportation, shaping the world as we know it. Understanding how this marvel of engineering works not only deepens our appreciation for its complexity but also sheds light on the remarkable strides humanity has made in harnessing the power of combustion.

VOCABULARY

aircraft [ˋɛr.kræft] *n.* 飛機
engineering [.ɛndʒəˋnɪrɪŋ] *n.* 工程學
internal [ɪnˋtɝnl] *adj.* 內部的
combustion [kəmˋbʌstʃən] *n.* 燃燒
mobility [moˋbɪlətɪ] *n.* 流動性
contraption [kənˋtræpʃən] *n.* 新奇裝置
mechanics [məˋkænɪks] *n.* 機械學
convert [kənˋvɝt] *v.* 轉換
mechanical [məˋkænɪkl] *adj.* 機械的
explosion [ɪkˋsploʒən] *n.* 爆炸
chamber [ˋtʃembɚ] *n.* 機械腔室
gasoline [ˋgæsə.lin] *n.* 汽油
vaporize [ˋvepə.raɪz] *v.*（使）蒸發
diesel [ˋdizl̩] *n.* 柴油
reactive [rɪˋæktɪv] *adj.* 反應性的
conducive [kənˋdjusɪv] *adj.* 有利的
piston [ˋpɪstn] *n.* 活塞
crankshaft [ˋkræŋk.ʃæft] *n.* 引擎曲軸
transmission [trænsˋmɪʃən] *n.* 變速箱
drivetrain [ˋdraɪv.tren] *n.* 傳動系統
exhaust [ɪgˋzɔst] *n.* 廢氣
expel [ɪkˋspɛl] *v.* 排出

Comprehension questions

Q1: What is the main topic of the article?

A. engines and how they work

B. the internal combustion engine and how it works

C. combustion and how it works

Q2: What is the combustion chamber?

A. a place where you can burn things

B. a place where air and fuel mixture is compressed and ignited

C. a place where the engine sits

Q3: What is the difference between petrol engines and diesel engines?

A. diesel engines have no spark plug

B. diesel engines do not use internal combustion

C. diesel engines are smaller

Q4: What does the text say about pistons?

A. pistons are the most important part of the engine

B. the downward movement of the piston turns a crankshaft

C. it's part of a long process

Q5: What does the text say about a V8 engine?

A. it can pull large loads

B. it can go very fast

C. it makes a loud noise

答案在本單元最後一頁。如果答錯了，請再確認一次文章內容。

中譯

每一輛汽車、船隻、機車和飛機的核心都蘊藏著一個工程奇蹟——內燃機。自發明以來，這項標誌性發明就徹底改變了交通運輸，推動人類進入前所未有的兼具流動性和進步的時代。然而，這個巧妙的裝置是如何運作的？讓我們深入探討驅動內燃機的複雜機制。

內燃機的關鍵原理是將燃料的化學能轉換為機械能，此過程藉由一系列在燃燒室內受控的爆炸來實現。

首先，空氣和燃料混合物會被引入燃燒室。在大多數汽油引擎中，這種混合物由汽油蒸氣與空氣組成；在柴油引擎中，則僅吸入空氣，燃料隨後直接注入壓縮的空氣中。

當混合物進入燃燒室後，下一步是將其壓縮。這種壓縮會提升混合物的壓力與溫度，使其更具反應性並有利於燃燒。值得注意的是，此過程是透過引擎中的活塞運動來完成的。

當活塞到達其衝程的頂端時，汽油引擎內的火星塞會點燃壓縮後的混合物。隨著燃燒的爆炸擴張，高壓氣體向下推動活塞，從而將燃料的化學能轉換為機械能。

在柴油引擎中，燃燒的發生方式則有所不同。燃燒室內的高溫高壓使柴油燃料自燃，無需火星塞點火，這種壓燃過程是柴油引擎的最大特徵。

無論採用何種點火方式，活塞的向下運動最終都會在引擎曲軸中驅動旋轉運動。這股旋轉能量透過變速箱與傳動系統傳遞，推動車輛前進，但這個過程並沒有就此結束。每次燃燒後，廢氣經由排氣系統從燃燒室排出，再讓新鮮空氣進入以進行下一個循環，確保引擎持續運作。

內燃機因其能夠高效地將燃料轉換為機械能，成為現代交通的基石。無論是 V8 引擎的轟鳴，還是渦輪增壓四缸引擎的嗡嗡聲，其運作原理在各種應用中始終如一。

總而言之，內燃機是人類智慧與創新精神的象徵，其優雅的設計與卓越的效率持續推動著交通運輸技術的進步，也塑造了我們所知的世界。了解此工程奇蹟的運作方式讓我們更懂得其複雜性，並見證人類在燃燒能量利用上的非凡成就。

文法甦活區

Task 2

請用上篇文章中的 word partnerships 完成下表。見範例。

iconic	invention
unprecedented	
	contraption
chemical	
	chamber
vaporized	
	air
mechanical	
	temperature
modern	

只要對照文章，便可輕鬆找出答案。

接下來，我們要利用上列 word partnerships 練習寫作。

Task 3

請用 Task 2 表格中的 word partnerships 填入下列空格。見範例。

1. The smartphone is an ___iconic invention___ that revolutionized communication and transformed modern life.

2. The 3D printer is an ____________________ that can create complex objects layer by layer, transforming digital designs into physical realities.

3. Electric scooters have provided urban commuters with ____________ ______________, allowing them to navigate city streets quickly and efficiently.

4. When __________________ mixes with air in the engine, it is ignited to create the explosion that powers the pistons.

5. The rocket's engines reached an incredibly ____________________ as they burned fuel during the launch, generating enough thrust to escape Earth's gravity.

6. The mechanic used _______________ to power the pneumatic tools, making repairs faster and more efficient.

7. The wind turbine converts the energy of the wind into ____________ ______________, which is then transformed into electricity.

8. __________________ has evolved dramatically, with electric vehicles and high-speed trains offering sustainable alternatives to traditional travel methods.

9. In a jet engine, fuel is ignited in the ____________________, creating high-pressure gases that propel the aircraft forward.

10. The combustion of gasoline in a car engine converts _____________ ______________ into mechanical energy, powering the vehicle's movement.

答案在本單元最後一頁。

再作一個文法練習吧！透過練習，你會更清楚本單元的文法重點。

Task 4

請再看一遍文章，找出下列動詞並劃底線。

- lies
- operates
- accomplishes
- involves
- forces

這些都是描述機械的動詞。請注意，字尾都綴有「s/es」，因為文章內容是在描寫一個過程，並且主詞是第三人稱。

Task 5

請用 Task 4 的詞組填入下列空格。

1. The advanced robotics in the factory ______________ intricate tasks with precision and speed, greatly enhancing the overall productivity of the manufacturing process.
2. The automated assembly line ______________ seamlessly, allowing machines to work in harmony and significantly increase production efficiency.
3. The operator __________ the machine to restart by manually overriding the safety lock.
4. The power plant ________ on the outskirts of the city, where multiple engines generate electricity for thousands of homes.
5. The production process ______________ several machines working together, including conveyor belts, robotic arms, and quality control scanners, to ensure efficiency and accuracy.

答案在本單元最後一頁。

Listening

Task 6 25-2

請聽讀下列對話，你聽出了哪些前面 tasks 用到的詞彙？

A: Hey Jamie, I just finished reading this fascinating article about internal combustion engines. Did you know how they work?

B: Yeah, I've heard a bit about them! It's amazing how they convert chemical energy into mechanical energy through controlled explosions. But I never really understood the details.

A: Exactly! The article explained how the process starts with a mixture of air and fuel entering the combustion chamber. In gasoline engines, it's vaporized gasoline and air, but diesel engines do it differently.

B: Right, diesel engines use compression ignition, don't they? The fuel ignites just from the high temperature and pressure without a spark plug.

A: You got it! I found that pretty interesting. It's like they operate on a different principle but still achieve the same goal—powering vehicles.

B: Definitely. And the way the pistons compress the air-fuel mixture before ignition is crucial. That pressure makes the compressed air explosion more powerful.

A: Yes! When the spark plug ignites the mixture, it expands rapidly, forcing the piston down and creating rotational energy. That's what ultimately drives the wheels, right?

B: Exactly! And I loved how the article described the continuous cycle of intake and exhaust. Once the combustion happens, the exhaust gases are expelled to make room for more air.

A: It's like a well-oiled machine—literally! The efficiency of internal combustion engines has shaped modern transportation so much. From cars to airplanes, it's incredible.

B: It really is. The roar of a V8 engine or the hum of a turbocharged engine can be so exhilarating. It's hard to believe all that power comes from such an ingenious contraption.

A: For sure! The article highlighted how understanding this technology helps us appreciate the engineering behind it all. It's not just about unprecedented mobility; there's so much more going on.

B: I completely agree. And with the push for electric vehicles nowadays, I wonder how the iconic invention will evolve.

A: That's an interesting thought! While electric engines are gaining popularity, the internal combustion engine still holds a significant place in our history and future transportation.

B: Absolutely! It's a testament to human innovation. I'll have to read that article you mentioned; it sounds really insightful.

A: You should! It dives deep into the mechanics and history. I think you'd enjoy it!

B: I can't wait! Thanks for the recommendation, Alex.

請先確實聆聽音檔，了解後再看翻譯喔。

中譯

A：嘿，Jamie，我剛看完一篇有關內燃機的文章，很有趣！妳知道它們是怎麼運作的嗎？

B：有聽過一些！這些引擎居然能透過受控的爆炸，把化學能轉換成機械能，超厲害。不過，我對細節不是很了解。

A：對啊！文章裡提到，整個流程是從空氣和燃料的混合物進入燃燒室開始的。汽油引擎用的是汽油蒸氣和空氣，但柴油引擎有點不一樣。

B：嗯，柴油引擎是靠壓縮來點火的吧？高溫高壓下，燃料自己就能點燃，不用火星塞。

A：沒錯！我覺得這很酷。雖然它們的運作方式不同，但最後都是為了讓車輛動起來。

B：是啊，而且活塞在點火前壓縮空燃混合物的過程也很關鍵，這種壓縮讓爆炸更有力。

A：沒錯！當火星塞點燃混合物後，它迅速膨脹，把活塞往下推，產生旋轉能量，然後傳到車輪上，讓車子動起來。

B：正是如此！而且我覺得文章裡提到的進氣和排氣循環也很有意思。每次燃燒後，廢氣被排出，新的空氣進來，準備下一次燃燒。

A：就像一台運轉順暢的機器！內燃機的高效運轉深深影響了現代交通，從汽車到飛機都少不了它。

B：確實如此。V8 引擎的轟鳴聲或渦輪增壓引擎的低沉嗡嗡聲真的很讓人振奮。很難想像這些聲音和力量全都來自這麼精巧的裝置。

A：就是啊！這篇文章讓我更了解內燃機，也更佩服這技術背後的工程智慧。內燃機不僅讓我們擁有交通的便利，其中還涉及好多科技細節。

B：完全同意。現在大家都在推電動車，我也很好奇這個經典發明將來會如何發展。

A：對啊，這是一個很有趣的問題。儘管電動引擎愈來愈受歡迎，但內燃機在我們的歷史和未來交通中仍然佔有重要地位。

B：說得對！內燃機實在是人類創新的見證。我一定要去看看你說的那篇文章，聽起來很有啓發性。

A：妳一定要看！裡面深入探討了內燃機的機械原理和歷史。我想妳會喜歡的！

B：好啊，謝謝推薦，Alex！

Answers

Task 1:

Q1: B Q2: B Q3: A Q4: B Q5: C

Task 2:

iconic	invention
unprecedented	mobility
ingenious	contraption
chemical	energy
combustion	chamber
vaporized	gasoline
compressed	air
mechanical	energy
high	temperature
modern	transportation

Task 3:

1. iconic invention
2. ingenious contraption
3. unprecedented mobility
4. vaporized gasoline
5. high temperature
6. compressed air
7. mechanical energy
8. Modern transportation
9. combustion chamber
10. chemical energy

Task 5:

1. accomplishes
2. operates
3. forces
4. lies
5. involves

NOTES

Part 6

Designed by Freepik

議題

ISSUES

Unit 26

全民基本收入 UBI

Universal Basic Income

本單元的學習目標包括：

☐ 學到一些可用以談論本主題的詞組

☐ 針對描述動作目的做一些文法語塊練習

Reading

Task 1 26-1

請閱聽這篇文章並回答下面的問題。

In an era defined by technological advancements and economic uncertainties, the concept of **Universal** Basic **Income** (UBI) has emerged as a compelling solution to address **poverty**, inequality, and the changing nature of work. With growing interest from policymakers and public figures, UBI has become a subject of intense debate and **contemplation**.

At its core, Universal Basic Income is a social **welfare** program that **guarantees** a **periodic**, **unconditional** cash payment to every individual within a given population, regardless of their employment status or income level. The primary aim of UBI is to provide a financial safety net that enables citizens to meet their basic needs, such as food, **shelter**, and healthcare, without facing the **dire** consequences of poverty.

Proponents of UBI argue that this approach can create economic **stability** and foster innovation. By providing a **stable** income, UBI can help lift people out of poverty, reduce income inequality, and **stimulate consumer** spending, thereby boosting the economy. Moreover, UBI may encourage **entrepreneurship** and risk-taking as individuals have a safety net to fall back on during times of uncertainty.

As automation and artificial intelligence continue to reshape the job market, concerns over job **displacement** have become more **pronounced**. UBI is seen by some as a **viable** response to the **potential** mass **unemployment** caused by technological disruption. By guaranteeing a basic income, individuals may have the means to retrain, **pursue** higher education, or engage in creative **endeavors**, leading to a more **adaptable** and **resilient** **workforce**.

While the idea of UBI is **appealing**, **critics** raise various concerns. One of the most significant challenges is the cost of implementing such a program. Financing UBI would require **substantial** public **funds**, and the method of **funding** remains a **contentious** issue. Critics also argue that providing a universal income could **disincentivize** work, leading to reduced labor force participation and potential negative impacts on productivity. Additionally, some critics suggest that a targeted approach to social welfare programs may be more effective, ensuring resources reach those who need them most, rather than providing a universal benefit.

To better understand the potential effects of UBI, numerous **pilot** programs and experiments have been **conducted** around the world. Countries like Finland, Canada, and Kenya have implemented UBI **trials**, with mixed results. These experiments have provided valuable insights into the real-world impact of UBI, shedding light on its **implications** for labor markets, poverty reduction, and overall **well-being**.

As societies grapple with economic uncertainties and income **disparities**, Universal Basic Income remains a topic of conversation at local, national, and global levels. The future of UBI **hinges** on further research, experimentation, and thoughtful policy design. While the concept may not be a **panacea** for all **societal** challenges, it has undeniably sparked essential discussions about the evolving nature of work, social welfare, and economic security in the modern world.

VOCABULARY

universal [ˌjunəˋvɝsl̩] *adj.* 普遍的；一致的
income [ˋɪnˌkʌm] *n.* 收入；所得
poverty [ˋpɑvɚtɪ] *n.* 貧窮
contemplation [ˌkɑntɛmˋpleʃən] *n.* 沉思
welfare [ˋwɛlˌfɛr] *n.* 福利
guarantee [ˌgærənˋti] *v.* 保證；保障
periodic [ˌpɪrɪˋɑdɪk] *adj.* 定期的
unconditional [ˌʌnkənˋdɪʃənl̩] *adj.* 無條件的
shelter [ˋʃɛltɚ] *n.* 住所
dire [daɪr] *adj.* 緊迫的
proponent [prəˋponənt] *n.* 支持者；倡議者
stability [stəˋbɪlətɪ] *n.* 穩定性
stable [ˋstebl̩] *adj.* 穩定的
stimulate [ˋstɪmjəˌlet] *v.* 促進
consumer [kənˋsjumɚ] *n.* 消費者
entrepreneurship [ˌɑntrəprəˋnɝʃɪp] *n.* 企業家精神
displacement [dɪsˋplesmənt] *n.* 取代
pronounce [prəˋnaʊns] *v.* 宣布
viable [ˋvaɪəbl̩] *adj.* 可行的
potential [pəˋtɛnʃəl] *adj./n.* 潛在的；可能性
unemployment [ˌʌnɪmˋplɔɪmənt] *n.* 失業
pursue [pɚˋsu] *v.* 追求；從事
endeavor [ɪnˋdɛvɚ] *n.* 努力
adaptable [əˋdæptəbl̩] *adj.* 適應性強的
resilient [rɪˋzɪlɪənt] *adj.* 有韌性的
workforce [ˋwɝkˌfɔrs] *n.* 勞動力
appealing [əˋpilɪŋ] *adj.* 有吸引力的
critic [ˋkrɪtɪk] *n.* 評論家
substantial [səbˋstænʃəl] *adj.* 大量的
fund [fʌnd] *n./v.* 資金；融資
contentious [kənˋtɛnʃəs] *adj.* 有爭議的
disincentivize [ˌdɪsɪnˋsɛntɪvaɪz] *v.* 抑制
pilot [ˋpaɪlət] *adj.* 小規模的
conduct [kənˋdʌkt] *v.* 實施；進行
trial [ˋtraɪəl] *n.* 試用；試驗
implication [ˌɪmplɪˋkeʃən] *n.* 含意；影響
well-being [ˋwɛlˋbiɪŋ] *n.* 福利
disparity [dɪsˋpærətɪ] *n.* 差距
hinge [hɪndʒ] *v.* 決定於
panacea [ˌpænəˋsɪə] *n.* 萬靈丹
societal [səˋsaɪətl̩] *adj.* 社會的

Comprehension questions

Q1: What is the main topic of the article?

A. Universal Basic Income

B. the job market

C. social welfare

Q2: What is UBI and how does it work?

A. everyone will earn the same amount of money

B. everyone will get a cash payment from the government

C. people living in poverty will get a cash payment from the government

Q3: What are the benefits of UBI?

A. it will reduce income inequality

B. it will get rid of poverty

C. it will help citizens in times of hardship

Q4: What is the main concern of critics of UBI?

A. it won't help to lift people out of poverty

B. it will have mixed results

C. the cost of implementing it

Q5: Which countries have tried some form of UBI?

A. the US and the UK

B. Finland and Canada

C. Africa

答案在本單元最後一頁。如果答錯了，請再確認一次文章內容。

PART 1
PART 2
PART 3
PART 4
PART 5
PART 6
Unit 26
Unit 27
Unit 28
Unit 29
Unit 30

中譯

在這個科技進步和經濟不穩定的時代，全民基本收入 (UBI) 此概念逐漸浮現，作為解決貧困、不平等與因應工作型態改變的解決方案，相當具有吸引力。隨著政策制定者和公眾人物的關注度不斷提升，UBI 已成為激烈辯論和深入思考的焦點。

UBI 本質上是一種社會福利計畫，保障向特定人口中的每個人定期、無條件地支付現金，無論其就業狀況或所得水準如何。UBI 的主旨為提供一個財務安全網，使公民能夠滿足基本需求，例如食物、住所和醫療保健，而不必面臨貧困的可怕後果。

UBI 的支持者認為，這麼做可促進經濟穩定，並激發創新。穩定的收入不僅能幫助人們擺脫貧困，還能減少收入不平等，並刺激消費支出，從而振興經濟。此外，UBI 可能鼓勵創業和承擔風險，因為在不確定時期仍有能夠依靠的安全網。

隨著自動化和人工智慧持續重塑就業市場，對工作流失的擔憂變得更加明顯。有些人認為，UBI 是因應科技顛覆造成大規模失業的可行方案。透過確保基本收入，個人得以接受再培訓、接受高等教育或從事創造性活動，從而培養出更具適應性和韌性的勞動力。

儘管 UBI 的構思頗具吸引力，但也面臨各種批評。最大的挑戰之一是推行此計畫的成本問題。UBI 的融資需要大量公共資金，而資金來源的安排充滿爭議。批評者還指出，發放定期補助可能會削弱工作動機，導致勞動力參與下降，並對生產力產生不良影響。此外，有人認為，針對特定人群的福利計畫可能更具成效，確保資源惠及最需要的人，而不是普發全民福利。

為了更了解 UBI 的潛在影響，世界各地開展了大量試行計畫和實驗。芬蘭、加拿大和肯亞等國家都有推行過類似的試驗，結果好壞不一。這些試驗幫助我們更了解 UBI 在現實生活中的效果，以及其對勞動市場、減貧和整體福祉的影響。

隨著社會努力應對經濟不確定性和貧富差距，UBI 仍是地方、國家和全世界的熱門話題。 UBI 的未來取決於進一步的研究、實驗和深思熟慮的政策設計。儘管這個概念並非解決所有社會問題的靈丹妙藥，但不可否認的是，它引發了人們對工作性質改變、社會福利和經濟保障的重要討論。

文法甦活區

Task 2

請用上篇文章中的 word partnerships 完成下表。見範例。

technological	advancements
economic	
	program
cash	
	needs
financial	
	inequality
consumer	
	unemployment
pilot	

只要對照文章，便可輕鬆找出答案。

接下來，我們要利用上列 word partnerships 練習寫作。

Task 3

請用 Task 2 表格中的 word partnerships 填入下列空格。見範例。

1. Access to clean water, nutritious food, and adequate shelter are fundamental ___basic needs___ for every individual to thrive.

2. ____________________ surged during the holiday season, reflecting optimism in the economy and indicating strong purchasing power among households.

3. Having a robust savings account serves as a ____________________, providing peace of mind during times of uncertainty or unexpected expenses.

4. ________________ remains a pressing issue globally, as differences in earnings persist among different socioeconomic groups despite efforts to address them.

5. ___________________, exacerbated by economic downturns, poses significant challenges for both individuals and governments as they seek to stabilize labor markets and support affected communities.

6. _____________________ in artificial intelligence have revolutionized industries by automating processes and enhancing efficiency.

7. The customer opted for a __________________ method to settle the bill at the restaurant.

8. The global economy faces increasing _________________________ due to geopolitical tensions and fluctuating market conditions.

9. The government implemented a new ____________________ aimed at providing financial assistance to low-income families in need.

10. The government initiated _________________ to test the feasibility and effectiveness of new policies before implementing them nationwide.

答案在本單元最後一頁。

再作一個文法練習吧！透過練習，你會更清楚本單元的文法重點。

Task 4

請再看一遍文章，找出下列文法 chunks 並劃底線。

- to address
- to provide
- to fall back on
- leading to
- to better understand

請注意，我們用「to V」來說明行動的目的。不過，「leading to」不一樣，它是描述一個行動的結果。通常會先講某動作之目的，再提及該動作，但也有例外。

Task 5

請用 Task 4 的詞組填入下列空格。

1. During times of uncertainty, having a solid education ______________ can provide individuals with the skills and confidence needed to navigate changing economic landscapes.

2. Scientists are conducting extensive research ______________ the intricate workings of the human brain and its complexities.

3. There is a prolonged drought in the region, ______________ crop failures and food shortages for local communities.

4. ______________ climate change, governments worldwide are implementing policies aimed at reducing carbon emissions and promoting renewable energy sources.

5. ______________ better healthcare access in rural areas, the government is establishing mobile clinics to reach underserved populations.

答案在本單元最後一頁。請注意，有時目的寫於句子開頭、動作之前，有時則是在句中、動作之後。

Listening

Task 6 26-2

請聽讀下列對話，你聽出了哪些前面 tasks 用到的詞彙？

A: Hey, have you heard about Universal Basic Income—UBI? It seems to be gaining a lot of attention lately.

B: Yeah, I've read a bit about it. It's basically a social welfare program where everyone gets a regular cash payment from the government, right?

A: Exactly. It's meant to provide a financial safety net for people, ensuring everyone has enough to cover their basic needs, like food and shelter, regardless of their employment status.

B: Hmm, that sounds interesting. But wouldn't that be really expensive for the government?

A: That's one of the main concerns. Funding UBI would require a significant amount of public money, and there's still debate about how to finance it effectively.

B: And what about the potential impact on work? If people are getting money regardless of whether they work or not, wouldn't that discourage some from working?

A: That's a valid point. Critics worry that UBI could lead to decreased motivation to work, which could have negative effects on productivity and the economy overall.

B: But on the other hand, it could also encourage consumer spending, encourage people to take risks, like starting their own businesses or pursuing further education, knowing they have a safety net to fall back on.

A: Exactly. And with technological advancements and AI creating mass unemployment, UBI might be a way to help people transition to new types of work without facing economic uncertainties.

B: That makes sense. But I guess we won't really know how effective UBI is until we see it in action, right?

A: Absolutely. That's why there have been pilot programs and experiments in different countries to test out UBI and see how it affects things like poverty rates and income inequality.

B: It'll be interesting to see what those experiments reveal. UBI could have a big impact on how we think about work and social welfare in the future.

A: Definitely. Whether or not UBI becomes a widespread policy, it's definitely got people talking about some important issues in our society.

請先聆聽音檔，再看翻譯喔！

中譯

A：嘿，你有聽過全民基本收入，UBI 嗎？最近好像受到不少關注。

B：有啊，我讀過一些相關內容。那基本上是一個社會福利計畫，讓每個人都能定期從政府那裡拿到現金補助嘛？

A：對。UBI 是要提供一個財務安全網，保障每個人都有基本生活所需的錢，像吃飯和住的地方，不用擔心沒工作就活不下去。

B：嗯，聽起來很有趣。但這對政府來說成本應該很高吧？

A：這也是大家擔心的點。推行 UBI 需要大量的公共資金，目前還在討論怎麼有效地籌措資金。

B：那對就業的潛在影響呢？假如不管有沒有工作都能拿錢，會不會有人因此不想工作了？

A：這是個很合理的擔憂。批評者擔心 UBI 會降低民眾工作的意願，進而影響生產力，對整體經濟造成負面影響。

B：但話說回來，UBI 也可能鼓勵消費者支出，鼓勵人們承擔風險，例如創業或進修，反正有個安全網在後面會接住大家。

A：沒錯。而且現在自動化和 AI 讓很多人失業，UBI 也許能幫助人們轉型到新工作，減少經濟上的不確定性。

B：有道理。但我想，UBI 到底有沒有效果，還是要看實際執行的情況吧？

A：當然。所以很多國家在進行試行計畫，比如在不同地方測試 UBI，看它對貧窮和收入差距的影響。

B：真期待看看這些實驗有什麼樣的結果。UBI 可能會大大改變將來我們對工作和社會福利的想法。

A：是啊。無論 UBI 最終能不能成為政策上路，它確實已經讓大家開始思考一些重要的社會議題了。

Answers

Task 1:

Q1: A   Q2: B   Q3: A   Q4: C   Q5: B

Task 2:

technological	advancements
economic	uncertainties
social welfare	program
cash	payment
basic	needs
financial	safety net
income	inequality
consumer	spending
mass	unemployment
pilot	programs

Task 3:

1. basic needs
2. Consumer spending
3. financial safety net
4. Income inequality
5. Mass unemployment
6. Technological advancements
7. cash payment
8. economic uncertainties
9. social welfare program
10. pilot programs

Task 5:

1. to fall back on
2. to better understand
3. leading to
4. To address
5. To provide

Unit 27 週休三日
The Four-Day Working Week

本單元的學習目標包括：

☐ 學到一些可用以談論本主題的詞組
☐ 熟悉一些詞組以描述組織內的成功

Reading

Task 1 27-1

請閱聽這篇文章並回答下面的問題。

In a bold move towards a more **flexible** and balanced work environment, numerous companies across various industries are adopting the four-day working week, with **astounding** success. This innovative approach has not only enhanced the well-being and job **satisfaction** of employees but has also proven to increase productivity levels, sparking a conversation about redefining the traditional workweek.

The four-day working week, which involves compressing the **typical** 40-hour **workload** into four days, has been a **resounding** triumph for both employees and employers alike. Research conducted by renowned labor economists **reveals** that this approach significantly boosts employee **morale** and job satisfaction, leading to reduced **burnout** and increased **retention** rates.

Moreover, companies **embracing** the four-day working week have reported a surge in productivity levels. By encouraging employees to focus on efficiency and prioritizing their tasks within a **condensed timeframe**, workers have shown remarkable dedication and heightened performance. The shortened workweek has also fostered creativity and innovation, as employees feel more energized and have additional time for personal pursuits and family commitments.

Industry leaders such as TechX Solutions and ProHealth Industries have enthusiastically embraced the four-day working week, **reaping** the rewards of their **progressive mindset**. TechX Solutions, a **prominent** software development company, reported a **staggering** 20% increase in productivity within the first month of implementing the new work schedule. CEO Rachel Thompson **attributes** this success to the improved work-life balance and enhanced focus of her employees.

ProHealth Industries, a leading healthcare provider, found that the four-day working week led to a significant reduction in **staff turnover** and **absenteeism**. The company's HR director emphasized that employees' well-being and job satisfaction are crucial for delivering exceptional patient care, making the **shift** to a shorter workweek a win-win situation for both employees and clients.

The growing momentum behind the four-day working week has **prompted** calls for further exploration and support from policymakers. Advocates argue that this innovative approach not only improves individual lives but also benefits society as a whole. A reduced workweek allows for more **leisure** time, fosters better **mental** and **physical** health, and promotes a healthier work-life balance, which is essential for the well-being and resilience of employees.

As the four-day working week gains **traction**, more companies are expected to adopt this progressive model. With the potential to revolutionize the traditional work structure and enhance the overall quality of life for workers, it is no surprise that this concept is receiving widespread **acclaim**. With ongoing studies and real-world success stories, the four-day working week may soon become the new norm, **heralding** a brighter future for the world of work.

VOCABULARY

flexible [ˋflɛksəbl̩] *adj.* 有彈性的；靈活的
astounding [əˋstaʊndɪŋ] *adj.* 令人震驚的
satisfaction [ˌsætɪsˋfækʃən] *n.* 滿意；滿足
typical [ˋtɪpɪkl̩] *adj.* 典型的
workload [ˋwɝkˌlod] *n.* 工作量
resounding [rɪˋzaʊndɪŋ] *adj.* 響亮的；成功的
reveal [rɪˋvil] *v.* 揭示；洩露
morale [məˋræl] *n.* 士氣
burnout [ˋbɝnˌaʊt] *n.* 精疲力盡
retention [rɪˋtɛnʃən] *n.* 保留；保持
embrace [ɪmˋbres] *v.* 擁抱；接受
condensed [kənˋdɛnst] *adj.* 濃縮的；壓縮的
timeframe [ˋtaɪmˌfrem] *n.* 時間範圍
reap [rip] *v.* 收穫；獲得
progressive [prəˋgrɛsɪv] *adj.* 進步的
mindset [ˋmaɪndˌsɛt] *n.* 心態；思維模式
prominent [ˋprɑmənənt] *adj.* 著名的
staggering [ˋstægərɪŋ] *adj.* 驚人的
attribute [əˋtrɪbjʊt] *v.* 把……歸因於
staff [stæf] *n.* 職員；工作人員
turnover [ˋtɝnˌovɚ] *n.* 人員流動率
absenteeism [ˌæbsnˋtiɪzm] *n.* 曠工
shift [ʃɪft] *n.* 輪班；轉變
prompt [prɑmpt] *v.* 促使；激起
leisure [ˋliʒɚ] *adj.* 空閒的
mental [ˋmɛntl̩] *adj.* 精神的；心理的
physical [ˋfɪzɪkl̩] *adj.* 身體的
traction [ˋtrækʃən] *n.* 被接受
acclaim [əˋklem] *n.* 讚賞；歡迎
herald [ˋhɛrəld] *v.* 預示……的來臨；宣告

Comprehension questions

Q1: What is the main topic of the article?

A. work-life balance

B. the four-day working week

C. increasing productivity levels

Q2: What have companies who introduced a four-day working week found?

A. people complained about it

B. employee moral went up

C. employee burnout went up

Q3: What did TechX Solutions report after they introduced the four-day week?

A. they reported a 20% decrease in productivity

B. they only tried it for one month

C. they reported a 20% increase in productivity

Q4: What did ProHealth industries find when they introduced the four-day working week?

A. employee turnover went up

B. employee turnover went down

C. employee turnover was not affected by the change

Q5: What do advocates of the idea claim?

A. it doesn't make a difference to people's lives

B. it makes a big difference to people's lives

C. it has no impact on society

答案在本單元最後一頁。如果答錯了，請再確認一次文章內容。

中譯

為打造更具彈性、更平衡的工作環境，許多不同產業的公司大膽地推行了週休三日制，並取得驚人的成功。此一創新舉措不僅改善了員工的福祉和工作滿意度，而且事實證明能增加生產力，引發了重新定義傳統工作週的討論。

週休三日制將典型的 40 小時工作量壓縮在四天內完成，對員工和雇主來說都是一個成功的嘗試。著名勞動經濟學家的研究顯示，這種做法可顯著提高員工士氣，從而減少倦怠並降低離職率。

此外，採用週休三日制的公司指出，他們的生產力大幅提升。這項制度鼓勵員工更有效率地完成工作，並在有限的時間內優先處理重要任務，展現出高度的專注力與卓越的工作表現。縮短的工作週還激發了員工的創新，因為他們擁有更多精力，以及更多時間投入個人興趣與家庭活動。

TechX Solutions 和 ProHealth Industries 等領頭企業已積極採納週休三日制，並從中受益。知名軟體開發公司 TechX Solutions 在實施新工作制度的第一個月內，生產力就增長了 20%。執行長 Rachel Thompson 將這一成功歸功於更平衡的生活方式和更集中的專注力。

醫療保健供應商龍頭 ProHealth Industries 發現，週休三日制明顯降低了員工流動率和缺勤率。該公司的人力資源總監強調，員工福利和工作滿意度對於提供優質病患照護至關重要，縮短工作週對員工和客戶而言是雙贏的局面。

週休三日制的聲勢日益壯大促使政策制定者呼籲更多的試驗和支持。倡議者認為，這種模式不光是有利於個人生活，而且能造福社會。減少每週工作時間讓人們擁有更多休閒時間，促進身心健康與較佳的工作生活平衡，這些都是強化員工幸福感和韌性的關鍵。

隨著週休三日制的接受度愈來愈高，今後預計會有更多公司採用這種進步的模式。此概念有望顛覆傳統的工作結構並提升員工的生活品質，難怪會獲得那麼多好評。將來當更多研究和實際成功案例出現時，週休三日制可能很快就會成為新常態，預示著職場的正向發展。

文法甦活區

Task 2

請用上篇文章中的 word partnerships 完成下表。見範例。

job	satisfaction
	levels
traditional	
retention	
work	
	balance
	turnover
leisure	
	of life
success	

只要對照文章，便可輕鬆找出答案。

接下來，我們要利用上列 word partnerships 練習寫作。

Task 3

請用 Task 2 表格中的 word partnerships 填入下列空格。見範例。

1. After a busy week, employees eagerly anticipate their __leisure time__ to unwind, pursue hobbies, and spend quality moments with loved ones.

2. Maintaining a healthy ________________ is essential for employee well-being, productivity, and overall job satisfaction.

3. Many employees find ________________ when their work aligns with their passions and allows for meaningful contributions to their organization.

4. ________________ soared after the implementation of new workflow strategies and training programs within the company.

5. The company's commitment to employee well-being extends beyond the workplace, striving to enhance their overall ________________ through flexible work arrangements and comprehensive benefits packages.

6. The company's efforts to improve workplace culture and offer competitive benefits have led to a significant reduction in ________________ rates over the past year.

7. The company's high ________________ are a testament to its strong company culture and commitment to employee development and satisfaction.

8. The company's newsletter regularly features ________________ of employees who have overcome challenges and achieved remarkable milestones in their careers, inspiring their colleagues and fostering a culture of growth and achievement.

9. The HR department is currently reviewing employees' preferences to adjust the ____________________ for better efficiency and work-life balance.

10. The ________________________ typically consists of Monday through Friday, totaling 40 hours of work.

答案在本單元最後一頁。

再作一個文法練習吧！透過練習，你會更清楚本單元的文法重點。

Task 4

請再看一遍文章，找出下列 word partnerships 並劃底線。

· bold move
· innovative approach
· progressive mindset
· attributes this success
· win-win situation
· progressive model

這些詞組皆用以描述對某組織所做的成功變革。

Task 5

連連看：請將左右兩邊的句子合理地連在一起。注意必要的標點符號。見範例。

1 Despite the risks, the CEO's decision to enter a new market was hailed as a bold	approach to problem-solving revolutionized the industry, leading to breakthroughs in technology and setting new standards for efficiency and creativity
2 Embracing a progressive	mindset, the company continuously seeks out new ideas and perspectives to adapt and thrive in an ever-evolving business landscape
3 Negotiating a fair deal that satisfies both parties' interests is the epitome of a win-win	model, blending sustainability initiatives with innovative technologies, sets a new standard for responsible business practices in the industry
4 One could attribute	move that ultimately propelled the company to unprecedented growth and success
5 The company's adoption of a progressive	situation, fostering mutual benefit and long-lasting partnerships
6 The team's innovative	this success to the cohesive teamwork, visionary leadership, and unwavering dedication exhibited by every member of the organization

答案在本單元最後一頁。

Listening

Task 6 27-2

請聽讀下列對話，你聽出了哪些前面 tasks 用到的詞彙？

A: Have you heard about companies adopting a four-day working week lately?

B: Yes, it's fascinating! They compress the usual traditional working week into just four days.

A: That sounds like a bold move. How's it working out for them?

B: Surprisingly well! Employees love it. It's improved their well-being and job satisfaction.

A: That's great to hear. But does it affect productivity?

B: Not at all, actually. In fact, productivity levels have soared. Employees are more focused and efficient.

A: Interesting. I wonder how companies are managing to pull this off.

B: It seems they're encouraging employees to prioritize tasks and work smarter within the condensed timeframe.

A: I can see how that would foster creativity and innovation.

B: Exactly! And employees have more time for personal pursuits and family commitments.

A: That must make for a better work-life balance!

B: Yes it does.

A: I bet companies are seeing benefits beyond just happier employees.

B: Absolutely. Increased retention rates and absenteeism are just some of the perks. The new work schedule is leading to reduced staff turnover.

A: It sounds like a win-win situation for everyone involved. More leisure time and a better quality of life.

B: Definitely. Plus, it's prompting discussions about redefining the traditional workweek.

A: I hope policymakers take note. This could be a game-changer for society as a whole.

B: Agreed. A shorter workweek could lead to better mental and physical health for everyone.

A: With all these benefits, I wouldn't be surprised if more companies start adopting this progressive model.

B: It's definitely gaining momentum. Who knows, maybe the four-day workweek will become the new norm soon.

A: It's an exciting concept with a lot of potential. Let's hope it turns into a success story.

請先聆聽音檔，再看翻譯喔！

中譯

A：你最近有聽說一些公司開始推行週休三日制嗎？
B：有啊，很酷欸！他們把傳統的工作週壓縮成四天。
A：聽起來很大膽。成效怎麼樣呢？
B：出奇地好！員工都很喜歡，福利變好了，對工作也更滿意。
A：讚喔。不過，這樣會不會影響生產力？
B：完全不會。生產力反而提高了。員工工作起來更專心，也更有效率。
A：有意思。我好奇公司是怎麼做到的？
B：他們鼓勵員工優先處理重要任務，並在縮短的工時內更聰明地工作。
A：難怪這樣能激發更多創意和點子。
B：沒錯！而且員工有更多時間投入個人興趣和家庭活動。
A：這一定能讓大家的工作和生活更平衡！
B：確實如此。
A：我猜除了員工開心之外，公司應該還有其他好處吧？
B：當然。留任率的提升和缺勤率的下降就是其中幾個好處。新的工作模式還減少了員工流動率。

A：聽起來是雙贏局面。更多休閒時間、更好的生活品質。
B：對啊，而且有些人還在討論要不要把傳統工作週改一改呢。
A：希望政策制定者能注意到這點，這對整個社會來說可能會是個重大改變。
B：同意。縮短每週工時對身心健康都有幫助。
A：有這麼多優點，不意外更多公司會開始跟進。
B：這模式確實愈來愈受歡迎。搞不好四天工作週很快就會變成新常態。
A：這個令人興奮的概念感覺有很大的潛力，希望它能成真。

Answers

Task 1:

Q1: B Q2: B Q3: C Q4: B Q5: B

Task 2:

job	satisfaction
productivity	levels
traditional	workweek
retention	rates
work	schedule
work-life	balance
staff	turnover
leisure	time
quality	of life
success	stories

Task 3:

1. leisure time
2. work-life balance
3. job satisfaction
4. Productivity levels
5. quality of life
6. staff turnover
7. retention rates
8. success stories
9. work schedule
10. traditional workweek

Task 5:

1. Despite the risks, the CEO's decision to enter a new market was hailed as a **bold move** that ultimately propelled the company to unprecedented growth and success.
2. Embracing a **progressive mindset**, the company continuously seeks out new ideas and perspectives to adapt and thrive in an ever-evolving business landscape.
3. Negotiating a fair deal that satisfies both parties' interests is the epitome of a **win-win situation**, fostering mutual benefit and long-lasting partnerships.
4. One could **attribute this success** to the cohesive teamwork, visionary leadership, and unwavering dedication exhibited by every member of the organization.
5. The company's adoption of a **progressive model**, blending sustainability initiatives with innovative technologies, sets a new standard for responsible business practices in the industry.
6. The team's **innovative approach** to problem-solving revolutionized the industry, leading to breakthroughs in technology and setting new standards for efficiency and creativity.

Unit 28

再生能源
Renewable Energy

本單元的學習目標包括：

- □ 學到一些可用以談論本主題的 word partnerships
- □ 複習動詞時態，對描述當前趨勢或結果有更好的掌握

Reading

Task 1 28-1

請閱聽這篇文章並回答下面的問題。

In a remarkable and pivotal shift towards a more sustainable future, renewable energy sources have emerged as the driving force behind a global transformation in the energy landscape. As the world grapples with the urgent need to combat climate change and reduce carbon emissions, renewable energy technologies have taken center stage, heralding a new era of cleaner, greener power generation.

Renewable energy, often referred to as "clean energy," **encompasses** a diverse range of sources such as solar, wind, **hydroelectric**, **geothermal**, and **biomass**. These sources offer a stark contrast to traditional fossil fuels like coal, oil, and natural gas that have long been the **dominant** energy providers, contributing significantly to environmental degradation and global warming.

One of the brightest stars in the renewable energy constellation is solar power. Solar panels, composed of **photovoltaic** cells, convert sunlight directly into electricity. With advancements in technology and **plummeting** costs, solar power has become increasingly accessible and economically viable. From sprawling solar farms in sun-soaked deserts to rooftop **installations** on residential homes, solar energy is making its mark worldwide.

Another key player in renewable energy is wind power. **Gigantic** wind **turbines**, resembling modern-day giants, harness the energy of wind to generate electricity. Offshore wind farms are rapidly expanding, **capitalizing** on strong and consistent sea breezes. Wind energy has not only proven its environmental **credentials** but has also established itself as a job creator, **invigorating** local economies and providing clean energy alternatives.

Hydropower, the **conversion** of flowing water into electricity, has been a renewable **stalwart** for decades. From **colossal dams** to small-scale run-of-the-river installations, hydropower provides reliable energy with minimal emissions. Similarly, geothermal energy taps into the Earth's internal heat, offering a consistent and sustainable power source that is independent of weather conditions.

Bioenergy, derived from organic materials like **agricultural residues**, forest waste, and even **municipal** solid waste, offers a unique solution to energy generation and waste management. Through processes like **anaerobic digestion** and combustion, bioenergy systems produce electricity and heat while simultaneously reducing the burden on landfills.

While the strides made in renewable energy are **commendable**, challenges persist. Energy storage, for instance, remains a puzzle to solve, as renewable sources like solar and wind are **intermittent**. Researchers are actively developing advanced battery technologies to store **excess** energy and bridge gaps in supply. Furthermore, the transition to a renewable-dominated energy mix **necessitates** significant infrastructure investments and policy support.

Governments, businesses, and individuals around the globe are stepping up to accelerate the adoption of renewable energy. Ambitious renewable energy targets, incentives for clean energy projects, and international collaboration are forming the **bedrock** of this transition.

The renewable revolution is not merely about adopting alternative energy sources; it is a **fundamental** shift towards a more sustainable, equitable, and resilient future. As the sun continues to shine, the wind keeps blowing, and the Earth's inner heat remains, humanity finds itself at the cusp of a renewable **renaissance**, **poised** to power generations to come while safeguarding the planet we all call home.

VOCABULARY

encompass [ɪnˋkʌmpəs] *v.* 包含
hydroelectric [ˌhaɪdro ɪˋlɛktrɪk] *adj.* 水力發電的
geothermal [ˌdʒioˋθɝml̩] *adj.* 地熱的
biomass [ˋbaɪoˌmæs] *n.* 生物質
dominant [ˋdɑmənənt] *adj.* 主要的
photovoltaic [ˌfoto vɑlˋteɪk] *adj.* 光伏的
plummet [ˋplʌmɪt] *v.* 大幅下降
installation [ˌɪnstəˋleʃən] *n.* 安裝；建置
gigantic [dʒaɪˋgæntɪk] *adj.* 龐大的
turbine [ˋtɝbaɪn] *n.* 渦輪機
capitalize [ˋkæpətl̩ˌaɪz] *v.* 利用
credential [krɪˋdɛnʃəl] *n.* 信譽；資格
invigorate [ɪnˋvɪgəˌret] *v.* 提振
conversion [kənˋvɝʃən] *n.* 轉變；轉化
stalwart [ˋstɔlwɚt] *n.* 堅定分子
colossal [kəˋlɑsl̩] *adj.* 龐大的
dam [dæm] *n.* 水壩
agricultural [ˌægrɪˋkʌltʃərəl] *adj.* 農業的
residue [ˋrɛzəˌdju] *n.* 剩餘物
municipal [mjuˋnɪsəpl̩] *adj.* 都市的
anaerobic [ænˌeəˋrobɪk] *adj.* 厭氧的
digestion [dəˋdʒɛstʃən] *n.* 消化
commendable [kəˋmɛndəbl̩] *adj.* 值得稱許的
intermittent [ˌɪntɚˋmɪtnt] *adj.* 時斷時續的
excess [ɪkˋsɛs] *adj.* 多餘的
necessitate [nɪˋsɛsəˌtet] *v.* 使成爲必要
bedrock [ˋbɛdˌrɑk] *n.* 根基
fundamental [ˌfʌndəˋmɛntl̩] *adj.* 根本的
renaissance [rəˋnesns] *n.* 復興
poised [pɔɪzd] *adj.* 準備就緒的

Comprehension questions

Q1: What is the main topic of the article?

A. solar energy

B. wind energy

C. renewable energy

Q2: What are some of the types of renewable energy?

A. oil and coal energy

B. solar and wind energy

C. natural gas

Q3: What does the text say about solar energy?

A. it's becoming cheaper to use

B. it only works in deserts

C. there is a worldwide market for it

Q4: What does the text say about wind power?

A. it only works in windy places

B. there are more and more wind farms at sea

C. it's like a modern-day giant

Q5: What are some of the challenges of renewable energy?

A. it produces a lot of waste

B. it's difficult to store energy

C. it doesn't have any support from government

答案在本單元最後一頁。如果答錯了，請再確認一次文章內容。

中譯

在邁向永續未來的關鍵轉捩點上，再生能源已成為全球能源轉型的主力。隨著世界迫切需要應對氣候變遷和減少碳排放，再生能源技術現正崛起，開啟了更乾淨的綠能發電新時代。

再生能源通常被稱為「乾淨能源」，涵蓋多種來源，例如太陽能、風能、水力發電、地熱能和生質能。這些能源與煤炭、石油和天然氣等長期以來的傳統化石燃料形成鮮明對比，後者是環境破壞和全球暖化的主要元兇。

再生能源中最引人注目的是太陽能。太陽能板由光伏電池組成，將陽光直接轉化為電能。隨著技術的進步和成本大幅下降，太陽能變得愈來愈普及且經濟可行。不論是建置於沙漠中的大型太陽能光電場，還是安裝在屋頂上的小設備，太陽能正在全世界嶄露頭角。

另一個再生能源的重要角色是風能。巨大的風力渦輪機如同現代巨人，藉由風的能量發電。離岸風電場利用強勁且穩定的海風供電，也正在迅速擴張。風能不僅環保，還創造了許多就業機會並振興地方經濟，也是乾淨能源的替代方案之一。

水力發電將流動的水轉化為電力，幾十年來一直是再生能源的支柱。從大型水壩到小型河流發電設施，水力發電以最低的排放量提供可靠的能源。同樣地，地熱能利用地球內部的熱能，提供穩定且不受天氣影響的永續能源。

生質能則來自農業剩餘物、森林廢棄物甚至都市固體廢棄物等有機材料，為能源生產和廢棄物管理提供了獨特的解決方案。透過厭氧消化和燃燒等過程，生質能系統能在發電與供熱的同時減輕垃圾掩埋場的負擔。

儘管再生能源的進展值得稱讚，但挑戰依舊存在。比方說，能源儲存仍是一個需要解決的難題，因為太陽能和風能等再生能源是間歇性的。研究人員正在積極開發先進的電池技術，以儲存多餘的能源並填補供應缺口。此外，過渡到以再生能源為主的能源結構需要大量的基礎設施投資和政策支持。

全球各地的政府、企業和個人正在加速推廣再生能源。野心勃勃的再生能源目標、乾潔能源專案激勵措施，以及國際合作構成了這項轉型的基石。

再生能源革命不僅僅是換個能源那麼簡單，它代表的是一種邁向永續、公平、韌性未來的全新轉變。只要太陽還在照，風還在吹，地球內部的熱能還在，我們就站在再生能源復興的最前線，準備好為未來發電，並守護我們的家園——地球。

文法甦活區

Task 2

請用上篇文章中的 word partnerships 完成下表。見範例。

renewable	energy
	degradation
solar	
solar	
	turbines
offshore	
	dams
	energy
bioenergy	
international	

只要對照文章，便可輕鬆找出答案。

接下來，我們要利用上列 word partnerships 練習寫作。

Task 3

請用 Task 2 表格中的 word partnerships 填入下列空格。見範例。

1. Bioenergy systems utilize organic materials such as crop residues and waste to produce renewable energy, offering a sustainable solution for both power generation and waste management.

2. ___________________ harnesses the Earth's natural heat to generate electricity and provide heating, offering a sustainable and reliable alternative to fossil fuels.

3. _____________________ provide a reliable source of renewable energy by harnessing the force of flowing water to generate electricity, contributing significantly to global energy production and water resource management.

4. ____________________________ is vital for addressing complex global challenges such as climate change, as they foster knowledge sharing, innovation, and collective action among nations towards sustainable solutions.

5. ______________________, situated in coastal waters, play a crucial role in expanding renewable energy capacity and mitigating climate change by harnessing powerful offshore winds to generate electricity on a large scale.

6. ________________________ sources such as solar and wind power are vital for transitioning towards a sustainable future.

7. _______________________ is rapidly becoming a mainstream source of electricity due to its abundant availability and environmentally friendly attributes.

8. The installation of ______________________ on rooftops has become increasingly popular among homeowners seeking to reduce their carbon footprint and lower energy bills.

9. The rapid industrialization and unchecked pollution have led to severe ________________________, threatening biodiversity and exacerbating climate change effects worldwide.

10. ____________________ dotting the landscape harness the power of the wind to generate clean, renewable electricity for communities worldwide.

答案在本單元最後一頁。

再作一個文法練習吧！透過練習，你會更清楚本單元的文法重點。

Task 4

請再看一遍文章並在所有動詞下劃線。

- have emerged
- have taken center stage
- have long been
- has become
- is making
- are rapidly expanding

這兩種動詞型態皆與現在有關。現在完成式用來描述某件事的「結果」；現在進行式則用來形容「正在發生的趨勢」。閱讀文章時，請以這兩個角度去思考。

Task 5

下列句子是指結果 (RESULT) 還是趨勢 (TREND) ？請圈出正確答案。見範例。

1. **RESULT** (circled) / **TREND**
   Efforts to protect endangered species and preserve biodiversity have long been integral components of conservation strategies worldwide.

2. **RESULT / TREND**
   In recent years, renewable energy sources like solar and wind power have taken center stage in discussions about combating climate change and transitioning to a sustainable energy future.

3. **RESULT / TREND**

New technologies for carbon capture and storage have emerged, showing promise in mitigating greenhouse gas emissions from industrial processes.

4. **RESULT / TREND**

Renewable energy technologies, such as solar and wind power, are rapidly expanding globally as countries seek to transition to more sustainable and environmentally friendly energy sources.

5. **RESULT / TREND**

The advancement of artificial intelligence is making significant strides in revolutionizing various industries, from healthcare to finance, by streamlining processes and enhancing decision-making capabilities.

6. **RESULT / TREND**

The transition to electric vehicles has become increasingly popular as society strives to reduce carbon emissions and combat climate change.

答案在本單元最後一頁。

Listening

Task 6 28-2

請聽讀下列對話，你聽出了哪些前面 tasks 用到的詞彙？

A: Have you noticed how renewable energy sources are becoming increasingly prominent in the global energy landscape?

B: Absolutely! It's remarkable how solar power and wind power, among others, are reshaping our approach to energy generation.

A: Solar power, in particular, seems to be gaining traction. I've seen more rooftop solar panels and large-scale solar farms popping up everywhere.

B: Yeah, advancements in technology have made solar energy much more accessible and cost-effective. It's fantastic to see it becoming a mainstream option.

A: And let's not forget about wind power. Those massive wind turbines are hard to miss, especially in areas with strong wind currents.

B: Definitely. Offshore wind farms are especially promising. They not only harness abundant wind resources but also create jobs and stimulate local economies.

A: True. And let's not overlook hydropower and geothermal energy. They've been around for a while but are still vital components of the renewable energy mix.

B: Absolutely. Hydropower dams and bioenergy systems provide reliable energy with minimal environmental degradation. It's great to have such diverse options.

A: Agreed. But challenges remain, like energy storage and infrastructure upgrades. It'll take concerted efforts from governments, businesses, and individuals to overcome them.

B: Definitely. But seeing the commitment and collaboration happening globally gives me hope. We're definitely headed towards a cleaner, more sustainable future.

A: Absolutely. The renewable energy revolution isn't just about powering our homes; it's about safeguarding our planet for future generations.

B: Well said. With continued innovation and international collaboration, we can ensure a brighter, greener future for all.

請先聆聽音檔，再看翻譯喔！

中譯

A：你有沒有發現，再生能源在全球能源格局中變得愈來愈重要？

B：有啊！像太陽能和風能等能源顯然正在改變發電的方式。

A：特別是太陽能，發展得很快。我看到屋頂太陽能板和大型光電場愈來愈多。

B：嗯，科技進步讓太陽能變得更便宜、更容易取得。看到它逐漸變成主流能源，覺得好厲害。

A：還有風能也不容忽視。那些巨大的風力渦輪機，超級壯觀，尤其是在風大的地方。

B：對啊，離岸風電場尤其有前景。不僅能充分利用豐富的風力資源，還能創造工作機會，帶動當地經濟。

A：說得對。還有水力發電和地熱能也很重要。雖然它們歷史悠久，但也是重要的綠能來源。

B：沒錯。像水力發電壩和生質能系統不僅能提供穩定的能源，對環境的破壞也是最少的。有這麼多不同的選擇真不錯。

A：同意，但像能源儲存和基礎建設升級這些問題還是要解決，這得靠政府、企業和大家共同的力量。

B：確實如此。不過，看到全球各地的努力，真的讓人覺得有希望。我們正在往更乾淨、更永續的未來前進。

A：我也覺得。再生能源革命不僅僅是為了供電，也是為了子孫後代保護我們的地球。

B：說得好。只要我們繼續創新和加強國際合作，就能打造更美好、更綠色的未來。

Answers

Task 1:

Q1: C　　Q2: B　　Q3: A　　Q4: B　　Q5: B

Task 2:

renewable	energy
environmental	degradation
solar	power
solar	panels
wind	turbines
offshore	wind farms
hydropower	dams
geothermal	energy
bioenergy	systems
international	collaboration

Task 3:

1. Bioenergy systems
2. Geothermal energy
3. Hydropower dams
4. International collaboration
5. Offshore wind farms
6. Renewable energy
7. Solar power
8. solar panels
9. environmental degradation
10. Wind turbines

Task 5:

1. RESULT
2. RESULT
3. RESULT
4. TREND
5. TREND
6. RESULT

過度旅遊
Overtourism

本單元的學習目標包括：

- ☐ 學到一些可用以談論本主題的詞組
- ☐ 對從屬介系詞 chunks 有更精確的掌握

Reading

Task 1 29-1

請閱聽這篇文章並回答下面的問題。

As travel enthusiasts flock to picturesque **destinations** worldwide, the term "overtourism" has gained **prominence** in recent years. Overtourism, characterized by **excessive** visitor numbers that **overwhelm** local communities and their infrastructure, has become a global concern. This article looks at the causes, consequences, and potential solutions surrounding the issue of overtourism.

The allure of iconic landmarks, stunning landscapes, and rich cultural experiences has led to an unprecedented surge in global tourism. Factors such as affordable air travel, the sharing economy, and social media have all contributed to this **phenomenon**. As a result, previously untouched corners of the world are now grappling with the negative consequences of overtourism.

Overtourism can strain essential resources such as water, energy, and waste management in tourist-heavy areas. This strain often falls **disproportionately** on local communities, leading to water shortages, energy **deficits**, and improper waste **disposal**.

Communities in overtouristed areas may experience a loss of their cultural identity as they cater to the **preferences** of tourists. Traditional businesses are sometimes replaced by **souvenir** shops and fast-food chains, **eroding** the **authenticity** of the destination.

Fragile ecosystems can suffer due to excessive foot traffic, pollution, and habitat **destruction**. Overtourism often leads to the degradation of natural wonders, threatening biodiversity and ecosystems.

Skyrocketing demand for **accommodation** can drive up housing costs, pushing local residents out of their neighborhoods. This **gentrification** process can disrupt communities and **jeopardize** the **livelihoods** of those who depend on tourism for income.

Addressing overtourism requires a **multifaceted** approach that involves cooperation between governments, businesses, and travelers themselves:

- Local governments and tourism authorities must implement responsible destination management plans. This includes setting limits on the number of tourists, promoting sustainable practices, and **enforcing** regulations to protect local culture and the environment.

- Tourists should be encouraged to explore less-visited regions and promote **off-peak** travel to **distribute** the benefits of tourism more evenly.

- Investing in infrastructure that can handle increased tourism, such as efficient public transportation and waste management systems, can mitigate some of the negative impacts.

- We need to educate travelers about responsible tourism practices, such as respecting local customs, minimizing waste, and supporting local businesses.

- Businesses should be encouraged in the tourism industry to adopt sustainable practices, from eco-friendly accommodations to responsible tour operators.

Overtourism is a complex issue that requires the collective efforts of governments, businesses, and travelers to address. As we explore the world's wonders, it's crucial to do so with respect for the communities and environments we visit. By adopting sustainable and responsible tourism practices, we can preserve the beauty and authenticity of our cherished destinations for generations to come. In the end, the responsibility to combat overtourism rests on all our shoulders, as the choices we make as tourists can shape the future of the places we love to visit.

VOCABULARY

destination [ˌdɛstəˋneʃən] *n.* 目的地
prominence [ˋprɑmənəns] *n.* 顯著；突出
excessive [ɪkˋsɛsɪv] *adj.* 過度的；過多的
overwhelm [ˌovɚˋhwɛlm] *v.* 壓垮；淹沒
phenomenon [fəˋnɑməˌnɑn] *n.* 現象
disproportionately [ˌdɪsprəˋpɔrʃənɪtlɪ] *adv.* 不成比例地
deficit [ˋdɛfɪsɪt] *n.* 赤字；虧損
disposal [dɪˋspozḷ] *n.* 處理
preference [ˋprɛfərəns] *n.* 偏愛；喜好
souvenir [ˋsuvəˌnɪr] *n.* 紀念品
erode [ɪˋrod] *v.* 侵蝕；破壞
authenticity [ˌɔθɛnˋtɪsətɪ] *n.* 眞實性
fragile [ˋfrædʒəl] *adj.* 脆弱的
destruction [dɪˋstrʌkʃən] *n.* 破壞
skyrocketing [ˋskaɪˌrɑkɪtɪŋ] *adj.* 飆升的
accommodation [əˌkɑməˋdeʃən] *n.* 住宿
gentrification [ˌdʒɛntrɪfɪˋkeʃən] *n.* 仕紳化
jeopardize [ˋdʒɛpɚdˌaɪz] *v.* 危及
livelihood [ˋlaɪvlɪˌhud] *n.* 生計
multifaceted [ˌmʌltɪˋfæsɪtɪd] *adj.* 多面向的
enforce [ɪnˋfors] *v.* 強制實施
off-peak [ˋɔfˋpik] *adj.* 淡季的
distribute [dɪˋstrɪbjut] *v.* 分配

Comprehension questions

Q1: What is the main topic of the article?

A. tourism

B. overtourism

C. traveling abroad

Q2: What factors have contributed to overtourism?

A. Instagram

B. expensive air travel

C. cheap accommodation

Q3: What does overtourism do to natural wonders?

A. increased traffic

B. they are slowly destroyed

C. biodiversity

Q4: What problems does overtourism cause to local places?

A. water, energy, and waste management problems

B. not enough souvenir shops and fast-food chains

C. not enough foot traffic

Q5: How can overtourism be solved?

A. ask people not to come

B. warn people not to come

C. restrict the number of tourists

答案在本單元最後一頁。如果答錯了，請再確認一次文章內容。

中譯

隨著旅遊愛好者湧向世界各地風景如畫的目的地，「過度旅遊 (overtourism)」一詞近年來愈來愈受到關注。過度旅遊指的是遊客數量過多，使得當地社區和基礎設施不堪負荷，已成為全球熱門議題。本文將探討過度旅遊的成因、後果與潛在的解決方案。

著名地標、壯麗景觀和豐富的文化體驗吸引大批遊客，助長了全世界旅遊業出現前所未有的大爆發。廉價航空、共享經濟和社群媒體等因素也推波助瀾，讓原本未受旅遊影響的角落如今也面臨過度旅遊帶來的負面影響。

過度旅遊會使遊客集中地區的水資源、能源和廢棄物管理等基本資源承受極大的壓力。這些壓力往往不成比例地落在當地社區上，導致水資源短缺、能源短缺和廢棄物處理不當等問題。

在遊客擁擠的地區，當地的文化認同可能會因迎合遊客需求而遭到破壞。傳統商店有時會被紀念品店或速食連鎖店取代，削弱了該地的真實性。

脆弱的生態系統也可能因過多的人流、污染和棲息地破壞而受到損害。過度旅遊常導致自然景觀的退化，威脅生物多樣性及生態平衡。

住宿需求的飆升可能抬高房價，迫使當地居民離開原本的社區。這種「仕紳化」過程會擾亂社區生活，並危及依賴旅遊業維持生計的居民。

解決過度旅遊需要政府、企業和旅客的共同合作，採取多方面的應對措施：

- 地方政府和旅遊主管機關須制定負責任的景點管理計畫，包括限制遊客數量、推廣永續旅遊，並透過法規保護當地文化和環境。
- 鼓勵旅客多去人少的地方觀光，推廣淡季旅行，讓旅遊收益分配得更平均。
- 投資能夠應對旅遊業成長的基礎設施，例如高效的大眾運輸和廢棄物管理系統，以減輕負面影響。
- 教育旅客遵守負責任的旅遊行為，例如尊重當地習俗、減少垃圾，並支持當地商家。
- 鼓勵旅遊業者採用永續經營模式，從環保住宿到負責任的旅遊業務均涵蓋在內。

過度旅遊是一個複雜的問題，需要政府、企業和旅客的共同努力來解決。當探索世界的美景時，也要記得尊重當地社區和環境。透過採取永續且負責任的旅遊方式，方可保留大家所愛的景點的美麗與真實，讓未來世代也能欣賞。最後，打擊過度旅遊的責任落在所有人的肩上，因為我們作為遊客的選擇將決定這些地方的未來。

文法甦活區

Task 2

請用上篇文章中的 word partnerships 完成下表。見範例。

travel	enthusiasts
global	
iconic	
	landscapes
	economy
social	
	consequences
local	
	identity
sustainable	

只要對照文章，便可輕鬆找出答案。

接下來，我們要利用上列 word partnerships 練習寫作。

Task 3

請用 Task 2 表格中的 word partnerships 填入下列空格。見範例。

1. Climate change remains a critical ___global concern___, urging nations to collaborate on sustainable solutions for a healthier planet.

2. Exploring ______________________, such as the majestic mountains of the Himalayas or the breathtaking beaches of the Maldives, can leave travelers in awe of the natural beauty of the world.

3. Implementing ______________________, such as renewable energy usage and reduced waste generation, is essential for mitigating environmental impact and ensuring a brighter future for generations to come.

4. ________________ play a crucial role in preserving cultural heritage, fostering social cohesion, and driving sustainable development initiatives.

5. Preserving ____________________ is paramount for many indigenous communities, as it represents a rich tapestry of traditions, languages, and customs passed down through generations.

6. __________________ platforms like Facebook, Instagram, and Twitter have transformed the way people connect, communicate, and share information across the globe.

7. The misuse of social media can have ________________________, including cyberbullying, misinformation spreading, and a detrimental impact on mental health.

8. The ______________________, characterized by platforms like Airbnb and Uber, has revolutionized the way people utilize resources and services, promoting a culture of collaborative consumption.

9. ____________________ often spend countless hours planning their next adventure to far-flung destinations.

10. Visiting ______________________ like the Eiffel Tower or the Statue of Liberty is a dream for many travelers seeking unforgettable experiences.

答案在本單元最後一頁。

再作一個文法練習吧！透過練習，你會更清楚本單元的文法重點。

Task 4

請再看一遍文章，找出下列從屬介系詞 chunks 並劃底線。

· cater to
· are replaced by
· the degradation of
· demand for
· limits on
· investing in

這個練習並不困難，問題是要記住所搭配的介系詞，最好將它們視為固定的語塊來記憶便事半功倍。

Task 5

連連看：請將左右兩邊的句子合理地連在一起。注意必要的標點符號。見範例。

1 Investing	of natural habitats due to deforestation and urbanization poses a significant threat to biodiversity and ecosystem stability
2 The degradation	for sustainable products reflects a shifting consumer mindset towards environmentally-friendly options
3 The growing demand	on the amount of carbon emissions that industries can release into the atmosphere to combat climate change effectively
4 There are limits	by innovative automation technologies, streamlining production processes and improving efficiency
5 Traditional manufacturing methods are gradually being replaced	to the diverse needs and preferences of its guests, ensuring a comfortable and personalized stay for everyone
6 The hotel's extensive amenities cater	in renewable energy technologies is crucial for reducing our reliance on fossil fuels and transitioning towards a more sustainable future

答案在本單元最後一頁。注意其中所搭配的介系詞。

Listening

Task 6 29-2

請聽讀下列對話，你聽出了哪些前面 tasks 用到的詞彙？

A: Have you noticed how crowded our favorite travel spots have become lately? It's like everywhere we go, there are just too many travel enthusiasts.

B: Absolutely, it's becoming a real problem. I think they call it "overtourism," right?

A: Yeah, that's the term. It's when there are so many visitors that it overwhelms the local communities and infrastructure.

B: So what's causing it, do you think?

A: Well apparently, it's a combination of social media, you know, people sharing pictures of tourist sights.

B: Right.

A: And the sharing economy is another problem. Websites like Airbnb make it easier to rent out your place for tourists.

B: It's sad to see how it affects the places we love to visit. I mean, all these iconic landmarks and stunning landscapes are getting trampled on.

A: Exactly, and it's not just about the environment. Overtourism puts a strain on resources like water and energy, and it disrupts the local way of life.

B: I've read that some places are even losing their cultural identity because they're catering too much to tourists. Traditional businesses are disappearing, replaced by souvenir shops and fast-food joints.

A: That's terrible. And you know what's even worse? All the negative consequences, for example, the damage it does to fragile ecosystems. Excessive foot traffic, pollution—it's devastating for the environment.

B: And let's not forget about the local communities. Skyrocketing housing costs drive them out of their own neighborhoods.

A: So, what can we do about it? It seems like such a global concern.

B: Well, there are some steps we can take. Governments and tourism authorities need to set limits on the number of tourists and promote sustainable practices.

A: Yeah, and we as travelers can do our part too. Like exploring less-visited regions and traveling during off-peak times.

B: And we should definitely support businesses that prioritize sustainability. Eco-friendly accommodations and responsible tour operators can make a big difference.

A: Absolutely. At the end of the day, it's up to all of us to combat overtourism. We have to be mindful of the impact our travels have on the places we visit.

B: Agreed. Let's make sure we preserve the beauty and authenticity of these destinations for future generations to enjoy.

請先確實聆聽音檔，了解後再看翻譯喔。

中譯

A：你有沒有發現，最近有一些熱門旅遊景點變得好擠呢？不管去哪裡，都是滿滿的遊客。

B：有啊，這真的是個大問題。我記得這叫「過度旅遊」，對吧？

A：對，就是那個詞。指的是遊客太多，當地的社區和設施都被搞得吃不消。

B：你覺得是什麼原因造成的呢？

A：顯然跟社群媒體有關係，你知道，大家分享旅遊景點的照片。

B：也對。

A：還有共享經濟也是一個因素。像 Airbnb 這些網站，讓房子更容易出租給遊客。

B：看著我們喜歡的地方受到影響，真的很難過。那些著名的地標和壯麗的景觀都快被踩壞了。

A：對啊，而且這不只是環境的問題。過度旅遊也會對當地的水資源和能源造成壓力，並擾亂當地人的生活。

B：我有看過一些文章寫說，有些地方因為太迎合遊客，連文化特色都快沒了。傳統商店都被紀念品店和速食店取代了。

A：那太糟糕了。你知道更糟的是什麼嗎？所有的負面結果，例如，它對脆弱的生態系統造成的損害。遊客太多、污染增加，對環境造成了巨大的傷害。

B：當地社區也受到影響。房價飆升，本地人被迫搬家。

A：那我們能做些什麼？這感覺是個全球性的問題。

B：有一些解決辦法啦。政府和旅遊機構應該限制遊客數量，還有推廣永續旅遊。

A：對啊，我們旅客也能盡一份力，比如去人少的地方玩，或者選擇淡季出遊。

B：然後，我們也應該多支持優先考量永續發展的業者。選擇環保住宿和負責任的旅行社，其實能帶來很大的改變。

A：沒錯。說到底，解決過度旅遊還是要靠大家。我們要多注意自己的旅行會對當地造成什麼影響。

B：同意。我們一定要保護這些地方的美麗和原貌，讓下一代也能好好享受。

Answers

Task 1:

Q1: B　Q2: A　Q3: B　Q4: A　Q5: C

Task 2:

travel	enthusiasts
global	concern
iconic	landmarks
stunning	landscapes
sharing	economy
social	media
negative	consequences
local	communities
cultural	identity
sustainable	practices

Task 3:

1. global concern
2. stunning landscapes
3. sustainable practices
4. Local communities
5. cultural identity
6. Social media
7. negative consequences
8. sharing economy
9. Travel enthusiasts
10. iconic landmarks

Task 5:

1. **Investing in** renewable energy technologies is crucial for reducing our reliance on fossil fuels and transitioning towards a more sustainable future.
2. The **degradation of** natural habitats due to deforestation and urbanization poses a significant threat to biodiversity and ecosystem stability.
3. The growing **demand for** sustainable products reflects a shifting consumer mindset towards environmentally-friendly options.
4. The hotel's extensive amenities **cater to** the diverse needs and preferences of its guests, ensuring a comfortable and personalized stay for everyone.
5. There are **limits on** the amount of carbon emissions that industries can release into the atmosphere to combat climate change effectively.
6. Traditional manufacturing methods **are** gradually being **replaced by** innovative automation technologies, streamlining production processes and improving efficiency.

Unit 30 台灣的 #MeToo 運動
Taiwan's #MeToo

本單元的學習目標包括：

- ☐ 學到一些可用以談論本主題的詞組
- ☐ 熟悉一些用於揭發政府腐敗的片語

Reading

Task 1 30-1

請閱聽這篇文章並回答下面的問題。

Taiwan's progressive credentials are being tested as the nation grapples with a wave of #MeToo **scandals** that have rocked its political establishment and public figures just months before the upcoming national **elections**. The surge of **sexual harassment** claims has prompted apologies, **resignations**, and internal **reforms** within the ruling Democratic Progressive Party (DPP) and the main opposition Kuomintang (KMT), while also shedding light on broader issues of **sexism** within Taiwanese society.

The recent scandals have dominated media headlines and public discussions, casting a spotlight on the country's commitment to gender equality. Taiwan, known for its progressive **stance** on issues like same-sex marriage, has been grappling with the impact of the #MeToo movement, which gained momentum following the release of the popular Netflix show "Wave Makers." The series exposed the struggle of harassment **victims** in Taiwan against powerful **perpetrators** and a work culture that often prioritizes silence.

President Tsai Ing-wen, Taiwan's first female leader, and her DPP have been compelled to apologize for **misconduct allegations** against party members. Several officials have stepped down, including the deputy secretary-general who was **suspended** for **mishandling** a victim's case in the past. The KMT, aiming to position itself as an alternative to the DPP, has pledged to **investigate** a former reporter's allegations of sexual harassment against a party **grandee** and **lawmaker**. The impact of these harassment scandals on the January elections remains uncertain, as experts believe that China-Taiwan relations will continue to dominate the **campaign**. However, recent **polls** suggest that the DPP's popularity has suffered, dropping to 24.6% from 31.1% in May, while the KMT has fallen to third place behind the Taiwan People's Party (TPP). The TPP has capitalized on the ruling party's **abuse** scandals and is attracting younger **voters**.

Taiwan's #MeToo movement is unique in several ways. Unlike in other countries, it was not an immediate response to the global movement in 2017 but gained traction in recent months. One distinctive aspect is the inclusion of male **accusers** and public **denials** from some of the **accused**. Taiwanese society's cultural norms around physical contact and boundaries have also posed challenges for defining harassment. Actions that may be deemed inappropriate in other countries have often been dismissed or normalized in Taiwan as merely "eating tofu."

Nevertheless, the movement has initiated changes in Taiwanese culture, prompting self-reflection and challenging long-established power imbalances. **Survivors** continue to come forward with their stories, despite the potential for **backlash** and denial from some perpetrators. Social media has played a significant role in providing a platform for victims to share their experiences and **bypass** institutional **barriers**.

Comprehension questions

Q1: What is the main topic of the article?

A. the recent #MeToo scandals in Taiwan

B. the upcoming election in Taiwan

C. the DPP

Q2: What is Taiwan known for?

A. its progressive stance

B. its position near China

C. its relationship with the US

Q3: What started the #MeToo movement in Taiwan?

A. President Tsai Ing-wen apologised

B. a TV show

C. harassment victims speaking out

Q4: What happened to the deputy secretary general of the DPP?

A. he was accused of sexual harassment

B. he had to resign

C. he had a lot of cases

Q5: Why is Taiwan's #MeToo movement unique?

A. some of the victims have been male

B. it's illegal

C. the DPP's popularity has suffered

答案在本單元最後一頁。如果答錯了，請再確認一次文章內容。

VOCABULARY

scandal [ˋskændḷ] *n.* 醜聞
election [ɪˋlɛkʃən] *n.* 選舉
sexual [ˋsɛkʃuəl] *adj.* 性方面的
harassment [ˋhærəsmənt] *n.* 騷擾
resignation [ˏrɛzɪgˋneʃən] *n.* 辭職
reform [ˏrɪˋfɔrm] *n.* 改革
sexism [ˋsɛksˏɪzəm] *n.* 性別歧視
stance [stæns] *n.* 立場；態度
victim [ˋvɪktɪm] *n.* 受害者
perpetrator [ˏpɝpəˋtretɚ] *n.* 犯罪者
misconduct [mɪsˋkandʌkt] *n.* 不當行爲
allegation [ˏæləˋgeʃən] *n.* 指控

中譯

台灣的進步形象正面臨考驗，隨著一連串 #MeToo 醜聞震撼政壇及多位公眾人物，而此時距離全國大選僅剩數月。性騷擾指控的激增迫使執政的民進黨 (DPP) 和主要反對黨國民黨 (KMT) 道歉、官員辭職，以及內部改革，同時也揭示了台灣社會中更廣泛的性別歧視問題。

這些醜聞成為媒體和大眾討論的焦點，讓人民開始檢視台灣對性別平等的承諾。台灣以同婚合法化等進步立場聞名，但如今正面臨 #MeToo 運動的衝擊。Netflix 爆紅台劇《人選之人—造浪者》播出後推波助瀾，揭露了受害者面對強勢加害者及默許沉默的職場文化時的無助。

台灣首位女性領袖、總統蔡英文與其所屬的民進黨，因黨內成員的性騷擾指控被迫道歉，包括曾因處理受害者案件不當而遭停職的副秘書長在內的多位官員相繼辭職。國民黨希望將自己定位為民進黨的替代選擇，承諾調查黨內大老和立委的性騷擾指控。雖然選舉結果會不會因這些醜聞而改變還不好說，但專家普遍認為，中台關係仍是選戰的主軸。然而，根據最新民調，民進黨的支持度從五月的 31.1% 跌到了 24.6%，國民黨也掉到第三名，落後於台灣民眾黨 (TPP)。台灣民眾黨則利用這波執政黨醜聞吸引了年輕選民的支持。

台灣的 #MeToo 運動在許多方面顯得相當獨特。與其他國家不同的是，這場運動並非 2017 年全球浪潮的延伸，而是近期才開始發酵。其特色之一在於出現男性指控者，以及部分被指控者公開否認指控。此外，台灣社會對肢體接觸和界限的文化認知也對騷擾的定義帶來了挑戰。在其他國家可能被視為不當的行為，在台灣卻往往會被駁回或正常化為僅是「吃豆腐」。

儘管如此，這場運動已促使台灣社會進行文化反思，並挑戰長期以來的權力不對等。即便有些加害者會否認並可能反撲，仍有許多受害者勇敢站出來發聲。對此，社群媒體也扮演了重要角色，為受害者提供了繞過制度障礙的平台。

VOCABULARY

suspend [səˋspɛnd] *v.* 使停職
mishandle [mɪsˋhændl̩] *v.* 處理不當
investigate [ɪnˋvɛstəˏget] *v.* 調查
grandee [grænˋdi] *n.* 重要人物
lawmaker [ˋlɔˏmekɚ] *n.* 立法者
campaign [kæmˋpen] *n.* 競選運動
poll [pol] *n.* 民調
abuse [əˋbjus] *n.* 濫用
voter [ˋvotɚ] *n.* 選民
accuser [əˋkjuzɚ] *n.* 指控者
denial [dɪˋnaɪəl] *n.* 否認
accused [əˋkjuzd] *n.* 被指控者
survivor [sɚˋvaɪvɚ] *n.* 倖存者
backlash [ˋbækˏlæʃ] *n.* 強烈反對
bypass [ˋbaɪˏpæs] *v.* 越過
barrier [ˋbærɪr] *n.* 障礙

文法甦活區

Task 2

請用上篇文章中的 word partnerships 完成下表。見範例。

political	establishment
public	
	harassment
internal	
	issues
progressive	
	culture
misconduct	
	members
male	

只要對照文章，便可輕鬆找出答案。

接下來，我們要利用上列 word partnerships 練習寫作。

Task 3

請用 Task 2 表格中的 word partnerships 填入下列空格。見範例。

1. Addressing climate change requires not only immediate action on reducing carbon emissions but also tackling __broader issues__ such as deforestation and sustainable resource management.

2. ____________________ have increasingly come forward to share their experiences of harassment and abuse, challenging societal stereotypes and norms surrounding victimhood.

3. __________________ rallied together to strategize and mobilize support for their candidate in the upcoming election.

4. _______________ often face intense scrutiny and media attention due to their prominent roles in society.

5. _________________ in the workplace continues to be a pervasive issue, necessitating comprehensive policies and education to address and prevent such misconduct.

6. The CEO's sudden resignation followed a wave of _____________, prompting an internal investigation into the company's workplace environment.

7. The company's _______________ aimed to streamline processes and enhance transparency, leading to improved efficiency and accountability across all departments.

8. The company's positive and collaborative ___________________ fosters innovation, employee satisfaction, and long-term success.

9. The party's __________________ on social issues advocates for inclusive policies that prioritize equity and justice for all marginalized communities.

10. The ____________________ remains deeply entrenched despite calls for reform and change from various segments of society.

答案在本單元最後一頁。

再作一個文法練習吧！透過練習，你會更清楚本單元的文法重點。

Task 4

請再看一遍文章，找出下列片語並劃底線。

· shedding light
· casting a spotlight
· has been grappling
· exposed the struggle
· gained traction
· initiated changes

若要討論某事、某組織的弊端以及因應作為時，上面這些片語皆能派上用場。

Task 5

請用 Task 4 的片語填入下列空格。

1. The documentary aims at ____________________ on environmental degradation in urban areas, urging viewers to take action towards sustainable living practices.

2. The documentary ____________________ of indigenous communities fighting for land rights against powerful corporations encroaching on their territories.

3. The government ____________________ with economic instability, trying to implement measures to stimulate growth and alleviate unemployment.

4. The grassroots movement advocating for renewable energy sources has ________________, attracting widespread support and prompting policymakers to consider more sustainable energy policies.

5. The investigative report ________________ on systemic flaws within the healthcare system, sparking calls for urgent reforms to ensure patient safety and quality of care.

6. The new CEO ________________ within the company's management structure to foster innovation and adaptability in response to evolving market trends.

答案在本單元最後一頁。

Listening

Task 6 30-2

請聽讀下列對話，你聽出了哪些前面 tasks 用到的詞彙？

A: Have you heard about the #MeToo scandals rocking Taiwan lately?

B: Yeah, it's been all over the news. The political establishment and public figures are really feeling the heat just months before the national elections.

A: It's crazy how the surge of sexual harassment claims has led to apologies, resignations, and even internal reforms within the ruling party and the opposition.

B: Definitely. It's shedding light on broader issues of sexism within Taiwanese society, despite Taiwan's progressive stance on other issues like same-sex marriage.

A: Right. And did you know that President Tsai Ing-wen and her party have had to apologize for misconduct allegations against party members?

B: Yeah, I heard about that. It's a tough situation for them. And the opposition party is trying to position itself as an alternative by promising to investigate misconduct allegations against its own party members.

A: I wonder how all of this will affect the upcoming elections.

B: Hard to say. Experts think China-Taiwan relations will still be the main focus, but recent polls show a drop in popularity for the ruling party, while a new party is gaining ground.

A: It's interesting how Taiwan's #MeToo movement has its own unique characteristics, like including male accusers and facing cultural challenges around defining harassment.

B: Definitely. But despite the challenges, it's clear that the movement is bringing about some much-needed changes in Taiwanese work culture.

A: Absolutely. It's inspiring to see survivors coming forward despite the risks, and social media is playing a big role in giving them a platform to speak out.

B: Let's hope this momentum continues and leads to lasting change.

請先確實聆聽音檔，了解後再看翻譯喔。

中譯

A：你有沒有聽說最近台灣爆發的 #MeToo 事件？

B：有啊，新聞上鬧得沸沸揚揚。就在全國大選前幾個月，政治圈和公眾人物都面臨巨大壓力。

A：對啊，這波性騷擾的指控害得不少人公開道歉、辭職，還逼得執政黨跟在野黨開始內部改革。

B：真的。這也讓大家看到台灣社會還有不少性別歧視的問題，即便台灣在像同性婚姻這些議題上相當進步。

A：是啊，你知道嗎？蔡英文總統和她的政黨還為了黨內的性騷擾指控出來道歉了。

B：對，我有聽說。這對他們來說真的很棘手。而在野黨正試圖透過承諾調查針對其黨員的不當行為指控，將自己定位為另一種選擇。

A：你覺得這些事情會不會影響到大選結果？

B：很難說。專家認為中台關係仍會是選戰焦點，但最近民調顯示執政黨的支持率下滑，有一個新興政黨正在崛起。

A：有趣的是，我覺得台灣的 #MeToo 運動很有自己的特色，像是有男性站出來指控，還有大家在文化上對騷擾定義的爭議。

B：真的。不過儘管有挑戰，這場運動的確讓台灣職場文化有了不小的改變。

A：完全同意，看到受害者不畏風險站出來真的很令人敬佩，社群媒體在這當中也幫了很大的忙。

B：希望這股力量能持續下去，帶來長遠的改變。

Answers

Task 1:

Q1: A Q2: A Q3: B Q4: B Q5: A

Task 2:

political	establishment
public	figures
sexual	harassment
internal	reforms
broader	issues
progressive	stance
work	culture
misconduct	allegations
party	members
male	accusers

Task 3:

1. broader issues
2. Male accusers
3. Party members
4. Public figures
5. Sexual harassment
6. misconduct allegations
7. internal reforms
8. work culture
9. progressive stance
10. political establishment

Task 5:

1. casting a spotlight
2. exposed the struggle
3. has been grappling
4. gained traction
5. shed light
6. initiated changes

NOTES

國家圖書館出版品預行編目（CIP）資料

Jazz up your English 英文閱讀能力養成 / Quentin Brand
作. -- 初版. -- 臺北市：波斯納出版有限公司, 2025.01
面；　公分
ISBN 978-626-7570-07-4（平裝）

1. CST：英語　2. CST：讀本

805.18　　113017693

Jazz Up Your English
英文閱讀能力養成

作　　者 / Quentin Brand
執行編輯 / 游玉旻

出　　版 / 波斯納出版有限公司
地　　址 / 100 台北市館前路 26 號 6 樓
電　　話 / (02) 2314-2525
傳　　真 / (02) 2312-3535
客服專線 / (02) 2314-3535
客服信箱 / btservice@betamedia.com.tw
郵撥帳號 / 19493777
帳戶名稱 / 波斯納出版有限公司

總 經 銷 / 時報文化出版企業股份有限公司
地　　址 / 桃園市龜山區萬壽路二段 351 號
電　　話 / (02) 2306-6842

出版日期 / 2025 年 1 月初版一刷
定　　價 / 500 元
I S B N / 978-626-7570-07-4

貝塔網址：www.betamedia.com.tw